Welcome!

[illegible]

Gina "Storm" Grant

SHIFT HAPPENS

Shift Happens

...A streak of lightning split the sky, illuminating the deadly standoff. Startled, his hands clenched. He felt rather than heard the shot. Had he hit anything? Anyone? He'd never even held a gun before, let alone fired one.

When his blurring and burning vision returned, the echoes of light silhouetted a screaming shape as it descended on the attackers. Dagger-claws flashed red as first one, then the other, went down beneath the black velvet onslaught, guns forgotten in primal panic.

The jaguar released the man's throat—Adrian would never know if he'd shot one of them or if the jaguar had taken out both. Three bodies lay in the muck, two with great red gashes where their throats had been. The one Adrian had clobbered with the sharp stone groaned and shifted, catching the cat's attention. Adrian clenched his eyes shut, wishing he could do the same with his ears, as groans became screams, then gurgles, then silence.

Three bodies. Three only. Montoya had escaped.

Surveying the carnage, Adrian gasped, bile rising in his throat. "Oh, God!" he whispered, but apparently not quietly enough.

The great cat lifted his head and faced Adrian. Bits of flesh dripped from its scarlet maw. It tossed its head, sending bloody droplets to join their purer cousins in the puddles below. Slowly, head lowered, it advanced. Cat eyes met human eyes. Adrian took a shaky step backward, then another.

The rain-saturated embankment melted beneath his feet. Adrian gasped instinctively for air as he plunged into the river where the angry current snatched him under.

Gray spots danced in his vision. Moments of his life spun across his consciousness. *How the hell did I end up here?...*

SHIFT HAPPENS

BY

STORM GRANT

AMBER QUILL PRESS, LLC
http://www.amberquill.com

SHIFT HAPPENS
AN AMBER QUILL PRESS BOOK

Amber Quill Press, LLC
http://www.amberquill.com

ISBN 978-1-61124-986-6

PUBLISHED IN THE UNITED STATES OF AMERICA

This book is dedicated to all those people
who helped me learn to write and find my own voice and style.
An early version was edited by Rentgirl2, Etui, and Valentin.
More recently I received input from Cat Grant, Angela Fiddler,
and Joan Leacott. The final proofing was courtesy of
Jenny Saypaw. I learned so much writing Shift Happens.
I can't wait to see what you think of it!

CHAPTER 1

ALL CADS ARE GRAY IN THE DARK

The dying girl staggered down the endless, grimy corridor, giggling and choking as bile slithered up her throat. Twice she fell, coarse fibers sawing at her bare knees as she crawled toward rescue. Pain stabbed her gut. Her moan descended into sobbing as the drug sang in her brain.

Reaching her destination, she collapsed on the filthy carpet, faux marble doorsill digging into her tear-tracked cheek. She mumbled, "Help." Tried again, a little louder. The words felt indigo, and tickled the back of her eyes.

"Blue, blue. My love is..." Half-remembered lyrics replaced her too-soft calls for help.

She hauled herself to her feet by gumption and the doorknob, raising her fist to knock. Dizzy and disoriented, she missed the apartment door entirely. Wild momentum spun her 'round to slam her shoulder against the solid pressboard surface.

She slid down the door to puddle in a sad heap; crooning, crying, trying not to die.

* * *

Inside, Adrian rolled his eyes. The stoner neighbors were at it again. When the low off-key singing started, he blocked one ear with his finger, and pressed the phone more tightly to the other.

"Sorry, Doc. You'll have to go searching for lost temples without me," Adrian's voice rose. He shook his head, not that Doc Soc could see him over a thousand miles of telephone lines.

"Plus there's outrageous flora and fauna," Doc Soc continued, disregarding Adrian's negative response.

Adrian paced his living room, wincing as he freed his ponytail from its leather tie. The tuneless serenade from the hall stopped. *Good.* "I'm saying no, Doc. Put on your listening ears."

"Like the *carnero* fish. It swims up your urine stream and into your penis. The local Indians sometimes use it to determine guilt—you live, you're innocent. You die… Let me email you the article, *Bottom-feeders at Their Best*. I can—"

"Whoa, Doc! Time out." Tired of the sales pitch, no matter how flattering—and tempting, Adrian needed to end this conversation now. "Sorry, Doc. Fascinating as your dick-fish sounds, not to mention the monkey-brain salad and all the other fun jungle stuff you've mentioned, I can't just take off to go tooling around the rain forest."

"C'mon, Adrian. We're talking Amazon jungle here. Think of the cave paintings, the ancient cures, the shamanic miracles. You can't say no to shamanic miracles!"

Professor Socrates Kawasaki hit all Adrian Thornapples's anthropological hot buttons. Except maybe the dick-fish. Adrian felt pretty sure he preferred his dick fish-free. Finny parasites aside, Adrian heard the siren call of all things rain forest, shamanic, and miraculous.

He straightened, shook out his hair, nearly dropping the phone. "I've got a job—no, a career!" He stripped off his shoes and socks, flexing his toes in the soft carpet pile.

"At least say you'll think about it, Adrian. Please. I could really use someone with your talent for languages and photography."

"Photography, yeah. I…" Adrian ceased his pacing near the window where his camera rested on the wide sill. He ran one finger over the case, leaving a faint streak in the dust. The extra memory chip lay beside it, equally dusty. He picked it up, fiddled with it, scratching at the label where one corner had come unglued.

On the street below, an attractive man stopped to let his dog sniff a hydrant. No, wait. Not a dog. This hot guy was walking his cat! *Click!* went Adrian's mental camera.

"What happened to your dreams, Adrian?" Doc's staticy voice crackled in Adrian's ear.

Dreams, indeed. Adrian had been having some weird ones lately.

Some were hot and sexy, while others starred cats. He shuddered. He wasn't fond of felines. He liked sex, though. Well, he was pretty sure he did. It had been a while. Maybe that was the problem. He just hoped he didn't start dreaming about having sex *with cats*!

Whump!

Something heavy hit the apartment door again—a hard crack this time, like a skull banging against wood. Even Doc Soc heard it. "What was that?"

"Dunno," Adrian answered, startled, heart thudding. "I'll go check."

The harsh knock came again, tapering to a soft rapping. Peering through the peephole, he saw nothing but the faded wallpaper across the way.

Another crash against his door. Adrian rocked back a step. "Hang on, Doc."

Panting a little, he checked the peephole again. Still nothing!

He swallowed hard. "Who's there?"

A muted "A— Adrian?" A woman's voice, raspy and weak.

Shoving the memory stick in his pocket, he opened the door a crack. His neighbor from down the hall slumped on the carpet, her eyes red-rimmed and slitted. "Adrian?" she repeated.

Adrian pushed the door closed again. It took two tries to wiggle the safety chain along its rusty track. He yanked the door open.

"Violet? Are you okay?"

Her head lolled, her fine red hair sweat-matted and messy. White foam crusted one corner of her mouth. She wore only shorts and a pink T-shirt imprinted with a faded white blob—possibly a kitten.

Adrian reached down to brush Violet's hair from her eyes, but discovered he still held the cordless phone. "Call you back, Doc," he said, hitting the disconnect button and tossing the handset on the grubby carpet. He squatted beside her. Dredging up details of a first aid course he'd once taken, he asked, "Did you hit your head?"

The brand new bruise painting her forehead crimson told him she had.

Smiling up at him, eyes closed, she sang, *"Blue, blue. My love is blue,"* segueing into something that may have been *Blue Suede Shoes.*

A sickly sweet scent tickled Adrian's nose. His explosive sneeze rocked Violet back to reality. Her eyes flew open. "Oh, my God! Where's Skip?"

She struggled to sit up, bracing herself against the doorframe. He checked her pulse, finding it thin and thready, her breathing erratic.

Well, given the circumstances, his was, too. He snatched his phone off the floor. It took three tries to dial 9-1-1. Why did the number have to be so complicated?

"Emergency Services. Do you need police, fire, or ambulance?"

"I need an ambulance. My neighbor…" He sketched out the situation, trying for calm. The operator assured him the ambulance was on its way, asking Adrian questions that were probably routine. How would he know? He'd never called 9-1-1 before. "Yes. My name is Adrian Thornapple. I live down the hall." He glanced toward Violet's apartment. The door hung open, a wispy cloud of blue smoke drifting out.

"My name is Danielle." The operator managed to convey a sense of calm urgency. "I need you to check her breathing."

"She's breathing okay. In fact, she's singing again!"

"She wore bluuu-uue velvet," Violet crooned, ending with a giggle.

"That's a good sign. Now check her eyes, please."

Calling her name and snapping his fingers, Adrian managed to get Violet's attention. "They're brown, but have a weird blue ring around them. I don't think it was there before. What's it mean?"

Danielle drew a sharp breath. "Is anyone else involved?"

"Yeah. Skip. Her boyfriend. He's back in her apartment, I think."

"Since Violet appears stable, are you comfortable checking on Skip?"

"I hate to leave her." Violet rocked slowly back and forth as if keeping time with music only she could hear. "I've never seen her like this."

"You don't have to go, Adrian. However, there appears to be a traffic accident on the only route to your area, and the paramedics may be delayed. It would be helpful for them to know what to expect when they get there. It could speed things up."

Couldn't Danielle just say what she meant? Everything was "appears" and "may" and "could." It was all so scripted and noncommittal. He needed action, goddamn it! "Okay. I'll go. Just, please tell them to hurry."

Adrian sprinted down the hall, the sickly scent of lavender growing stronger as he approached. "Hey, Skip," he called, dashing through the open door. "Violet's down by my place. She needs help. I called 9-1-1."

Skip sprawled on the sofa, headphones mashed over his mullet, eyes shut, foot tapping to the beat.

"Skip! Skip!" Adrian shouted.

Skip rocked on, oblivious. Tinny spill-over music from his enormous headphones gnawed at Adrian's already frazzled nerves. Following the wires, Adrian located the docking station perched on the coffee table. He shut it off with enough force to send it shooting across the table and over the edge. It hit the floor with the kind of smash-crunch that voided any warranty.

"Hey! Where's my tunes?" Skip peered at Adrian hazily. "Yo, Adrian! Come to party? Check out my new merchandise. All natural. Made in the rain forest. You're a big fan of that all-natural shit, eh?"

"Adrian?" Danielle said, reminding him she was still on the phone. "I need you to look into his eyes. Can you do that for me? Tell me what you see."

"Uh, yeah, Skip. Look at me, buddy." Adrian tapped his own temple. Skip blinked up at him.

"Same blue ring around the iris," Adrian reported. "It kinda glows. Like it's iridescent. It's more pronounced than Violet's."

"Does he appear to be in any physical distress? No? Then you should leave."

Something gray flashed at the edge of Adrian's vision. He spun toward the door, but saw nothing. Oh, God. Was he beginning to hallucinate on the second-hand fumes?

Racing toward the door, he noticed the gym bag too late to stop, smashing his bare foot against it painfully. He reeled forward, managing to keep upright by clutching the doorframe. *I've broken my fucking toe!* A soft-sided gym bag shouldn't be that solid. Looking behind him, the open zipper showed a stack of shrink-wrapped blue bricks.

Blue bricks, lavender smell, rings around the eyes. Suddenly, it all came together. A half-remembered newscast about a new designer drug, shipping up from South America. *Oh, God. Skip, what the hell have you gotten yourself into now?*

Sirens wailed in the distance, signaling the arrival of emergency services—finally! Turning his back on Skip, Adrian hobbled toward Violet. The hallway had never seemed so long.

The sirens must have triggered Skip's lizard brain. Behind Adrian, he came charging down the hall, over-stuffed gym bag in hand. He body-checked Adrian into the wall, leapt over Violet, and shot through the stairwell door.

"Skip!" Toe throbbing, shoulder aching, Adrian shouted after him.

"You asshole. Come back here!"

He might have chased after Skip, but Violet began to wretch—a horrible grating sound like tearing metal. She lay in his half-open doorway, arms wrapped around her stomach, heaving and choking. Ignoring the puddle he knelt in, he rolled her on to her side in the recovery position, counting the seconds until the paramedics arrived. The goddamn sirens weren't getting any closer!

"The baby, Adrian." Violet panted between spasms. "The baby."

"Oh, my God. Violet. You're pregnant?" Adrian brushed a tear from Violet's sweaty cheek. It may have been his own.

Violet nodded, circling Adrian's wrist with her small hand, grip tight enough to bruise. His office-pale skin seemed rosy compared to her blue-white fingers. "Skip said it'd be safe. Be fun."

"Hold on, Violet. Hold on. The ambulance is almost here." Adrian hoped to God Violet and the baby would be all right. He even hoped Skip would survive, too—survive to go to jail for endangering Violet and her baby with his stupid, partying ways!

"Hurts." Violet released Adrian's wrist and moved her hand down to her belly. Horrified, Adrian watched the dark stain spread across Violet's shorts, the over-sweet smell of blood merging with the lavender scent drifting down the hallway and from Violet herself. He yanked off his jacket, balling it up under Violet's head. He'd never wear this suit again.

She thanked him so softly he barely heard her, her gaze growing unfocused, the iridescent ring around her irises clearly visible now. She sighed once and closed her eyes. Feeling frantically for a pulse and finding none, Adrian began CPR, pumping Violet's chest rhythmically, clamping his lips over the dying girl's, careless of bio-hazards or inhaling drug residue. His long curls hung like curtains around them and he tasted lavender with every breath. One, two, three… He counted off the seconds of Violet's life. He pumped until his arms ached, and continued until the paramedics pulled him off. They assumed control with reassuring efficiency. How much later that was—seconds, hours—he hadn't a clue.

Wretched and numb, Adrian shivered against the grimy wallpaper, the emergency blanket draped across his shoulders offering no comfort at all. The racket of emergency services in action faded to a rhythmic pounding in his brain. He watched dully as a young policewoman wove her way around other cops and paramedics, reaching his side. She stared earnestly into his eyes.

"Hi. I'm Officer Robyn Warner. Call me Robyn. I need to ask you a few questions."

Adrian answered her litany of questions as best he could. "Yes. We were friends. I met them when they moved in and—" He choked a little as the paramedics pulled back from Violet, slowing their frantic motions. "Is she…"

The slumped shoulders of the medical crew told the story as they began re-packing their equipment. There was no sense of urgency now.

"Why'd you guys take so long?" he asked Robyn.

"Jack-knifed tractor trailer on Yonge. We had to cut around it." She shrugged, somehow making it a gesture of helplessness and apology. "I'm so sorry we couldn't get here any sooner."

Adrian looked away. She stayed with him, checking her notes, asking him a few more questions.

The forensic team arrived with silver suitcases stuffed with little orange cones and containers of powders and liquids. Their photographer shot enough pictures to fill a memory card. Adrian toyed with the one in his pocket. The camera flashes and the similarity to TV crime dramas lent an unreal feel to the scene.

"If there was a guy there—" Another cop jerked his thumb over his shoulder in the direction of Violet's apartment. POLICE LINE—DO NOT CROSS tape now bannered the door. "He's gone now. No trace of him, 'cept some clothes and a smashed mp3 player. Let's hope the forensics guys find somethin'." He narrowed his eyes at Adrian. "A bag of drugs, you say? You didn't happen to remove it, did you? Say, for safekeeping? It's okay, you can tell me."

"I saw the drugs. I tripped over the bag and have the bruised toe to prove it." Adrian gestured at his stubbed toe—it felt hot and swollen. A little dried blood gave him a *pedicurus interuptus* look. He hadn't even noticed he was bleeding. "I told you. Skip charged out of here with the bag of—"

"Musta gone down the stairs," a third cop interrupted. Adrian was pretty sure he'd already told them that.

The cops all seemed to loom over Adrian, even the one shorter than him. At five-foot-ten, Adrian wasn't exactly short, but given the circumstances, he found the uniforms and their accusatory posture more than a little insulting. They were obviously going for intimidating, but only succeeded in pissing him off.

He took a deep breath, getting a grip before he told them off, knowing that wouldn't help anybody, especially poor Violet. His gaze strayed downward to the tallest cop's utility belt heavy with law enforcement equipment—gun, nightstick, Taser. He framed another shot in his mind, wishing he had his camera. He found it calming sometimes. Taking pictures lent him a sense of distance he could have really used right about then.

The police stepped a few yards down the hall, conversing as if he couldn't hear them.

"About five-ten, Caucasian male, late twenties. Hazel eyes, slim but fit." Robyn dictated to another cop who took notes. "Shoulder-length brown hair. Curly."

What the hell? They were taking down *his* details.

"Hey, what are you—"

Another camera flashed, momentarily blinding him. "Just routine, buddy."

He ground his teeth. He didn't deserve this! *He* was the good guy here. It wasn't like he was a big scoff-law rebel. Well, maybe he'd parked illegally a few times, smuggled some designer clothing back to Canada from the Buffalo outlet mall without paying duty. But overall, he was a law-abiding citizen. He crossed at the lights, drove at the speed limit, even returned his freakin' library books on time. He hadn't thought twice about granting them permission to search his place.

"Can I go back into my apartment now?"

Nobody answered, or even acknowledged he'd spoken.

The paramedics finished repacking their equipment. They loaded Violet's body onto a gurney, strapping her down. They had to angle it a bit to fit the old building's tiny elevator. The doors shuddered closed.

Bye-bye, Violet. Adrian's throat clenched and his stomach roiled. *If I puke now I'll choke.* Maybe I should call the paramedics back. He stared at the chalk outline, empty now, but for a small dark stain.

He couldn't believe Violet was gone. He really liked her. Had liked her. She'd been upbeat and kind with a wry, self-deprecating sense of humor. He felt her presence, as if her body had left the building, but her spirit remained nearby. How cliché was that? He let the fantasy run, though, imagining her floating up near the ceiling, looking down at the whole crime-scene circus. Always insecure about her figure, she was probably chewing her lower lip, worrying, *"Does this chalk outline make me look fat?"*

Adrian snorted, instantly appalled at his own lack of decorum.

"Sumpthin' funny?" the big cop asked, peering into Adrian's eyes again.

Jeeze, thought Adrian, I hadn't had this much eye contact since that gay cruise I took a few years ago. Guess they're just checking for blue rings.

Radios crackled, startling Adrian each time. "You're sure jumpy, mister," one of the cops said. "Something you want to tell me?"

"I'm just a little shook up. I—"

"Sure, guy. Sure." The cop's eyes narrowed. "Is that lavender I smell?"

"Buzz off, Eddy." Officer Robyn laid a hand on Adrian's shoulder. "I know you were just trying to help." She peered so sincerely into Adrian's eyes that he could practically see "Good Cop" engraved on her eyeballs.

"Okay, that's it." Adrian declared to anyone listening. "I'm tired, hungry, upset, and desperately need to pee. I'm going back into my apartment and if anyone has a problem with that, they can take it up with…" He'd been going to say "my lawyer," but since he didn't have a lawyer, it felt like a lie.

"They can take it up with me," Officer Robyn announced, gesturing for Adrian to precede her into his own apartment.

Stepping around the stains and numbered day-glo pyramids, Adrian hurried to the bathroom. He quickly locked the door behind him, more than a little afraid Robyn would want to "be there for him." And make sure he didn't flush anything incriminating.

When he entered the kitchen, she was examining the notes and photos stuck to the fridge. He started a pot of coffee while the cops finished searching his place.

"It's just routine," Robyn said. "No coffee. I'm good. Thanks."

Adrian nodded. He stared at the coffee maker as if it required all his attention, the last of his composure draining away while the pot filled. He sniffled. Poor Violet, dead for the crime of liking the wrong guy. *There but for the grace of God.* He'd been attracted to the wrong man a time or two, himself, and had the missing stereo equipment to prove it.

A few minutes later, he carried his steaming *Save the Whales* mug to the kitchen table, slumping into his usual chair. Something dug into his hip. He extracted the memory chip, recalling how he'd pocketed it earlier for no good reason. Not wanting to misplace it, he rose, re-entered his living room and placed it back on the window sill. A young forensic tech glanced up from where he was scrolling through Adrian's phone, making note of all the incoming and outgoing calls Adrian had received in the last few days. Adrian rolled his eyes and returned to the kitchen, Robyn tailing him a few paces behind.

He dropped into his chair again and reached for his coffee.

"Can I move this?" Robyn gestured at the cardboard box occupying the only other chair.

"Sure." Adrian reached for it, but she grabbed it first. She set the box on the table.

Staring at the box, he gulped a huge sip of coffee—a huge sip of *scalding* coffee. For the next half-hour, his tongue toyed painfully with the strips of skin hanging from the roof of his mouth. It gave him something to do.

Robyn stayed with him, keeping close watch. Was she there to make sure he didn't make a break for it or in case he, too, collapsed? The paramedics had given him a quick once over—blood pressure, respiration—and thoroughly checked his eyes. They'd declared him fine, although fine was the last thing he felt. His mug clattered slightly as he set it on the table. He had to use both hands to keep it steady.

Adrian picked at the cardboard box on the table between them. It overflowed with awards and framed pictures and other office memorabilia.

"I spent the day processing lay-off paperwork," he babbled. "We're doing an employee *harvest* tomorrow. As far as I know, my job's safe, but I brought most of my personal stuff home just in case."

She nodded. "So not your best day ever, then?"

Adrian tried to smile at the dry, sympathetic comment, but his face remained frozen.

The young forensic tech brought Adrian's camera into the room. "We'd like to take these pictures with us. You're not going to make us get a warrant or anything are you?" He looked nearly as tired as Adrian felt.

Adrian knew his brain was fried but couldn't image why shots of his friend Wendy's birthday bash last month would be of interest. "What pictures?" He scratched his knee.

"The ones of the crime scene on that memory stick you dropped off."

"Pictures?" Robyn narrowed her eyes. "You should have told us about them. Tell me you weren't planning to sell them to a tabloid?"

"I have no idea what pictures you're talking about." Adrian's chair squealed on the linoleum as he pushed back from the table. He scrubbed his hand across his brow. "Show me."

The tech wasn't about to release the camera, but he held it where

Adrian could see the little display screen. Robyn moved to stand behind him so she could see, too.

Pictures of the evening flashed by in reverse order as the tech pushed the "previous image" button. The cop's utility belt, heavy with law enforcement equipment. Violet curled in on herself, clutching her stomach on the floor. Skip in his chair, bopping to the beat. The bag of drugs, full to bursting. There were half a dozen shots, the final shot of a handsome man three stories down, walking his cat.

"What the—" Adrian reached for the camera, but the tech pulled it out of reach.

"You took these? You should have told us." Robyn slid back into her chair and crossed her arms across her chest.

"I guess I… I have no idea. I must have. I was the only one here. I mean, I thought about taking those pictures. When I see something, it gets captured in my brain like a picture. But I don't think I even brought my camera with me down the hall. Wasn't it dusty when you picked it up?"

The tech scratched his chin with one gloved finger. "We dusted it for fingerprints." He shrugged. "Everything's got black dust on it now."

Robyn stared deeply into Adrian's eyes again. "Maybe you inhaled more of that stuff than you thought. Do you want to go to the hospital?"

"I don't think so. I—"

"Sir, we need your permission to take this camera and memory card. If you could sign here?"

"Sure. Sure." He read the form carefully, so distracted he had to read it three times. Finally he signed, telling himself he must have taken them—he'd been alone after all, and they were set up in his style.

"Sorry," he said to Robyn. She raised one shoulder in a half-shrug, although what she meant by it, he didn't know.

Nearly six hours after Violet's first desperate bang on his door, the cops and CSIs packed up, telling Adrian his apartment had been cleared.

"Don't leave town!" the tallest cop ordered.

"Knock it off, Eddy." Officer Robyn glared at her colleague. "He's a witness, not a suspect."

Eddy's accusing gaze never faltered. "Yeah, well. He may not have committed *this* crime…" The cop looked at him suspiciously. "But I'm sure he's done something." He glared one more time before striding away.

"That's our Eddy and his keen sense of humor." Robyn rolled her eyes. "He puts the *fun* in *dysfunctional*." She patted Adrian's hand. "You weren't actually involved, were you, Adrian?"

Under different circumstances, Adrian would have liked her. Shaking his head, he withdrew his hand.

"Here's my card." Robyn placed a business card on the table, next to the box of workplace memories. "Call me if you think of anything that might help."

Adrian fingered the card, sweaty fingers dampening the corner. "I don't know how much more I can tell you. I'm not sure I've been much help at all. I don't even know Skip's real name. I'm sorry. I'm just… so…sorry." He stared at the table top, no idea what he had just apologized for.

Robyn reached for his hand again, but stopped halfway. "Just come to the precinct tomorrow to approve and sign your statement. We'll have it typed up by then. That'll help a lot. Really."

Adrian nodded. Of course he would. It was his duty. He'd miss the big meeting at work, but so what? In light of Violet's death, he could feel his priorities shifting like his own personal tectonic plates.

The lettering and Toronto P.D. logo on her card blurred. When he looked up, Officer Robyn was gone.

CHAPTER 2

BEAUTY SLEEP: RESULTS MAY VARY

For the next couple of hours, Adrian checked his eyes every five minutes even though the paramedics had told him not to worry. When his greeny-hazel irises remained ring-free, he eventually stopped looking.

His toe throbbed and his shoulder ached where Skip had body-checked him into the hall wall. He downed a couple of aspirin and wandered into his bedroom.

His suit was history—the jacket gone—with the forensics guys maybe. And the pants... He tossed them in the garbage. He'd never wear them again even if they weren't stained. He pulled on an old pair of shorts, the elastic almost shot. He returned to the living room, curling up in his big, comfy chair. Although he wasn't cold, he felt better with a blanket wrapped around him.

He tried TV and he tried a book. He called his friend Wendy but her voice mail said she was traveling for a couple of days. Looking up her new cell number seemed like way too much effort. Despite his best efforts to distract himself, his thoughts kept returning to Violet.

His throat felt tight and he figured he might feel better if he cried. He scrunched up his face and sniffled, but the tears refused to come. Too exhausted to haul himself in the other room, he drifted off in his chair.

Muzzy, fuzzy. Colors echo. Noises stink. I rise from my comfy chair, blanket misting away. I stride across the acres of clover in my living room. A dream, I think. One I've had before.

I see a man. On the horizon. No. Now he's here, before me, with me. I touch his chest. He's naked. Good. Now I am, too.

Nice hard body. Handsome face, super-short hair, and nasty scar across his abs. He cups my chin and kisses me. It's good, so good. Gentle, tender, caring. A loving stranger.

He tugs at my hair, playfully using a handful to pull me to him. Kissing, stroking, teasing. My cock aches for his touch. Enough with the foreplay! We rut against each other, too urgent for patience. No time for condoms, no need. He's in me. I'm in him. Even though he's taking me, it feels like I'm taking him.

He's got me. I've got him, too. A two-person daisy chain. Impossible sixty-nine. Yin Yang. Big bang. Gonna come. Gonna... Gonna...

Tom jerked awake, heart racing, breath heaving in rough gasps, the last of his orgasm still thrumming through his system. What the hell? A wet dream? He hadn't had a wet dream since his teens.

Cute guy, though. Not his usual type, but after what had happened with Lazlo, Tom never wanted another muscle-bound blond man again. Maybe that was why his subconscious had drummed up a long-haired gen-Xer. The brown curls were a novelty in Tom's world, not to mention a real turn-on. But then, it was a wet dream. What wasn't a turn-on? Just so long as the guy wasn't blond. Tom shuddered and turned his mind from the past.

His skin tingled, his shorts damp. His fine dusting of dark body hair stood on end. The room was warm, despite the cool breeze soughing in through the open window. A giant cicada clung to the screen, buzzing faintly. The weather here on the tiny island nation of Azunya was great. No wonder BOO had chosen to headquarter there.

Sitting up, he glanced around his private quarters, cheeks heating, very glad barracks days were long behind him. Despite the darkness, he could make out the details of his bedroom, the digital clock illuminating the room. And also telling him it was too early to get up.

He lay back, brain churning. Rumor had it he'd be getting new orders in the morning. Not orders, he corrected. Requests. Offers. *Would you care to undertake this assignment?*

He could always turn down the mission. He found that a little unsettling. He'd been in the army most of his adult life and was conditioned to: *Sir-yes-sir! Go where I'm told, sir! Risk my life for my country, sir! Kill anyone you say I should, sir!* Well, sure, you could say no, if you had a good reason, but don't expect any more promotions, any more plum assignments. He'd learned to say yes early and often. Hadn't hurt his social life any, either.

But now the army was in the past and three months ago he'd signed on with a weird paramilitary group who called themselves the Borderless Observers Organization, making it conditional that he not be sent on any magical missions. Just human problems. Human strife.

At first, some of his colleagues shocked him—vampires, were-beasts, seers, and a bunch he hadn't yet identified. It's not like they wore name badges. *Hi. My name is Crystal. I'm an accounts payable clerk... and a kitsune.*

He never trusted magic, but then humans hadn't been all that good to him either. He preferred to work solo. It hadn't always been that way. Once he'd thought he could trust his teammates, that they'd always have his back. He rolled over and punched the pillow a few times. *I don't need anybody.*

Middle of the night or not, he wasn't getting back to sleep. He headed for the bathroom, tossed the sticky shorts on the floor, turned on the shower, and stepped in.

CHAPTER 3

ESCAPE CLAWS

Adrian awoke from the best sex he'd had in ages. Slowly it dawned on him that he'd fallen asleep in his living room chair, and his dreamy lover was only a dream. Military type, eh? He hadn't had the generic soldier fantasy in a while. After the day he'd had, his subconscious probably felt it needed to surrender control to an authority figure. Or maybe it had been inspired by all those uniformed cops who'd poked around last night. He'd thought Officer Eddy kind of cute, if only the guy hadn't taken the role of *bad cop* quite so seriously. Anyway, his dream lover's buzz cut and hard body had been sexy as hell.

He sighed and stretched, his neck cracking painfully. The room was inky dark. A glance at the window said morning was still a long way away. He really should go lie down, but somehow he just couldn't. How could he lie in the comfort of his warm, soft bed when Violet lay on a cold metal table somewhere? His only knowledge of morgues came from TV, but they'd pretty consistently been cold rooms filled with lockers of dead people. His throat ached and his eyes burned.

Shifting a bit, Adrian realized he needed to change his pants and went to clean up without turning on the light.

He returned to his chair sporting fresh shorts. He curled up again, hooking the hassock closer and tucking the blanket around him again. Deliberately not thinking about the evening's tragic events, he dozed...

Only to startle awake, fog-headed and panicky. *What was that? A scratching noise? What the hell?* One more shock and he'd shoot right out of his chair, and end up hanging from the ceiling, nails dug into the plaster like some cartoon kitty.

The scratching noise became a clicking. He could hear it coming across the floor toward him. Unable to parse the darkness, he huddled deeper beneath the blanket. Still groggy with sleep, he childishly hoped the thin fabric would shield him from whatever evil moved inexorably his way.

Closer, closer it came, halting in the shadows right before his chair. Suddenly, something landed in his lap. Something hard and sharp! He leapt from the chair with a squawk, tripping on his failed security blanket.

His third pass at the lamp illuminated the room, throwing a pool of light on the blanket that bubbled and hissed on the floor.

His eyes adjusted and he watched in groggy confusion as the discarded blanket writhed about like some boneless ghost seizing on his apartment floor. Adrian's stomach flip-flopped and it wasn't exactly his heart that came up into his mouth.

Eventually, the truth sank into his foggy brain, and he realized it wasn't the blanket itself that was possessed, but that it was wrapped *around* something—something that struggled and hissed. Too big for a mouse, it must be a rat. How could he contain it? He couldn't just grab the blanket since the...whatever-it-was could probably bite right through it. He'd get rabies for sure. Or bubonic plague!

As he watched, the thing under the blanket managed to work its way to one side, finally nosing its whiskery little face out from under. It surveyed the room once before streaking toward the kitchen and disappearing under the little table.

A cat. Adrian shuddered. How had a freakin' cat gotten into the apartment? It had to go. Now.

He headed toward the apartment door, trying to figure how he'd coax the damn thing back out. It was probably someone's beloved pet and they'd be worried sick. It must have sneaked inside last night during all the...

And then he remembered. It was Violet's cat, Pixel. And Violet wasn't going to be able to care for him ever again. This, more than anything else, finally brought home the grim reality of Violet's death. He fell back in the chair, wrapping the not-possessed blanket around himself again. He couldn't really be blamed if, when the cat jumped in his lap a second time, he let it stay, maybe even scratched it behind the ears a little.

Nor did Pixel seem to mind if he got a little tear-stained.

CHAPTER 4

THE QUALM BEFORE THE STORM

Thomas J. Ferrell had joined the army at eighteen, starting at private, obtaining a degree in military history, and eventually rising to captain.

Ten years in, an off-the-record recruiting officer had approached him. He'd listened to the guy's pitch, then made the switch from regular army to Special Ops. During the last years of his military career, he'd successfully completed nearly two dozen covert missions that, according to official records, had never happened. His final mission so secret, his superiors granted him early retirement to prevent difficult questions from being asked. And even they didn't know the whole story.

Over the course of his military career, he'd faced some terrifying enemies, and served under some scary commanding officers. They were nothing compared to his new boss, Jacqueline Batique, head of Borderless Observers Org.

He entered her office, determined not to let her see him sweat. Luckily her office was well air-conditioned or all the determination in the world wouldn't have kept the sweat stains at bay here in their tropical island complex.

She rose to greet him, easily matching his six feet two inches. She wore a light business suit, chunky gold jewelry, and little makeup as far as Tom could tell. A trio of black-on-brown scars adorned each cheek.

"Welcome, Captain Ferrell. I may call you Thomas, may I not?" She spoke with a rich cultured accent, probably from expensive finishing schools and private tutors. Gossip ran high at BOO, but nobody seemed to know anything about Ms. Batique, except that she'd been Director of BOO for a long, long time. In fact, there was no record of anyone else ever being Director since its founding as The Royal Society for the Investigation of Natural and Unnatural Phenomena back in the 1800s.

"Yes, ma'am. Uh, it's Tom, actually."

"Of course," she responded, a stiff little smile replacing the welcoming one. He felt he'd disappointed her, although he wasn't sure how. "Or Thomas is fine, too. Uh, ma'am."

Her smile warmed again. Seating herself, she indicated he should take the wicker chair before her desk. She didn't invite him to call her Jacqueline, and no one in their right mind would ever call her Jackie.

His new boss cleared her throat. "I have a favor to ask of you. Would you care to go on a journey? Perhaps see some of the equatorial rain forest?"

What a sales pitch. Couldn't she just tell him what she wanted? "Yes, ma'am." He figured he couldn't go wrong with that.

"Excellent. Thank you. You would care for additional details? Yes? There is a scientist in the Amazon jungle. He is doing good work, devoting his life to a noble cause. He has spent his entire family fortune to further his research. But our sources tell us he has now turned to less savory methods of funding."

Tom wondered what those sources were. He wasn't sure he'd like the answer. This was one weird organization, and for all he knew they used crystal balls and blind seers to obtain their intel. They did have massive banks of computers with radar and satellite hookups and all kinds of blinking lights and beeping screens—NORAD eat your heart out! Tom figured BOO could not only track Santa, but had him on their payroll. Santa wouldn't be the strangest co-worker Tom had met. Besides, BOO's intel was way more accurate than the army's, so he sat up a little straighter and paid attention.

"Dr. Deerborne is…" Ms. Batique frowned down at the thin manila file on her desk, laying the flat of one hand on it as if trying to contain its contents. "Or at least he *was* a good man, but I fear for his sanity. We have provided him with funding and protection in the past, but apparently not enough for his vast ambitions."

She raised her eyes to meet Tom's. The early morning light

streamed in the windows, making her brown eyes glow golden. Tom heard wicker creaking and realized he was fidgeting. Hell, first a wet dream and now a return to the principal's bench. When had he entered his second childhood? He was thirty-four years old, for Chrissake!

He steeled himself to meet her eyes, but ended up focusing on her wide metal choker instead. It gleamed in the light, mesmerizing, hypnotizing... He yanked his gaze away, suddenly finding his own knee fascinating.

"Dr. Deerborne has been approached and manipulated by a very bad man. Elvis Montoya is the son of a cocaine dynasty, but he was too unscrupulous even for them and they have ousted him from the family business. Together, Dr. Deerborne and Señor Montoya are manufacturing and distributing the new drug known as indigo. You have seen the news reports, yes? This drug is fast becoming popular among those people who favor a dangerous lifestyle. Yet it is of deadly consequence to some individuals. In addition to foisting their illegal drug on the world, they are also using involuntary labor to manufacture it. Rain forest Indians are captured and forced to work in their drug factory, beaten, starved. This is Montoya's doing. I have hope yet for Basil Deerborne."

"Rain forest's a pretty big place. Whereabouts will I be going?"

"The details are in this file I shall give you. You have asked specifically for assignments in which no magic is involved in the commission of the crime. This is a very human problem."

Tom nodded. Yes, he only wanted to deal with human bad guys. Magic had been the downfall of his last career. Bad enough he had to work with all these "supernaturals," as they liked to call themselves.

She inclined her head in acknowledgment. "You must be discreet, circumspect, and unobtrusive. Not a breath of scandal may touch his family. You are authorized to use judicious force, should you deem it necessary."

"A license to kill, you mean?" The words were out before Tom could think. Words had never been his strong point, especially when nervous. It was why he used them so sparingly. His psych appraisals always read, "concise and efficient" if the shrinks liked him, "curt and secretive" if they didn't. Special Ops had liked a guy who kept his trap shut.

"I would not phrase it quite so succinctly, but yes."

"But—"

She raised a hand. "There is a reason we are located on this tiny island, other than the clement weather. It is owned not by one government, but shared by many. We act under the auspices of the world's superpowers, and most other nations as well."

"Why wasn't I told any of this when I signed up?"

"You are told what you need to know, when you need to know it." She rose and handed him the file folder. "We are not entirely unlike your army, yes?

He closed his mouth and opened the folder. The first item was a travel itinerary that would take him to Bogotá, Colombia via Atlanta.

"Now I must inform you, Thomas…" She raised an eyebrow "We have adopted a warning policy. I believe you Americans would call it *three strikes and one is out*."

Tom opened his mouth to correct her, but on second, smarter thought, he snapped it closed again. His teeth were beginning to hurt.

"We have spoken once already with Dr. Deerborne. He has refused our offer of controlled funding and supervision, instead choosing to partner with Elvis Montoya. You will find this Montoya and give him this warning as well. If Señor Montoya is not receptive, then you will travel to Tanpu where Dr. Deerborne has his lab and speak with him. Please be sure he grasps that this is his final warning."

"And if he doesn't agree?"

She tapped the desk, her fingernails short and blunt. "You will use your satellite phone to contact us. Your team will be comprised of a telepath, a werewolf for tracking on land, and a selkie for underwater work. To this end, I'll put Josie, Chai-Li, and Eric on standby. In that file you'll find a list of—"

"No," Tom interrupted, before he could think.

The tapping ceased. "No?" She raised an eyebrow.

Now he was sweating, but he'd faced graver threats. "No. I do this one alone." He leaned forward. "Let me do this. I can take down the drug operation alone." Even as he said it, he realized how preposterous it sounded.

She gazed at him, toying with the choker at her neck. Her gaze grew distant. The clock on her desk ticked. Finally she refocused on him, nodding once. "You cannot take down the operation alone, but you will not need us. Should Deerborne and Montoya continue the indigo production, you must use your own judgment to resolve the situation. Do you understand?"

Tom nodded again, but she seemed to be waiting for more. "Yes, ma'am. Understood, ma'am."

"You will find allies when you need them. And you may find you feel differently about magic following this mission." A tiny smile played at the corners of her dark lips. "Thank you."

Tom didn't need a translator to know that her gracious "thank you" was the civilian equivalent of *"DIS-missed!"*

No one was more surprised than Tom when he found himself bowing slightly as he took the folder and left. Bowing? Who the hell bowed in this day and age?

* * *

Tom flipped to the next page in the file. It was a brief account of the most recently reported death by indigo. A twenty-four-year-old woman in Toronto had died in her home. Tom felt the unsettling mixture of judgmental and sympathetic. She'd taken the damn drug like a fool, and while pregnant, according to the article. He tried for righteous indignation, but just felt sorry for the two wasted lives.

If he'd been waffling over taking this mission before, he certainly wasn't now. Deerborne and Montoya had to be stopped—by any means necessary, as Ms. Batique had made so clear.

Tom turned to the next document in the file, a CIA report.

> *First reported in January of last year, Indigo is a powerful stimulant directly affecting the brain. Like cocaine, reports indicate it is shipping from South America. Authorities believe it is being manufactured deep within the rain forest, although neither aerial nor infrared tracking have managed to locate the manufacturing facility(s).*

Great. All the spy technology in the world and they can't find a manufacturing plant in the rain forest. Well, they couldn't find weapons of mass destruction, either, he groused. But he wasn't at all bitter about the abrupt way his military career had ended. Not him. He scratched his stomach and moved on.

Indigo users are often identifiable by the iridescent blue ring that circles the iris when using the drug—not just during the immediate ingestion period, but building up cumulatively.

The article went on to talk about trafficking trends, arrests and sentencing, and legislation.

The new drug dealt in dreams and delusions, death and destruction.

Yet people lined up to try it. Tom clenched his teeth, grinding them in fury as he turned to his computer and googled the drug. He clicked links, followed threads, read on about this new threat, the havoc it created. If it followed the patterns of previous drug infestations, it would soon spread across the world, thanks to a few entitled, greedy men with no value for human lives other than their own.

He couldn't wait to take the bastards down. The question, now, was how? And how soon?

CHAPTER 5

A Change Is As Good As A Quest

The sun was just rising when Pierre passed Adrian's cubicle. Adrian grabbed a stack of envelopes and followed his boss into his office.

"Oh. It's you." Pierre tugged at his collar, loosening his tie. "Big day, today, eh? Got the rest of the layoff paperwork done?"

Adrian set the envelopes on Pierre's desk, each one labeled with the name of some unlucky soon-to-be-ex-employee. "It's all here, Pierre."

"Good. Good. I'm glad you're in early. I've got something—"

"Hey, Pierre." Adrian swallowed. He pulled the top envelope off the pile, gripping it so tightly his knuckles blanched white. "Listen. You asked me to give some thought to how we could trim the fat in our department, and I have an idea for another lay off." He paused.

A huge smile bloomed on Pierre's face. "Yes, yes? Who is it? No one in our senior leadership team. You know those guys are hands-off."

"No. Just another small fry who won't even be missed. Me."

"You. Well, uh." Pierre adjusted his tie, drawing the knot up tight against his throat. "It's actually good you bring it up. I was going to keep you on till the end of the week. That'd give you a few more days' pay. But since you mentioned it, I happen to have the paperwork here." He handed Adrian a folder, running a finger under his collar. "I guess you know where to sign." He chuckled, but wouldn't meet Adrian's eyes.

So they were going to keep me long enough to process the layoffs, then give me the boot, too. Doc Soc's offer couldn't have come at a better time. Adrian flipped through the folder quickly. Nobody knew layoff paperwork like he did. "Nuh-uh." He slapped his termination form on the desk. "That's *three* weeks a year severance for every year worked, not two. I'm a Stratum Three now. *You* promoted me."

"No, but…" Pierre fingered his tie but didn't loosen it again. "You haven't been in your new role three months yet. You're still on, uh, probation."

"Probation's only for new hires, not promotions. You should know. The policies I wrote all have *your* name on them as author."

Pierre sputtered, yanking his tie off completely. He rose and pointed at Adrian. "Now, you listen here. You should be grateful—"

"You know…" Adrian swallowed hard, hoping to hell he looked calm. Swimming with the sharks wasn't his strong suit, but no way was he going to let them get away with this. "I never asked you how that HR conference in Vegas was last month. Did you and Devorah enjoy yourselves? I didn't realize her customer service job involved so much HR."

Pierre sat hard, wheeled chair rolling back, smacking lightly into his credenza.

"Okay. Okay. Three weeks for each year." His personal shredder whirred as he fed his version of Adrian's layoff documents into its gaping maw. "Will you require a termination bonus? Because I—"

"Nope. I only want what's coming to me. In fact, I have the paperwork right here." He presented the termination form he'd prepared. It was a little damp from his sweaty palms. "I guess *you* know where to sign."

He'd only meant to take an office job for a few months while he saved enough to pursue a career in anthropology. Well, here he was three years later, actually doing it. "Thanks, Pierre. It's been swell. I have to go see some law enforcement agents."

"Law enforcement—"

Without a backward glance, Adrian walked out, leaving Pierre, kisser of management ass, to sweat over it.

Adrian reached the street, elated and shaking just the tiniest bit. He walked quickly away. It was still so early the streets were almost empty. Two blocks later, he leaned up against a building, relief spreading through him like a shot of tequila. Braced against the cool brick, he flipped open his cell phone, found the number and hit send.

"Hello. You have reached the voice mail of Professor Socrates

Kawasaki. I'm not—"

Adrian pressed five to bypass the rest.

"Hey, Doc Soc. How's it hanging? Still fish-free, I hope. Listen, I've changed my mind. Set a place for me at the tribal campfire 'cause I'm going to the rain forest with you!" He whooped and disconnected.

Next on the morning's agenda, 52 Division to sign his statement about last night. Then off to PetSmart to stock up on Kitti-Feast. And definitely a real litterbox. He'd lined a cardboard box with plastic and newspaper, but both he and Pixel would be much happier with the real thing.

CHAPTER 6

A QUEER AND PLEASANT DANGER

Adrian yawned. The enforced inactivity of long flights left him stiff. He stretched, pushing his arms straight down toward his knees instead of out at the sides since he'd been assigned the middle seat in a three-seat grouping. A proper stretch would mean cauliflower ears for his neighbors. And speaking of ears, his popped painfully.

His seatmates ignored him.

The Avianca Airlines plane was an older model, without any entertainment. Every seatback on the Air Canada flight from Toronto to Atlanta had sported those individual computerized screens. It had taken him nearly the entire flight to select a program. After this one, he had a puddlejumper flight to catch in Bogotá that would take him a little closer to the village of Tanpu where Professor Kawasaki awaited him.

Adrian pressed the seat button and pushed back, making sure his seatback was as far from its upright position as possible, mind still racing despite his fatigue.

There'd been planning and packing. He'd had to get approval to leave Toronto, but since Skip hadn't been arrested or found yet, they couldn't object. He gave the cops his email address and promised to return if they needed him to testify. He was only going to be gone a couple of weeks, after all. His friend Wendy had agreed to look after Pixel for him. The cat took one look at her and abandoned his skinny lap for her generous one. Adrian had been a little hurt. Especially when

Wendy, too, seemed to prefer her newfound friend to Adrian. The cat had grown on him, and he had every intention of keeping the cute little thing. It wasn't like he'd learned to trust cats, but Pixel was obviously the exception...at least in his eyes.

Doc Soc had emailed that he'd secured an excellent guide and a couple of other local Indians who knew the area and were willing function as scouts, guards, porters, and cooks.

Adrian's musings left him determined and restless. He glanced at his seatmates. Both were engrossed in their own interests, the guy in the window seat napping, the woman on the aisle doing something with a Blackberry.

He was tired, yet too excited to doze. A bunch of friends had surprised him with a "congratulations on following your dreams" party the evening before. It left him yawning and, after a few of the more heated goodbye hugs and kisses, a little turned on. A friend of a friend had wanted to hook up, but Adrian had begged off, claiming an early flight. He wasn't sure why he'd said no. It was almost as if he was waiting for someone.

He'd sworn off men after a heart-wrenching break-up from which he'd never quite recovered—never quite recovered his iPod, never quite recovered his Nintendo DS, never quite recovered the two hundred and fifty dollars in cash he'd received from his parents for his birthday. "From now on," he'd sworn, "I'm going to be dynamic, strong, and successful." And for the past year, he'd been all these things. And also? He'd been alone.

He stretched one more time and, while he didn't actually need to pee, he did need to get up and walk around. Climbing over his grumpy seatmate, he headed for the lavatory, actually hoping there was a line-up so he'd have an excuse to stand around for a bit.

The line consisted of only one other person, a tall, handsome man in his mid-thirties dressed in khaki sweater and cargo pants. It did wonderful things for his blue, blue eyes. Blue eyes without any weird, iridescent rings, Adrian noted. He'd gotten in the habit of checking every time he met someone. All that intense eye contact had gotten him some interesting offers and a few unnecessary rejections, but he'd kept checking anyway. Adrian figured this bathroom line-up guy for military, basing his conclusion on the short spiky haircut. And the all-khaki outfit. The muscular body and the short hair reminded him of the sex dream he'd had a few days ago.

The guy looked at Adrian expectantly, probably bored, too. "First time in Bogotá?"

"Just passing through," Adrian answered. Although it was none of this stranger's business, Adrian was so excited about his big trip he couldn't help but add, "I'm on my way to the rain forest."

The guy's eyes widened. "Me, too."

He seemed sincere, not just making conversation. Adrian didn't mind a bit of distraction, and the guy was really handsome. He caught himself staring at the guy's pretty mouth. *Uh-oh. Busted.* The guy caught him at it, too. And smiled back, looking both predatory and very cute. Adrian felt his dick harden and his cheeks redden. He blurted the first thing he thought of. "I'm going to find a lost temple and hopefully—"

The plane hit turbulence. Adrian jerked and swayed right into the broad khaki chest.

"Whoa!" The man shot one arm around Adrian and grasped a bulkhead handhold with the other.

He held Adrian tightly as the plane bucked and swayed, Adrian's arms crushed awkwardly between them. The man loosened his grip as the turbulence subsided. Adrian pushed off his chest, only to be tossed forward again by the next dip. His arms flailed outward, instinctively grabbing for support. His right arm ended up wrapped around the man's neck, his left hand fisting the khaki sweater.

The plane gave another sickening lurch, this time sending the plane—and Adrian—to one side. Adrian felt the warm, hard pressure of a muscular bicep against his chest. He leaned into the touch as the other man's hands tightening on him.

Against all good judgment and common sense, the lavatory's current occupant chose that moment to fling open the door and, using the doorframe for leverage, propelled himself past them. He continued up the aisle, using seatbacks as handholds, until a gut-wrenching drop sent him flying into an unsuspecting row of passengers, while simultaneously tossing Adrian and his companion into the open bathroom.

The khaki-clad man landed with his ass half in the tiny sink, Adrian half-sprawled in his lap. Apparently he thought this was the moment for introductions, beginning, "Hi, I'm T—" His words were over-ridden by the crash of the bathroom door slamming shut, barely missing Adrian's backside. "Tom," he repeated.

"Adrian," he replied, sliding across Tom's broad chest as the plane tipped to the left. It seemed important to him, all of a sudden, to do something daring and different. To prove he was capable of doing anything he pleased. To prove it to himself. And also to take the edge off before he landed in Colombia. That was the one thing he'd forgotten to take care of last night! He had no idea what the bunking and showering arrangements might be like in Colombia. It might be a while before he had enough privacy to jerk off again.

The pilot's calm voice grated from the loudspeaker above their heads, assuring them there was nothing to worry about, first in Spanish and then in accented English. Immediately following his reassuring announcement, the main lights winked out, leaving Adrian and Tom in the tiny cubicle with nothing but dim emergency lighting thrown by the small backup fixture over the mirror.

Even in the faint glow, Adrian was aware Tom was staring at his mouth. Tom raised one hand to brush Adrian's long curls back from his face.

Adrian gazed into Tom's eyes, so blue they still shone even in the dim emergency lighting. "Now's the time to tell me you're going off to war and might not make it back."

"Funny you should mention that." Tom lowered his mouth over Adrian's. Adrian kissed back hungrily for a few long, languid seconds before Tom pulled back.

"I—" Tom began.

"Shhh!" Adrian hoped he'd been right about Tom being military, and that he was good at taking orders. He twisted to one side and slid the little lever across to lock the door changing the sign to *Occupied/Ocupado.*

Turning back to Tom, Adrian asked, "Wanna join the Mile High Club?"

"Hell, yeah," Tom breathed, nipping at Adrian's lower lip. "I want frequent flyer points."

Although he'd been holding on to Adrian for the last few minutes, his entire demeanor changed, and he now seemed to envelop him in a whole new and sexy way. Tom's sheer size was a turn-on, and his long arms were everywhere. Adrian moaned and arched backward as long fingers trailed down the back seam of his jeans. Tom sucked lightly on Adrian's neck and closed his teeth gently over the tendon beneath his ear.

Adrian moaned, feeling breathless and dizzy and more turned on than he'd been in months. Possibly years.

"I've never done this before." Adrian meant many things by that—

sex on a plane, sex in public, sex with a stranger. It didn't matter if Tom interpreted him correctly, or if he even heard him at all over the roar of the engines. Tom so wasn't going to respect him in the morning, and Adrian really didn't care. This was exactly what he needed—no strings attached sex from someone he'd never see again. Hell, if the guy's Midwestern twang was anything to go on, they probably weren't even from the same country. This was good. So good.

"Fuck me," Adrian moaned, feeling free and daring.

Tom froze, clutching at Adrian's arms and resting his forehead against Adrian's. "Oh, God. Keep saying things like that, and I won't get a chance to." He stayed still another moment, apparently groping for control, before returning to his task of driving Adrian crazy, rubbing his hands across Adrian's nipples, then reaching down to rub his aching erection. The touch felt great even through his jeans. Adrian gasped, pushing against his hand.

"So good." He murmured. "So—"

"Turn around!" Tom growled.

Shivering with excitement, Adrian did as instructed. Lightning quick, Tom dealt with Adrian's zipper, sending his jeans into a denim puddle around his ankles.

Both men turned so they were facing the shadowy mirror, Adrian in front, Tom pressed right up against his now bare ass. For a long moment Adrian just stared into the mirror, panting and meeting Tom's hungry gaze. Adrian read desire in Tom's eyes and in his own. Tom reached around, his erection pressing against Adrian's ass while he jerked Adrian's cock, the heel of his hand thwapping the thigh-high countertop with every stroke.

Tom removed his hand from Adrian's cock only long enough to position his hard-on so the head was pressing inward, but just the head. Panting, he drew back. "Condom," he said desperately, a pleading looking in his eyes.

"In my knapsack."

Tom looked hopeful.

"Back at my seat," Adrian finished, dashing both their hopes.

"Oh, God. Oh, God. What will we…" He moaned and pushed himself forward so the slippery tip of his cock pressed another millimeter inside.

Blow jobs it is, then, Adrian figured, trying to clear his head, although he'd really been in the mood to get well and truly fucked. He considered the logistics of the tiny bathroom. "If I sit on the—"

"Oh! I almost forgot." Tom's reflection turned smug. He reached awkwardly into his back pocket, his khakis drooping low, hanging precariously from his narrow hips, and drew out a wallet. "For emergencies." He produced a flattened foil packet, squinting at it. "Uh. It's nearly expired. Guess I should get out more, huh? That okay?"

Panting, Adrian nodded at the mirror. "Live dangerously!"

"Oh, man, you have no idea." He tore the packet open with his teeth. (And how far gone was Adrian that that was just about the sexiest thing he'd ever seen?) "Pre-lubed," he said, slipping it on. Suddenly in a rush, Tom began working his way inside. Using both hands now, he gripped Adrian's body, hip and ass, crushing him against the sink, driving in as far as possible.

Once fully seated, Tom began to slide in and out, gently at first. Their eyes locked in the dark depths of the mirror, lips parted and panting. As Adrian opened up for him, Tom began to move faster and faster until he was slamming in.

But the position was wrong for Adrian. He needed friction, and there was nothing to press against. He took one hand off the mirror and wrapped it around his straining dick, relying on the other arm for support. Tom slapped his hand away. The big man wrapped his own huge paw around Adrian's cock and began to jerk him in time with his rhythm, giving it a hot twist over the head with every stroke. It was exactly what Adrian needed. He could feel his orgasm swirling in his balls, building, building…

Suddenly, Tom bit possessively on the back of Adrian neck hard enough to leave marks. Pain tangoed with pleasure, and with a gasp that was almost a shout, Adrian came and came and came, barely aware of Tom's orgasm when it hit.

Tom lost his erection quickly, and it felt like the end of something when he slipped from Adrian's body. He disposed of the condom and, turning Adrian to face him, kissed him deeply.

Men are always grateful, Adrian thought as his mind returned to earth, for about five minutes before they get all smug and superior. Adrian steeled himself for some kind of unpleasant aftermath that would ruin his afterglow.

Instead, Tom kissed him almost shyly, smiling boyishly despite looking around thirty-five—maybe five or six years older than Adrian. His charm put paid to all thoughts of resistance. Something cold and damaged inside Adrian began to melt. He surprised himself by saying, "Should we try and get together again? Talk a bit."

Tom smiled and nuzzled his neck. "I'd like that, but I'm leaving Bogotá and don't know when I'll be back. Give me your email address, and I'll write you when I can." Tom produced a Blackberry and thumbed through to the address book. "Okay, what is it?"

"It's anthro.adrian@rogers.ca." He leaned in. "No, that's *anthro* as in *anthropology*."

"Got it." He tucked the device back in its holster. Adrian could picture Tom with a gun, instead.

"I had a dream the other night," Tom continued. "I dreamed about a guy a lot like you." He tugged on Adrian's ponytail for emphasis. "The long hair is hot."

Adrian barked out a laugh. "That's funny, 'cause the other night I dreamed about a guy with a crew cut. Which is weird because—"

The bathroom lights flickered on, seeming horribly bright after the dim emergency lights. Adrian lost his train of thought as he shifted against the cold countertop, the edge digging into his thighs. He pulled up his pants and yanked down his shirt.

Tom straightened his own clothing. Adrian gave him as much room as possible by jamming himself into the corner by the door. Tom turned to the sink, scrubbing his hands thoroughly. Although a big fan of personal hygiene, Adrian thought that much anti-bacterial soap was rather insulting. He felt kind of slutty, but wasn't that why he'd hooked up in the first place?

He felt satiated, adult, and proud of his little rebellion against the celibate life he'd been living for a long time now—a nice safe lifestyle that left him sad and lonely.

His friends had been telling him for months he needed to get out and meet a nice boy.

And now he had met a nice boy—a nice man, really. One who he'd probably never see again. Well, now he'd ruined his own afterglow. Men. Couldn't live with them…

Once more they shuffled around the tiny bathroom until Adrian sat on the closed toilet so Tom could get at the door. Before pulling the latch, he surprised Adrian by leaning in and kissing him one more time.

Adrian pulled back and admired the handsome man. He framed a shot in his mind, *click*, his inner sound effects supplied.

Tom smiled and left, closing the door quickly behind him.

Adrian made use of the facilities, cleaning up as best he could. He made sure there were no telltale white splotches on the counter or the floor, then tried wiping the hand prints from the mirror where he'd braced himself. He left big smudges, but it wasn't like glass cleaner was provided among the complimentary products.

He left the lavatory with a spring in his step (not really noticeable with the residual turbulence). He felt better than he had in a long time.

He wondered if he'd find the scent of airline deodorizers arousing for the rest of his life, deeply grateful it was pine and not lavender.

* * *

Tom navigated back to his row, glad he'd picked the aisle seat so he wouldn't have to climb over his dozing seatmates. He seated himself gingerly, as if he were the one who'd just bottomed. His skin felt tingly and taut, like it fit again after months of feeling awkward and strange—since he'd left the army. Maybe even before that.

He realized he was grinning and rearranged his features to hide his "got some" smile. Pretending to yawn, he sniffed at one armpit, hoping he didn't reek of sex.

His seatmates dozed on.

Congratulating himself on getting laid in the middle of a crowded airplane without anyone noticing, he allowed his grin to re-emerge. He was still admiring his stealth skills when, unexpectedly, the airline steward presented him with a huge shrimp cocktail probably reserved for first class, where Tom was very definitely not sitting.

"I didn't order this," Tom told the smiling steward.

"My compliments," the man answered, winking. "Just consider me a fan. Besides, you may need to keep up your strength."

Tom meant to be indignant and outraged, but for some reason, he grinned and winked back instead.

Leaning in, the steward whispered, "He's a real cutie." He nodded knowingly, glancing toward the back of the plane, probably where Adrian was seated.

Tom blushed, focusing on the shrimp cocktail, furious at himself for blushing. "Thanks," he mumbled.

The steward rested his palm on Tom's shoulder for a second, whispering, "I certainly hope you got that one's number," and wheeled his trolley on down the aisle.

Tom feasted on his jumbo shrimp, feeling like he'd won something…something more than just a festive dish of seafood.

Finally surfacing, his seatmate blinked at him owlishly, a twenties-something guy, wearing designer-ripped jeans and a T-shirt with the logo of a band that had broken up before he'd been born. "Hey, man." The guy eyed Tom's rapidly disappearing shrimp. "Who you gotta blow to get one of those?"

Without missing a beat, Tom responded, "You might try the steward. And just so you know, the bathrooms are bigger than they look."

The guy's mouth hung open. Obviously he'd only meant it as a crack, not a request for hook-up advice. Tom munched on happily, ignoring everything but his shrimp and his very recent, very fond memories. He patted his Blackberry, but knew he'd never use that email address. Sadly, they must never meet again. No entanglements for this secret operative, that was for damn sure!

* * *

Returning to his seat, Adrian lay back and closed his eyes, savoring the memory of his bathroom tryst. Before long, he began to get hard again. So to take his mind off all things arousing, he reviewed his notes about the expedition.

Adrian had scoured the library and the Internet, prepping for his trip. A couple of the more far-out sources claimed Amazon witch doctors performed weird acts of magic and miracle cures. Not just the poultices and elixirs that modern men of science were looking into, but real magic, like transmogrification. He'd had to look that one up. It meant shape-shifting, like werewolves. Of course that was fiction, but there might be some interesting folklore. If he could get paid by some of the travel magazines or even new age publications, then he could support himself for a while without having to return to office work.

Having acquired some Spanish in high school, Adrian had devoted his prep time for this trip to Quechua, a fusion of the original language of the Incas mixed with conquistador Spanish, with a dash of forest Indian as well. Some scholars were finding connections with ancient Hebrew, which Adrian, Jewish on his dad's side, found fascinating. Although most of the aboriginal jungle tribes had their own dialects, they managed a sort of Quechua-based trade tongue to communicate with each other. Adrian had memorized as many basic words and phrases as he could. He had a remarkable facility for language, but it had only been a few days since he'd agreed to go... *Since Violet's death,* a tiny voice in his mind whispered.

He'd called Officer Robyn yesterday morning, but there had been no leads on the missing boyfriend. Skip was *officially* wanted for questioning in regard to Violet's death, but Officer Robyn had confided that they planned to charge him with manslaughter the instant they found him.

It had been nice of Robyn to put in an appearance at Violet's memorial service. Adrian hadn't known anyone else, so they'd kind of hung back at the edges. Violet's parents had thanked them both for coming. It had fallen on Robyn to inform them of their daughter's death. Then she'd had to question them about Skip. It seemed that Violet had neglected to mention either Skip or their impending grandparent-hood. How awful for Robyn to have to break it to them; how awful for them to have to hear it that way. Adrian found new respect for Robyn and her fellow officers.

In preparation for his trip, he'd exercised his crack google-fu to scout out the rain forest, finding Doc Soc's team wasn't the only researcher group interested in the area. A British scientist, Dr. Basil Deerborne, had established a lab in Tanpu, where he was investigating traditional anti-malarials and other jungle cures. Adrian had emailed Dr. Deerborne requesting an interview, but had received a discouraging reply. The doctor had, in fact, told him—no, *ordered* him—to stay away. Yeah, Adrian thought, I'll get right on that. As if the guy was lord of the rain forest or something.

Still, they'd be in the same village—Tanpu, Colombia, population three hundred fifty—so he was sure to run into the guy. Adrian could still snoop around Deerborne's lab. He might write yet another article he could sell to *National Geographic—Dedicated Jungle Doctor Seeks Witch Doctor Cure*. More like *National Inquirer*. Still, ego aside, if it paid, Adrian was up for it. And maybe some exposure would help Dr. Deerborne with his fundraising. Not that Adrian had been able to find a fundraising website for Deerborne, but he had to be getting his funding somewhere. A tiny article on the *UK Guardian's* website reported Deerborne's family had cut him off once he'd burned through his personal fortune. Nice of them to support his research. No wonder Deerborne had sent him that curt email ordering him away. He had every right to be pissed, poor guy. Adrian couldn't wait to meet the noble scientist. He just knew they'd get along.

In addition to the article on the jungle doctor, Adrian planned to shoot pictures of rubber collection and local industry, native flora and fauna, possibly the infamous dick-fish as well. Some sources said the *carnero* was real, while others decried it as an urban legend, er, rural legend, er, jungle… apocryphal tale. Still, Adrian had no intention of peeing in any Amazonian body of water. He'd find a nice tree somewhere and hope there weren't dick-lizards or something. He'd spent a half-hour googling dick-parasites after that, then parasites in general. He'd itched for hours afterward.

Anyway, he wanted to photograph a whole whack of different subjects so he could write articles on everything from the rain forest itself to local religious rites. While getting published in *Anthropologist Digest* would win him the admiration of his peers, it was the commercial publications that would keep a roof over his head and Pixel in Finicky Feast, an important commitment now that he intended to keep the cat. That was assuming he could extract his fuzzy new roommate from Wendy's warm and nurturing clutches when he got back.

One googled link had taken him to the CIA website where he read with growing horror of the evils of indigo. He wasn't worried about running into the drug lords, though. South America was, after all, a huge continent. What were the chances?

The very last thing he had done was call his parents. From the airport. Just before his flight.

"You're going where?" they'd shrieked. "It's not safe. You could get hurt. We read in *National Geographic* about this fish that swims up your…your *you know*. Did you buy travel insurance?"

His parents were so risk averse they never left their southern Ontario hamlet. They'd both stayed in unfulfilling jobs from high school to retirement, hating it when their only son had moved to big, bad Toronto to attend U of T. They unplugged the TV during thunderstorms, and lived in fear of cell phones and Americans. Adrian had been twelve before he clued in they weren't like normal parents who took their kids hunting and snowmobiling. He'd had to learn to ride a bicycle in secret. When he'd come out to them about being gay, they'd showered him with a rainbow array of condoms and literature about safe sex—and at that point, he hadn't even gotten laid yet!

Speaking loudly over the intermittent flight announcements, he'd assured them repeatedly he'd be fine. And that he'd bought Blue Cross travel insurance. When his mother began to cry, he held the phone up toward the ceiling speaker and told them he had to run to catch his plane.

"You're going via Alaska?" his dad asked. Great. The one time the airport sound system was intelligible. His flight didn't actually leave for another hour. "You know, son. Hundreds of people die in polar bear related accidents every year."

"Gotta run. Mom, Dad. I love you." He'd clicked the phone shut, feeling guilty he'd lied to them—even a tiny white lie to cut the call short. It had taken him a long time to learn to take risks. Besides, he was just going for a stroll through the rain forest. What could possibly happen?

CHAPTER 7

LOOK WHO'S STALKING

Adrian had plenty of time to make his connection with the small private airline that would take him to San Arbol. It was the closest town to Tanpu with a landing strip. Air Carlos consisted of one pristine six-seater Cessna that was nicer than either the Avianca or the Air Canada planes that had carried him this far, although bobble-head Jesus stuck on the dashboard was a tad nervous-making.

Passengers were greeted warmly at the counter by Carlos himself and warned in several languages to use the bathroom before they left. Adrian sighed. Well, he didn't intend to repeat his recent tryst anyway. The handsome Mr. Tom had last been seen heading across the tarmac toward a private helicopter at the Bogotá terminal. At least he'd waved goodbye.

The flight lasted an uneventful forty minutes, landing in San Arbol on schedule.

Adrian's driver arrived at the San Arbol airport's dusty equivalent to a kiss'n'ride promptly—if by promptly you meant forty-five minutes after Adrian had begun to worry. He'd paid a deposit via PayPal and was mentally composing the stern (but probably futile) letter demanding reimbursement when a dirt-encrusted Jeep pulled into the waiting area, honking madly. It might have been dark blue or black, but it was hard to tell under a thick coat of red mud. But the top was down and it was a beautiful day. Adrian decided not to mention the driver's tardiness and climbed in.

The driver, Elvis, creeped Adrian out for no apparent reason. He was probably a nice enough fellow, and he spoke good, although heavily accented, English. He wore a well tailored outfit, complemented by wraparound sunglasses.

"Got supplies already." He hooked his thumb toward the back of the Jeep, which was crammed with crates and boxes. "One stop. Den we go."

Elvis shoved some of the boxes around, unlashing two small suitcases. Grunting, he hauled them into the backseat, treating them with extreme care. The bags strained at their zippers, threatening to burst at the first good pothole. At Elvis's command, Adrian plopped his own luggage in the space left by the bags. He opened the hard-sided case and extracted his favorite digital Nikon, looping it around his neck.

Elvis bound Adrian's backpack and equipment case securely, using a thick web of bungee cords. Exactly how rough was this ride going to be?

Fifteen minutes later, Adrian thought he knew the answer as they moved slowly across town in stop-and-start traffic. The mix of old world and new was eclectic and terrifying, with German-made cars and oxcarts, motorbikes and bicycles all vying for one opening that wouldn't fit a unicycle. The Jeep's engine zoomed to life for five seconds, followed by the shrill squeal of brakes, both theirs and those of the vehicles they cut off. The shouts and honks and even moos wore on Adrian's nerves as they progressed slowly through the endless traffic, bouncing over heaved and broken pavement. Adrian wished he were as well strapped in as his equipment in the back.

"I make one queek stop, A-dreen," Elvis announced. "Wait een Jeep, *por favor.*"

Elvis grabbed the two suitcases from the backseat, lugging them into the one well-maintained home in the middle of a rundown *barrio.* Five minutes passed, then ten. Adrian began to sweat…and not only from the heat, when he thought he saw a familiar form loitering in the shadows. He unbuckled, planning on stepping across the street for a closer look. He chose to stay put though, when he realized anyone could just reach in, unstrap his stuff and be gone in seconds. He elected to "wait een Jeep," as Elvis had directed.

No stranger to travel to foreign places, Adrian knew that when you're away from home, nervous and lonely, you see familiar faces everywhere. That Tom, the guy from the plane, was actually in South America only made it slightly more likely Adrian might actually see him. He would have *liked* to see him again. But there were thousands of places to go in Colombia. It would be way too much of a coincidence for Tom to end up in San Arbol.

There! Wasn't that…in the shadows again? He was almost sure this time—the short, light brown hair, the military bearing, the wide shoulders, the khaki. It was Tom, definitely.

Tom approached Elvis as he exited the building. Their exchange was brief, but the angry gestures and voices were loud enough for Adrian to catch the tone if not the words. It was clearly a confrontation. Tom laid a hand on Elvis's shoulder, but Elvis shrugged him off and headed back toward the Jeep. Tom followed, calling after him, his tone threatening. Elvis ignored him, swinging back into the driver's side, looking grim and turning the key in the ignition as the door slammed shut behind him.

Tom reached the Jeep. His eyes widened at seeing Adrian, then narrowed. "You! What the hell are you doing here?"

Elvis squealed away from the curb, shoving his way into traffic, ignoring honks and shouts, not to mention explicit and universal hand gestures.

"Be careful, Adrian!" Tom shouted after them.

Elvis clutched the wheel, eyes on the road, or at least Adrian hoped he was watching the road; it was impossible to tell with the sunglasses on.

"How you know this man?" Elvis demanded.

"We met on the plane. We, uh, talked a bit."

Taking his eyes off traffic long enough to look at Adrian, Elvis asked, "You not know him before?"

"Nope. Just met him— Look out!"

Elvis swerved, narrowly missing a flower-seller who apparently thought the middle of the road was a great place to set up shop.

Adrian decided it was his turn to ask a question. "What was that about?"

Elvis's stormy look halted further inquiry.

"Oh, look. An oxcart!" Adrian finished, not asking any more about Tom.

* * *

Tom returned to his rented Jeep and started the long drive to Tanpu, feeling like he'd been sucker-punched in the soul.

Why the hell was Adrian traveling with Elvis Montoya? Adrian had seemed like a nice guy on the plane. If only Tom had known Adrian associated with drug dealers, he'd never have gone with him. Talk about buzz-kill. Can you un-enjoy sex retroactively? He shuddered. Or maybe it was just the vibration of the Jeep.

Hooking his satellite phone up to the headset, he called in his report, although yelling in his report over the noise of the drive would be more accurate.

"Borderless Observers Organization," the receptionist sing-songed.

It always shocked him when this super-secret operation made no effort to be cagey.

"Try googling Borderless Observers Organization sometime," Frieda Koffler, his Field Liaison had said over drinks one night in the island's only bar. Frieda was a succubus, and she preferred to hang out with gay men since her overdose of pheromones didn't render them horny fools. "There's a number of places calling themselves that. We hide in plain sight." She picked at her scarlet nail polish. "Besides, who'd believe in us anyway? I work here, and I'm not sure I believe in us."

Tom asked to be connected to Frieda now, making his report brief and to the point. Yes, he'd given the requested warning. No, Montoya hadn't agreed to close down. Tom was on his way to Tanpu now.

"Carry on, Captain," Frieda said. He could hear her sultry smile even over the crackling long distance connection.

"Hey, Frieda. Can you check on something for me?" It was his professional duty to ask; no way was it personal interest. "There was a guy with Elvis Montoya. I was…I met him on the plane from Atlanta. Only got his first name—Adrian—if that's even his real name. I think he's Canadian. Said *eh* a coupla times. I got his email address, though." Tom pulled over. No way could he juggle steering wheel, satellite phone, and Blackberry. He read her off the email address.

"Give me a sec."

Tom thought he heard keys clacking over the static.

"Yeah, here he is. Homeland Security says he boarded in Toronto, changed flights in Atlanta and again in Bogotá, landing in San Arbol. That's where you are, right?"

"Just left," Tom replied, wondering when the long arm of BOO would stop surprising him. Of course they would have access to

Homeland Security's data. Probably Interpol and the CIA as well. And that Canadian agency, too—CSIS, or whatever. That was the one with the Mounties, right?

"His name is Adrian Thornapple. He's a Canadian citizen, no priors. Kinda cute. Oh, wait. Apparently he was involved in a recent indigo-related death in Toronto. The report says he's a witness, but doesn't that strike you as a little too much of a coincidence? Of course, as Ms. Batique says, there are no coincidences. Want me to look further into it?"

"Would you? That'd be great. Thanks." Tom didn't much like the conclusions he was drawing. Adrian either owned the Canadian indigo franchise, or he was a vigilante come to avenge his friend's death. Whichever it was, he was trouble. Tom was disgusted at himself. He was usually a better judge of character, and he hoped Frieda would find something that proved Adrian was a good guy after all.

Tom signed off the call, barely side-stepping a commitment to let Frieda take him shopping on his return trip. What was so goddamn wrong with khaki?

Starting the Jeep up again, Tom pulled back out into traffic. He was far enough out of San Arbol now that there was a lot less.

Next stop, the tiny village of Tanpu, home to Dr. Deerborne. Tom had no idea where the "three strikes you're dead" policy came from, but he was glad to give the warnings. He'd had to take people down before, but usually in time of war. Well, they called this the drug war, and these were major players. Any qualms he might have felt before were fading fast. Seeing Adrian with Montoya pissed him off. He put the pedal to the metal, sending a shower of debris onto the road behind him.

Since Montoya and Deerborne were in cahoots, they'd get three warnings between them, and they'd better share. God forbid they even think about having a "going out of business" sale. *They better just close up shop before I get my hands on them.*

* * *

Elvis drove wordlessly and recklessly, tires squealing, brakes shrieking. Eventually they pulled clear of city traffic, merging onto a narrow highway. Unlike the city streets, here the asphalt was well maintained. The Jeep sped along with a lot less bumps and grinds. Still, Elvis's driving left Adrian clinging to the vehicle's conveniently placed handholds as they flew along at... Did they even have speed limits here? Adrian hadn't seen any road signs in any language, except one that might have been "Water Buffalo Crossing." It was hard to tell from the peeling and obscure icon. It could just have easily meant "Pick Up After Your Ox."

Rather than watch their alarming progress, Adrian stared at the countryside. They passed vast tracks of bleak landscape, shorn of trees for lumber and cleared for cattle. Farther on, past the farmlands, stood great stands of weeping trees sporting deep scars and fresh wounds strung together by plastic tubing. Rubber collection. He recognized it instantly. It was the same technology used back in Canada for maple syrup collection; the only thing missing was the snow. Except here, many trees lay fallen, their lifeblood siphoned away to make tires and condoms and rubberbands like the one that tied back Adrian's hair.

He also saw the endless stretches of shanty towns, with ill-fed children living in unwholesome poverty, playing in streams running yellow and brown.

Like everyone of his generation, Adrian hated the way technology raped and laid waste to the land, but in the back of his mind, he couldn't help but wonder if maybe the new industry was exactly what these people needed. They were so primitive, so poor. They were just getting their industrial revolution later than the old world and the new world. Wasn't that why it was called the third world? They'd just had to wait their turn. He snapped a few pictures and turned away, adjusting the camera strap, ensuring the memory chip was well seated. He'd only brought a couple more, although this one was the largest by far.

In a shocking transition, the road suddenly cut through dense vegetation, branches slapping the windshield, smearing the bug guts that festooned the glass. It reminded Adrian of rock cuts back home in Ontario, where portions of highway had been blasted through massive boulders. Here, instead of grays and browns, dull pinks and rusty streaks, the claustrophobic channel had been hacked through walls of brilliant green. Here and there a scarlet bloom garnished their emerald canyon.

They drove in silence for about an hour. Adrian grew bored and antsy. "Why don't they cut these trees and vines back?" he asked, leaning inward, palming his cheek where a leaf had smacked him through the open passenger window.

"The *jardinero* cut dis back all de time. But, dey grow like weeds." He gave Adrian a huge grin. Adrian wished Elvis would keep his eyes on the road before they became one with the weeds.

"The weeds grow like weeds, eh?" Adrian smiled back, trying another line of inquiry. "What did we stop for back there?"

Elvis didn't respond. Probably didn't hear the question over the noise of the engine and the uneven rhythm of branches slapping the car as it passed. Adrian couldn't think of another thing to say, so settled into his seat and stared at the passing landscape some more.

*　　*　　*

They spent the night at a relatively clean way station, sort of a Budget Inn whose budget hadn't included plumbing or privacy or walls. Adrian did have his very own mosquito netting, though, and glad of it. Bugs chirped and whined all night. He hoped that jungle doctor Deerborne was really close to finding that malaria cure.

They set out upon their bumpy journey at dawn on day two. Before departing, Elvis had secured a tarp around their baggage. By the time the afternoon rains fell, Adrian had a headache, a sunburn, and a butt both wet and numb (not to mention a little sore from yesterday's dalliance).

"Shouldn't we put the top back up?" he asked when the first fat drops plopped and steamed on the hood.

"Top gone. Was stolen. Damn Indians." Elvis spat out the window. "Is just a little rain. Is *rain* forest. What you expect?" He seemed to enjoy the rain, and his fine linen clothing was bone dry again twenty minutes after the downpour. Adrian's jeans and T-shirt were not.

By the time they finally pulled into Tanpu in the late afternoon, all Adrian wanted was a shower, a meal, and a chance at some real plumbing. He now wore a fine freckling of mud all over. First he'd gotten soaked. Then the mud had dried to dust. *Then* he'd started sweating again, and it had turned back into mud, collecting in all the most uncomfortable places.

Personal hygiene issues aside, he felt pretty good. While the rain forest in principle was fascinating, the green monotony had finally sung him to sleep, and he'd managed to snooze through the final hours of their journey.

Elvis pulled to a stop in a deforested area that, judging from the churned up earth and multiple tire marks, served as a Tanpu's municipal parking lot. Clambering out of the Jeep, Adrian stretched and looked around. They'd parked not far from a charming antebellum-style building complete with pillars and a two-story wraparound porch. Whoever lived there had gone to a lot of trouble to bring the trappings of civilization to the jungle. He hoped against hope that he was staying in the rain forest mansion, but Elvis grabbed his bags and led him to a row of small, thatched cabins.

"You get own lee-zurd." Elvis proclaimed pointing to the sleepy gecko stuck on a wooden support beam. "Like bug zapper." Pursing his lips, Elvis executed a very realistic imitation of electronic bug death. Repeatedly.

"Ah, thanks." Adrian handed him an American twenty. Elvis accepted it with a final huge grin and slapped Adrian so heartily on the shoulder that he'd have a small bruise come morning.

"Ta-ta, señor. Enjoy your stay at Chez Montoya."

"You're the owner?"

"*Sí*. I own everyting around here." He leaned in close, breath reeking of the spicy stew they'd called breakfast. "Every. Ting." He pulled back, grinning. He punched Adrian in the shoulder in that way macho men have of really hurting each other while pretending it's just a friendly nudge. "You need anyting…" He trailed off and shrugged. Adrian figured he'd better not need anything.

Elvis was an odd mix, and Adrian still wasn't sure after two days of constant togetherness if he liked or disliked the secretive Colombian. He didn't trust Elvis, though, and not just because Tom had confronted him. After all, what did he know about Tom anyway? Other than that fact that he was gentle and kind and handsome. And good in bed, er, bathroom. Maybe Tom was the bad guy here. Thoughts about good guys and bad swirled through his brain as he lugged his bags into the charming hut.

A note from Doc Soc lay on his bed. Adrian smiled at the handwriting, familiar from the blackboards and whiteboards of college days. And a lot of red ink, as well.

> *Sorry I'm not here to meet you. I'm tied up in negotiations for certain privileges with Tanpu's shaman and some tribal elders. Entertain yourself. The public showers are just down the path. You'll want to skip dinner, as we have a "walk on the spirit side" planned for the evening. And by the way, it's just you and me, kid. Nick, Tracy, and Fritz blew us off for Dr. Rubenstein's Mexican dig. Mayan Riviera, my saggy,*

middle-aged ass!

Chuckling, Adrian unpacked his wrinkled clothes and went to find whatever bathing facility his jungle "resort" had to offer. He slung a towel over his shoulder, grabbed his travel kit, and a complete change of clothes. There was no lock on the door, so he slung his favorite camera around his neck.

A hand-drawn sign reading *baño* (complete with an icon of a Western toilet that would only lead to disappointment) pointed Adrian westward along the rutted road.

He walked slowly, glad to stretch his legs and get a look around. The area appeared more like a small factory town than what Adrian had envisioned as a jungle village. It was less *National Geographic* and more like a *Time Magazine* report on a one-industry town. It looked dreary and depressed.

A few of those quick-assemble industrial type buildings huddled along the road. Farther back some dilapidated ones decayed in the sun. Along the path he found some pretty little cottages with flowers in their window boxes. Behind those were a lot of the little shacks like poor people all over the world call home. Where did poor people acquire so much corrugated iron? Ringing the clearing, barely discernable from the surrounding vegetation, were some conical little huts that looked like they'd grown there. Their builders had made clever use of the native flora to build the kind of things you see on *Discovery Channel* specials about lost tribes. Adrian snapped a few pictures. Ironically, nearly all of the local residences, regardless of income bracket, sported satellite dishes. Metallic antennae sprouted from aluminum siding, tar-paper shingles, and even thatch and wattle.

Each step he took, Adrian was assailed by different scents—rotting garbage, fragrant flowers, putrid outhouses, appetizing cooking. The long drive had gifted him with a sore neck and an empty stomach that growled like a jungle beast.

Off to one side, a cluster of factory-like buildings huddled, completely enclosed by high chain link fencing topped with barbed wire. Diamond-shaped signs featuring a blue lightning bolt hung from the fencing. Adrian couldn't imagine why they'd need such security in the jungle. Perhaps the electrified fence kept out animals, like the huge snakes and killer jaguars he'd read about in his pre-expedition research.

There appeared to be only one break in the fence, a gated entryway with a guardhouse surrounded by a lot of vehicles. The area outside the fence was devoid of vegetation, as if the jungle shunned the very ground nearby. Vehicles had churned the red earth until it looked like a blood-soaked moonscape. Here and there pieces of abandoned equipment lay rusting. Smoke belched from a trio of short smoke stacks, sending dark trails across the sky. It stank—a mixture of chemicals and carbon. He sneezed, sending nearby lizards scuttling for shelter.

A cellular tower competed with the surrounding jungle for tallest freestanding structure and made him wish he'd brought his cell phone. He'd left it in Toronto, anxious to save a few bucks by putting his plan on hold until he returned.

Adrian shuddered. Something about that fenced-off compound reminded him of those factory ships that had gutted and processed whales on the open seas in the past century. It felt like an old and ancient evil had descended upon the land and raped away its decency. The whole thing reeked and was just the type of civilization that should never have been introduced to the rain forest. Or anywhere for that matter. Sure, on the drive out he'd thought the land could benefit from some modern technology, but now that he saw it, against the lush background of virgin rain forest, he wasn't so sure.

He'd be sure to write an article about the factory. He'd check it out later, find out what they made. He took a few pictures on the way to the shower, and a lot more on his stroll back, a stroll that took him all over the tiny hamlet.

He tried to question the locals, but his Quechua was limited, and they seemed reluctant to talk. He probably needed to win their trust first. Anthropology 101—no problemo. He'd brought a lot of dollar store items—toys and crayons and comics and such.

He circled around the village, ending up back at the large whitewashed mansion. A young boy leaned on a tree nearby.

"Who lives there?" Adrian asked in Quechua, not even trying for correct grammar or syntax. The boy understood him though. "*Jampiri* Deerborne," the child answered, pantomiming injecting himself in the bicep. "*Llik'ichiri,*" he added, running off. Adrian had no idea what *licky-cheery* meant, but he knew *jampiri* was shaman. So the good doctor lived in the nicest house in town. Medical research must pay pretty well. Perhaps Deerborne had private funding. After all, Adrian's googling had turned up no fundraising campaigns or even a donation page—just some rather self-aggrandizing articles and the one about his family cutting him off.

Since he didn't know how long they'd be staying in Tanpu before heading into the interior, Adrian decided now was a good time to meet Dr. Deerborne. He hesitated a moment at the door, suddenly nervous, before grasping the brass jaguar knocker and rapping soundly.

A nervous-looking native housekeeper answered, using gestures and broken English to shush him and send him away.

"But I'm sure Dr. Deerborne will want to talk to me. I'm Adrian Thornapple. We exchanged emails," he proclaimed loudly, wiggling his fingers to mime typing. He was sure she wouldn't understand, but he thought someone was hovering in the shadowy hallway behind her. "I'm going to write articles. News of his work could really help with the fundraising."

Dr. Deerborne—Adrian recognized him from his photos on the Internet—stormed forward, knocking the housekeeper aside. "Get away! Get away from here!" The upper-crust British accent did nothing to temper the harsh words. "I need no reporters poking around. I want nothing from the outside world. Go away!" He shook his fist in the air theatrically, and Adrian would have laughed if he hadn't noticed a heavily armed man stepping up the wraparound porch to his left.

"I'm an anthropologist, not a reporter."

"I don't care if you're a secret agent. Go away!" He slammed the door in Adrian's face, the heavy knocker banging the door in an echo of finality.

Adrian didn't need to be told twice, charging away from the mansion as if his hiking boots had sprouted wings. It wasn't the gunned-up henchmen that struck cold fear into his heart. It was the madness he'd seen in Deerborne's blue-ringed eyes.

CHAPTER 8

REIGN FOREST

Tom stretched as much as he dared, afraid he'd fall off his little makeshift platform. Must be fifty, sixty feet down, he calculated. Nice to know his tree-climbing skills hadn't atrophied in the twenty-five years since he'd last used them. He'd lashed a few smaller branches across the fork of a huge cypress, but the off-shooting limbs grew unevenly, and he'd listed to the right so long the world seemed angled and weird.

A howler monkey whooped just off to his left. At first their echoing barks had been creepy, then irritating, but had faded into just so much jungle soundtrack as the day wore on. At least he could report back to the banshee contingent at work that these monkeys didn't sound at all like their own eerie wails. More of a barking sound, really, almost like a big dog.

He surveyed the jungle floor. The carpeting of creepers, rotting vegetation, and rotting less-appealing things probably made for a soft landing, but he wasn't anxious to find out. Something stung his cheek. Slapping at it smeared his fingers with sticky, sweat-dampened face-paint. He chuckled, picturing himself as some sort of demented camo-mime. Perched on his numb butt in a tree for eight hours was probably on a par with being trapped in an invisible box.

He rubbed at his eyes, blotting the face-paint a little more. It was mostly sweated and rubbed off anyway. His eye-sockets ached from the binoculars. Even the miniature ones BOO handed out got heavy after a while. He wished for another canteen, but the balance of his water supply was stashed in his Jeep, hidden deep in the jungle a couple of miles back.

He needed to pee. He worried the noise of his personal cascade might attract human attention, but so far had managed to time his elimination with the noisy arrival of a vehicle bouncing into the parking area or the grinding of some industrial equipment at the factory. It was late afternoon now, and pretty quiet. He could have peed directly against the tree trunk, silencing the stream, but he was, after all, planning on shimmying back down again. *Funny, how there isn't a section in the Special Ops handbook about how to handle bladder demand when on observation detail.* He arched his stream out into the jungle, hoping anyone listening would think monkey, imagining handbook subsections such as:

Need to pee? Keep your edge.

In a tree, Or on a ledge.

On the quay, or behind a hedge.

Okay, so maybe Dr. Seuss never wrote training manuals for Special Ops, but Tom was bored and antsy and knew you took your entertainment where you found it. Life was nasty, brutal and short. As was Elvis Montoya, who was just pulling into the parking lot…with Adrian in the passenger seat. Well, that pretty much ended any hope Tom had had of filing their airplane meeting under "fond memories."

He watched as the younger man clambered out of Elvis's Jeep and hauled his luggage into a little hut. Tom tried to read the body language, hoping to find no connection between Montoya and Adrian. He almost wished he had one of the psychics with him. Almost. He'd had dealings with psychics before, and it never ended well.

He watched as Deerborne sent Adrian packing. Good news.

Frieda had emailed a report to Tom's Blackberry not long after they'd spoken. Adrian checked out. According to a blog post made by some professor, Adrian was accompanying him on a research trip through the rain forest. That explained his presence in Tanpu.

Tom shifted again, reminding himself he was here to observe Deerborne, not Adrian. Although his orders were to warn Deerborne, he wasn't expecting it to go well and needed to get the lay of the land before confronting the not-so-good doctor.

Someone coughed. Close by from the sound of it. He froze.

Not someone—some*thing.* A rangy jaguar peered at him from the next tree.

Tom palmed a knife; gunfire would only alert the guards patrolling below.

An aerial scuffle between man and beast might be pretty noisy, too, especially if one of them crashed to the ground. He weighed his options as he stared back, meeting the cat's yellowy eyes. Would the cat back down? He hefted the blade, ready for battle.

The big cat gazed at him, nodded once and vanished into the foliage. That was so weird. It was almost as if it had acknowledged him.

* * *

Adrian explored, snapped pictures, and made notes. Just after sunset, as he worked by Coleman lantern, a young man scratched at the hut door—you can't exactly knock on thatch. He was about Adrian's age and stature, but much more fit, which was obvious since he wore only a pair of beat-up shorts and a sprinkling of tattoos. Adrian tried to be restrained as he checked out the jungle hottie. No need to get himself gay-bashed if the locals didn't embrace "two-spirit" culture. In his experience, most aboriginal peoples didn't have a problem with alternative sexualities, but who knew how a few hundred years of Catholic conquistadors and missionaries might have affected their beliefs?

The young man gestured for Adrian to follow him, leading him to a large hut where a group of villagers sat around an unlit firepit. Dr. Kawasaki stepped out of the shadows and enveloped Adrian in a huge hug.

"I'm so glad to see you, Adrian. I knew I could count on you. Everyone else reneged."

Before Adrian could say much more than "glad to see you, too, Doc," the Professor was introducing him around. Adrian missed most of the names, which may have been ranks or job descriptions as far as he knew. He'd have plenty of time to ask Doc Soc about it later.

"Come. Sit. Join the circle." Adrian sat hard on the faded and none-too-clean pallet he was offered. He hoped if it housed any occupants, his awkward landing had squashed them. He crossed his legs like the other men in the circle, grateful for that yoga class at the Y.

A wise-looking elder covered in tattoos and scarification and wearing the bone necklace of a shaman nodded and addressed Adrian.

Adrian had memorized a chunk of the basic Quechua phrasebook, but each tribe spoke their own dialect, and he could only catch every third of the old man's words.

He was aged and dried-out looking, his near-hairless head shaped like a peanut. To Adrian, he looked about eighty, but what did he know of the aging process away from civilization—no moisturizers or under-eye night creams here. Or were there? The shaman could have been fifty or one hundred fifty for all Adrian knew.

"Alberto," the old man said, laying both hands over his heart.

"Adrian," he responded, aping the gesture. Across the circle, Doc Soc smiled approvingly.

Alberto retrieved a dried gourd from the hard-packed floor beside him. *"Ayahuasca,"* he said, holding it up and twisting off a cleverly carved little cap.

Adrian recognized the name, vaguely recalling that *ayahuasca* was credited with many medicinal properties. He thought it might have been hallucinogenic as well.

Alberto took a swig from the gourd. Adrian was impressed at how watertight the container was. Not a drop spilled as it was handed to each man in the circle. The man on Adrian's left drank deep and passed it on, indicating Adrian, too, should drink.

Doc Soc had taken his share without hesitating and now nodded solemnly, raising an imaginary glass.

"L'chaim," the Indians chorused. Adrian barked out a shocked laugh. Just where had they learned the Hebrew toast? He loved the ways of the world coming together in multi-cultural celebration.

It wasn't the first time Adrian had felt it necessary to indulge in local foods and homebrew. He'd taken peyote among some First Nations people and some odd beans from Tibetan refugees in Burma. He knew exactly why Doc Soc's note had advised him against dinner. He didn't figure this for a drink-the-Kool-Aid kind of massacre nor hemlock on the rocks. He took a sniff. It had a pleasant lavender scent. He'd noticed a similar, but much less pleasant odor coming from the electrified compound at the far end of the village—burnt lavender, he decided. Not entirely dissimilar to the rotting lavender smell that had accompanied Violet's death. Indigo must be *ayahuasca*-based. He thought of Deerborne's blue-ringed irises and shuddered.

He tried for a tiny sip, but Alberto was ready for him and, with surprising strength for one so frail-looking, he seized Adrian by the ponytail, tipping his head back, keeping the gourd to his lips by force.

Adrian swallowed way more than he'd intended, choking and coughing. Some of it escaped and trickled down his neck. Alberto pulled the gourd away, carefully recapping it, although from the weight of it, it was nearly empty. Still, it was obviously precious to these people, and Adrian felt a little sick and a little flattered that they'd shared this with him. And a lot worried that he'd been forced to drink so much. Just what was in store for him now? At least there were no high-rises handy in case he suddenly became convinced he could fly.

Adrian had never been one for religion, either traditional or new-age, but suddenly he felt very spiritual. It was as if he'd left his real self behind when changing planes in the Atlanta airport. Or maybe he'd lost himself somewhere since leaving university.

His thoughts sputtered and flew. His vision wavered. Alberto sat back on his pallet, smiling. Superimposed on him, Adrian saw flashes of darkness, and of light. Of snakes and dragons. He struggled to sit up, realizing he already was.

"I'm soooo stoned," he announced, leaping into song, *"Stoned. Stoned on the range."* He giggled, his soft laughter transmuting into a thick sob.

Alberto began to chant softly, his foreign-toned music soothing if unfamiliar. Instinctively, Adrian knew the words were holy and spiritual. Literal meaning wasn't necessary.

He lost track of the room with its thatch walls and chanting men. Instead, he descended level after level, climbing down stairways set at crazed angles, like that M.C. Escher drawing. He wondered if Escher had ever been to South America. Adrian's thoughts swirled and sparkled. His vision narrowed to a tiny pinpoint, then suddenly shot widescreen and Technicolor.

Walking, walking. Well, staggering, to be honest. I peer around, one hand on the banister for support. Strange. You'd think I'd have noticed a staircase in the single-story hut. I stroke the old wood. It's exactly like the one we had in our house on Davisville when I was a kid. I step from the landing. Mommy. Where's my mommy? Duck. Duck. The bats will get stuck in my hair.

There's Mommy. But she doesn't see me. She's busy polishing Daddy's piano. Polishing, polishing. Ignoring me. I'm trying to get to her, but every step is swimming through syrup, and Mommy seems to get farther away. One step, another. The floor suddenly gives way. I should scream, but my teeth snap together, and I can only make mmm noises. I crash through the hardwood into the basement, then crash through the cement floor, plunging down through the earth and down into a cavern...falling, falling, never-ending. Raptor bats and monster earthworms attack, tangling in my hair, forcing themselves into my nose, mouth, ears, eyes. Lower.

So full of blackness, so full. Full to overflowing. I'm gonna be sick. I'm gonna puke.

Someone puts a bucket in my hands—whether real or dream, I don't know. I do vomit, filling the container with black, writhing snakes and roaches as big as my ear. My throat feels raw, but I have more to purge. Next into the bucket I upchuck a cell phone, a camera, a wristwatch. Next comes a steam of keys—car keys, house keys, keys to every lock in the world. Blood mixed with vomit, then a rainbow of liquids—wine, beer, cola, coffee, petroleum. All the addictions of the modern world.

The last thing I heave is a set of dog tags, their long, stainless steel chain eeling out in a silvery trail.

Empty now, Adrian fell back against the wall. The bucket—real, apparently—was taken from his shaking hands before its vile contents could spill.

The dream grows lighter now, brighter, as Alberto's song grows less dirge-like.

Blackness flies at me, now unable to penetrate. I wear a shield of light. When did I stop falling? I'm standing in a field, safe in the warmth of the sun.

There's my mother again, welcoming this time with an ephemeral embrace, then gone. Another woman joins her, young and beautiful. I know her. My grandmother when she was young, long before I was born. I see in her a long line of grandmothers. Of ancestors I've never met, never even heard of. All-powerful women, earth mothers, wishing me well, sending me their strength, youth, beauty, and purpose.

I feel protected, virtuous, glowing. The women morph into men now, reversing from ancient ancestors to my grandfather, father, the brothers who'd never been born. My first love, first lover. And my last, Tom. I smile at Tom, wishing he could have been more to me. I cherish the brief moments we had together.

A blue Cheshire cat ghosts in, growing into a dark-skinned Indian—Alberto but younger. No, not Alberto at all, a different shaman—young, handsome, self-assured. The shaman laughs, slapping Tom on the back so hard he falls forward, arms extending, reaching the ground, body twisting and warping into the shape of a cat, a giant black cat. Tom roars and morphs again, into Pixel, the orphaned kitty I adopted and left behind with my beloved friend Wendy. How long ago now? I have no idea. Pixel crosses the void instantly, climbs into my lap and settles in warm against my belly. I stroke the soft fur, gray-black but at the same time glowing blue. Pixel's purring merges and blends with Alberto's slowing song.

Adrian returned to the world around him, feeling both woozy and content. He thought he saw a giant black jaguar prowling in the corner, but when he turned his head to look, it scream-coughed and dissipated into a cloud of inky smoke.

"Weird," he said. Then, *"Blech!"* at the foul taste in his mouth.

Alberto laughed and handed him a yellowish ball to eat—it was sweet and sour at once, with a hint of licorice. It was a huge improvement and settled his stomach. Comforted, Adrian rested, dreams at an end, peaceful, dozing. And when he awoke, he knew a lot more Quechua.

* * *

After dropping (damn near literally) Doc Soc at his hut, Adrian staggered back to his own. He collapsed on the bed, head and stomach spinning. The *ayahuasca* concoction hit hard and fast, but exited pretty quickly. Mostly he felt drained. Better than the single peyote trip he'd once taken. They had told him later he'd been out of it for three days, but his walk on the spirit plane had seemed to last only a few hours. Now it was the reverse. Only an hour had passed, but he'd lived several lifetimes in his dream state.

He awoke in the night with an awful headache, his *ayahuasca* hangover not having the courtesy to wait until the morning after. He pawed through his travel case, locating a couple of Tylenol. He felt far too dehydrated to dry-swallow them; he'd have to go find some water. He pulled on a T-shirt and a pair of safari pants he'd bought for its multitude of pockets. He located his boots and grabbed his largest memory card as backup to the one already in the camera. Ensuring its hard plastic, waterproof case was closed tightly, he shoved it deep into the hidden pocket on the inside of his waistband, smoothing down the Velcro flap so it couldn't get lost.

He didn't bother with a flashlight, finding his way to the cabins' communal kitchen by the moon's generous brightness. He liberated a bottle of water from the old fridge humming dutifully in one corner. He swallowed his Tylenol quickly, chugging half the water in one long draught.

Taking the rest of the bottle with him, he curled up in a big wicker chair on the porch, impatient for the painkillers to kick in. The chair creaked threateningly, but held together. The rain forest humidity—not to mention the actual rain—must play hell with everything. Metal rusted, fabric and wood rotted. It seemed only stone and certain alloys would last a decent length of time in the jungle.

He hoped his camera was constructed of stainless steel or titanium parts. Even electronics could be ruined by humidity. Turning his Nikon so the view screen faced him, he examined the pictures he'd taken so far. There were some stunning beauty shots and a bunch of pictures of cute kids in a mish-mash of native and modern clothing. The fenced-off factory grated in comparison. But wait. What was that? He flipped through the pictures quickly, hands shaking, to a bunch he'd shot with the long-range lens.

He'd filmed a group of Indians unloading woven baskets of bluish-green plant leaves from a pickup truck, then reloading crates marked "Coffee." One of the crates had fallen, dropped by an old man—a man so frail he shouldn't have been working at all. Adrian enlarged the bottom left corner. The crate had collapsed, spilling bright blue, almost iridescent bricks shrink-wrapped in plastic onto the hard-packed ground, exactly like the ones he'd seen in Violet's apartment that night.

"Coffee, my ass," Adrian spoke aloud, his words echoing through the nighttime quiet.

He enlarged the corner of the shot a little more, sharpening the focus. The display showed the foreman brandishing a whip. In the final picture, the old man lay in the dirt, red stripes crisscrossing his skin.

Adrian drew deep, centering breaths trying to get to a place where he could cope. Trying not to heave up the water he'd just swallowed. His stomach had been through enough upheavals already tonight.

Eyes closed, he listened to the night. The squawks and chuffs of the rain forest denizens laid down a jarring soundtrack. He needed to get out of there, get to the nearest authorities, and report them—these manufacturers of indigo. He wondered who was involved. Deerborne? Montoya? Damn it. They might have nothing to do with it. He needed more facts. He'd go to the authorities at first light. Let them investigate. Now how would he get back to San Arbol? He didn't know the way, didn't have a vehicle. If Elvis was involved, he could hardly ask him for a ride back so soon.

Everyone in the tiny village knew he and Doc Soc were heading into the rain forest tomorrow morning. Whoever it was making the indigo would be suspicious if he suddenly changed plans. He needed to think, damn it. He—

Voices off to his left by the parking lot jerked him out of his panic. An argument. In English. What if they were coming for him? And who, exactly, were *they*? Until he knew who was involved, he'd be safer keeping a low profile. Hiding was one thing, but who was he hiding from? The voices grew louder; maybe these were the bad guys! He thought about sneaking off into the jungle, but the scream of a nighttime predator reminded him of warnings he'd received not to stray near the village edge after dark.

Calm the hell down. He drew a few more deep breaths. Nobody needed to know he was on to them. He'd just go back to his hut and try and get some sleep. In the morning he'd discuss options with Doc Soc. The professor would know what to do.

Unfortunately, Adrian needed to cross the parking lot to return to his hut. He didn't want to draw attention to himself, so he'd try to sneak by the arguing men without being seen.

Shaking a little, Adrian crept forward, one vehicle at a time. He could make out a word or two. The voice with the upper crust British accent was clearly Dr. Deerborne. The other voice had a slight American drawl. Tom! What the hell was he doing here? Oh, God. What if he was stalking him? How likely was it he'd run into him on the plane to Bogotá, then San Arbol, then again in the Tanpu?

Cheeks burning and stomach roiling, he crouched behind a beat-up Land Rover, but he was still too visible. Anyone coming down the road would see him. He wove his way through the tangle of parked vehicles, staying low, slaloming around muddy moguls until just a couple of Jeeps separated him from the combatants.

Curiosity overcame fear, and he eavesdropped, hoping to gain some knowledge of the situation if only for the sake of his own safety and

Doc Soc's. As he tuned into the argument in progress, he heard Tom say, "You're just a drug dealer, Deerborne. The science stuff doesn't change that. You have to stop. I'm here to stop you."

"You? Alone?" Deerborne laughed—it sounded both cultured and crazed.

Adrian knelt up, peering around the Jeep, dry earth digging into his knees. The full moon illuminated the clearing as well as any streetlight. Deerborne was easy to see, dressed in light-colored clothing. He stood with his back to Adrian, legs spread wide, and arms crossed. Tom wore camouflage. Within the jungle, he would be impossible to see, but now he was clearly silhouetted against a background of torn red earth. He stood before Deerborne, hands on his hips. Tom stood too far away for Adrian to make out the expression on his face, and the smeared black streaks didn't help. Adrian went with the working hypothesis that Tom was mad as hell.

"Yeah, just me. For now. I've been sent to give you a warning, Doctor. This is your last. Jacqueline Batique gave you plenty of time to back off on your own. I gave the same message to Montoya in San Arbol a few days ago. Stop manufacturing indigo now, and we'll let you go back to your research. That research is the only reason you get a second chance. We're on to you, and we're watching."

Oh, so not about me then, Adrian realized, ego just a little punctured. Who did Tom mean when he said *we*? Who was Jocelyn Batista or whatever he'd said?

Deerborne stood his ground. "How do you imagine I'm funding my research? It's not as if your society of do-gooders provided me with much. I was barely able to afford a new spectrometer with the last check your superiors saw fit to send me."

"We've supplied you with—" Tom began, but Deerborne lectured right over Tom's words.

"It all made so much sense once Elvis explained it to me. No more time wasted on fundraising. No more leaving my laboratory for endless rounds of black tie dinners. No more talk-show appearances. He runs the production and distribution side of the business, while I concern myself with research and development. Indigo is just the first of many new creations to come from my lab. With Elvis's assistance, I'm able to stay here and focus on pure research. The rain forest holds amazing flora and fauna! Even the deadly can be useful. Indigo is just a fortuitous by-product of my research."

"You're insane. There's nothing fortuitous about a drug that kills!

Right now you're the sole manufacturer of indigo. Stop now before more people die."

Deerborne ignored Tom, carrying on with his self-serving rationalization. "I'm doing the world a favor. If indigo removes a few of the unwanted element from this earth, then so be it. The herd requires culling. One has only to look at your great United States to know that. Your cities are rotten things, decaying and dying. Your government only exacerbates the situation by continual cuts in education and health care. America doesn't even have a socialized medical system." He spat on the ground, stepping a little to the right so Adrian could now see both men in profile.

No wonder Deerborne's eyes are blue-ringed. He's not just a user, he's the inventor! Adrian gasped, fingers spasming, ripping up clods of dirt and gravel.

"You're playing God!" Tom shouted, taking a step closer to Deerborne. "Who decides people in third world countries get to live and Americas die?"

And Canadians, Adrian added silently, heart clenching as he thought of Violet's last moments retching and dying on the dirty carpet back in Toronto.

"I do! I decide who lives and dies." Deerborne nodded, smug expression clear even from Adrian's hiding place. "These innocents of the jungle deserve a chance. Nobody forces your citizens to take indigo. They have choices where my Indians do not."

"And is it the choice of *your Indians* to slave away in your drug factory? Are they volunteers?"

"Yes. Most of them are, at least initially." Deerborne shifted, uncrossing his arms. "Some desperate father brings me his dying child and promises me he'll work for a year. Then no sooner is the child cured, the parents disappear back into the jungle, leaving their debt to me unpaid. I need workers, and they need to learn responsibility. What choice do I have? Should I let their child die? What kind of man would I be then? These are primitive people, without a strong sense of time or commitment. I'm merely helping them understand what it means to give one's word. I'm teaching them honor. They're so childlike. I'm like a father to them. It's an important lesson."

"A lesson that usually ends in death," Tom ground out, voice tight. "This is your last chance, Deerborne. I report back to BOO in the morning. If you don't agree to stop immediately, I'll tell them you didn't see reason. We'll take you down by force if we have to."

Deerborne's laugh went on way too long for any sane person. "You'll do no such thing!" He produced a gun from some hidden holster, pointing it at Tom.

"I know you carry a weapon, agent. Please lay it on the ground."

Tom hesitated. Deerborne fired. Clods of red earth geysered up terrifyingly near Tom's boot.

"The next bullet will shatter your leg so completely *even I* will be hard pressed to repair it."

The indigo may had affected Deerborne's brain, but it hadn't affected his aim. The gun inched a little farther left, pointing straight at Tom's leg. Tom drew a gun from the back of his waistband with his fingertips, laying it on the hard-packed ground.

Deerborne cackled—Snidley Whiplash of the jungle—drug-induced insanity in every bark of laughter. "Hands in the air and step away from the gun. Good. I'm sure Elvis can use a strong man like you in the factory. If you'd be so good as to head toward the compound." He gestured toward the fenced-off area. Tom turned toward the factory, arms raised.

Once his back was to Deerborne, the doctor raised his weapon and pointed it straight at Tom's shoulder blades.

"Nooo!" Adrian shot up from his hiding place, heaving the handful of gravel he hadn't even noticed he'd snatched. The stones clattered like gunfire as they bounced off the Jeeps and trucks.

Distracted only a split second, Deerborne fired at the spot where Tom had stood a moment before. He took careful aim a second time as the Tom sprinted across the clearing toward the jungle. The gun popped, sounding nothing like the loud bam in the movies.

Tom grunted and stumbled.

"You bastard!" Adrian shouted. "You shot him! You're insane."

Deerborne swung his gun in Adrian's direction. "Well, if it isn't the journalist. You think I'm going to let you write about this?"

"Anthropologist, you asshole!"

A sharp crack sounded behind Adrian, like someone stepping on a dry twig. For a moment he mistook it for rescue. His left butt cheek burned, which was weird because Deerborne stood in front of him. What the…

Adrian reached behind him and plucked the offending item from his backside, examining it in the dimming light. *Wow. You know you only ever see these on TV, but you recognize...* The dart dropped from numbing fingers.

"Yo, A-dreen!" Elvis jogged toward them, moonlight glinting off what had to be a tranquilizer gun. He wore a delighted smile, as if he'd been just waiting for a chance to quote *Rocky*. Adrian's thoughts skittered and spun—it was the *Ayahuasca* trip all over again.

"Leave the journalist… Oh, forgive me. I meant *anthropologist,"* Deerborne ordered, making "anthropologist" sound akin to "piece of shit." "Find the agent. I wounded him. Do not let him escape."

"Run, Tom, run. See Tom run," Adrian murmured, sinking into woozy darkness.

CHAPTER 9

BLOOD IS SLICKER THAN WATER

"C'mon. C'mon. You're supposed to be in good shape. Get your fuckin' ass in gear!" ordered Tom's inner cheerleader, spawned from the vicious drill sergeant he'd had for Basic. "Jeep's just a little farther. Only a pussy would cop out now!"

He charged on through the jungle, dodging trees and rocks, hoping the smell of blood didn't draw jungle predators the way it did sharks in the ocean. He tripped on a vine, green on green blending into a huge monochromatic mosaic, like the hardest jigsaw puzzle ever.

Pain shot through his side as he danced a few awkward steps, regaining his balance without actually eating another mouthful of forest floor. He spat loam from a previous tumble, wishing again for water. And he thought he'd been uncomfortable perched in the tree all day. He'd give anything to be back up there now.

"Loser!" he chided himself.

Why the hell had he told Jacqueline he'd go in alone. He could so use a vampire or shape-shifter right about now. He really had to get over his phobia about supernatural beings and magic.

His feet pounded the uneven earth, each step sending cascades of agony through his side, pain and blood loss rendering him dizzy and disoriented. He needed to stop, just to collect his bearings. He should have reached the Jeep by now. Slowing, he slipped behind a huge up-jutting rock formation, leaning into its cool, solid bulk, drawing great gulps of humid air. He drew his bloody shirt away from the wound. Fresh blood painted new trails over old. He'd been running long enough for the initial flow to dry. Where was the goddamn Jeep? It held his satellite phone. He needed help. He needed…to sit down. Now. He folded in on himself, sliding down the rock wall, puddling in a heap. The world tilted and seemed far away. So did the pain. He floated, whole body as numb as his butt had been in the tree. Blessed relief. But no, he had to…needed to…to do something. Right. Right. Stop the drugs. Save the…Adrian.

"Doncha worry, Adrian. I'm coming," he said out loud to no one in particular. "I'm going to get him. He needs me," Tom told the three warriors who stepped from the jungle and surrounded him, bows and blowguns at the ready. "But maybe not right now."

Warriors, rocks, jungle all stuttered away as blood-loss won the day.

*　　*　　*

After their initial hazy meeting, the first clear words Tom spoke to his rain forest benefactors were, "Holy fuck, that tastes like shit!" He spit most of the concoction back into the bowl, sloshing some on his lap. "What the hell is this?"

They didn't seem to hold it against him, though. A small, round woman with laughing eyes just smiled and removed the bowl from his trembling hands. *"Tomay! Tomay!"* she ordered, forcing the bowl to his lips, backwash and all.

Against his better judgment and all willpower, Tom swallowed. He was terribly thirsty and terribly weak. And more than a little nauseated. He flopped back against the hard pallet. "My phone. My gear. My…"

His rain forest orderlies peered at him, obviously not understanding a word. They stepped aside as a new person entered the hut. He was young, maybe a little younger than Tom's thirty-four years—closer to Adrian's age, Tom guessed, recalling the other man was twenty-nine from the report Frieda had sent from BOO headquarters. The new guy had a jolly, open face, or at least that was Tom's feverish impression. It was hard to tell under the face-paint. Somehow, on this guy, the makeup looked less like a transvestite clown and more like a badge of office. Since Tom probably still sported a little face-paint of his own, he couldn't really criticize.

The new guy placed his fingertips on Tom's temple. Tom jerked away. "You're not reading my fucking mind!" he shouted.

The Indian grinned. *"K'aja onqoy,"* he explained, demonstrating on a convenient attendant that he merely wanted to feel Tom's forehead. *"K'aja onqoy,"* he repeated, fanning himself as if hot, then wrapping his arms around himself and chattering his teeth.

"Okay. Fever. What was your first clue?" Tom jerked the rough blanket up around his neck, his own teeth chattering now.

The witch doctor reached out again, this time moving slowly. Warily, Tom allowed his forehead to be palmed, gritting his teeth against any possible mental invasion. But good to his miming, the man merely gauged Tom's temperature, drawing his hand back and consulting with the orderlies in rapid… Quechua, Tom's spotty memory supplied. He could feel himself slipping away again, whether from the fever or the shit-tastic beverage, he couldn't tell. He was only too glad to pass out, although his conscience nagged at him that he had something to do, somewhere to go, someone to be with. He needed to…

His side throbbed, derailing his train of thought and his journey back into dreamland. He peeled back the covers, too hot now anyway, and checked the bullet wound. A poultice of some sort stuck to it, stinking worse than that stuff in the bowl had tasted. He picked at the sticky mess, but the medicine man grabbed his hand.

"Uh, uh," he told Tom, wagging his finger at him in a universal gesture for "don't touch."

Tom began to protest, but found he couldn't make sense. Didn't matter anyway since these people couldn't understand him any more than he could them. If only he were better at languages. Now there was a talent he could use. They needed someone like that at BOO—a human universal translator.

The room whirled and swirled, and a rainbow of colors danced at the edge of his vision. He figured he was going to get better or die, but he was too exhausted to care. "Catch you back," he muttered, and the world went away.

Or rather, *that* world went away, to be replaced by one painted in as many shades of blue as the rain forest had been green. He looked down from where he floated.

Blue. Blue. My love is blue.

I look around me. Okay. Not my first walk on the spirit plane. Make that flight on the spirit plane—spirit airplane. Ha!

I ricochet off the occasional tree, but it doesn't hurt, just sends me in another direction like a ghostly pinball. Am I dead? Probably. Last I remember I wasn't in great shape. Hope someone sends my dog tags...back to BOO, I guess. Haven't had a home or family or anyone in a long, long time. It's better that way.

I float over some buildings, now, a factory or something. Looks nasty against the brutalized red earth. Looks familiar. I drift over a wire fence, brushing against the vicious barbs. They tickle, and the sparks look nice. I float through a window. Not an open window, either. This is pretty cool. I didn't know I could do this, although I think my mother could.

I'm in the drug lab now. I remember. Sort of. I am here to do something, but how can I if I'm a ghost? I watch the operation. I see fleeting scenarios of mistreatment and cruelty.

"Adrian!" I whisper as the handsome young man enters the production area. Is he associated with Deerborne's operation after all?

Arian moves slowly, stiffly, eyes downcast. He climbs on a stool at the long stainless steel workbench and grabs a pile of leaves. He winces, hands blistered and raw. I ache for him, but I'm also insanely glad to find he's a victim and not an ally. Now all I have to do is rescue him. But wait. I think I'm dead. Or not. I haven't seen any bright light or a scythed reaper. I do see Adrian though.

He's thin. Thinner. "How long?" I ask, but he can't see or hear me.

How long does it take to lose weight like that? A week? Two? How long have I been unconscious? Is this a vision of the now? Of the future? I survey the scene, but can locate no handy newspapers lying date-up, no wall-calendar with days struck off.

My attention returns to Adrian. Red streaks crisscross his arms just below the sleeves of his once-white T-shirt—whip blows fallen wide. Filth and black gunk mark the back of the shirt—probably dried blood.

A man, fat and greasy, strides back and forth behind the row of workers, a nasty whip dangling from his belt. "No los negros!" *He clouts the worker on Adrian's left on the ear hard enough to send the man sprawling on the dirt floor.*

"Okay, Doc?" Adrian asks, helping the older Asian man back to his stool. He grabs onto the work bench, remaining upright when the overseer clouts him, too. A little blood trickles down his neck as he returns to the task of leaf sorting.

Apparently this concludes the clouting portion of the demonstration.

Now the greasy overseer moves to the pretty young woman on Adrian's right.

"Allinchay," *he says approvingly, stroking her arm. She flinches away, not looking at him. He laughs, cupping her breast instead. He pinches her nipple and massages her breast roughly while she continues to work, trying not to touch him with her arms. It's a game he's played before, and she knows the rules.*

Adrian's shoulders hunch in. The muscles in his jaw twitch. His fists clench, crushing the perfect green leaves he's holding. The sweet smell of lavender clouds the air...lavender in color to my spirit-eyes.

"Don't try anything," Doc whispers to Adrian. "They'll only beat you again."

Adrian nods, fury rolling off him in waves. Now I can see their emotions in color, stark against the LCD blue of the vision: Adrian projecting waves of fiery red anger; the overseer, burnt and rusty-looking with lust and evil. Tiny auras of cool gray radiate from Doc, the girl, the other workers. Fear, humiliation, hunger.

When the girl begins to cry, the overseer lets go of her breast, laughing.

Elvis Montoya enters the lab. He watches a moment, assessing, calculating. He laughs with the greasy man. Walking down the row of workers, he slaps Adrian soundly on the back. Adrian gasps in pain, a fresh bubble of blood seeping through the T-shirt. Montoya wipes his hand on the girls back, stroking longer than necessary to remove any residue.

I'm furious. This can't go on. Jacqueline Batique must have had no idea what goes on here or she'd have skipped the three-strikes bullshit and gone right to "You're out!" I must fix this. The girl. The Asian man—must be the professor who blogged about their expedition. All of them. Adrian—you're there because of me. You risked your life saving me from Deerborne. I try to control my drift, needing to reconnoiter the place for my rescue mission.

"No! No!" I cry as I realize I'm floating not around the compound, but up, upward, unable to stop myself. Up through the ceiling, up through the clouds. My vision fading and blurring as I rise. "No!" But it's gone. It's all gone. All except my resolve.

"No!" Tom shouted, sitting up, sweat coating his body.

A woman sitting on the floor near the door put down her beadwork and shifted to his bedside, or pallet-side to be more precise. Tom watched her, panting a little, dream-fear and frustration receding, replaced with determination and impatience. He threw back the blankets. A tiny spider scuttled away from the poultice still stuck to his side. He ripped the stinking bandage off, finding a fine mesh of spider web knitting his wound as tightly as modern gauze. The woman babbled at him in Quechua, probably telling him to settle down.

The shaman entered. He had great timing, Tom would give him that.

"Where're my clothes?" Tom demanded, standing and taking a step toward the shaman.

The shaman just smiled and held out his arms to support Tom as he swayed unsteadily. "Head rush," he explained as the shaman guided him to a carved bench running along the far wall. Tom sat heavily. "Thanks," he muttered.

"Well-come." The shaman smiled almost shyly. Perhaps he knew enough English to help Tom figure out where he was, where his vehicle was, and of immediate interest, "Where are my clothes?"

The shaman smiled and pointed to his heart. "Yuyaychaj."

So, introductions first. Okay. "Tom," he replied, pointing to his own chest.

"Ta'am," the shaman tried.

"Tom," Tom corrected.

It took several tries, but eventually the Indian got it. He pointed at himself, then back at Tom. "Yuyaychaj," he said again. When Tom still couldn't master it, he said something that Tom guessed meant, "But you can call me Chaj.'"

Tom's clothing was brought to him, relatively clean, bullet hole nicely repaired with a crisscrossing of thick green threads. Retrieving his few possessions proved somewhat harder as they'd already been spoken for.

"Sorry I didn't die," he said to a pouty teenager who'd woven feathers and beads onto his dog tags. His knife was a little more difficult, since a warrior named Appo had won it fair and square in the local equivalent to Russian roulette, involving, Tom learned, live piranha tossing. He was almost inclined to let anyone who won a game involving maneating fish keep the knife, but he thought he might need it. They finally settled on an arrangement whereby Tom was just borrowing Appo's new knife. Tom was okay with that, since he found the handle's newly carved symbols threw the balance a little off.

A small child marched up to him and solemnly returned his compass. It was a little grubby, but otherwise fine. Apparently watching the needle tremble hadn't been a terribly entertaining activity.

That was pretty much it. He'd surrendered his gun to Deerborne back in Tanpu, but had several others back in the Jeep. The Jeep's keys had been stashed in a knothole close by where he'd hidden it. Now he just needed to figure out where he'd left it.

"I gotta go," he told Chaj. "It can't wait." He shivered, the fowl liquid they'd made him drink again bouncing around his stomach. He could feel the fever returning. His wound felt hot and itchy and he wondered if infection had set in. Maybe they could retrieve the spider. "I gotta stop the drugs being made."

Chaj looked confused.

In a moment of inspiration, Tom pointed to a section of the woven fabric draped over their table. "Blue," he said. He pointed to some bright feathers worn in a passing child's hair. "Blue," he repeated. Chaj held up a glossy stone, possibly turquoise, *"Azul?"* he asked.

"Yeah, yeah. *Azul."* He carved bricks in the air with his hands, repeating the Quechua word for blue.

Chaj crossed his eyes, rose, and staggered around the firepit. *"Azul,"* he said again, drawing circles in front of his eyes.

"Exactly," Tom said, nodding vigorously, which really didn't help his stomach at all.

"Azul," Chaj repeated. He spat into the fire.

Tom couldn't agree more and spat into the fire as well.

Appo and another warrior joined them by the fire, and the four men discussed plans. They managed to communicate using a combination of insight, pantomime, and the fact that Chaj was pretty damn psychic.

Tom learned that the tribe was called the Perqua, that Appo and the other man, Addo, were brothers and also the head warriors of the village.

"I have to go now, Chaj. The longer I wait, the more people will suffer and probably die."

"But you're not yet strong again, Tom. And what can one man do against so many? You have strong magic?"

"If I can get to my satellite phone, many will come. Many with strong magic." He knew Chaj was being literal. Well, so was he.

The concept of phone was lost on them. They understood long distance communication, but failed to grasp why Tom needed a device to reach out and touch someone. Wouldn't a short nap do the trick?

Tom had never found the spirit plane an effective communication method. Maybe if there was some sort of psychic 4-1-1... He'd have to check with BOO when he next was in touch with them. Why hadn't he asked for some sort of psychic link before heading out on this mission? Again his paranoia about magic had interfered with his ability to get the job done. That was never going to happen again!

Finally Chaj rose. As leader and shaman of the Perqua, he'd made his decision. They would wait for Tom to regain his strength. There were neighboring tribes such as the Wallpa and the Eek who would help. No tribes had escaped unscathed, their people enslaved in the drug factory, too.

They would formulate a plan that involved stealth and many warriors and possibly their wives, who were not only fiercer than the men, but also smarter, which was why they tended to stay out of dangerous situations like battles. Chaj seemed to think they might be convinced to join the men this time.

Tom thought he'd maybe missed something. He felt his own forehead. He was dizzy and hot. Yet he'd understood every word the young shaman had said.

Gritting his teeth in frustration, he rose and went toe to toe with the shaman. "Look, Chaj. I'm sure your guys are great warriors. Gals, too," he added at the glare from Addo's wife. "But I gotta go now. And I gotta go alone. You don't need me, and frankly, I don't need you!"

He pushed his way past Chaj, pretty sure he could find his Jeep. He would have made it, too, if he hadn't keeled over halfway across the village square. Luckily good ol' psychic Chaj was there to catch him.

"No. I gotta go, I gotta—" His head pounded, and his wound throbbed. Chaj eased him to the ground where he knelt in the hard-packed dirt, supporting his weight on his outstretched arms. His fever raged, muscles and joints aching beyond the telling of it. The village wavered—the same, only different—a village superimposed on a village. The hair on his arms crackled as if static electricity danced around him.

"Yes. I see you must go. Go with my blessings, then. Go knowing the Perqua have done what they can for you."

Tom's skin itched and burned. He grunted, tearing off his clothing. Horrified, he watched his skin darken and char. No, not burnt. His body hair was thickening, new hairs sprouting from every pore, rushing out to form a coat—hell, a pelt!

"What have you done to me?" he screamed. It sounded raw and

hoarse to his own sensitive ears. He clawed at them. It hurt, and he realized he had real claws. And paws. He rolled on his side, pain and shock too awful to bear. He felt a touch on his shoulder. Chaj, holding up a piece of glass—a mirror, cracked and crazed. A black face looked back at him. Cat-like. Regaining his feet, he snarled and pawed the air, smashing the mirror, ungainly in his new inhuman form. He roared—more of a scream-cough.

Around him the warriors circled, spears and knives at the ready.

Tom backed up, too panicked to even try and understand Chaj's soothing flow of words. *What the hell have you done to me?* The cat form's natural grace took over, and he leapt into the jungle and ran, feeling strong, powerful, no sign at all of fever or gunshot wound. He screamed again. No point in finding the Jeep now—keys, locks, guns and phones beyond his ability since he'd swapped his opposable thumbs for killer claws.

He needed no compass to find his way back to Tanpu and the drug lab. The rotting lavender scent drew him like an olfactory signpost—*Drug Lab This Way.*

CHAPTER 10

FATAL DISTRACTION

Rain thrashed the jungle. Slashes of lightning split the dark sky, blinding blue-ringed eyes, ears deafened by thunder. *Run! Get away!* The sole clear thoughts in Adrian's drug-addled mind.

Greedy fronds clutched at him. Mud oozed around every step, sucking at his boots and leeching his strength, each footprint a puddled signpost to those tracking him.

His overlong sopping hair whipped his face, blinding him. Were they behind? Ahead? Circling back in ambush?

He stumbled, hit the trail chin first.

"I need a moment. Just a moment," he begged, lying in the downpour. A Sunday school sentence screamed in his brain—*My God, my God. Why hast thou forsaken me?*

Dismal skies might have been dawn, might have been dusk. It was hard to tell, living mostly underground for days. Or weeks. He no longer knew. Dusk, he decided, recalling he and the other workers had been brought their evening meal—one scant bowl of watery stew grudgingly allotted by fattened guards. He'd gulped it down in three slimy mouthfuls when something had disrupted the compound. Something shadowy and violent—screams, roars, blood, death. A guard and an overseer down, throats shredded to fleshy chunks—a fitting end for the cruel captors.

When a jaguar had attacked the compound, he'd seen his chance and fled, squeezing his way painfully out a tiny ventilation window. He sought freedom, not so much for his own safety, but for the sake of Doc Soc, the young girl, and the other Indians who toiled beside him. He'd be pursued, of course—by his captors, by their attacker. Either. Both. But he had to try. Duty, not heroism. It was the right thing to do. Find the authorities. Report the drug lab. Hope the local cops weren't in cahoots.

More likely, he'd be hunted, killed, or recaptured. Punished. Made example of. Or slaughtered like a beast in the rain. His captors could never allow him to reach the outside world. Ever.

There'd be hell to pay for his escape attempt, when he was caught. Thinking this, he prayed the jungle beast would find him first. Suicide or escape? The fates would decide.

Adrian shivered. Who knew the rain forest, stiflingly hot by day, could be so cold at night? He felt he could drown just lying on his back in the mud. The bloated raindrops seemed to spring full-blown from the air around him.

What was that? Voices, calling in Spanish. The indigo men were coming. The *azul-runa* as the Indians called them.

He harbored some dim hope of finding a local tribe, of throwing himself on their mercy. Help me. *Yanaparuwanki-manchu!* You're my only hope. Though he'd heard the locals weren't always friendly.

The truth was he had no hope. No plan. Just run. Get away. From the drugs, the beatings, the starvation. Run now while he still could, before the brutal labor, before the *azul*—the indigo, along with the filth and the violence, brought about his untimely end. Before his jailers decided to risk Montoya's wrath. He'd rather die fleeing than lying in a pool of his own waste in the disease-ridden compound.

Only now, hours away from the drug labs, was his head starting to clear, life-giving rain expunging the indigo residue. It had entered through his pores and with every breath, and was being shed in his sweat and his urine and his tears. The purer form, the dream-inducing liquid old Alberto had given him, had hit harder, but receded quicker. Something about Montoya's concoction made it dally in the bloodstream. And not in a good way.

Obviously, I'm still not thinking straight. His mind was wandering despite his life and death flight. Rising from the earth, mud dripping from his hair and clothing, he ran on in the darkening gloom. The fetid jungle grew thicker, near impenetrable. It leeched away his energy, his life force, his *chi.* He felt his very soul being sucked away.

Thrusting through a thicket of vines and thorny undergrowth, Adrian stumbled into a clearing. Petrified, he drew a slightly fresher breath of air. A brief reconnoiter revealed not a clearing but a shoreline. A turbulent river filled the chasm before him, unheard over the storm. Its seething whitewater blocked his flight as effectively as any prison wall.

Cries in Spanish just behind him.

"There he is!"

"*¡Sí! ¡Sí!*"

"I see him!"

"Get him! *¡Consígalo!*"

Adrian understood it all now. His crash course in Spanish and Quechua—begun with phrasebooks and trips to the spirit plane—had become a matter of survival in the work camp, where disobedience meant brutal punishment and ignorance of the language had been no excuse.

Panicked, Adrian spun, frantically seeking escape. To his left a massive rockfall blocked his path, insurmountable as a stone glacier rising from the earth. To his right ran a tributary as riotous as its wild parent. He was cut off, hemmed in, his captors almost upon him. A bullet cracked rock by his ankle—no tranquilizer dart this time. His instinctive recoil sent him sprawling, halting at the edge of the steep embankment. Another inch and he'd have toppled into the river below.

Over the thunder and the rhythmic tattoo of rain on the leafy canopy came the sound of a new pursuer—the ragged scream of a jungle cat perched on a rocky outcrop nearby—perhaps the same one that had attacked the compound, providing deadly distraction, allowing Adrian to escape. Was his rescuer now to be his executioner?

Adrian snarled at his pursuers—men before him, jaguar looming on the rocks above him. Searching the dirt, his fingers curled around a solid, jagged stone. He'd be damned if he was going down without a fight. Hell, he'd be damned anyway. Escape or death? Escape now surely meant death later.

"Jose!" a voice called in Spanish. "Don't waste the bullet. He's still got work left in him. Catch him and bring him back with us."

"Nah. I shoot him. Once a runner, always a runner."

A third voice, ominously clear above the resonance of the storm, ordered, "Take him. We'll march him back and *dificultelo* him there. An example for others who might think to run."

A soulless laugh echoed in the dampness, like a stick dragged across corrugated iron.

No way would Adrian let this happen to him. He'd seen the recaptured runners, their ankle bones broken and fused at ungainly angles. "Go fuck yourselves!" he screamed, voice harsh against the storm.

The others laughed with their leader, a devil's lieutenants currying favor.

"Maybe have some fun with him first, no? While he's still pretty."

"Or after we hobble him with the sledgehammer. He'll be only too glad to kneel." Their laughter grated on his already shredded nerves.

The moonlight painted his pursuers' faces in sickly light—three grinning death masks just yards from his defenseless position. The fourth, Elvis Montoya, a shadow behind them, staying well back from the violence—violence of which he was the ultimate creator. The men fanned out before him, three against one, a constellation of doom in the growing darkness.

"Venido aquí, pequeño querido. Give up now and we'll be gentle." Wheedling tones, followed by more sadistic laughter. Montoya snapped his fingers, the sound eerily loud. One of the men handed him a camera. *Adrian's own camera!* Montoya laughed and brought the camera up to his chest, checking the flash. "Now!" he ordered the men.

I don't think so! Adrian answered silently. Out loud, he shouted, "Hobble this, you bastard!" He flew from his prone position, dashing directly at the nearest assailant. By the time the surprised Colombian thought to raise his automatic weapon, Adrian was upon him, a seething ball of fury and desperation. Gun rendered clumsy and useless at such close quarters, the son of a bitch swung his weapon at Adrian instead. Ducking a clout from the rifle barrel, Adrian seized his moment, striking with deadly accuracy, bashing the man's face with the jagged rock he'd grabbed when he'd fallen. A shadowy fissure appeared where a cruel, blue-ringed eyeball had been.

Adrian yanked the rifle from his enemy's spasming clutch and gifted the prone man with a brutal kick, payment in kind for harsh beatings received.

The other two advanced on him. Adrian swung the gun butt like a club, keeping them at bay, knowing it was all over even as he stepped backward, pinned again between the enemy and the churning river.

"¡Olvídese de él! Just shoot the sum'bitch!"

Good, Adrian thought. A clean death.

"No. I want him alive! Capture him!"

Montoya's words sent snakes of fear slithering down Adrian's spine, squirming in the depths of his bowels. He stood his ground, still holding the purloined rifle like a Louisville Slugger. Any attempt to shoot one man would result in his instant death by the other.

And suddenly, that sounded good. Very good, in fact. He turned the gun barrel outward, aiming for Montoya. At least he could do this last good deed for the world—if, in fact, good could arise from murder.

Montoya sneered, raising Adrian's camera in answer, obviously confident his henchmen would protect him.

A streak of lightning split the sky, illuminating the deadly standoff. Startled, his hands clenched. He felt rather than heard the shot. Had he hit anything? Anyone? He'd never even held a gun before, let alone fired one.

When his blurring and burning vision returned, the echoes of light silhouetted a screaming shape as it descended on the attackers. Dagger-claws flashed red as first one, then the other, went down beneath the black velvet onslaught, guns forgotten in primal panic.

The jaguar released the man's throat—Adrian would never know if he'd shot one of them or if the jaguar had taken out both. Three bodies lay in the muck, two with great red gashes where their throats had been. The one Adrian had clobbered with the sharp stone groaned and shifted, catching the cat's attention. Adrian clenched his eyes shut, wishing he could do the same with his ears, as groans became screams, then gurgles, then silence.

Three bodies. Three only. Montoya had escaped.

Surveying the carnage, Adrian gasped, bile rising in his throat. "Oh, God!" he whispered, but apparently not quietly enough.

The great cat lifted his head and faced Adrian. Bits of flesh dripped from its scarlet maw. It tossed its head, sending bloody droplets to join their purer cousins in the puddles below. Slowly, head lowered, it advanced. Cat eyes met human eyes. Adrian took a shaky step backward, then another.

The rain-saturated embankment melted beneath his feet. Adrian gasped instinctively for air as he plunged into the river where the angry current snatched him under.

Gray spots danced in his vision. Moments of his life spun across his consciousness. *How the hell did I end up here?*

* * *

"I'm hungry, Mom. Smells good." Still half asleep, Adrian cuddled closer to the warmth and comfort of the soft bulk beside him. "Mac'roni and cheese for lunch, Mom?" he asked, salivating hungrily for his favorite comfort food.

Instead Adrian's dream-Mom began to wash his face, a warm pink washcloth painfully rough over his abraded skin.

"Macaroni and— What the—" he scuttled backward like a beach crab, uncaring of lacerated palms in this new escape. His flight stopped abruptly when his back smacked against stone.

The jaguar regarded him, Sphinx-like, if the Sphinx had been designed to flop to one side. And animated. Its tail lashed the ground rhythmically.

"Uh. Good kitty." Adrian desperately tried to recall if feline tail wagging meant friendly or hungry. He now had a cat of his own, after all. What would Pixel do? He strove to control his frantic breathing, afraid of disturbing the thing. He shuddered, heart beating so loud he could barely think. Well, panicking wouldn't help either his situation or his calming down, which wouldn't help the… His thoughts chased themselves in frantic loops. He panted a little less noisily and tried not to move.

Interminable minutes passed. The great beast made itself more comfortable, shifting around so it could lie down again, resting its head on its paws, never taking its eyes off Adrian.

More time passed. Adrian's bladder demanded attention. Telling it to get over itself, he surveyed his surroundings. His pulse had settled a bit, and flight-or-fight had been replaced with some sane thinking about escape. He checked his surroundings.

So, a cave. Yes. Very typically cave-like, with rock walls, floor, ceiling. An unseen back wall and an obvious front entrance bleeding a little weak daylight. Outside it was drizzling. Again.

"Guess that's why they call it the rain forest." His hand flew to his mouth. *Oh, shit! Was that out loud?* But his silent watchman just carried on with licking itself—himself, Adrian could now plainly see—so maybe he hadn't spoken aloud after all. He felt kinda woozy and disoriented. His stomach growled. The jaguar raised its head and blinked at him before resuming its exercise in personal hygiene.

From the angle of the sun peeking in through the opening, he guessed he'd been out for a good ten hours, whether asleep or unconscious or possibly dead he couldn't guess. Fleeting recollections of strange dreams of witch doctors and cats sent shivers crawling down his spine.

But how had he gotten here? To this cave? Last thing he remembered was pitching into the river—being dragged along by the current, dragged under, and then…dragged out again. By whom? Or by what? He glanced down at his pants. Straight parallel tears marred the fabric on one leg. And now that he noticed, the leg began to burn. Pulling apart one of the larger tears, he saw angry scratches on his thigh. They didn't look deep. In fact they seemed identical to the ones Pixel had inflicted the night he'd acquired the cat, but those had hurt disproportionately, too. He wished he had some disinfectant with him and hoped that rain and river had washed away any bacteria. And not washed it in. He felt his forehead and cheeks with the back of his hand, but he was cool to the touch. So was his leg. The cuts were well scabbed over, so he turned his mind to more pressing matters, like maybe, possibly, staying alive.

Adrian eased his cramped legs a bit. The big cat, tongue-bathing done, remained motionless except for its tail. Adrian shifted a bit more. No response to that, either. Moving very, very slowly, grateful for those yoga classes, he eased aching muscles upward until he was standing. He stayed still a long time.

The jaguar yawned, showing huge, pointy incisors. He plopped his magnificent head on his paws and closed his eyes.

Adrian waited and waited… *I wish I had a watch.* Time seemed to be standing still, not unlike himself. He inched his way toward the cavern opening. *Maybe the cat's just pretending to be asleep. Don't cats like to toy with their prey before…* He couldn't bring himself to finish the thought. Or maybe that was spiders. The thought of bugs and other things that hung out in caves opened up a whole new avenue of worry.

Sweating profusely, Adrian had just reached the entrance when the jaguar moved. Adrian froze. The big cat rose and stretched. Nostrils quivering, it drifted over, butting Adrian's hip once, nearly knocking him over. It strode to the rocky opening and flopped back down, effectively blocking the way out.

Aching, thirsty, hungry, scared, caution be damned, he began to babble. "I just want to pee. I wasn't going to run away or anything." *Why am I justifying my behavior to a dumb animal?*

Whoa. Maybe not so dumb after all. The jaguar heaved to its feet and exited the cavern. Adrian followed quickly, staying just inside and peering out at the rain. Last night's deluge had tapered off to a mere sprinkle, the tinkling sound of which only made his bladder more insistent.

The big cat paced around the small ledge twice, three times, then squatted and peed copiously. Adrian had expected him to lift his leg like a dog, but perhaps cats didn't. He'd bought Pixel the kind of litter box that had a little house over it. No way did he want to know what went on in there, plus the guy needed his privacy. Adrian had meant to buy a book on cats, but with all the activity of Violet's death, quitting his job, going on expedition, it had just slipped to the bottom of the priority list.

Having finished peeing, the big cat scraped up huge clods of dirt and scree with his back legs, flinging them out over the edge of their little rock balcony. They knocked and clattered down the side of the mountain long enough for Adrian to realize just how high up they were and how unlikely it was he was going to escape downward.

The jaguar returned to the cave entrance, standing to one side as if to let Adrian follow his example.

"I don't believe this!" Adrian's bladder didn't need a second invitation. He stepped onto the ledge. "Well, you could at least turn your back." The jaguar stepped back into the cave, and with tremendous relief, Adrian moved to the cliff wall, his back to the drop.

Long moments later, feeling much relieved, he decided to investigate his surroundings. He zipped up and crept closer to the lip of the ledge. The cliff plunged nearly straight down. A hundred feet? Yards? Meters? He knocked another pebble off the edge. It noisily bounced and scrabbled down to join the others. He'd never been good with distance and had never really made the conversion to metric, but he knew a drop like this would kill. How the hell had he ever gotten up here? He doubted he could have accomplished the journey while conscious and equipped with the latest in rock-climbing gear, let alone knocked out and half drowned.

The big cat padded over to stand beside him, staring out over the dense green canopy below. What was that? Something below shook the branches. Adrian shot back to the solid rocky comfort of the mountain. As his heart once again calmed, the disturbance reminded him that somewhere out there Montoya and his small army of *azul*-men were searching for him. Last night's battle during which several of his men had been ripped to shreds would only have made the deranged Colombian angrier. Already Montoya would have his hired killers out stalking Adrian—they could not let him live to report them.

And report them he would, just as soon as he escaped his newest captor and found his way back to some sort of civilizations. He only hoped the other factory workers survived until then. He had to get to the authorities. Had to!

Compared to the horror of recapture, Adrian felt oddly safe standing on the dangerous cliff beside the maneater.

"Maybe I'm safer here with you."

At the irony of that thought, a massive shudder rocked him to the core. He needed to form a plan for escape. But how could he even get out of the cave? No way could he climb down from the ledge.

He gazed out across the sea of leaves. He'd done the research, read about the disappearing rain forest, but from this perspective, it looked like the entire world was one big primeval jungle. He wished he was one of those gay men who had fifty words for a single color. Like emerald and khaki and hunter. And chartreuse. Wasn't chartreuse a kind of green? What a great shot this amazing vista would make. He raised an invisible camera, squinting at the nonexistent viewscreen. Beside him the jaguar coughed.

Adrian dropped his hands to his sides, embarrassed at being caught playing with an imaginary camera. Then he felt even more embarrassed at being embarrassed in front of a wild animal. The jaguar shook its head and coughed again.

"Guess there's another way out, right?" Adrian spoke aloud for the poor company it offered.

The jaguar met his eyes and turned to re-enter the cave. Adrian followed.

"Now what?"

With liquid grace, the cat moved to the back of the cavern, stepping into the shadows on one side. Adrian's thirst redoubled as he listened to soft splashes. The jaguar padded back to the center of the cave and licked its right front paw twice before lying down again. Even in the dim light, Adrian could see the paw was wet, the fur flattened right up to the ankle, wrist, or whatever it was cats called the first bend in their front legs.

Adrian sidled to the back of the cave, gaze never leaving the sprawling cat, which meant he wasn't watching where he stepped and nearly tripped into the small basin of water in the shadowy reaches of the cave. Rain or spring water seeped in along a narrow crack in the rock. Instead of the expected stalactite and stalagmite, the eons of droplets had worn a shallow depression in the floor. Adrian recalled something about minerals, salts, or something, that were needed for the stone icicles to form. Guess there weren't any here. Thirst loomed large on his personal horizon and, losing interest in geology, he threw himself down and drank heartily. His body ached and shivered. He knew he should take only sips, but it was beyond his self-control to hold back now. He guzzled sweet water until his stomach hurt.

Since the water appeared to replenish itself, he washed up as best he could, he returned, dripping, to the larger area, to find the big cat asleep again.

Eventually he followed suit, because being damp, hungry, sore, and scared only held one's interest for so long.

* * *

Tom watched Adrian sleep for a while, mind racing, tail lashing. "What now?" Adrian had asked. That was the question. What the fuck was he supposed to do now?

He looking down at himself, startled anew to see legs and paws—nicely equipped with lethal claws, but paws nonetheless. *Wolverine, eat your heart out!*

He'd run on panic and instinct, frantic to take down the drug lab and save Adrian. Now at rest, he saw his mistakes. If he'd planned better, he might have taken out the entire place. All he'd thought was protect, mate, mine, kill. He needed to get the cat impulses under control. How the hell was he supposed to do that? He curled into a U-shape and began to lick his balls. Now here was something he could get used to! Although it was still much nicer when someone else did it.

Straightening out again, he lay, sphinx-like, on the rocky floor, resisting the urge to nap. He would have thought he was already asleep, dreaming about being changed into a jaguar, if he hadn't encountered magic and shape-shifters before. At BOO, there were a couple of werewolves, not to mention Chuck, the were-raccoon. He licked a paw, chewing on one claw, stripping away a sliver, leaving it sharper, deadlier, than ever.

He cursed Chaj, and at the same time knew there'd been no choice. Despite the care he'd received from the witch doctor (and the spider), the gunshot wound had been serious and crippling. The fever probably meant infection—he might have died. If he'd lolled about waiting to be healthy again (or to die), stupidly brave Adrian would have gone and got himself killed trying to protect the people he was enslaved with. So timing was everything. With the added bonus that Tom had managed to take out several of the assholes who worked for Deerborne and Montoya.

The human part of him shuddered at the thought he'd taken out several men with his bare hands—and teeth! It wasn't the first time he'd killed a man in the line of duty, but a gun from a distance, or even a knife, was still not the same as accidently swallowing bloody chunks of their flesh. And liking it.

He hadn't even kept count. Maybe it was seven. Two or three at the compound, three more in the jungle. That was… He concentrated hard. Six. The cat's brain was not designed for math. He recalled the old joke about how cats count—one, two, many.

Thoughts of ripping throats out with his teeth had his stomach roiling and also growling as the human's conscience and cat's entitlement battled. He was starving. He flowed up into a standing position, stretched forward and back like the most graceful yoga master, and headed toward the tunnel at the back of the cave.

But not before checking on Adrian one more time, ensuring the young man was sleeping as peacefully as one could in a cave high above the rain forest.

When he got back, he'd figure out how to communicate with the guy. He padded off.

CHAPTER 11

NOTES FROM THE UNDERGROWTH

Adrian awoke in the late afternoon, the angling rays of the sun searing his eyelids. He stretched, gasping with pain as his ill-treated muscles and skin ached and burned.

He was alone. No great furry beasts in sight. Why the beast hadn't already killed him he had no idea. Now was his chance at escape. He'd get away from the cave and the jaguar first, then worry about avoiding recapture from the indigo men, reporting them, and rescuing the workers.

He crept to the entrance, surveying again the impossible drop from the ledge to the jungle floor below. There must be another exit, then. He searched the cave as quickly as griping muscles would allow. A shaft of inward-slanting sunlight now illuminated the back of the cavern. He found the trickle-fed basin again, drinking and sluicing water over his head and neck. He couldn't clean up as well as he'd like, but he was still cleaner than he'd been back in the drug factory where a good dose of body odor was a guy's best defense against unwanted attentions. Some of the workers let themselves get really ripe—it kept the handsy guards at bay.

His stomach rumbled like yesterday's thunder—at least, he thought it had been yesterday. Not knowing how long he'd been unconscious, he really couldn't tell how much time had passed since his impromptu flight. His heart clenched; he needed to get moving.

Rising from the stone drinking fountain, he investigated the rear of the cave more thoroughly. A darker shadow to one side hinted at a passageway. It had to be large enough to accommodate one oversized jungle cat dragging an unconscious man. He picked at a scab on one elbow, grateful for the rescue, but bruised and scraped in so many places.

Not wanting to come face to face with said cat in the narrow rock tunnel, Adrian edged toward the back slowly, listening for signs of...whatever noises a jaguar would make. As his ears strained, his eyes strayed—and found odd markings on the walls.

Holy crap! Cave paintings! An anthropologist's wet dream. It could prove to be the symbology of an ancient people, the record of their history and culture, a spectacular find that could land him on the cover of *National Geographic* and establish his career. He must be the first person to see these in hundreds, perhaps thousands of years!

Hunger, maneater, and drug lords forgotten in his intellectual ecstasy, Adrian followed the patterns and cadences of the pictographs along the rocky chamber. He snapped mental photos, imaginary flashes illuminating the carvings.

He translated where he could, guessing at the rest, unraveling a tale he could hardly believe. Didn't believe, in fact, mentally categorizing it as myth, allegory, and parable. He examined and scrutinized until his eyes burned and his head ached and the sun took its light away for another day. Shit! Now how was he to escape? Sure, the passage would be dark either way, but what was he supposed to do once he'd reached the jungle floor? He shouldn't have wasted this precious time!

He faced the front of the cavern once again, knowing the way only by the dim glow limning the opening. He considered finding the exit by feel and trying to make his way in the rain forest night. Animal noises peppered the humid air. A jungle cat screamed; his bunkmate or another, less friendly beast? That settles it, he thought. Better the known evil. Or at least the single evil. He'd be wiser to stay put, although if the cat didn't kill him soon, hunger just might.

He decided to try to leave the cave at dawn, assuming his jailor hadn't returned. There must be fruit and berries and edible plants in the immediate area.

He took a few steps and struck something metallic with his foot. He fumbled for it. It felt sort of like a rusty football, only square-ish. He carried his find over to the dying light at the cave's mouth. A lantern! And probably not more than a decade old, he guessed, judging from the rust and the dust. So, he wasn't the cave's first modern visitor, then. The previous visitors must not have reported the cave art, or it would have been crawling with academics and tourists by now. It could still be the great find of the decade. He couldn't wait to inform the local historical society. Maybe they'd let him photograph it, or write an article about it.

What happened to the lantern's original owner, though? He decided he'd better not poke around too much in the dark. Thousand-year-old skeletons might be his field of study, but recent ones…not so much.

The lantern creaked on its hinged handle. The swish of sloshing liquid within sounded like the best thing to happen to him in weeks. *Please let it be oil.* A quick search located a drawer-like compartment in the base of the lamp. In it Adrian found two squares of some hard material on a short chain, similar in configuration to military dog tags. No stranger to outdoor living, thanks to some of the digs he'd been on while in college, Adrian recognized the flint and magnesium lighter immediately.

Fear and urgency hounded him to try the lantern immediately, but he knew he should save it for an emergency, although he was loath to think how his circumstances could possibly be any more dire.

Cradling the rusty lantern, he eased back down on the hard-packed ground, leaning up against the cave wall. He closed his eyes and waited—for dawn, for the cat's return, for death—he didn't know. But even pain and fear and hunger get old after a while, and Adrian grew bored waiting for the next day—or whatever—to arrive. His clothing and hair felt stiff and starchy with dirt. To pass time in the last of the light, he attempted to work some of the snarls from his hair. He unwound a bit of thread from a tear in his T-shirt, and, ascertaining first that he couldn't eat it, used it to tie back his filthy tangles.

Adrian was no longer tired, but hungry and sore and restless. It was too dark to explore, so he passed the time in painful yoga stretches. He was just thinking he might jerk off when cat's eyes appeared in the darkness, coming closer. Closer.

Something plopped in his lap. He jumped away, shrieking in surprise. Snatching up the lamp, he ordered quaking fingers to find the flint lighter and strike the lantern to life. The sparks spat in all directions as he swiped the flint across the magnesium bar repeatedly until the lantern thankfully, dutifully, provided a sliver of light. His eyes adjusted and he saw…a bunch of bananas? *No. Not possible.* He was already into the second banana while his mind raced to deny what he'd read in the pictographs at the back of the cave. *No. No. You can't change a human being into a...*

The jaguar padded off again.

* * *

Over the course of the next few hours the cat deposited several more types of fruit, a sizable sweet potato, and a crawfish-like water creature that Adrian tried to cook over the lamp flame, but ended up eating mostly raw. The last thing the jaguar fetched, strangely, was a warm and rather dented can of *cerveza.*

Adrian devoured most of the cat-catered repast, saving the warm beer for dessert. He washed his face again in the stone basin and settled down for the duration of the darkness, back braced against a relatively comfortable rock. Now that he'd lit it, he couldn't bring himself to douse the lantern, even though he knew he should be husbanding the minimal store of oil. He settled for turning the wick way down, illuminating only a tiny radius. Still, he found it hugely reassuring, and he needed all the comfort he could get right now. He'd been through hell in the last few weeks.

He was almost unstartled when the jaguar flopped down beside him, curving spine propped against his right hip. It seemed...normal, somehow. He reached out and stroked the furry flank. The hair was coarse but satiny, like the mink coat his Granny had been so proud of when he'd been a child.

Taking liberties with the maneater seemed unwise, but what the hell? The entire situation was a surreal nightmare, from his captivity to his personal jungle-cat rescue. He often had incredibly complex dreams, and this seemed like a particularly long and lucid one. Maybe he was still back in the lab, and this was just another drug-induced dream.

He stroked his hand up the creature's neck, where his fingers became entangled in a bit of chain. Holding the lantern up to illuminate the taut metal, he observed tiny silver balls strung together to form hardy links, like the chain that leashes the plug to the bathtub, or...military-issue dog tags. He pulled the tags closer and peered through the gloom, the lantern almost in the cat's face. He read:

FERRELL, Thomas J., Spcl Agnt.
Borderless Observers Organization

IDC: 129-45-6009 O POS

"Huh. Must be my week for Toms. So you're somebody's pet," he told the cat. "Or were when you were smaller, I'll bet. Some dumb soldier— Hey, easy now!" The cat ceased hissing, and Adrian continued his speculation. "The guy probably bought you for five American dollars and a carton of Marlboros, thinking you were just *sooo* cute. Then when you got too big, he turned you loose. I've heard of that happening."

He picked at another banana even though his stomach, shrunken from weeks of sparse meals, was really too full to eat any more. "I guess that's why you're really huge, too. Good nutrition during your formative years."

The cat sprawled back against his leg, making a sound—half-purr, half-meow—that might have been cat laughter. It turned to regard Adrian, then slowly moved its head left to right then left again.

"No, huh? That's not your story. So tell me what is, then?"

No response. What had he expected? *Curriculum vitae?*

"You'll never believe what the graffiti at the back of the bar says," he kidded, thumbing over his shoulder in the direction of the pictographs. "It says that a man who needs to learn a lesson… Or maybe he was dying," he interrupted himself, "I'm not entirely clear on that part. Anyway, it says he got turned into an animal. You know, like a man into, say, a jaguar."

The jaguar was nodding now. No, really. It almost looked like…

"That's ridiculous, right?"

The beast shook its head, eyes never leaving Adrian's.

"That's a no, right? So *no* that's not ridiculous or *no* that's not your story?"

The cat hissed, scaring the crap out of Adrian. Again.

"Sorry. Sorry." Adrian slowly lowered the arm he'd raised in instinctive defense. "You want only yes-or-no questions, right?"

The cat slitted his eyes, then nodded once.

"Boy, were you well trained. That's a great parlor trick!" And, chuckling at the preposterousness of it, Adrian lay back against his new roommate and waited for sleep.

CHAPTER 12

THE ROUTE OF ALL EVIL

Running. Running. Through thick, sweltering jungle pursued by shadowy shapes—men, beasts, feathers, leaves.

A man in war paint—not war paint, camouflage—dogs my steps, not threatening, not attacking. Not acknowledging me at all, in fact.

On we run. We pass by many odd things along the trail—a camera, a cell phone, a fax machine and a house, a blow dryer, a sleek gray cat, a knapsack and a laptop, a pine tree and a maple. A monkey and my first boyfriend, the monkey pointing and screaming.

I know I'm dreaming. I must be.

After covering many dream-miles, the trail ends. We've arrived at a derelict temple. Vines and vegetation obscure much of its surface, its neglected stone façade crumbled and worn. The soldier finally speaks, not to me, but to a painted Amerindian who's suddenly appeared.

"Why am I here?" the soldier asks. He speaks an unfamiliar Quechua dialect with a distinctly Midwestern twang, but in my dream I understand every word. "Why have you done this to me? Fix it. Now!"

The Indian just stands there, observing the soldier, ignoring me. "You ask too many questions, Qollpa." Qollpa, I know, means salt. It strikes me as a funny thing to call the man. It strikes me as odd that I understand.

"I want answers, Yuyaychaj." I'm not sure quite what this word means, Yuyaychaj. Teacher or counselor, I think. From the looks of

him, he's a shaman, I guess.

They know each other. They ignore me.

"You know the answers."

"'Follow the Yanapaj.' I know. I know. What the fuck does that mean?" The American is curt, frustrated. "Change me back, goddamn it! I've learned whatever lesson you thought I should learn. Change me back." The vision swirls and clears. I see now the handsome soldier has taken on the appearance of Tom from the airplane and from the confrontation with Deerborne. Power of suggestion, no doubt.

"You've learned nothing, Qollpa, except to lick your own sogay." Yuyaychaj laughs, but not meanly. "And I have not known you long enough to know what lessons you need to learn."

"Is he the one?" Qollpa jerks his head in my direction. I want to interject, but my mouth is glued shut. Instead, I make underwater noises, but neither of my dream-companions hears.

Yuyaychaj just smiles.

"Hey, Chaj." Tom shortens the Indian's title—or is it his name?—to only the final syllable. The two men must be familiar, or is it the American way of making everything informal, intimate? "Why am I having this dream-vision if you're not actually going to tell me anything?" Tom demands. Sarcastic. Desperate.

Again, Chaj laughs. "I will tell you this. This is not your dream at all. It is his. And mine. You are merely a self-important guest, Qollpa." Like a rain forest Cheshire cat, Chaj begins to fade from the feet up. He's shoulders and head only when Tom calls out to him, "Wait! Tell me what I must do."

The shaman continues to disappear.

"Please, Chaj. Please!" Tom begs, desperate. "I'm starting to lose myself. I'm beginning to be the cat."

"You must find the Temple of Cambiay, the Temple of Transfiguration. Prepare the Tears of Truth and bring some to me. You must also learn to trust the Yanapaj." Just the fading smile is left now, lips stained blue with tribal paint. Or maybe it was something he ate. "Then we shall see about restoring your man-form."

"But... But..."

But Chaj is gone. The American—Tom, Qollpa—finally turns to me.

"So, Adrian..." He runs an appraising gaze over me. "Are you the Yanapaj? The one?"

I feel like I've been judged and found wanting, like I haven't been all that I can be. I think maybe the shaman has a point about this guy's arrogance. I try to speak again and find this time I can. "No, actually I'm the Keymaster." I say, paraphrasing from a favorite movie without a trace of irony. It's my dream, and I'll plagiarize if I want to. Besides, who are you gonna call in a situation like this?

The startled look on his face is amusing. Then, before my eyes, he stoops over and in one smooth transition morphs into the great black jaguar. It roars at me, showing dripping, razor-sharp teeth.

* * *

Adrian opened his eyes, feeling like he'd gone a round with the spirit world and won. Adrian, one. *Qollpa,* zero. He felt almost good this morning, although hungry once more. Muscles protested less as he eased himself into a sitting position. The jaguar sat to one side looking pissed, tail slapping the ground like an angry, furry metronome. Adrian hummed the *Ghostbusters* theme softly.

The cat rose and headed for the back of the cave, where it stopped, looking at Adrian expectantly.

"Time to leave? Okay. Lemme get a drink and pee, and I'll be right with you." He tried it on for size. *"Qollpa."* The cat paced toward him. "That's you, then. *Qollpa."* The cat nodded.

"And you used to be a man."

Nod.

"And you're a U.S. soldier?"

The cat shimmied and whined, neither a nod nor a shake of that great head.

That didn't seem like a clear no. "You were a soldier, and now you're not?"

The big cat nodded.

"So you're what, then?" Adrian cast about his mental dictionary for just the right word. After his dream last night, Tom was very much on his mind. "An agent?" he prompted, remembering that's what Deerborne had called Tom back in the parking lot.

The beast nodded, again.

"Named Thomas Ferrett?"

The cat roared. Adrian jumped up and back, heart hammering. "What? What?" he asked, panting a little.

The cat stalked closer and held up its great head, showing its neck in a gesture that might have meant submission in another context.

Adrian re-read the dog tags. "Ferrell. Sorry. Ferrell, Thomas J." The cat stepped back and nodded.

"Why does he call you *Qollpa*—salty?"

The cat swatted at him, nails catching his T-shirt. He extracted them carefully, looking as close to chagrined as any feline ever could.

"Right. Right. Only yes-or-no questions." Adrian examined his shirt. The lethal claws had left pinprick holes, but no actual rips. He smoothed a hand down the fabric. He only had the one to last him… Who knew how long? It wasn't torn, but four little dents marred the cotton. They'd probably work their way out in the humidity. He reached out gingerly and scratched the cat on its huge black head. "So, do you want to be called *Qollpa?"*

The reaction was another sort of a cat shrug.

"How 'bout Thomas, then? After the owner of the dog tags you wear." *And the man of my dreams—literally.* "Again with the shrug, huh? How 'bout Tom?"

The cat rubbed its great head hard against Adrian's hand, purring.

Adrian chuckled. "So, Tom. Pleased to meet you. I had a dream about a guy named Tom just last night. I'm Thornapple, Adrian H." He held out one hand and the cat high-fived it, nearly sending him sprawling in the dirt. "Great. Tom. Great. You are so well trained. High five me again! What a great trick!"

A virtual shaman, a dream-lover, a jaguar that understands English. Adrian knew that indigo caused hallucinations and flashbacks. He chided himself for thinking any of this was real. He realized he was buying into some things and not others, but he needed to believe in something—something other than he was sick or dying back in the drug lab.

He did believe he'd escaped, with the help, deliberate or otherwise, of a well-trained jaguar. He knew he had to get to the authorities and report Deerborne and Montoya's illegal operation. He also knew he couldn't stay where he was.

He splashed more water on his face and neck, picked up the old lantern along with two leftover bananas. He hummed a bar or two of "I Will Survive" as he followed the now-pacing jaguar from their temporary shelter. What other option did he have, after all?

* * *

It had been early morning when they'd departed the cave through the shadowy back passage Adrian had noticed the night before. They hiked along a rocky tunnel, heading steadily downward. Adrian counted the steps, but lost his place somewhere around three hundred and sixty when something icky brushed his arm. He shrieked, jumping back against the cave wall, only to jump away again upon finding the wall slimy and *warm.* Some sort of glowing mildew painted the rocks in greenish light. The word "bio-luminescence" swam up from the depths of his memory. His subscription to *National Geographic* was certainly paying off. The glowing...plant (he refused to even think it might be alive—a *colony* of something), kept it from ever being completely dark, so head bashes were kept to a minimum, although not entirely prevented.

Adrian's chest grew tight and his breathing shallow. If he'd had enough oxygen, he would have asked Tom, or rather Tom's receding backside, how much farther. He might have been experiencing a touch of claustrophobia. Spelunking had never been his thing.

Eventually, they exited the cave's backdoor, stepping onto a barren rocky shelf, not unlike the one above that had served as both balcony and bathroom. There were a few more harrowing minutes while they followed a path that traced the side of the mountain, complete with washouts and switchbacks and other stuff that would have made your average suicidal rock climber ecstatic, but didn't do a lot for Adrian.

Finally their descent reached the treetops, a bumpy green topography stretching out to the horizon in every direction. Hoping to return someday to examine the pictographs further, Adrian carefully noted the cave's location. He memorized the shape of the crags and surrounding hills, hoping that satellite imaging and local legend would help him find his way back—it had certainly worked for archaeologists and explorers before him.

He didn't, of course, have any actual idea where he was. His pell-mell flight through the jungle followed by his trip downstream and his unconscious rescue had disoriented him to say the least. He had no clue how long he'd been in the river or of how far he'd been dragged while unconscious, first by the raging current, and then by the jungle cat.

The next few steps took them into the forest canopy. It was a lot like an airplane entering a cloud, except this cloud was green and filled with hoots and howls.

After having gazed out over the jungle for miles, suddenly Adrian could only see a few feet in any direction. His heart banged, and sweat trickled down his back, making it itch exactly where he couldn't reach it. Apparently claustrophobia wasn't just for caves anymore.

The canopy above was so thick it shut out the morning sunlight, bathing the paths where Adrian and Tom walked in eternal twilight. The trees grew close together, competing viciously for sunlight. Their branches intertwined, not in loving embrace, but in the ultimate death-match. Vines and parasitic plants wound their way among the massive trees. Here and there Adrian saw gray trunks, leafless and lifeless, strangled by their compatriots, long dead, but unable to lie down and rot in peace.

Many of the trees had complicated root systems to support their massive bulks. Roots like arms reached out to snag his ankles, and in the pale dappling of light, they seemed menacing, grasping, slowing his passage. He was glad it had been too dark to see much the night of his jungle flight from the compound.

So, since he didn't know where he was or in which direction to head, he might as well stick with Tom-the-Jaguar. Tom had proved to be protector and provider, both of which Adrian could really use right now. He figured he'd eventually find a clue that would lead him back to civilization, where he could report the indigo manufacturing plant and all its horrors. Until then he was pretty much without alternatives, and so he trotted dutifully behind his furry escort, wishing Tom would pick up the pace a little.

His stomach clutched painfully, not with hunger this time, but with panic about Doc Soc and the other captives back in the drug factory. The sooner he reported their illicit activities to the authorities, the sooner the workers would be free. He attempted to communicate both his goal and his urgency to Tom, trying commands like "home" and "casa." The cat sped up a bit, and Adrian trotted to keep up, grateful he'd been allowed to keep his sturdy hiking boots during his time in the factory. Eventually his dual panics—the claustrophobia and the need for urgency, receded into a manageable level of anxiety.

He'd eaten the last banana hours ago and grabbed some other fruit along the way. While it was the best food he'd had in weeks, and the largest quantity as well, he was quickly becoming less than enamored with Mother Nature's high fiber diet. He didn't mean to appear ungrateful, but he was tired of stopping every half-hour to use nature's port-a-potty. He'd keep his eye out for more solid food, maybe share in one of Tom's kills—provided it didn't include humans. He shivered despite the heat.

It did feel good to be walking again after two days of enforced rest.

His muscles, stiff at first, welcomed the pace the jaguar set for them. The big cat moved surely along jungle trails that were sometimes well established and sometimes of a more obscure design.

Tom glanced back often to ensure Adrian was in tow, switching his tail impatiently each time he needed to stop.

"Hold your horses, Tom. I can't help it. Find me something more substantial to eat than fruit, and we'll be stopping less often."

The growls of annoyance and Tom's pacing were suddenly noticeable by their absence. "Oh, shit. I've scared him off," Adrian mumbled as he searched for the Charmin of jungle leaves, praying he didn't accidentally find the Colombian equivalent of poison ivy. He emerged from the handy bush, looking for Tom. Failing to see him, he was considering his options, not excluding sheer panic as one of them, when a small bloody heap dropped at his feet.

"Oh. Uh. Thanks."

Simultaneously salivating and grossed out, he carried the slaughtered lizard to the next major clearing. Using a few small rocks, Adrian assembled a make-shift firepit. He loaded it up with burnables and used the flint and magnesium striker that had been with the lantern to get a small fire going. Eventually he managed to cook himself a greasy meal that tasted as good as anything he'd ever eaten. He knew that carbon and dirt and bits of scaly skin would probably not be the seasonings of choice in the finer restaurants back home, but right here, right now, it was heaven on a sharp stick. He'd only burned one finger in the process and he was almost positive eyelashes grew back. He'd offered a share to Tom, but Tom had declined as politely as a jungle cat could, which is to say he looked horrified and bounded off into the jungle, not returning until Adrian had finished his *lizard du jour.*

Having satisfied his hunger for now, Adrian reconnoitered his surroundings. He gasped in awe and fear at the jungle's overwhelming beauty, while his index finger twitched, camera-less, aching to snap shot after shot of nature at its most raw. He wondered who or what had worn the trails they were following. In the next breath, he hoped they wouldn't find out.

With most of his basic needs looked after, he began to think about weaponry. He'd done terrible things the other night with a sharp rock—he'd never know if he'd killed that man, or if Tom had. He had to admit, though, he'd do it again, if he had to. Being out in the wilderness changed how a man looked at life. And death. He made a mental note to get lots of therapy when he got home.

A machete, however, would come in very, very handy for a variety of tasks not limited to self-defense. The rifles of the other evening might be retrievable, but he didn't know where the confrontation had taken place and dearly hoped old Tommy-the-Cat was taking them in the most opposite of directions from Montoya's operation.

A bow and arrow he could probably fashion, given a bit of time, but his insistent guide had him up and traveling again the instant he'd taken the last bite of roast lizard. Perhaps they were on a schedule. Adrian was only too glad of the haste. The sooner he could report to the authorities, the less those poor people who were still laboring in the drug factory would suffer.

But he needed a weapon. He watched the trail for a suitable stick.

A piece of sturdy bamboo presented itself before long, and he was able to twist it free of the ground. He employed it as a walking staff for now, but as soon as he could, he'd find a rock and sharpen it into a serviceable spear. He felt better just carrying it, and Tom seemed to approve as well. Or at least he hadn't hurried Adrian along once he'd seen what he was doing.

"What am I thinking?" Adrian asked out loud. "I'm starting to buy into the human-to-jaguar transformation crap! This is nothing more than someone's abandoned pet."

Tom looked back at him. He almost appeared amused.

"Anthropomorphizing R Us," Adrian muttered, hurrying to catch up with the disappearing cat.

* * *

Adrian felt better than he'd felt in weeks. He hefted his new spear, enjoying the weight and balance of it. He executed a few practice throws. Tom lolled on a sunny rock watching him in what Adrian had come to regard as jaguar-amusement.

"Adrian Thornapple steps up to the javelin toss. The crowd goes wild! *Hhhhaaaa!*" A roar from Tom echoed Adrian's faux-cheer, scaring the crap out of him. Heart racing, he turned, hands on hips, and addressed the cat. "What? *What?*"

He'd long since given up being afraid of his maneating escort. He had so many other things to fear, from boas to bandits, piranhas to parasites. Not to mention the annoying bugs. He might as well be back in northern Ontario in blackfly season. He swatted another as it hummed near his ear. Strangely he wasn't getting bitten and he recalled one of the guards saying that indigo had an insect repellant property. On one hand he couldn't wait for the stuff to leave his system so he could be sure what was real again, but he wasn't looking forward to being bug-fodder once more. He eyed the buzzing cloud hovering above him, convinced they were just waiting for the hallucinogenic bug spray to wear off.

He had no worry left for a giant kitty that seemed to have his welfare at heart. His lifelong distrust of cats was melting away, first at home with Pixel, and now with Tom of the jungle. Learning to like cats—to trust them even—was just one more life-altering change in his long and recently compiled list.

"I like you, Tom, but you've got to stop with the roaring, unless you want a heart-attack victim on your hands." He wondered if CPR was among the cat's many surprising skills. What a great trainer his first owner must have been—a real cat whisperer. Adrian scratched at a healing and itchy scab on his elbow while considering that. Was he beginning to think of himself as Tom's owner? Because if anyone owned anyone in this jungle, it certainly wasn't him.

After startling Adrian with his roar, Tom looked properly ashamed, head down, peeking up at Adrian in contrition.

"I know, big guy. I know." He stepped over and petted the soft fur. "You were just playing along. It's just, you know, a bit…overwhelming." The cat rolled on his back and allowed Adrian to scratch the great expanse of chest.

Looking at the sky while he scratched, Adrian announced, "I could go a little farther before dark, I think." Straightening up, he shifted the spear to his left hand and grabbed a bundle of items strung together on cable-like vine. The lantern rattled against a sharp stone that was secured to it with more vines. Next to it was a broken arrow he'd found, which was carefully wrapped in smelly lizard skin to keep Adrian from accidentally poking himself or Tom with the tip. It might or might not be curare-dipped, but Adrian wasn't anxious to find out through experimentation. His scavenged prizes were mostly weapons, the pointy stone also serving as a knife for dressing and eating Tom's kills.

"What the…" Tom had grasped Adrian's right wrist gently in his immense jaws. The big cat tugged the man back toward the clearing. "Okay…I guess we're down for the count."

The jaguar herded Adrian into a small space between a couple of large rocks overgrown with stunted vegetation and lay down in front of the opening.

Not stupid by any means, Adrian lay quietly. Although sunset was an hour or so off, he figured now was as good a time to sleep as any. The moon would be pretty bright after it rose, hanging low in the sky. Perhaps they'd travel on after a brief nap.

Dozing intermittently, he started awake at the sound of voices.

Oh, God! Spanish! Oh, crap! He pressed himself back into the unyielding rocks, shaking violently, clutching his tiny arsenal. He'd felt confident and proud of his weapons earlier. Now they just seemed pretentious and woefully inadequate when compared with, oh, say, guns.

A low rumbling from Tom reminded him he wasn't alone in this…or so he needed to believe. Tom had heard the men approach long before Adrian had.

The voices came close, closer. Close enough for Adrian to make out a few snatches of their conversation.

"Useless. We'll never find *Americano* on foot. He's probably *mort* anyway." Elvis Montoya's voice. "But if he's not, we finish him. Remember. No more indigo means no more *denary.*"

So Montoya had survived their confrontation by the river. Bad kitty.

"*El doctored ill loco,*" said Juan Carlos, another of the guards who'd made Adrian's time in the lab a waking nightmare.

Adrian agreed the doctor was crazy.

"El doctored wants to dismantle the lab, set all the workers free," Juan Carlos added.

Adrian's heart leapt. Release the prisoners! He heaved a great sigh. He'd still report Deerborne and his crew to the authorities. They had to pay for the enslavement, torture, and murders he'd witnessed, but at least the enslavement and the drug production would cease.

"Set free?" Elvis's laugh prickled down Adrian's spine like a scorpion crawling along it. He hoped that was just a simile. "Okay for him to say. He'll be far away, but for us, no way. Free workers means death for us. A blow dart or a knife. Or a jail term. *Non.* We'll use the grenades left from clearing the jungle and just drop them in the underground lab. *Boom boom!* No more workers. No more tellers of tales."

Several other cruel voices joined in the laughter this time. Adrian choked. It would be all his fault if these men killed the workers—Doc Soc and the others. Adrian would give himself up. That would fix things. Shaking so hard his teeth rattled, he tried to cry out, but his voice failed him—like trying to scream in a dream.

Tom's head shot round to stare at him.

"I have to," Adrian croaked, tears doing nothing to lubricate his rusty vocal cords. "If I give myself up…"

Tom shifted his great soft bulk, pinning Adrian firmly against the rock. He hissed, very quietly, but there was no mistaking the anger. Awkwardly as he was perched, Tom reached one giant, razor-clawed paw up and placed it none-too-gently across Adrian's mouth. One sharp claw pricked Adrian's cheek piercing the tender skin.

Startled, Adrian rocked backward, smacking his head on the rock wall behind him. The impact left him dizzy and gasping with pain, tears and now blood dripping from his face. He laid his head on Tom's velvet-soft shoulder, just for a moment, to collect himself before trying again to gain the attention of Deerborne's men.

He must have passed out, whether from hyperventilating or from the clonk on the head, he didn't know. Either way, the men were gone when he came back to herself. His head throbbed.

"We have to hurry, Tom. We have to hurry." He spoke only for himself, but the great cat seemed to nod in agreement. Tom sniffed at the scratch on Adrian's cheek, and a warm wet tongue snaked out to soothe away blood and tears.

"Ow." Adrian pulled his head away, careful not to smack it again on the rock behind him. "I know you mean well, big guy, but your tongue is like a rasp." Adrian wiped his damp face on the warm fur, soft but not very absorbent. He swiped at his face with his filthy T-shirt, probably adding more grime than he was wiping away.

Once Montoya and his men had passed, so did Adrian's quaking. He crawled shakily from his hiding place and followed Tom along the trail.

The sun set and the moon rose, and on they traveled through the jungle. Tom picked up the pace, a new sense of urgency clear in his ground-eating strides. Adrian hurried to keep up, one eye on the vine and root-strewn ground, and the other on the familiar figure he followed, a darker shape among the shadows.

*   *   *

Tom fumed as he led Adrian through the jungle.

If I'd been alone, I could have attacked Montoya and taken those sons of bitches down. But Adrian has to decide he wants to do the sacrifice thing. The guy doesn't have the sense God gave a goat!

Adrian was turning out to be a real burden. Tom needed to drop him off somewhere safe and go tear those fuckers to shreds. Maybe the next village would be—

Hearing a weird choking noise behind him, Tom flew back down the trail.

"You okay, buddy?" he asked, although it came out more as, "Whreroo?"

"I—" Adrian horked loudly, spitting the resultant wad on the trail. "I swallowed—" He cleared his throat once more. "A bug the size of a bird. In fact…" He poked at the mess with the toe of his hiking boot. "I'm not sure it wasn't a bird."

Tom ambled over and sniffed at the yellowy goo. Something large and metallic black floundered in it. He butted Adrian in the arm to get him moving again, but not before sniffing him, delighted to find the young man unharmed.

Okay, so maybe he wasn't a burden, after all.

* * *

"I'm sorry, Tom. I'm trying, but I just can't." Adrian sighed, almost as frustrated as the big cat appeared to be. Tom stood on the trail, towering over Adrian, tail switching back and forth in the manner Adrian had learned meant impatience. "I'm trying, but my ankle… Jeeze. I'm apologizing to a cat here. I am so losing my mind!" He yanked a grimy tangle back from his face in annoyance. "What are we going to do now? We sure can't stay here." He glanced around, rain forest to the left and right, well-worn trail ahead and behind. Well-worn meant something or somebody came this way regularly, and he was really not interested in meeting up with something or somebody now that he'd probably busted his ankle.

After two days of racing through the jungle, he had felt he needed to get his bearings—*any* bearings—so he decided to climb the tallest tree on the tallest hill. First, he'd removed his boots as he'd seen the locals do, to get a better purchase on the rough bark. Now he was sorry he'd tried. Especially since the only thing he'd been able to see had been miles and miles of dense, green jungle in all directions. Sure, the vista was beautiful, inspiring a dozen mental photographs, but he remained unenlightened in terms of their whereabouts. It had been a waste of time and effort, and then he'd slipped on the way back down, landing painfully on his right foot. He'd panicked at the horrifying *pop!* accompanying his fall. Since running and screaming weren't an option, he'd been stuck with just screaming. Well, manly screaming in which the words "fuck" and "goddamn" had featured heavily.

Two minutes of cursing had left his throat raw and Tom hovering. Somehow the cat had managed to convey "be quiet and try not to attract attention" as well as concern and caring.

Adrian sat on the trail in a sorry lump, poking his ankle occasionally as it puffed up to twice its normal size. He put his tattered sock and boot back on his good foot and tied his other to his belt along with his makeshift tools and the lantern. No way was he able to get his hiking boot on over that ankle.

Tom had nuzzled Adrian's cheek before pushing at him with his enormous head and starting to walk down the trail again.

"You'll have to leave me. There's no freakin' way I can walk," he told the cat, watching Tom closely, not so much expecting a solution as hoping for inspiration. He'd come to warily trust Tom's guidance, although he was still not buying any of the shape-shifter nonsense. This was just an exceptionally well trained and intelligent animal who had developed some sort of pack attitude toward him.

Tom gazed at Adrian for long, unblinking moments, then padded over to his side. A velvet paw pushed away Adrian's hand. He sandpapered his rough tongue over the sore and swollen ankle, simultaneously balm and sledgehammer.

"Guess I didn't need Montoya to hobble me after all. All that son of a bitch needed to do was wait a couple of days, and I'd take care of it myself." He poked his ankle again, trying to ascertain if it was broken. "Wish I had some ice. And I need something to wrap it with." He examined the nearby jungle for vines and leaves that might serve.

Tom turned his back on Adrian, facing down the trail in the direction they'd been heading before Adrian's bungled high wire act. He shifted from paw to paw, peering back over his shoulder at Adrian.

When Adrian failed to acknowledge him, Tom growled low and menacing. To Adrian it sounded like the annoyed-cat equivalent of "A-dri-an Thorn-ap-ple!" Six distinct syllables, just the way his mother had said it when he'd been in trouble as a child. He could swear he heard teeth grinding—sharp, pointy teeth.

"Just how well trained are you, Tom?" he asked, not for the first time. "Okay. I get it. I get it. Just…" He really hoped he did get it. It seemed pretty preposterous. And also pretty obviously their only solution.

Tom's roar split the jungle. Birds scattered with caws and screeches, small animals skittered away unseen. One of those freaky howler monkeys let loose with a cascade of eerie barks, sending shivers along Adrian's spine.

"Jesus, Tom. Keep your pelt on, will you? I'll give it a shot, although I've mostly ridden English, not bareback."

Using his sturdy spear as a staff once again, he hoisted himself upright, trying not to put any strain on his ankle. He lurched toward Tom, who relented and backed up a pace or two, meeting him in the middle of the dusty pathway.

"Here goes nothing." Adrian took the ring of vine-lashed gear in his teeth, leaned the spear against a nearby bush and grabbed Tom's soft coat. Using only his left foot, he sprang high, determined to make it on the first try. Tom flinched, probably from the fistfuls of jaguar pelt Adrian used to haul himself up. There. He sat astride Tom's broad, warm back, his thighs muscles straining for purchase. He wondered if Tom had been ridden before. For once in his life, he was glad he wasn't some big muscular dude. As it was, he wasn't sure how long Tom could bear his weight.

Adrian let go of one furry handle long enough to grab his spear. At some point during his scramble onto the cat's back, the spear had lodged against Tom's neck, a rough bit of bark snagging on Tom's dog tags. He untangled it gingerly, careful not to break the little metal chain, although it seemed very sturdy.

Tom set off slowly, as if trying to get the feel of his new burden. Adrian knew he'd treasure the memory of his ride on this oversized maneater until the day he died. He just hoped that day was a long way off.

God, it was weird. Unbelievable. Like it was all just some particularly vivid dream.

An hour later, though, the growing discomfort of his ride convinced him he was awake—reality was generally more uncomfortable than dreams in his experience. He shifted slightly so the keel-like spine wasn't rubbing quite so sharply against him, serving as the jungle version of "pinch me." He now understood the popularity of the saddle in many far-flung cultures he'd studied.

Adrian's damaged ankle felt hot and tight, but more numb than painful. He leaned to the right and peered down, trying to see how the bruising was coming along, wondering if the numbness were a good or bad sign. Tom chuffed back over his shoulder, and Adrian returned to his centered position. After a while his backside started to go numb as well, so he leaned forward a bit. The cat didn't seem to mind. Fifteen minutes later the awkward position left his lower back aching. He leaned a bit farther forward, until he was lying along the length of the broad back as he had when he'd first climbed aboard. It was pretty comfy, actually. Tom flowed along, and with nothing new to look at, the hot, humid jungle lulled Adrian into an early afternoon nap.

*   *   *

Why the hell did he climb that fuckin' tree? How can I take down a drug lab with the guy on my back. Maybe I should just dump him at the first village I come to and be done. Have a nice life.

Tom rolled his shoulders, trying not to dislodge the man riding on his back. Jaguars, he concluded, were not designed to be ridden, despite their structural similarity to horses. This guy was heavy, and it wouldn't help anyone if Tom couldn't move tomorrow.

Refusing to wimp out, Tom strode on, keeping his pace constant despite the uneven trail. He flowed over downed branches and across small streams.

Tom listened to Adrian's breath even out. *Oh, great. He's asleep now. He'll probably fall off and break his neck. Then I'll really be in trouble.*

Tom considered stopping, but what was the point? He knew this well-worn trail led somewhere. He only hoped it was somewhere that would help.

Tom padded on, one foot in front of the other, the close air within the jungle stifling and stale, the afternoon before the rains hot and humid. He felt his eyelids droop, the step-step-step hypnotic. He didn't so much fall asleep, as fall into a trance—a walking trance.

Adrian began to moan in his sleep.

Blue. Blue. Runny, inky blue. A fountain-pen drawing left in the rain. Chaj the shaman, Chaj the showman. Tom. Even me, good ol' Adrian. I hold my arms out before me. My hands and clothes are blue.

"Trust the Yanapaj. Follow him," the shaman tells Tom.

Haven't I already had this dream-vision?

"Screw him!" Tom responds.

Chaj nods. "That, too."

The shaman fades, and the dream becomes different—more like a normal dream, with regular colors and familiar surrealism.

Tom, no longer blue, leers at me.

I've obviously based this "man of my dreams" on Tom from the plane. I've always had a bit of a fantasy about anonymous sex—the zipless fuck of the 70s—although the airplane tryst was practically my first time having sex outside a relationship.

My imagination has done a fine job with my fantasy lover. He looks so good in khaki. This, too, is a vision—no, a dream—I've had before, although usually the man is ageless, nameless, faceless.

My dream-lover advances. I quiver with anticipation and wonder if my sleeping body is shaking, too.

"Screwing." He laughs lewdly. "I can get behind that."

He strips off the little clothing he's wearing. Behind him, palm fronds bounce and wave as they receive the pants, boxers, and gun belts he tosses at them. He's buck naked now except for camo face-paint, socks, and army boots. He strides toward me, erection bouncing. My heart beats wildly.

"C'mere," he orders. I can't seem to move. I'm breathless and willing, and excited, although I'd spurn such a crude approach in my waking life.

I'm naked now. My clothes have faded to nothingness. Or maybe they were never there.

As dreams will do, without transition or preparation, he's inside me, panting like a dog on a hundred-degree day. "Take it! Take it! Take it!"

This guy really likes giving orders. I don't mind sometimes. I've always been eager to please.

And I am taking it. And loving it, both the hot sex and the hot scene. It's great, I'm so close... So... Ohhhh.

Two handfuls of jaguar hair were all that kept Adrian from crashing to the jungle floor. "Ah, Jeeze," he said, sitting up. "Can we stop at the next stream, Tom? I've, uh, gotta go." He plucked the damp fabric of his pants. "I am such a perv." Adrian chided himself. "I think I just got off on a giant housecat. Damn."

The giant housecat padded on.

CHAPTER 13

MARRIED ALIVE

After a brief cleanup at a small stream, Adrian remounted Tom, carefully not thinking about the dream he'd just had. Funny, but the jaguar, too, looked a little embarrassed. *Must be my guilty conscience. No cat on the planet ever felt guilt or remorse.*

This time Adrian used a fallen tree as a stepstool and was able to seat himself on his velvet-covered perch without yanking out handfuls of fur. Tom seemed to appreciate this.

Having deftly avoided human contact over the last few days, Tom surprised Adrian by hauling him to a clearing obviously chopped out of the jungle by men. He surveyed the space. It housed a few scattered thatch dwellings and a number of outbuildings, all of which appeared occupied and well tended.

Adrian slid gingerly down from Tom's back.

Leaning heavily on his spear, he limped into the clearing. He clutched his paltry ring of belongings and hoped the inhabitants of this village were friendly—to him and not to the drug men who shared their jungle. He hated to think he might have made it this far only to be sold back to the foul indigo makers. At this point Montoya would probably have him crucified in the center of the compound.

"Tom, I don't think…" But Adrian found himself suddenly alone in the clearing, no sizable jungle cat to back him up.

Before he could worry too much, a forceful-looking Indian strode across the clearing toward him. The man was heavily tattooed, the intricate sunburst patterns indicating he was someone to be reckoned with, probably the village chieftain. Adrian held still, figuring he should wait for the chieftain to speak first, since he was the outsider entering this man's territory. Two anthropology degrees had taught him a thing or two about aboriginal cultures.

The chief halted a few yards away, speaking loudly in a Quechua patois. It took Adrian a few tries to pick up the gist of it.

"Maymantataq kanki taytay?" the man asked. As Adrian understood from his studies, this was a typical opening statement to strangers, part greeting, part interrogation. "Where do you come from?"

"Estados Unidos," Adrian replied in Spanish, then repeated in the Quechua dialect he was most familiar with, *"Estados Unidosmantan kani."* He didn't bother trying to explain that he was Canadian. He'd come to learn that people of the third world weren't all that familiar with the land that lay north of the forty-ninth parallel. America, however, everybody knew, although the degree to which they welcomed Americans differed, depending on the cultural climate. Everybody liked American commercialism, he knew, a theory borne out by the chief's next statement.

"Ahhh. *Americano,"* the chief acknowledged. "Coca-Cola?"

Adrian smiled uncertainly and nodded. *"Sí.* Coca-Cola. *Ari."*

The chief grinned back, deep laugh lines appearing amid a tracery of faded ink. He gestured to Adrian to come have a seat by the unlit firepit, no doubt the central hub of the village.

Leaning heavily on the spear-turned-crutch, Adrian hopped after the chief.

Tom had chosen well, or rather, Adrian corrected himself, they'd just lucked out. *He's just a dumb animal,* Adrian reminded himself. This particular chief seemed a happy kind of guy. His village appeared prosperous, the people healthy. The village sat far from the parts of the rain forest currently being logged. So far, this village's interactions with white men had probably been friendly. Adrian hoped that wouldn't change any time soon.

Chief Eek (or so it sounded to Adrian), summoned his people. The young warriors were quick to relieve Adrian of his possessions. They carried on a great mock-hunt with his amateur weaponry until a grandmotherly type appeared and told them to knock it off. Then Grandma fired a few questions at Chief Eek, their exchange too rapid for Adrian to follow. Having apparently decided Adrian was harmless, she summoned a beautiful young girl to bring food and drink.

"Lynelle," the woman-in-command said pointing to herself. "Gaya," she said, pointing to Adrian's delegated waitress. Gaya smiled and lowered her eyes in an appropriately maidenly manner.

Names were important. Adrian acknowledged the introductions gravely. He pointed at his own heart, following Lynelle's lead. "Adrian," he said, smiling. Neither Eek or Lynelle seemed pleased, so he figured a bow might be in order. Bowing seemed to be a pretty universal gesture of respect, humbling oneself before one's superiors, leaving oneself vulnerable.

In a college anthropology course, he'd once written an essay on pan-cultural body language, sort of the gesticulatory equivalent of Campbell's archetypal mythology theories, and he remembered it well. He grabbed his spear, which the warriors had returned, and heaved himself up on one foot. The surrounding warriors looked suspicious when he laid hands on his weapon, but scowls turned to laughter at his attempts to bow while standing on one foot. Their guffaws startled Adrian, and he ended up sprawled backward in the dusty soil, legs draped unglamorously over the log on which he'd been sitting.

The whole village joined in the laughter—toothless grannies, muddy toddlers, even pretty young Gaya who'd brought his food.

Adrian laughed, too, figuring making them laugh was a great start at making them friends.

His Chaplin-esque theatrics broke the ice (not that these people had probably ever seen ice), and a bit of dialogue in the Quechua trade tongue began. Adrian wasn't the least surprised when Lynnelle managed to convey that the tribe was called the Eek—same as the man who'd come out to meet him. Roughly translated, it meant "the only true people."

After a communal lunch of unidentified mashed stuff, Chief Eek summoned a shaman-type to examine Adrian's ankle. Speaking the same pigeon patois, the village healer asked Adrian many questions (some of which Adrian even understood), that seemed to focus largely on his health and spirituality. Adrian greatly admired the holistic approach to medicine, but was also relieved when the *jampiri*—who, oddly, was named Ko-hen, and pronounced it similarly to Adrian's own G.P. back home—finally tended his swollen ankle.

No longer numb, the hike across the village square had set it to throbbing again. Adrian sucked in a breath. Dr. Ko-hen wrapped his warm hands gently over Adrian's ankle. *"Manan p'akisqa,"* he proclaimed, although it took several iterations before Adrian realized the good doctor was declaring the ankle "not broken."

Ko-hen smiled, patting Adrian's knee. *"Allinchay. Allinchay."*

Adrian hoped he was promising to fix it and not that amputation was just the thing. He freaked a little when a sharp knife put in an appearance, but Ko-hen just used it to shred some bark into a tiny cauldron.

Over the next couple of hours, they watered, heated, and stirred the goopy mess. Removing it from the fire, Ko-hen spat into it and insisted Adrian do the same. Greenish and snotty, and not without a few drowned bugs, it smelled exactly as foul as it looked. It perfumed the entire area and drove away all the curious onlookers who had watched Ko-hen's open-air clinic like their favorite afternoon soap opera. Jungle Hospital, Adrian mused.

Ko-hen dabbed some of the gelatinous goo on the rest of Adrian's cuts and scrapes. Adrian tugged off his T-shirt so Ko-hen could also treat a couple of nasty whip marks left from his time on the indigo assembly line. Ko-hen cleaned and treated some swollen insect bites—it seems not all species were put off by the residual indigo in his system—and dolloped them liberally as well.

Lastly, he turned his attention to the ankle, coated it with the paste and wrapped it tightly with thick dried strips of some plant. He ordered Adrian to keep his weight off it for "three moons." This worried Adrian greatly, since "three moons" could mean three months. Looking for clarification, he tried to indicate a moon getting larger and smaller by drawing it in the dirt.

"Ama! Ama!" Ko-hen shook his head right to left. *"Iskay killa."* He pointed at the sun, then drew an arc across the sky from east to west, repeating the heavenly passage three times.

Oh, okay. Three *days* Adrian could handle, although he bitterly regretted any delays from rescuing the factory workers and stopping the indigo drug trade. Still, what choice did he have? He might have ridden Tom, but Tom had taken off. Maybe Tom was doing his best Lassie impression and had gone to get help. Adrian didn't believe that for a second and only hoped his feline tour guide hadn't abandoned him.

Lynelle installed Adrian in the single men's dorm, a thatched and airy longhouse on the far side of the clearing. It was probably set apart because young men were young men anywhere in the world, and their residence could be as loud as any frat house. Plus it was away from the single girls, like Gaya, who continued to live at home with their parents.

Under Lynelle's watchful eye, Gaya tended to Adrian, which initially caused some tension among the bachelors since nobody's beautiful daughter was waiting on their every whim. With her even white teeth, and shy manner, Gaya was the most attractive woman in town by their standards. No doubt many of Adrian's bunkmates dreamed of settling down with the chief's beautiful daughter.

Gaya's command of the common dialect was limited. Most of the villagers used an ancient, purer form of Quechua with which Adrian was unfamiliar, so his communication with Gaya was restricted to smiles and gestures.

On the evening of the third day, Ko-hen unwrapped Adrian's ankle. With Gaya by his side smiling encouragingly, Adrian tentatively put some weight on it. Okay. So far, so good. He tried a bit more. Then a few tentative steps. Whoa! It was completely healed. Not even a twinge.

He sat on the nearest log and examined it. There wasn't even a hint of bruising. Further investigation revealed all his other cuts and abrasions treated with Doc Ko-hen's magic elixir had also healed leaving only a tracery of scarring.

Wow. He should probably stay and check this out. See what other wonder drugs they might have. He could stay. It would be so simple. No more stressful career. No more big-city rat race.

Raising his gaze from his healed ankle, he found Gaya no longer smiling and blushing, but looking fearfully at the treetops. Ko-hen and the rest of the omnipresent gawkers focused in the same direction.

"What?" Adrian asked. *"Ima?"* He realized the tribe was listening to a sound so familiar to him he hadn't even noticed it. It was a sound of civilization, of technology, of home...and, he belatedly realized, of the captors he was fleeing. He dived into the nearest hut as the helicopter swung directly over the village, blasting treetops sideways with its vicious whirlwind, creating a cyclone of sand and dust. The chopper circled back a few times, but by then all the villagers had followed Adrian's lead and faded from view, although perhaps with somewhat more grace.

The clumsy swan dive left Adrian with a bruised shoulder, but it probably saved his life. The chopper could easily have set down in the middle of the Eek village to retrieve him. Instead, they circled a few times and began to pull away. Almost as an afterthought, they sprayed the village with a quick burst of machinegun fire. A child shrieked, a piercing squeal even over the chopper-blade racket. The helicopter pulled off into the distance, followed by chilling quiet. Thatch wasn't exactly bullet-proof.

When the child started to howl again, Adrian thought it was the prettiest sound he'd ever heard. Crying meant life. A woman charged from the hut toward Ko-hen, toddler clutched in her arms. Blood painted both mother and child, although after a minute, Adrian realized there wasn't enough to be life threatening.

The child kicked and screamed and refused to be touched. The next time he opened his mouth to wail, Ko-hen poured a measure of some blue liquid into the kid's mouth. A few moments later, his crying and struggling diminished enough to let the *jampiri* tend the shallow wound on his upper arm where a stray bullet had grazed him.

The casual brutality of the strafing horrified Adrian. He asked Chief Eek if this had happened before, but Eek's attention was on the child.

Eventually Ko-hen rendered a promising prognosis. The crowd of village gawkers moved on, and so, Adrian knew, should he. He really needed to get back to civilization as soon as possible—the sooner he reported the drug men to the authorities, the sooner they could help the suffering laborers.

He also missed Tom. Who knew a wild animal could come to mean so much so quickly? Sure, he was growing attached to Pixel, but the domestic cat depended on him. Here in the rain forest, Adrian was dependent on the big cat. He should ask if Dr. Ko-hen had an elixir to cure Stockholm syndrome.

The Eek people's normally upbeat communal dinner was a somber affair that night. It matched Adrian's mood, and he returned to his loaner lodgings early, glad of a good night's rest.

The village rose with the sun. Adrian dressed, delighted to be able to get both boots on again. He gathered his now-larger collection of belongings. He'd won his very own machete in a story-telling contest. He'd acted out *Singing in the Rain Forest,* substituting the Eek village for Paris, playing all the parts, and belting out a couple of half-remembered tunes inventing lyrics where memory failed. The machete now dangled from his belt loops, housed in a tie-on type sheath Gaya had constructed from some sort of heavy-duty cloth.

His rusty lantern, some food and a hollowed-out gourd of water were carefully packed in the decent leather satchel he'd also been given. He headed out to find his hosts.

"Buen día," he greeted each member of the Eek family.

"Buen díos," each replied, including their neighbor from the next hut, Dr. Ko-hen, who'd apparently dropped over for breakfast.

At Lynelle's bidding, Adrian seated himself at the family campfire. He'd barely sat when Gaya appeared, smiling and holding a full plate out to Adrian. Mmm! Fried monkey brains and mashed banana. Again. As quickly as he'd gotten used to the salty-sweet mixture, he was growing tired of it. South America possessed some of the most exotic flora and fauna on the planet. Why did this neck of the rain forest think monkey brains was the ultimate culinary delicacy? Oh, well, one last meal with his new friends.

"Buen día, A-dreen." Gaya greeted Adrian with a smile. The smile quickly faded, though, once Gaya noticed the pack lying in the dirt at Adrian's feet. She looked stricken. *"Maytataq...? Maytataq rinki?"* Gaya looked from Adrian to her parents in dismay.

"Yes, Adrian. Where *are* you going?" Chief Eek asked in the more familiar dialect.

"I've got to go." Adrian gestured at the sky with the spoon-like implement he was using to scoop banana-'n-brains into his mouth. "The drug runners... *sajra maytataq."* No. That didn't seem to be doing it. His hosts seemed to be going from puzzled to angry. *"Sajra qhari."* Adrian had no idea what he'd said wrong—bad crowd, bad man. *"Llik'ichiri."* There. That should do it. Surely evil-spirit-boogieman myths were common to every tribe in the world.

Chief Eek drew a wicked-sharp machete from the sheath at his waist.

"Ari! Ari!" He brandished the knife at Adrian, making cruel slices through the air just about neck level. *"Llik'ichiri!"*

"What'd I say? What'd I say?" Adrian asked, falling back into English. Chief Eek lapsed into the unfamiliar dialect, yelling at Adrian and gesturing menacingly with the machete. Lynelle grabbed a cooking knife. The dripping monkey blood and brains made it look far more threatening than the machete. Gaya looked both sad and angry. Afraid to say anything more for fear of making the situation worse, Adrian smiled, trying for innocence. The two blades gleamed in the sunlight.

In apparent frustration, Eek rose, stalked over to Gaya grabbing a fistful of her lush, brown hair. He mimed cutting it, the cruel machete dangerously close to Gaya's neck. *"Mujerña!"* Chief Eek shouted. *"Muru!"*

Hair cut. Woman. Adrian translated silently. He'd noticed before that in this tribe, short hair meant married. *Oh, no!*

"Qhari warmi?" Adrian asked, gesturing between Gaya and herself.

"Ari!" cried Chief Eek. *"Sí!"*

"Ari!" cried Lynelle. *"Sí!"*

Gaya began to cry.

Oh, God. Now what?

"Gaya chichu," Chief Eek informed Adrian, arms crossed over his chest, machete clearly in sight.

"Huh?" Adrian asked multilingually.

Lynelle mimed a great rounded belly followed by the rocking of an invisible baby. *Pregnant? How?* Well, he knew how, but not by him, obviously. He'd only been with the Eek people for a few days. Did the Eek have a way of telling if a woman was pregnant this early?

And again, not by him. He wasn't sure how he'd tell them that and if he did, would he be insulting her and making matters worse?

Dr. Ko-hen looked uncomfortable and began edging away from the firepit. Across the compound, Mrs. Ko-hen looked on with narrowed eyes.

Nerves on edge already, the nearby scream of a jungle cat sent Adrian's forgotten breakfast flying and Adrian sprawling in the dirt.

Just as the helicopter noises had barely registered on Adrian, the jungle noises failed to register on these rain forest dwellers. Adrian watched Chief Eek's intelligent face as he took a minute to figure out what had startled Adrian.

"Adrian *mancharikuy otorongo?"* the Chief asked sharply.

"No. *Mana.* Ummm..." Adrian replied, cautiously reseating himself on the log, but no longer hungry. He wasn't afraid of the *otorongo,* but he was afraid to commit to anything at this point.

"Adrian *kasarakuy* Gaya?"

"No. I can't stay and marry her. I..." He had to get going. Had to report the drug lab.

"Adrian *wañupuy."*

Die? Adrian die? So much for Chief Eek-the-friendly-and-welcoming-guy.

The chief stood, machete raised in threatening stance, or Adrian would have tried out his newly-healed ankle with a mad dash back into the jungle. *"Veni! Veni!"* The chief shouted toward the longhouse, and in moments, half a dozen more machetes fanned around Adrian like gleaming metal flower petals.

Adrian ran through escape plans, discarding them as quickly as they formed in his whirling brain. Distracted as he was, he flinched again when the jaguar screamed, even closer this time. The men of the tribe looked scathingly at him. Certainly, *they* weren't afraid of a mere *michi.* A mere kitty.

Adrian trembled, peering fearfully into the thick undergrowth surrounding the clearing. He sobbed openly the next time the jaguar coughed. "Oh, please," he implored in Quechua. "I'm so afraid of the *otorongo.* Please don't throw me to the *otorongo."*

"It has been long since *otorongo* received a sacrifice," Chief Eek replied in their native tongue, eyeing Adrian like a side of beef.

"Nooo. Nooo!" cried Adrian as the hostile mob hoisted him on their shoulders and lugged him into the jungle. It took all the fortitude and inner strength to keep from smiling at his own cleverness...until he remembered that there was more than one *otorongo* in the jungle.

* * *

Good plan, buddy, Tom thought as he let out another angry *otorongo* scream. *Saves me ripping the throats out of your new friends.* Although he would have done so had he deemed it necessary. But those machetes looked dangerous, and besides, he wasn't hungry.

He prowled around the edge of the clearing, watching the Eek haul Adrian through the jungle. The dense green-on-green foliage was no problem for the cat's enhanced vision, nor the whispered sounds to his superior hearing.

They dragged Adrian to a smaller clearing with a single tree growing in the center. The straight and sturdy trunk featured thick branches shooting out in pairs in opposite directions.

They'd shoved him up against it, back to the tree, lashing his waist to the trunk and each wrist to one of the off-shooting branches.

"What? No crown of thorns?" Adrian asked in English. Tom figured he was trying to keep up his own spirits. Or maybe attract his attention. *Don't give them any ideas, nitwit!*

The Eek stood around for a while, chucking the occasional stone in Adrian's direction. Tom watched from the jungle, awaiting his moment.

Can't leave you alone for five minutes. He shook his head. *Guess I can't leave him at some village after all. I'll just have to keep him with me.* Tom felt a sort of smile tugging at the corner of his mouth. He wasn't smiling at the prospect of staying with Adrian. Of course not!

How could he? Cats had no lips.

An hour passed, but no jaguar arrived to claim his sacrifice. The Eek grew bored and drifted away.

* * *

Sweat poured down Adrian's brow, stinging his eyes. An icy trickle traced down his back, joining the flood from his underarms, soaking his waistband and shirt. He shifted his weight again, trying without much success to flex his aching shoulders. He could see his arms, tied straight out to either side, but could no longer feel them at all.

The tribespeople had hung around a while before wandering off. Sounded to Adrian like these guys had a game they wanted to catch. Some sort of Jai-Alia, he guessed, although this one seemed to involve a rubber ball and a pit filled with stakes. Or maybe it was snakes. He didn't follow the conversation; he had other things on his mind.

Before leaving, though, one young warrior thrust the machete they'd given Adrian through the sheath Gaya had given him, taunting and laughing as he'd done so. Adrian figured they expected to get it back…shortly. If only he could…but no. It was tantalizingly out of reach and driving Adrian crazy, not unlike the insects that were making themselves at home in his pants. The indigo bug-spray effect was pretty much history. He thought he might have a lizard down there, too, and was more than a little worried about it—and its choice of luncheon meats.

He stood in the hot sun for what seemed like hours. It had been breakfast-time when he'd had his awkward and short-lived betrothal to Gaya, and now it was… Oh, the sun was still low in the eastern sky, so perhaps not that long had passed. Still, he really needed to pee. Plus that lizard was getting a little too friendly.

Directly behind him, a jaguar coughed. For a moment he felt relieved, but what if it wasn't Tom? Not every cat in the jungle was some soldier's tamed and trained pet. If he thought he'd been sweating before…

Adrian strained and struggled against his bonds, trying to see behind him. No good. The Eek were very good with knots.

Giving up, he faced forward again and nearly jumped out of his restrained skin. There, comfortably washing his right paw, sat none other than the jaguar of his dreams. If cats could laugh…

"Ah, Tom. Am I ever glad to see you! Good kitty. If you could just—"

The cat screamed and leapt toward Adrian. Adrian screamed, too.

Tom rose up on his back legs before Adrian, steaming breath blasting his face. *Carnivore!* Adrian's brain shouted. *Why now?*

Tom swayed toward him, unsteady on his back legs, front paws raised, cruel claws extended like blades.

"It's me, Tom. It's me. Don't hurt—"

Another scream, and Tom lashed out with his humongous paw. Adrian closed his eyes, hoping for a quick death.

Tom roared again, but no longer up close and personal. Adrian opened his eyes.

Tom stood a few feet away, a small greeny-black snake—clearly dead—lay on the ground before him. Adrian stared at the tree above his head, suddenly aware that the jungle held more dangers than he'd even begun to catalog. He thought he'd been maxed out on terror, but now he shivered and shook until his teeth rattled. If he hadn't been securely tied to the tree, he would have fallen into a gibbering heap at Tom's feet.

Tom paced over to Adrian gently now, licked him sloppily on the cheek, removing a layer of dirt and probably skin as well with that raspy tongue. Then he disappeared from view. A few moments later the ropes fell away. Adrian's arms dropped numbly to his sides. He collapsed to his knees, shaking.

"Oh, my God. Tom. Thank you. Thank you." He wanted to hug his rescuer—to cling to the big velvet cat—but his arms dangled uselessly at his sides.

Tom started away, turning back to glare at Adrian kneeling in the dirt. Tom's snarl sounded a lot like a question.

Adrian sighed. No time for a breakdown now. Who knew when the Eek, another snake, or some new danger would drop by? He sucked in a deep, slightly damp breath and pulled himself together.

Tom let out a sort of whiney, kittenish yowl.

"No need for sarcasm, Tom. Just give me a sec here. Ow! Ow! Ow!" The returning blood burned through his arms as if caustic and carbonated.

"It's just that—" Suddenly, he danced a merry jig around the clearing. "Get it out. Get it..." He shook his leg, glad he favored relaxed fit pants. A little lizard tumbled out. "Oh, my." He watched as the thing recovered and sidled away. Were there poisonous lizards in the rain forest? He couldn't remember. He'd crammed so much research into the last few weeks it was all starting to blur. And half of it was proving wrong anyway.

Tom whined again.

"I know I don't need my arms to walk, but I do need my arms to pick up my stuff." His attempt to point at his pack resulted only in a sort of dying fish flop on the part of his right arm.

The cat rolled his eyes and stalked over to the pack Adrian's hosts had flung in the dirt when they'd tied him up.

Tom snatched up the pack with his teeth and strode into the jungle, finding a nearly invisible path directing them away from the Eek settlement. This time Adrian followed, feeling rather humiliated.

"But it was my idea, Tom… The whole Br'er Rabbit thing." Jeeze. Was he looking for approval from a wild animal now? He really needed to work on his self-esteem when he got back to civilization. Thank God Ontario's medical system covered shrinks. He was so going to need one.

* * *

Once again, Tom led the way through the jungle.

Adrian marveled that they had encountered so few signs of civilization. There was so much rain forest, much more than he had ever grasped. He framed shot after shot in his mind, wishing for a camera and a cartload of memory sticks.

Although he had no concrete evidence, he was pretty sure Tom was leading him away from settled places and deeper into the jungle. This was not a good thing in terms of reaching the authorities, reporting the drug men, and getting home, but he knew he couldn't survive in the jungle on his own. Reluctantly, he followed Tom. He would make his way to civilization when the first opportunity presented itself.

On the second day after leaving the Eek, Adrian and Tom crossed a small river. A dead anaconda sprawled semi-submerged on the bank. Rotting and foul, it was nearly as big around as he was. He'd thought the ones in the horror movies were huge exaggerations and wasn't happy to be proved wrong by this huge and stinky carcass. Snakes had become his new least favorite thing. Cats had long since been bumped out of the number one spot on Adrian's personal phobia hit parade.

He had trouble sleeping that night. Thank God for Tom curled up and snoring softly beside him. If only he knew where Tom was taking them. Wherever it was, it certainly seemed important to the big cat, though.

The next day, Adrian saw another colossal dead anaconda in a river. It was a little more rotten and stank a little more, and he realized they'd gone in a big circle. Tom seemed to get that too, because he sat on his great fuzzy haunches and stared at the revolting snake carcass until his eyes watered. He relocated them upwind and sank down into a listless heap. If a jaguar could be depressed, Tom certainly was.

Adrian plunked down beside Tom, running his hands over the soft fur, caressing and whispering encouragements. He was frantic to tell him to hurry—that people were suffering, dying in the labs, but he knew that wouldn't help. The warm afternoon sun filtered through the leafy canopy. Tired from constant travel and sleeping poorly, Tom drifted off and Adrian followed soon after, head pillowed on the soft, muscular thigh.

* * *

Blue Blue Blue. If it's blues-day, I must be dreaming.

And here's Tom and Chaj bitching, as usual.

"I don't have a fucking clue where I'm going. Can I get a little help here, please?"

"You are not partnering with the Yanapaj—the companion."

"He's right there." Tom gestures at me.

"You're not following, Qollpa. You are leading."

Ah. So Tom doesn't play well with others. Figures. I decide to jump in and find my voice. "Where are we going, anyway?"

Chaj says something I don't understand, but I just know means we're big-time losers, and we need to get a brain. In something I do understand, he tells me, "To the Temple of Transfiguration. Bring me the Tears of Truth."

The Temple of Transfiguration! That's the temple I originally set out to find with Doc Soc. This gets weirder and weirder. At least I know something about the old T of T, having done my post-grad work on it.

"How the hell do we find it, Chaj?" Tom demands.

"You are not a man, Qollpa. Do what a not-man would do."

As Chaj fades out, the Technicolor kicks in. Instead of drifting off into a wet dream, pleasant as that is, I take control, intending to make good use of this one chance to talk to my kitty.

"I'm tired of being led around. The first thing we need to do is get to somewhere with a satellite phone or some other way of contacting

the outside world. A logging camp or a rubber processing center. I don't know. Everybody in Tanpu had a satellite dish. Somebody must have Internet."

I hope Tom can access a better poker face than he uses on me. Right now I can clearly tell he thinks I'm an idiot. "We can't go back to Tanpu. That's just—"

"No, I get that. Deerborne and Montoya have the whole place locked down. But Tanpu isn't unique. Well, that's not to say there are slave-labor drug factories all over the rain forest. But here must be other small towns with some technology. Hell, I don't care if they use smoke signals, we have to report the drug operation to the authorities."

Tom blinks at me, as if he's surprised by the depths of my idiocy. "And what authorities would those be? Don't you think Montoya's taken care of the local officials? He buys off those he can and threatens the rest. Sure, there's lots of honest officials in the Colombian government, but no matter how honest you are, if someone says they're going to kill your wife and kids, you keep your mouth shut. That's why my organization is here. Usually we restrict our investigations to the weird and wacky. There's nothing paranormal about a drug operation, but we're able to use methods others can't." He sits back, clamping his mouth shut, the muscles in his cheek jumping.

"But we'll find somebody. The United Nations. Canadian peacekeepers. The freakin' Coast Guard! I don't know. We have to go to the authorities. We'll do that first and then we'll change you back!"

"Don't you get it? I am the authorities!" Tom roars.

I snap my own mouth shut, unwilling to engage in pointless arguing. I stare down, checking out our surroundings, looking anywhere but at Tom. There isn't much to look at in this particular dream, just sort of a dirty marshmallow background. Probably just my own lack of imagination. I steel myself, and I lift my head and meet Tom's gaze. "I think we're going to have to agree to disagree."

"Right. Except you're outnumbered. It's me 'n' Chaj against you. So we're heading for the Temple."

"Two things." I hold up one finger. "One, we don't know the way, and two..." I hold up a second, hoping Tom gets the symbolism of the peace sign. I so don't want to fight with him, but this wasting time wandering has to stop. "Chaj assigned the role of leader to me, *and I say we find somewhere to report in."*

Tom looks as if he were about to really lose his temper when suddenly his features soften and his shoulders slump. "You're right. I don't know the way, and you're supposed to lead. Take us wherever, but I don't see why, since we don't really know where we're going, we can't do both. If we knew the goddamn way, we could just head for the Temple, and if we pass a pay phone or even a goddamn telegraph relay station on the way, we'll call anyone who'll listen."

I consider this plan for a moment. It's true I don't know how to get anywhere at all, either phone or civilization. Tom's plan has merit since it would solve all our problems.

"Okay," I reply, not sure who won the argument.

I look back at Tom. God, the man was a hottie. The informational portion of our program this evening is complete. The erotic portion commenceth.

Tom kisses to perfection, human mouth eating me alive. He's a maneater in cat form. I run my hands all over his naked body, toned, fit, and a perfect fit. I can't get enough of him, hands, mouth, chest to chest. Lying down, swallowing me whole. I can't believe how good this feels... feels good... feels good... feels...

CHAPTER 14

YIELD OF DREAMS

Adrian woke to the fading pleasure of his dream-induced orgasm…and also to the realization that somewhere Chaj existed, and that Tom really was a shape-shifted human with whom he'd been sharing dreams.

He reached out and stroked his big furry head. "That was great, Tom. Was it good for you, too?"

The cat coughed and looked away.

Arian quickly changed the subject to avoid the awkward "morning after" moment. "I know what Chaj meant," he said, adopting Tom's nickname for the shaman.

Tom blinked at him.

"Chaj said, 'Do what a not-man would do. Not-man,' right?"

The jaguar's head went up and down.

"You're not a man but a jaguar. So that could mean we're supposed to do a jaguar thing to locate the temple, right?" Tom looked noncommittal, but interested. "But that's what we have been doing, and frankly, I don't think I can stand to smell that putrefied snake a third time."

Tom nodded earnestly.

"So, these shamans are always tricksters, in love with their own cleverness. What else could be a not-man?"

Tom roared. Adrian wasn't sure if he'd figured it out as well or was just losing patience with the lecture. He quickly moved on to his conclusion.

"A not-man could also be a woman, which means he wants us to do something a man would never do, but a woman would."

Tom looked thoughtful, gaze leaving Adrian's to stare unseeing at the ground. Suddenly he raised his great velvet head, a look of triumph in his eyes. He butted Adrian's chest hard enough to send him sprawling in the dirt. The big cat jumped playfully on him, keeping his full weight on his own legs. Nuzzling Adrian's none-too-clean cheek.

"That's right, big guy. You got it." He pushed Tom's head away, and the great cat let him. "Chaj wants us to ask for directions."

They tussled in the dirt a few more seconds before sobering up again. Adrian stood and dusted himself off, then brushed Tom off as well. He cleaned up in the river, well used to dirt and other things staining his clothing by now.

"I guess the fact that men hate to ask for directions is pretty universal, eh? Let's you and I buck the stereotype and go look for the local information kiosk, shall we?"

Tom snorted, scented the air, and choked. He then moved them farther from the dead snake and scented again. He seemed to be on to something. They headed away from the river.

"Hey, Tom." The cat stopped. "You're supposed be letting me drive, anyway, remember."

The cat roared, but fell into step behind Adrian as Adrian chose the most well-worn path and headed down it.

CHAPTER 15

CIRQUE DU POULET

"La Iglesia de Cambiay, um..." Adrian tried again to communicate with Kepi, headman of the Wallpa tribe. So far all they'd managed was an exchange of names, and in Kepi's case, rank and job description. Plus the fact that "Wallpa" meant "chicken" and that they considered themselves *the only true people.* Adrian was anxious to get the information he and Tom needed to find the Temple of Transfiguration and get out of there. They'd lost so much time already. Who knew what had transpired while they were out charging around the rain forest? It was starting to feel like one of those dreams where you have to be somewhere, but can't seem to get there.

Kepi had welcomed him warmly when Adrian had hiked into the village, stopping respectfully at the edge of the encampment. Tom had faded, unseen, into the jungle. The chief had a physique that might have once been powerful, but now looked overfed and running toward fat. He had a nose like a toe and beady, close-set eyes.

Adrian and Kepi sat on a circle of stones around an unlit firepit. Chickens scratched in the dirt nearby. The occasional passer-by seemed only a little curious, unlike the Eek, who would have lived in each other's pockets—if they'd had pockets. Or pants for that matter.

"Sí. Sí. La Iglesia de K'anchay," Kepi said, nodding, speaking in a dialect similar to that of the Eek. Then he surprised Adrian by switching to passable English. "Temple of Change. Of Transfiguration,

as your church-men would say. Where those who are not themselves go to learn and…" He paused searching for the right word. "See *ñawi de cheqa.*"

"*Ñawi?* The something of truth," Adrian muttered.

Kepi nearly poked himself in the eye defining *ñawi.*

"You mean *eye* of truth?" Adrian clarified, pushing away a large hen that was pecking at his satchel. Chickens overran the village, and Adrian now had the guano-encrusted boots to prove it. It gave new meaning to the term shit-kickers.

"*Sí.* Yeah, boss." Chief Kepi reached protectively for the chicken, cradling it on his lap like a favored cat. It preened under the attention.

"How'd you learn English, *Kuraka* Kepi?" Adrian added the local word for chief out of respect, although a mostly naked man with a chicken in his lap might have been cause for disrespect in some cultures.

Kepi returned the prize hen to the ground, carefully disengaging its claws from the gold bracelets adorning his wrists. "Worked riverboats as boy. Bring men. Take men. Tree-men. Rock-men. City-men. Church-men." He spat in the firepit after the last, but Adrian wasn't sure if it applied to just the religious types or to all the visitors. Or whether Kepi just felt moved to spit. "You know a changed one? Lucky. Long time Wallpa no have met changed one." He spat again.

"Do I know a changed one?" Adrian thought hard on this crucial question. He'd been slow to believe in Tom's shape-shifting, the pragmatist in him declaring the very idea ridiculous. Eventually, though, he'd acknowledged what was being demonstrated for him day by day.

As a student, he'd often found he was more open to new and offbeat ideas than many of his peers, but perhaps he'd become a little stodgy over his years of working in a corporate environment. His manager in HR had liked new "initiatives," just as long as nothing really changed. Like renaming "Human Resources" to "Organizational Development." And then changing it back a few years later. Adrian looked around himself and wondered why he didn't really miss his corporate life back in Toronto. It had been so much safer. And so much duller.

"Where is this Temple?" Adrian asked, returning to the original topic, deliberately not answering Kepi's question about whether or not he knew a changed one. It had proved advantageous to keep Tom's existence a secret in the last village.

"*Sí. Sí.* Of course." The chief sat back, grinning, clearly satisfied with the way the conversation was going. Sunlight glinted from Kepi's gold ear and nose rings. Blinking, Adrian added the shiny chieftain to his mental photo shoot.

"Great!" Adrian sat forward eagerly, rubbing his eyes. He could hardly believe they'd been this fortunate, finding almost instantly someone who knew the way to their destination.

"So where is it? Can you draw me a map?" He smiled at his kind, if a little grimy, benefactor.

Kepi nodded, smile matching Adrian's, except for the missing teeth. "Yes, boss. I only man in village who know." He uncrossed one arm and made a sweeping gesture to take in the settlement, then tapped at his own temple knowingly, another archetypal gesture.

Adrian sighed with relief. Chaj hadn't steered them wrong.

"Great," Adrian repeated and waited. After an uneasy few moments of sitting and smiling in silence, Adrian prodded further, "So will you?"

Still smiling, Kepi answered, "No."

"But… But…" Adrian sputtered. "Why not?"

Now Kepi leaned forward conspiratorially. He looked right, then left, then directly at Adrian. "Why would Kepi tell secret for free? What in it for Kepi?"

"I need to go there. I…my friend…" Adrian motioned limply in the direction of the surrounding jungle. He sighed and patted his pockets. "I have nothing to pay you with."

"Kepi tell you now for free. You tell many people. Temple map not worth pay no more. I'm *sajwakuy.*" Kepi made a loose fist and moved it up and down just above his crotch.

Great. The universal gesture for "I'm so screwed." At the back of his mind an unrelated idea was forming—a coffee table book on universal gestures. He'd photograph people all over the world doing the same gestures to indicate agreement, disagreement, love, charity, masturbation, greed…

"Is there anything else I can do? Perform some service? Make something?"

Kepi laughed delightedly. This was obviously the best joke he'd heard in ages. "Kepi think on it." He rose and wandered away from the circle of rocks, still chuckling softly, wending his way nimbly among the many chickens he passed, careful not to disturb them.

* * *

Tom waited anxiously at the edge of the jungle, wishing his hearing and his Quechua were good enough to figure out what they were saying. So far it had mostly been about chickens. Chickens. Fat, delicious chicken. He scented the air, mouth watering. And something about jerking off, if the chief's hand gestures were anything to go on. Ah, jerking off. Something Tom missed greatly about having hands—those claws could be downright dangerous! Thank God for his dream-sex with Adrian, or he'd be going crazy by now.

As soon as Adrian re-entered the jungle, Tom went to him, accompanying him to the clearing they'd designated as their temporary encampment. Adrian sprawled next to the makeshift firepit, grabbing a swig of water from his hollowed-out gourd. He wiped his mouth.

Tom growled, meaning *hurry up! What'd I miss?* He lashed his tail back and forth. Adrian seemed to get that.

"Well, we're well and truly *sajway'*ed, Tom. And not in a good way." Adrian repeated Kepi's crude but expressive single-fisted gesture. "Any ideas?"

Tom lay down and closed his eyes. *Chickens. Nice fat chickens.*

After a few minutes, Adrian ran his hand over Tom's head. "Are you thinking, Tom, or just taking a nap? Sometimes you seem more cat than man."

Tom rolled on his back, encouraging Adrian to scratch under his chin, his neck. Adrian's fingers tangled in the dog tags, yanking out a few hairs. Ow! Why did a few hairs hurt more than a handful? Tom leapt to his feet, shaking the dirt and sticks from his coat.

"You told Chaj you were losing it. Becoming the cat. That's another reason we need to hurry."

Tom felt he should be distressed by this, but his tail itched, and that needed attending to right away.

Adrian sat in the dirt beside him. Tom sniffed him. A lot. He smelled very much of chicken. *Yum.*

"Tom! Are you even paying attention? We need a plan, goddamn it!"

Plan, right. We need plan. To buy time, Tom began to wash, the tongue-paw-coat rhythm so soothing. *Chickens. Need chickens...*

That's it! Now, how to tell Adrian? A nap maybe, but they only had dream-walks sometimes.

Instead, he rose onto his back legs and began to dance—the most awkward dance in the history of the world, flapping cat elbows and shimmying feline knees.

"Wow, Tom. Are you okay? That's like the worst dance ever. Like something they make you do at a wedding."

Tom dropped to his feet, nodding.

Adrian looked puzzled for a bit, then slowly a real shit-eating grin blossomed on his handsome, dirt-smeared face. He hugged Tom so suddenly the big cat flinched. "So, you like chicken, do you, Tom-cat?"

* * *

Two days later Adrian sauntered back into the village, requesting an audience with Kepi. The village was not the pastoral hamlet he'd last visited. It was more like a frontier fort under siege. They'd hastily erected some wattle fencing, but it would no more have kept Tom out than macramé.

"What's up, Chief?" Adrian asked when Kepi, dark circles shadowing his eyes, finally agreed to see him.

"Supay! Devil! It murders our chickens. *Our chickens!"*

Whoa, these people really like their chickens. Don't let the Colonel find out, or he'll sell the Wallpa a franchise. Adrian tried to calm the distraught chieftain.

"Take it easy, man. What devil—*supay*—do you mean? A snake? Another tribe? *Otorongo?*"

"Ari! Yes! *Otorongo.* Jaguar. Huge black monster. Comes night. Comes day." He looked wildly around him, then lowered his voice and leaned in close. "When no more chicken, *otorongo* eat child. Then man."

So, old What's-In-It-For-Me was ultimately worried about his own hide. Like most politicians. Adrian knew that the peoples of the rain forest were perfectly capable of defending themselves against the beasts of the jungle, but not without risk. So he appealed to Kepi's sense of self-preservation and his guardianship of his people.

"Just a jaguar, you say?" Adrian stretched expansively. "Why, I could take care of that for you."

Kepi turned his myopic focus to Adrian. "Oh, yes. Yes, please, Mis-tah Adrian. Thank you. Thank you. You great man!"

You expendable *man,* Adrian interpreted mentally. He sat on a nearby log, and began examining his cuticles. They were in really rough shape.

Kepi waited in agitation, shifting his weight from one leg to the other like a child needing to pee. "Ah. Mis-tah Adrian? You kill *otorongo* soon?"

Adrian looked up, meeting Kepi's eyes, holding his gaze. "Oh, no, Kepi. I didn't say *kill*. I said *take care of*." He went back to studying his nails.

There was a long pause while Kepi considered this statement. "Ah. Mis-tah Adrian? What mean 'take care of *otorongo*?' Not kill?"

"Not kill, Kepi. Tame. I could tame that ol' devil-cat. I could even ride it around the middle of the village."

The conversation was evidently progressing far too slowly for the headman, yet he obviously didn't want to offend the man who'd either come to save the village or be Tender Vittles for the hungry jungle cat, thereby delaying the chicken-slaughter a few days. Adrian supposed either was fine with the chieftain. Finally, Kepi asked, "Ah. Mis-tah Adrian? You tame *otorongo* soon?"

"You know, Kepi. I could do it right away. Tonight, even. But..." He paused dramatically. "Why should I? What's in it for Mis-tah Adrian?" He tossed Kepi's earlier words back at him, enjoying the shift in power. It reminded him a bit of the day he'd quit his HR job. He chuckled, picturing his former supervisor Pierre in a loincloth. It wasn't pretty.

Kepi looked horrified, then shrewd, then defeated. "I draw map to Temple. You tame jaguar, you get map." The canny look returned, and he held out his right hand. "Deal?" he asked in strangely accent-free English.

Adrian shook the proffered hand briefly—it was clammy and fishlike—then turned to go. He had a nice dinner of roast chicken waiting for him back at his temporary camp.

* * *

Adrian had always been a bright kid, whipping his way through the standard school curriculum far ahead of his peers. His guidance counselors and scholastic advisors had channeled his excessive energy and brainpower in any and every direction they could in hopes of preventing him from reaching his hooligan-ringleader potential. He'd taken after-school programs, advanced courses, and optional credits. He'd studied hard sciences and soft, languages and maths. He'd taken courses in a huge range of subjects and interests, and one he'd particularly excelled at had been theater arts and drama. He adored pomp, circumstance, and a really good soundtrack. He loved performing. He even loved the staging and choreography—lights, camera, action!

Only the brighter flame of anthropology and the grand sense of mankind's history had swayed him from pursuing a career in the theater. Tonight, he'd get a chance to live his dramatic dreams, scripting a "sacred" ceremony for the Wallpas such as they'd never seen before. No one had, in fact, since he was pulling bits and pieces from a whole raft of cultures and knitting them together in a bit of indie theater that would never see the lights of Broadway.

Now if he could just convince Tom that the play was the thing with which to catch a king, or in this case, win a map from a petty chieftain.

"Sorry, but it's what I came up with on the spot. You've let me ride you before." Adrian could feel his cheeks heating as he recalled his mounted wet dream. At the time, he'd hoped it might have escaped Tom's notice, but now he knew better. Jaguars have a keen sense of smell. Not to mention Tom's human brain capacity.

Adrian hid his blush by undoing his ponytail and letting his dirty hair fall over his face. It was coming undone anyway. He pulled it back again, tying it awkwardly with the leather thong Gaya had given him. "If you've got a better plan, Tom, I'm listening."

Tom stared at the ground for several minutes. The yelping of the toucans hidden in the dense green canopy marked the passage of time like a ticking clock. A tiny monkey face peeked from behind a leaf the size of a yoga mat. Adrian waved. It disappeared, screaming, apparently unaware of the monkey-see, monkey-do rule. Adrian felt strangely rejected. At least the tiny creature hadn't flung monkey poo at him, as they often did.

Tom snarled.

"C'mon, Tom. It only makes sense."

A one-sided argument can only go on so long, and eventually Tom acquiesced. It seemed being ridden wasn't something he much cared for.

"Pride goeth before a fall," Adrian reminded the big cat.

A deafening roar right in his ear adequately conveyed Tom's irritation.

Adrian shook his head to clear the ringing and refrained from any halitosis comments. No doubt his own breath reeked after all these days in the jungle, despite chewing a particular soapy-tasting root that Lynelle had shown him.

Focusing on the task at hand, he outlined his plan for obtaining the map to Temple Transfiguration.

"Okay. Here's what we're gonna do…"

* * *

The night was clear and bright. A fat moon shed pale light down on the Wallpa village clearing. A number of small fires ringed the perimeter, and a huge bonfire toasted those who stood in the center of town.

Adrian stood next to Kepi and his strongest warriors, holding the "magic" jaguar bridle he'd woven from vines that afternoon. Back in college, he'd worked on a dig on a reservation one summer and learned a little about weaving from the Navajo women. The bridle actually looked pretty good. He'd decorated it with some pretty jungle flowers, but they'd wilted quickly, so he'd used discarded chicken feathers instead. Kepi seemed to like this since they matched those piercing his wives' ears and noses. Kepi, of course, wore gold.

"No weapons, guys." Adrian warned one more time, shifting from foot to foot, hands sweaty on the bridle. "Remember, absolutely no weapons, or the jaguar god will become angry and kill us all!"

Kepi translated, but Adrian was pretty sure what he'd said was more along the lines of "No weapons until this brave-but-misguided shaman is jaguar food."

In accordance with Adrian's instructions, the remaining chickens were corralled in the longhouses, except a few of the most favored. These currently resided within a small wattle pen to one side of the village square. Only the smallest of fires, a mere burning bush, smoldered between the jungle and the chicken pen.

Hearing a jaguar roar not far away, Adrian clapped Kepi heartily on the shoulder, admonished him one more time "no weapons," and positioned himself between the chicken pen and the dark jungle.

The jaguar roared again, closer this time.

Adrian began to chant loudly, the secret, time-honored, jungle-cat ode that he'd learned at his mother's knee:

"In the jungle…" he began in a shaky but strong falsetto.

"The scary jungle…"

He raised his right hand, holding his unlit creosote-soaked torch high.

"Otorongo *comes tonight."*

His voice cracked slightly on a high note. He raised his left hand, which held the bridle.

"In the jungle, the bug-filled jungle..."

He dipped the end of the torch in the smoldering embers near his feet and raised it again. It burst into flame with a crisp roar and a blaze of rusty color, frightening both the tribesmen and the chickens. And singeing Adrian's eyebrows.

"Otorongo *comes tonight,"* he repeated, lowering his voice to a whisper.

Waving the torch like the Archangel Michael, Adrian launched into a full, if somewhat squeaky rendition of the song, eschewing the 1960s do-wop version for the more representative Zulu adaptation. The tribe might not know Zulu from Zuni, Disney from Dickens, but they'd recognize a good beat when they heard it.

"In the jungle, the bright green jungle,

Otorongo *comes tonight.*

In the jungle, the sweaty jungle,

Otorongo *comes tonight."*

The jaguar roared in time with the chorus:

"In the village, the stinky village,

Otorongo *comes tonight."*

Adrian waved the torch and the bridle at each of the four directions: north, south, east, and west.

"In the village, the chicken village.

Otorongo *comes tonight."*

The second time through the chorus, one of the dark shadows detached itself from the jungle and manifested as the most feared of beasts, its great head bobbing and weaving in time with the music. It appeared hypnotized, heading toward the torch singer in the clearing.

"Hush, my Wallpa. Don't fear, my Wallpa,

Adrian rides tonight."

Adrian threw back his head and let loose his best ululation, followed by, "*Here, kitty, kitty, kitty!"*

The great black chicken-killer lumbered forward, razor teeth flashing in the firelight, the buzz of a low growl chilling Adrian's soul. What if Tom really was hypnotized? Lately, there'd been times when the beast was more present than the man. Adrian squinted in the dimness. What if he'd managed to charm a different jaguar altogether and Tom was still out there waiting for his signal?

Adrian took a half step back, torch and bridle slippery in his sweaty hands.

He swallowed hard, deliberately shaking the bridle in the air to mask his trembling. He stood his ground, barely able to breathe. The black shape moved inexorably toward him, closer, closer.

So near now he could smell roast chicken on the beast's breath. He groaned with relief as the great bulk crouched at his feet. Adrian quickly bent to fasten on the rope halter, nearly clonking Tom on the head with the torch when he dropped it in the process. Luckily, the torch had burned low, and the crowd was unable to observe this minor gaffe in the theatrics.

Moving slowly, largely so he wouldn't trip, Adrian carefully stepped to Tom's side and threw one leg over his broad back.

"Rise up!" he shouted. The villagers, who had moved forward and formed a circle around him, hissed and stepped back. The jaguar didn't move. He lay dreamily on the ground like a black velvet Sphinx, seemingly unaware of the man straddling his back.

"Rise up!" Adrian called again. Still no response. The villagers moved a little closer. Despite Adrian's earlier orders, weapons sprouted among the warriors. An evil-looking machete glinted in Kepi's hand.

Shit! Somehow, he'd managed to really hypnotize Tom. The smell of chicken, the dance of the bonfires, the rhythm of the song… They must all have combined to send Tom off to commune with his inner beast.

"C'mon, Tom," he begged. "This is *so* not the moment, you big pussy!"

Nor was it the moment for finesse. Adrian executed several actions simultaneously. He kicked Tom hard in the flanks like a stubborn pony. At the same time, he jerked the rope halter. Although made for show, rope was rope, and it yanked the cat's head up. Lastly, he shouted, "Heigh-ho, Thomas, away!"

And it was all he could do to keep his seat when one startled jaguar returned to the land of the living and to the village of the rapidly scattering Wallpa.

"Whoa. Hey! Hold on, big fella!"

Faster than thought, Adrian shoved the halter lead between his teeth, chomping down so hard his vision blurred. He grabbed great furry handholds, clasping his knees tight to Tom's ribs.

Like some epileptics returning from a seizure, Tom seemed to have no recollection of his circumstances and just wanted out of there. In fact, Tom-the-man didn't seem to be present at all. Adrian really was dealing with the wild jungle cat! He hung on tightly, as Tom dashed around the clearing screaming and roaring, kept from the safety of the jungle by the circle of fires ringing the village clearing.

The second time they passed the chicken pen Adrian realized Tom wasn't bucking him off or executing a drop-and-roll. The third time around Tom halted in front of the terrified cluster of warriors that surrounded their headman.

Adrian looked down upon the villagers, grateful he hadn't screamed when Tom had first bolted. That really would have undermined his I'm-a-cool-shaman-who-can-control-the-wild-beasts persona. He removed the reins from his mouth, drawing a deep breath, trying to still his pounding heart by sheer force of will.

"I have delivered my half of the bargain." Softer, he murmured, "Yeah, Tom. You got me." He could feel Tom's sides heave beneath him, but whether the big cat was winded or laughing was hard to judge. Again, Adrian addressed the cluster of Wallpa. "This beast will trouble you no more."

"Here is your map, then, *jampiri* Adrian." Kepi handed Adrian a papyrus-like bundle. "You are great shaman. Great warrior." Kepi's few remaining teeth shone grayly in the weak light.

Adrian thrust the bundle into his shirt, reaching down to shake Kepi's hand.

The machete flashed in the direction of Tom's throat. The jaguar turned and dashed back into the jungle. Adrian clutched new fistfuls of cat hair as they fled the ungrateful Wallpa.

*　　*　　*

Tom allowed Adrian to remain on his back as far as their camp. Then he stood, trembling, barely able to contain his urge not to buck. *Off. Get off.* It hadn't been so bad the first time he'd had to carry Adrian, but the longer he remained in cat form, the more he felt like a cat.

Adrian slid to the ground, yanking the halter with him.

"It's okay, Tom. It's okay." He hugged Tom briefly, but Tom felt constrained and antsy, backing out of the circle of Adrian's arms. He growled low.

"Okay," Adrian said again. "Just give me a sec to get oriented." He kicked the banked embers to life, tilting Kepi's map toward the fire.

"It's way out of scale, but I think I can figure it out." He held it up for Tom to examine, but Tom just sniffed it. "Okay, I guess your orienteering is on hold for a bit." He chewed his lower lip, mumbling.

Tom was fast losing interest and thinking of going hunting instead when Adrian announced, "I've got it. We go this way." He pointed toward a pathway heading away from the Wallpa.

Keeping his ears peeled for pursuit, Tom headed toward the gap in the trees. Behind him, Adrian kicked the fire out entirely, picked up his pre-packed satchel, and followed.

"Aren't I supposed to be leading?"

CHAPTER 16

LIFE'S A WITCH

That Kepi's map proved an excellent guide came as something of a shock. After all Adrian'd been through in the last few weeks, it was only natural he'd be a bit paranoid. He supposed, though, that when Kepi had been deciding how to best handle the situation, he'd assumed he would be handing a map either to a dead guy, or to a shaman who commanded the beasts of the jungle. Kepi had no doubt weighed all his possible alternatives and, like an unwashed Spock-of-the-jungle, had undertaken the most logical course of action in giving them a true map to the temple.

The map brought them back to the river they'd been following. Tom looked vindicated, in an anthropomorphic way, of course. They took one last cruise by the now-crumbling anaconda. It looked like it had finally attained a nice squishy rottenness that appealed to whatever bottom feeders could reach the submerged half of the snake. The land-locked portion was being carried away in minuscule bits to feed thousands of gaping baby insect maws. Didn't help the smell much, though. Adrian was glad to see it becoming a link in the food chain and hoped to check out a less smelly skeleton on the return trip from the temple.

That there might not be a return trip didn't bear consideration. He framed a few shots in his mind, yearning once again for his long lost camera equipment.

They followed the river several miles, finding it curved to the right, just as the map indicated.

An odd formation of trees in a clearing appeared precisely as drawn.

A geyser, a naturally carbonated spring, and a great up-jutting plateau were all exactly as rendered.

One inky splotch resolved itself into a rocky inukshuk pointing them onward. It was an anthropological mitzvah. Adrian rambled on about race memory and inter-tribal communications, coffee table books and Pulitzer Prizes until Tom increased the pace to a jog, thus ending Adrian's dreams-of-glory monologue.

Adrian was glad it was dry season, although even that meant the occasional dousing with rainwater. Because of thick forest canopy, rain didn't fall so much as find its way earthward via natural troughs and rivulets formed of leaves, large and small. He got soaked on a semi-regular basis, and while it aided with his quest for personal hygiene, it was beginning to rot the soles off his boots. He bound them up with tough vines and hoped they'd last until he found civilization again.

A broken footbridge across a deep, wide canyon gave them some trouble, but eventually they circled around, scrambled down a scree-strewn ridge. They forded at a shallows, well upstream from a pool of piranha Tom was able to identify and avoid. (Although how Tom could differentiate one species of fish from another while they were underwater was something Adrian would have to save for later questioning.)

Adrian had been about to hop into the pool for a cool soak before dinner when Tom had intervened. They'd played charades until Adrian had narrowed it down to "deadly things beginning with *p*." "Piranha" had made the list only after "poisonous snakes" and "parasites." Adrian thanked Tom profusely and further demonstrated his gratitude in their shared dreams that night.

The erotic dreams recurred every now and then. When he closed his eyes, he never knew if he'd find herself in the arms of the very human, very amorous Thomas Ferrell. The more he dreamt, the more his mental picture of the man developed. His dreams moved farther away from the early "Generic Soldier Fantasy #6" to a portrait of a gentle and loving man who gave willingly and received with bliss. The skilful and satisfying love-play moved through a gamut of lust, desperation, playfulness, and whimsy. Adrian had no complaints about his dream lover's performance, and felt confident Tom had none about Adrian's own.

Initially, Adrian thought he'd just borrowed the face of Tom from the plane and projected it on Thomas Ferrell, his dream lover, but by now he knew they were actually one and the same. He grumbled about freaky coincidences, but had long since begun to believe in fate or karma or divine destiny or whatever. He'd ask Chaj if the young shaman ever showed up again.

The dreams were exciting and hot, but more than the sexual satisfaction, however, Adrian treasured their virtual pillow talk. He was developing a sense of closeness with Tom like none he'd ever experienced. His serial monogamy with a steady stream of boyfriends paled when compared to the growing connection between Adrian and Tom. As far as he could tell, Tom felt the same. He hoped so, anyway.

Adrian wondered if the real Tom Ferrell was as warm and open as the man of his dreams or if his mind—possibly still whirling with the residual drugs—was creating or skewing it. He recalled from their previous encounter in the airplane bathroom, Tom was capable of great warmth and affection, as well as great sex. In their dream conversations, they talked about their childhoods and growing up.

Tom, too, seemed to enjoy their time together on the spirit plane.

*   *   *

I tense, every muscle clenching tight. My body feels like a giant fist under Adrian's touch. My orgasm rips through me, leaving me gasping. Adrian thrusts one more time, before freezing in a taut arc, hard cock pulsing deep within me.

"Love you." Adrian groans, panting and shaking.

I pull away, ordering, "Don't." I wish we had clothes or condoms or clean-up to distract us, but dream sex is just so damn easy. Usually we wake up now. Wakey-wakey. Oh, God. He's going to want to talk about it.

"I'm sorry," Adrian whispers. There's a pause, then, "No, I'm not. I'm not sorry for falling in love with you. I didn't plan—"

"I know. No. It's just—"

"I know you've been hurt. Someone did a number on you, I guess." I shudder. Adrian's perceptiveness is too damn close to being psychic. Mind-reading terrifies me. Mental powers always do since...

"I want..." Should I go on? Should I tell him? I've never told anyone before. "I want to tell you. I want to tell you about it. I want

you to understand."

The tone of the dream changes. It feels like we've stumbled on a chunk of reality floating within the spirit world.

I face Adrian, eyes meeting. I'm going to do this. I really am.

"It's okay, Tom. I do understand, whether you tell me or not." Adrian raises his right hand, patting me like he would the jaguar.

I grab his hand and force it, palm-flat, against my temple, pinning it there like a moth to a cork.

I grab at Adrian's mind, drawing it into myself, wishing I enjoyed this invasion as much as I had the one a few minutes ago. Adrian shudders. I can feel the tips of his fingers sink into my skull just a little, which strangely, here on the spirit plane, isn't all that gross.

Our minds merge, memories swirling and meshing. I've done this before, but never as the initiator. But I can and I will. I'm in control, directing our strange ride. I force certain memories away, dredging up the ones I can't talk about, but need Adrian to know about anyway. He looks shocked. Can you puke on the astral plane? Maybe I should have warned him I was going to do this...

* * *

Oh, God. Oh, God. My fingers are actually sunk into Tom's brain! Why the hell didn't he warn me? What the hell are these wild images? They're not blue like the ayahuasca *dreams. These are more like memories...but not mine. They must be Tom's, but not as an adult. These must be from when he was a kid.*

I see things, half remembered, out of sequence, out of proportion, hissing and whirling around each other, around my brain. These are Tom's traumas, old and new. Bombs exploding, people dying, wars, backroom negotiations, covert missions, a stuffed animal in the shape of a cuddly black kitty.

The wash of memories settles on a room, seen from child-height.

A woman, crying, angry, the outline of a hand reddening her cheek. A man, furious, terrifying, calling her names, accusing her. "Witch!" he yells. "We could live like kings. Our own son could have anything he wants." He points at me. No, he's pointing at Tom, the kidlet-version. I can feel his terror as if remembering my own. Terror and hopelessness. "Mommy, Daddy. Please don't fight!" I/Tom/we remain in the doorway, watching, recording events in our brain like a freak-show home movie. The man—Tom's father—shouts some more. "The ponies.

The stock market. I don't care. Just do it!" He hoists his hand to strike her again.

Mommy raises her own hands, murmuring a few words we don't understand.

Daddy staggers backs. The images blur, now seen through our tears.

"Don't you dare turn your unholy powers on me!" Daddy grabs a lamp from the nearby dresser, charging toward her.

She rises, shouting her words this time. Untouched, Daddy is tossed back, head crunching against the doorframe. The lamp shatters into ceramic shards like bone fragments on the floor.

Mommy collapses in a heap. We sidle slowly, one unsure step at a time, to Mommy's side. We sit next there a long time—five minutes? Half-an-hour? A child's eternity. "Mommy, please wake up." Against the wall, Daddy's body slowly stiffens, bowels releasing in stinky eulogy.

A new collage of images rushes by at MTV speed: police, paramedics—a grim replay of the night Violet died—child-Tom taken away for a while. Fostered by a nice suburban family who preach discipline is next to Godliness, lessons taught with belts and straps. A mixed reunion with his mother—released on final appeal. Tardy neighbors testifying to previous violence. She never used magic again, cuts herself off from friends and family who did.

Awkward, confused, he joins the army at eighteen, finding a sense of belonging, of fitting in, until suddenly he doesn't anymore. Abandonment and betrayal like a recording set on repeat.

New images form: desert, pain, betrayal.

Tom yanks my hand away, gasping, sweat gleaming on his forehead. "I can't... That wasn't..." Tom seems to have lost his ability to complete a sentence. Well, who needs speech when you can plug directly into someone's brain?

"I'll never leave you," I tell him.

Tom surprises me by encircling me and pulling me close, just hanging on. "It's hard for me. Magic. I have..." He lets go, sitting back with a shaky smile. He raises his hands and makes little finger quotes in the air. "Issues," he concludes." I know I have issues."

"Issues around using magic? Well, after what you just showed me, I believe you're entitled to have some"—I mirror the finger quotes—"issues."

Tom barks out a rough laugh, swiping at his eyes. "Right. Except that wasn't what I meant to show you. I hardly remember that at all." He shudders. "No, I wanted to show you something more recent. But I guess I don't need a shrink to tell me these two events are connected. Here. Give me your hand again."

"You don't have to."

"I want to. It's just—"

I try to raise my hand as requested, but it won't move. "Tom! Tom!" But Tom is getting blurry, morphing back into the jaguar.

* * *

"Tom!" Adrian called one last time, sitting up. "Ow." A rock dug into his back, and the world's loudest mosquito whined by one ear. Tom padded over. "Guess we'll have to wait for a later showing, eh?"

Tom nuzzled Adrian's neck. It tickled, but Adrian didn't much feel like laughing. The cat scented the air and looked at Adrian. "Yeah. I could go for some breakfast right about now. Thanks." The cat padded off. "I won't let you down, Tom. I'll never desert you," he whispered to the retreating cat. The cat padded away, showing no sign of having heard.

CHAPTER 17

UNNATURAL SELECTION

Their journey to the temple was slow going, taking them three days that Adrian hated to lose. Adrian guesstimated they'd covered maybe twenty-five miles of dense foliage and irregular topography. Twice they'd run from the hated helicopter. As much as possible, they stayed away from clearings, depending on the jungle to hide them in its dense green bosom.

Adrian poked at a pile of leaves with the end of his spear. One large raggedy leaf sprouted legs and skittered away. He barked out a surprised laugh. "Wish I had camouflage like that." He looked down at himself. "Maybe I do." His skin had tanned dark like the tree trucks, his stained and dirty pants resembled the forest floor, and his T-shirt was more bare than thread.

Gaya had cleaned and mended his clothes (and shaved his short beard), during their brief, one-sided courtship. Now, days later, he once again wore grit like an extra layer of itchy skin.

Adrian continually cleaned his clothing and himself in any piranha-free pools he could find. A forest stands, however, on a foundation of dirt, which, when adding in the "rain" part of "rain forest," is an instant recipe for mud. He scratched his stubble and wished for a razor and a loofah.

The knowledge of their deadly pursuit spurred them on—what was a week-long walk for man and beast was only minutes of flying time—

and Adrian knew they wouldn't be safe until Deerborne's operation was destroyed and the cruel men brought to justice.

They stayed away from human settlements, too, not wanting to lead their pursuers into another innocent village. That and the fact that they kept running into people who wanted to kill them.

At last, they arrived at the Temple of Transfiguration, Kepi's map having led them honest and true.

It seemed almost surreal to Adrian to have reached this milestone in their journey. Their arrival filled him with a reeling mass of emotions. He was thrilled to have found this undocumented ruin in the jungle. If only he had a camera! But the absence of photographic equipment didn't stop him from framing award-winning shots in his mind. *Click! Click! Click!*

He was proud to have helped Tom to his destination. He was sure they would be able to gather the Tears of Truth—whatever they were—and, once they'd found their way back to Chaj, convince the tribal shaman to change him back.

But, Adrian barely admitted to himself, he was also deeply afraid that when once more a man, Tom would have no reason to stay with him. A trek back through the jungle together for sure, perhaps some hot sweaty nights on the agenda, then *poof,* Tom'd be back to his secret agent life while Adrian would return to Toronto and the reality of his life there. He sighed at the irony of it all. For most of their journey he'd longed to go home, and now, he just wanted to be with Tom, even if it meant never going back to Toronto. Home was where Tom was.

Still, they were here for a reason. Adrian turned his attention to surveying their surroundings.

Shaped like a standard-issue South American pyramid, the temple's thick patina of jungle made it seem like some giant flat-topped bush.

Tom and Adrian circled the structure until they stood before a steep stone stairway, typical of pyramidal buildings around the globe. Beneath the vines and creepers, the temple walls were pink and gray rock, probably sandstone and volcanic materials quarried locally. The doorway was offset by blue-green pillars and matching lintel which might have been mined far away. Adrian noted a familiarity between the doorframe design and the standing stones of Stonehenge. Stepping closer, Adrian examined the mortar-free masonry, the precision-fit stone blocks evidence of long-lost engineering techniques. Wouldn't an article or a book on the similarities of pyramids all over the world be worthwhile? He itched to take notes.

Where the jungle hadn't yet encroached, the walls, the pillars, the doorways were all carved with symbols of jaguars, warriors, and great eyes set with green crystals. He couldn't help feeling he was being watched. Watched and judged. He hoped he was up to whatever task these watchers—whether imaginary or real—had set for him.

Adrian turned toward the great mossy staircase, but halted immediately when Tom stepped in front of him, cutting him off. A spotted jaguar appeared on the rock wall above them. Adrian froze.

The newcomer roared that eerie jaguar scream-cough and leapt, landing on the stone pathway before them. The three creatures—cat, human, and man-cat—eyed each other warily as they stood in frozen tableau in the courtyard fronting the temple.

Lithe and beautiful, the other jaguar—a female—sidled up to Tom, touched noses, then stepped away.

For his part, Tom looked bemused. Or was that bewitched? Adrian felt a cold shiver at the base of his spine.

"C'mon, Tom. This is no time to get in touch with your inner kitty," Adrian whispered, not wanting to attract the attention of the other, wilder animal. "Nor outer," he added, glancing at the spotted lady.

She took another step away. Tom followed her, dazedly.

She turned to face him, and they touched noses a second time. This time she continued her forward motion, running her body along Tom's, front to back, her tail sliding by Tom's nose in passing. She repeated this maneuver several times. Tom staggered drunkenly. With a last look over her shoulder at her bewitched victim, the spotted jaguar turned and bounded away.

*   *   *

Tom trembled as the female rubbed her hot fur against his, her scent overpowering, mesmerizing. He'd never been attracted to the opposite sex before. He shook his head, but it remained foggy.

Mate. Protect mate.

He dashed after the female, leaving Adrian alone.

*   *   *

For three long days Adrian explored the temple solo. He clambered up the crumbling stone staircase, the footing treacherous under its camouflage of moss and lichen. He spent long hours figuring out the trick to opening the door panel. In desperation, he'd even tried saying "open sesame" and "friend" in a variety of languages. Eventually, he'd run out of literary incantations and resorted to brute force, accidentally palming the carved jaguar symbol in the middle. The door swung inward on creaking hinges hundreds-of-years rusty.

The original design of the temple had featured tiny pinholes to illuminate the interior. Now there was plenty of light for Adrian to see by during the day as it filtered in through cracks and holes in the aging—and possibly about-to-collapse—roof.

He explored the temple thoroughly, finding a great-room at its very center containing a large sunken tub. Built like a vaguely diamond-shaped polygon, it grew wider about four-fifths of the way up (or down, depending on where one was standing.) With a shudder, Adrian realized it was wider *at the shoulders* to accommodate a human lying down. It resembled a coffin far too much for Adrian's taste, but he marveled at the clear, algae-free liquid it held.

The mirror-like surface glistened. He gasped at his own tired reflection, having not seen himself in weeks. He'd thinned and hardened, and the beard didn't look half bad despite it desperately needing a trim. He looked older, surer, more decisive. He'd do what he had to do. He'd become an older version of the dynamic young man he'd been in college when the entire world had been his oyster, and he'd bounced around between majors and minors, studying drama and photojournalism before settling on anthropology. Gone was the slightly soft HR Specialist who meant to make better use of his neglected gym membership.

His knowledge of ideograms and petroglyphs served him well. The wall carvings translated into the recipe for the Tears of Truth, which just might be the bath oil to convert Tom to human again. No wonder Chaj had wanted them to come here. Perhaps the smug young shaman wasn't as self-serving as he seemed.

Near the pool he found an earthenware basin, ewer and cup, all carved with geometric symbols of cats, power, and life. Following the instructions carefully, he gathered herbs and plants and concocted the Tears of Truth, dumping some of it into the pool per the great stone Owner's Manual. He filled his two empty water gourds. He'd just have to drink directly from whatever body of water happened to be handy until he could replace them. The rest of it he poured into the ewer, which he placed, together with the cup, on the temple floor.

"Not for you," he told himself. It seemed senseless to have come all this way and *not* follow the directions left for him by those more knowledgeable in the ways of shape-shifting. It seemed senseless, too, to bother. Still, what else did he have to do to kill the time until Tom returned? Or until he got it through his own thick skull that Tom wasn't coming back.

In the jungle, in this holy place, he was pointless without Tom. Just a solitary man standing vigil in a temple not meant for him.

The nights were the worst. Inside the temple, only a modicum of moonlight trickled in. Outside was brighter, but less protected. He used up the last of the oil within the old lantern he'd found back in the cave… When? Just a couple of weeks? Not even? A few days here, a few days there. He'd lost track.

He slept fitfully in the stone entrance, fearful of becoming locked in the temple should the door suddenly swing shut—afraid he'd roll down the steep pitch of the stairway in his sleep; terrified he'd become dinner for a hungry jungle cat. Or two.

He didn't bother to set up any sort of camp, knowing he'd be leaving in a day or two with or without Tom Ferrell.

Not so long ago he'd promised Tom to stay with him forever. Now it was slowly becoming evident that Tom might not care. If a few of Adrian's own tears mixed in with the Tears of Truth, no one was there to notice.

Also absent were the spirit-walk visions—no shared erotic dreams, no wise and wily Chaj dispensing cryptic orders and cagey advice. He began to feel homesick, missing his bff Wendy and his own kitty-cat, Pixel. He missed Tom. His heart ached each time he caught the sounds of jaguars caterwauling under the moon.

The curious anthropologist within him tried to pass the time by exploring, but the man within him waited, heartsick, pining for the unlikely return of his protector. His dream-lover. His friend. His… What? Was there even a term for what they'd become to each other?

He had a great deal of time to think about things, like his life, his loves, his goals. He revisited his youth, remembering old friends and family. If this was his life flashing before his eyes, he found it awfully slow-going.

He sighed, remembering his first crush. Winston Johnston had been cute and smart, outgoing and talented. He'd carried a few extra pounds, which vicious schoolmates had declared an unforgivable sin. Winston had been Adrian's first kiss, and while nothing much had developed between them, it was a sweet memory, and Adrian cherished it, finding it comforting as he lay on the hard stone of the temple steps, comparing the harsh inflexibility of the stone to the behaviors of teenagers.

And female jaguars, he thought jealously. He'd vowed never to leave Tom, and here was Tom chasing after the first piece of tail to flash her dripping fangs his way. He was reminded of a character on one of his mother's favorite shows back in the '80s, and just as he dozed off, he dubbed the she-cat "Alexis," after the reigning bitch of the nighttime soaps.

* * *

The black jaguar prowled nearby, keeping close watch on the lolling female. Each time he approached, she snarled and hissed, driving him off. Yet her scent drew him back, mesmerizing. He shook his head to clear it, but that accomplished nothing. He paced the rocky outcrop, gazing at the sweeping view of the valley. Something about that green and stone mound across the way…

He prowled in circles, feeling trapped and bound as if he were in the wrong place at the wrong time. Life should be simple. *Eat. Sleep. Protect.*

Yet, something niggled at the back of his cat mind. *Be somewhere? With someone? Another…cat? Another mate? Almost rememb—Oh.* A new spicy odor caught his attention. He sniffed the air, turning this way and that, hunting the illusive trail. Got it! *Tapir. Chase. Catch. Kill.*

With a last glance at his new lady friend, he slinked off, one more black shadow in the night.

* * *

On the fourth morning, Adrian headed down to the nearby river to wash and maybe entice some nice, fat crustacean to join him for breakfast. He fancied that shrimp-like bottom-feeder he'd dined on once or twice. He'd grab a few for later, hoping they'd keep for a while; last thing he needed was a dose of food poisoning.

Just down the path from the temple lay a broad basin where he'd been lucky thus far, finding fruit and catching lizards and turtles easily. It appeared to be a natural formation enhanced by ancient architects.

Arriving at the pool's edge, he knelt by the waters and began his morning ablutions. When he raised his soaked head from the pool, he realized the two jaguars stood on the opposite side. The she-cat that he'd dubbed Alexis watched him warily while the black jaguar hovered nearby, focused possessively on her.

Adrian froze, thoughts racing. He knew the she-cat, at least, was a real threat to his safety. Plus there seemed to be very little of Tom Ferrell left in the larger cat now. Only the light glinting off the steel dog tags indicated he'd ever been anything other than the wildest of jungle beasts.

Hastily, fearing for his life, Adrian rose and took a single backward step up the path, away from the two predators. He recognized the truth now. He would have to come back later to the pond once the jaguars were gone, to collect as much food as he could to see him on the impossible journey back through the jungle alone.

He took another backward step, his foot slipping on a loose stone. He crashed to the ground, shocking the wind from his lungs with an ungainly, *"Umph."*

The skittish Alexis screamed and attacked, leaping the pond in a blur of tan and brown spots. She slammed Adrian sharply against the ground, knocking out what little air he'd managed to suck into his lungs. The spotted jaguar rolled away and crouched before him, poised to spring a second time. Adrian twisted to look at Tom. The black cat just stood there watching, as if in a drugged haze.

Alexis attacked again, this time knocking Adrian into the pool. His head struck a rock on the way down, and his vision narrowed to tiny pin-dots of white.

Following Adrian into the water, Alexis pinned him under, holding him there with cruel claws digging into his shoulders, raking his flesh. Black and brown spots danced before his eyes. Then blue. Blue. Vision-blue, but this time there was no instructional video, and the blue became fainter and fainter, the radiance whiter and farther off. He began to head into the light when something called him back.

Adrian had seen a lot in the last few months—mystical and tangible, cruel and precious—but nothing was more glorious than the huge black blur descending upon Alexis, knocking the spotted cat aside. It looked like hope. It looked like life. It looked like Tom.

Partially sheathed claws tangled in his T-shirt, raking one abraded shoulder, yanking him to the surface.

Gasping, coughing, and vomiting water, Adrian waited for the panic to subside. He was breathing. He was safe. He'd live. For now.

A warm tongue rasped over his face and neck. In a gesture of appreciation, he heaved another tsunami of water from his lungs and stomach.

Rising shakily, grasping a handful of black hide to help him stand,

Adrian checked his surroundings. The she-cat lay on her side, seemingly dead, until an obvious rise of her ribcage indicated Tom had only knocked her out.

A little blood ran down Tom's coat from a deep wound in his shoulder. Further examination showed Tom lacerated and deeply gouged in a number of places. What Adrian had originally taken to be water on the gray stone path now resolved itself into blood as his light-headedness passed. While Tom had merely used his superior weight to subdue her, Alexis had fought nastily, using tooth and claw where he—out of some insane sense of chivalry—would not.

"Oh, God. She sure did a number on you." *In more ways than one.* "Let's get you into that chamber." Adrian's voice creaked from disuse. "That'll fix everything."

Together, Adrian and Tom staggered away from the unconscious jaguar, supporting each other as best they could.

They struggled up the hill and the stone staircase. Tom grew weaker with each step. Adrian provided little more than moral support to the overgrown jaguar. Somehow, they made it, Adrian leading the way.

Upon reaching the great-room, instinct seemed to take over. Tom fell into the coffin-shaped pool with none of his usual grace. The waters splashed outward, the level rising to accommodate his bulk. He lay sprawled beneath the surface, one shoulder, two nostrils, three whiskers breaking the sparkling surface, sunlight pouring in through the crumbling ceiling.

Kneeling by the pool, Adrian reached for the earthenware cup. He trickled a little of the potion he'd made into Tom's muzzle, his own tears adding to the mixture.

The black cat coughed once, then stilled.

At first, the water within the pool reddened with the blood of Tom's many wounds. Only moments later (at least, it felt like moments to Adrian—time had ceased to have much meaning within the temple), it cleared again, and though the water distorted the view, the wounds appeared to be closing, knitting, healing before his eyes.

He blinked. Then again. He could almost see the… No, he could clearly see the translucent image of a human dancing on the water, superimposed upon the supine jaguar. The flickering image revealed a tall man, naked, glistening, muscled, and scarred, an angry gunshot wound appearing and closing as the more recent wounds had. The Tom Ferrell from the plane—and of Adrian's dreams and visions—gradually suffused the lines of the jaguar, the very bones shifting and realigning into ramrod spine, spherical skull, graceful fingers. Tom's eyes scrunched closed and his shifting teeth clenched. Adrian winced. That had to hurt.

As Tom's chest expanded and contracted with each breath, the waters jumped and sparkled, reflecting first black fur, then white flesh, fur, flesh, black, white.

Mesmerized, Adrian couldn't look away.

Without conscious thought, he spoke ancient words of power in languages older than English, Quechua, Latin, or Hebrew—the sounds so old they barely formed syllables, dating back to man's earliest time, before anyone told the sons of Adam and daughters of Eve that men could not change into animals, that dreams were meaningless, that magic and spirits were fairy tales.

The light danced on the pool's surface, sending glints of brilliance, interspersed with flutters of shadow, this way and that.

"Oohhmmm," Adrian murmured, assuming the mantle of Shaman of the Temple. *"Oohhmm."* Adrian drew a deep breath to continue, noting Tom was slightly more man than beast now, light triumphing over blackness.

"Oohhmm-oommph!" He smacked the ground hard, air leaving his lungs again as black and brown spots once again tangoed across his vision.

The spotted jaguar pinned him to the narrow rock floor between the wall and the pool. Sharp claws pierced his shoulders once more. Alexis threw back her head to roar in concert with Adrian's screams.

Gasping in pain, Adrian knew he had only seconds before Alexis used those vicious incisors to rip out his throat. Hell hath no fury…

At the edge of his vision, he saw Tom rise, standing tall, prepared to do battle nude, unarmed. The sound and motion of the man rising from the pool distracted the jaguar. Alexis kept Adrian pinned to the floor, but turned to scream at this new, confusing enemy.

For one long moment, Tom remained erect, water sheeting off his body, dog tags dangling from his human neck, polished steel sending flashes of reflected light bounding around the room. Then he bent over, hands reaching the edge of the pool for support, arms shrinking, face turning dark and re-forming outward. Skin turned black as pores sprouted inky hairs. He opened his mouth, screaming. Teeth and fingernails lengthened, spine curved, legs twisted, human screams became feline roar as the man morphed back into the jaguar once again, the unfinished transformation sluicing away with the sacred waters.

The black cat snarled and sprang.

The she-cat yowled, still crouching low over Adrian. Tom dashed around them, back to the temple wall. Alexis feinted forward, then crouched, growling low and dangerous. She slinked backward across the wet floor, eyes never leaving the black cat. Tom stepped across Adrian, possessive stance screaming, *"You want a piece of him? You'll have to go through me!"* He flowed forward, pushing Alexis backward step after step until her hind legs found the pool. Adrian raised himself on one elbow, dizzy and freaking, watching but unable to help.

Alexis glanced behind her, one foot faltering where it touched the waters, seeking solid ground. Taking advantage of her distraction, Tom sprang forward, knocking her into the pool, his momentum carrying him to the far side. Adrian lay weakly on the cold stone floor, watching the action and willing himself to rise and run, but fear, curiosity, and one too many shocks left him trembling on the floor, unable to rise. He lay on the damp rock, satisfied just to be breathing for now.

The spotted jaguar howled and spat, surging about the shallow pool as if trapped in a tar pit. Syrupy tentacles extended from the waters, embracing Alexis, welcoming her, restraining her like a liquid straightjacket. Although there was no visible ingress, the water level rose until only her razor-toothed muzzle and a few trembling whiskers remained above the surface. The cat mewled wetly once, then lay still.

As one, Adrian and Tom rose from their respective sides of the pool and came to stand together, peering down. Light dappled the walls. Adrian almost thought he could see the outline of a woman with light brown hair floating like a veil above the cat.

"The writing on the walls says she'll stay in 'a waking sleep'—a state of suspended animation, I guess—until someone comes to get her." Adrian buried his fingers in the soaked ruff of Tom's neck. "Was she a changed one, too?" he asked, using Kepi's term. He had no words of his own to describe this. Were-cat? Shape-shifter? Transfigured? He was a scientist, goddamn it. He'd never imagined he'd need words like this outside of the study of myth.

The black jaguar shook his head, eyes still on the pool.

"How could you... Never mind." Complicated answers would wait.

Adrian stared closely. Despite the shimmering surface, he was able to examine the trapped cat as he hadn't previously. At this close range, he saw the cat's enlarged belly and swollen teats. Although time seemed elastic in the jungle, Alexis's now-obvious pregnancy was so advanced Tom couldn't possibly be the father. So it hadn't been sexual instincts that had drawn Tom to her, but protective ones, a whole different set of pheromones at play. Maybe the same ones that kept him with Adrian.

Now Adrian understood why Tom had restricted his fighting technique to body-checks and head-butts. Well, he sort of understood. Something inside Adrian relaxed a little. “You ready to leave?”

The jaguar swiveled his great head toward Adrian, then back toward the pool.

“You can’t go back in again. It’ll fry your circuits if you try.” He gestured at the carved wall.

The jaguar nodded, as if he, too, knew this.

“I’m so sorry, Tom. I…” Words failed Adrian, and he laid a hand on Tom’s soft shoulder, stroking to comfort his companion and himself. His fingers felt sticky wetness, and he noticed blood on the fur, although careful observation told him the cuts and gashes that had marred the beautiful fur coat were gone as if they’d never been. At least the interrupted transformation had accomplished that much.

In a dreamlike state, Adrian realized the blood seeped from his own wounds, trickling down from the gouges in his shoulders. Suddenly the sense of timelessness shattered; his shoulders hurt like hell. His vision blurred, which was good because it made the spinning room easier to take.

He lowered himself on the wet stone gingerly, knowing he was about to fall down. “Back in a bit,” he informed the worried black face hovering above him, merging with dancing black dots that didn’t look worried at all. “I hope.”

*   *   *

Tom paced circles around the great-room, unsheathed claws clicking on the rough stone. He sniffed Adrian’s cheek. Between each slow breath, Tom panicked, fearing his companion had ceased breathing. He kept careful watch, although how he’d administer CPR, he hadn’t a clue.

His brain functioned clearly again. While the pregnant jaguar pheromones had pulled him unwillingly into the mindset of the wild beast form he wore, the aborted transformation had given his humanity a reboot. He was man in mind again, if not in body. And wasn’t he pissed about that? He’d almost made it, almost become a man again. So close, but…

What if that had been his one chance? His only chance, and he'd blown it? Maybe Chaj didn't have the power to turn him back. Fact was, the shaman had never admitted to working the change in the first place, now that Tom thought about it.

He paced over to the gourds lying in a corner. Sniffing them, he ascertained they were full of the same liquid Adrian had poured on his muzzle. So necessary to the transformation, then, he figured. But not here. Adrian had said he couldn't try again, here. Maybe elsewhere. He had hope. He had…nothing really.

Wake up, Adrian. Wake the fuck up!

Angry. Frustrated. He screamed, his rage bouncing off the walls, floor and ceiling, building an echo that caused Adrian to flinch, and a few stray stones to dislodge from the ceiling. One bounced into the pool, and bounced out again as if the surface were rubbery. The female jaguar sighed in her sleep, looking content.

Tom paced to the pool again and horked into it, making a grating noise. *If I have to stay a cat forever, then you can just stay in there forever.* "Bitch," he snarled, although it sounded nothing like the English word.

Even now, her pheromones drifted from the pool—pregnant female. He held his breath and moved as far away from the pool as he could without actually leaving Adrian.

Even though they weren't his cubs, he felt the instinctive imperative to protect. He'd hunted and brought her meat, fought off other predators, left Adrian alone. It had all been so confusing. If she hadn't gone after Adrian, he might have lived out his days as adoptive father to a bunch of jungle brats. Or maybe he would have killed them at birth, the males anyway. He had no idea how his humanity would mesh with his feline-side. Nor his sexuality. He'd been attracted to her as a protector, but not really wanted to mate. Could jaguars even be gay?

Adrian stirred and Tom paced to his side. Blood oozed from the cross-cut of slashes the spotted bitch had hacked into his shoulders. What if Adrian bled to death? Then what? Tom had lost comrades in arms in the past, but he'd never been quite as…attached, before. He nuzzled Adrian's hair.

Hey, what's this? Tom noticed that some of the cuts and scratches had healed more than they should have in the short time since the brawl in the grotto. Scabbed over, maybe, but some were already healing to pink scars. He circled the area, thinking logically. *What would do that? What was…*

Carefully, he locked his teeth around the ewer's handle, strode to Adrian's side and awkwardly dribbled a little of the contents onto one bleeding shoulder. Turning his head to peer around the pitcher, careful not to spill any, he watched the blood cease flowing almost instantly. Gradually, wishing he'd been transformed into a monkey or something with hands, instead, he managed to slosh the magic elixir onto most of Adrian's wounds. Knowing he couldn't set it down without spilling the rest of it, he dumped the last of it over Adrian's head.

Adrian stirred. Tom touched his forehead to Adrian's damp one. Without waking, Adrian reached up and patted Tom's head (hitting the cat squarely in the eye, but in Tom's joy, the blow barely registered).

"Come here of'n?" Adrian mumbled. Sighing, he rolled over in his magic potion puddle and went back to sleep.

I sure hope not. Reassured that Adrian had moved from unconsciousness to regular sleep, Tom padded off to check out the rest of the temple.

* * *

Adrian awoke some time later, lying on the hard ground near the pool. His shoulders burned and ached, and he had a hell of a headache. He checked quickly on Alexis, but the she-cat lay still in her watery sarcophagus, held safely in check by whatever magic possessed this ancient place.

Moving slowly, Adrian took careful inventory of his injuries. There was little blood now. He figured he hadn't been out of it too long, since the puddle he lay in, while smaller, hadn't dried completely even in the afternoon heat.

"Oh, yetch," he said, rolling slowly onto his knees. "I hate sleeping in the wet spot." He climbed to his feet, swaying a little. Tom appeared at his side, silent as a shadow. Adrian steadied himself against the warm bulk, and together they staggered out, a mirror of their entry a few hours earlier. Or maybe it was days. Time meant little in the rain forest, although he hoped it hadn't been so long that the workers in the indigo factory were all beyond hope and help.

His belongings lay in a pile near the gate—lamp, machete, gourds filled with the magic potion for Chaj. Scattered around his pack were several intricately carved gold bangles and a pair of emerald earrings that hadn't been there last time he looked. He glanced around, even though he knew he'd been alone the entire time he'd been there. Was it a gift? A test? Multiple choice or essay?

Gift, he decided, because he was too tired and sore to think further.

"*Diospagarasunki*" he whispered, like a prayer. "Thank you," to whatever benevolent spirits watched out for him. He felt grateful until he bumped his damaged shoulder against a rock. *Ow!* Why was his guardian angel doing such an on-again, off-again job of looking after him? Some fairy godmother he had! Maybe she was union or something, regularly clocking out for breaks and overtime.

Tom sauntered up, having checked on Alexis again.

"Hey, Tom. Something or somebody left a pile of jewelry with our stuff." He displayed the gold. "It's a miracle. It must have been…"

Adrian stopped. He could easily recognize cat mockage by now. "Oh, so you put them there." His cheeks burned. He'd gone from being cynical to seeing magic everywhere, even where it wasn't. "Where'd you find them?"

Tom led Adrian to a low chamber he hadn't noticed before. Bones and armor lay scattered about, along with a single skull, and a single breastplate. A lone soldier had died here.

"That could have been me," Adrian murmured. He knelt in the dust, throwing his arms around Tom. "There but for the grace of you." He whispered his thanks again— "*Diospagarasunki*"—not sure if he was thanking Tom or whoever had sent Tom to guide and protect him.

Adrian clutched Tom tightly, then the moment got awkward, and they pulled away. "Let's get some chow. I could eat a zebra."

Tom growled.

"Yeah, wrong continent. I know." And off they headed.

Returning to the grotto outside the temple where he'd scavenged for food, he forced himself to wash and drink. He managed to catch a couple of turtles. It was too late to start out that night, so he barbecued both turtles, eating one then, and wrapping the charred meat of the other in leaves to eat on the journey back. Tom could fend for himself since he preferred his meals raw and still warm.

* * *

The sun was only hinting at dawn when Adrian came awake to Tom's gentle prodding. "Right. Right. I'm up. I'm… Oh, God. I hurt all over." Adrian fingered one of his sore shoulders, instantly regretting having touched it at all. "Sure wish I had some of that stinky paste the Eek use." Twisting his head, he could just see that he now wore a crosshatch of faded whip scars and bright new claw marks. "You could play Xs and Os on my shoulders." He laughed. There was just a touch of hysteria in the sound. Miss Alexis Spotted Bitch had done a number on him, and he was very worried about infection.

* * *

Twenty-four hours later, Adrian was almost ready to declare he'd live. That he was aching less and not more, and not throwing a fever at all led him to believe he'd escaped infection. The claw marks were well scabbed over and, where he could reach, not hot to the touch, although they were still very, very sore. Which almost kept him from poking them every so often. Almost.

Adrian wiped sweat from his brow again and adjusted the strap that suspended his gear across his lower back. He'd re-strung his pack to avoid most of the cuts and bruising. The hollowed-out gourd containing the Tears of Truth for Chaj bounced uncomfortably against one hip with every step. He plodded along, almost sure he was leading them in the right direction, following Kepi's trusty map back the way they'd come.

They accidently wandered off the track a bit, which turned out to be serendipitous when they encountering a foul-smelling hermit living beneath the broken bridge they'd bypassed on their way to the temple. The trollish man pointed out a better way to cross the gorge, thereby cutting several days from their return trip.

One by one they'd ticked off all of the milestones rendered on their map, so despite being directionally impaired as a rule, Adrian felt they were nearing the Wallpa village. His plan was to skirt the village and continue on their journey. Whether their next stop was Chaj's village or somewhere with a phone, only the gods of these jungles knew.

On the pre-temple part of their journey, Tom had been anxious and frustrated, but very motivated. Now, though, he was despondent. He trailed uncaringly after Adrian, and although he still dumped fresh kills at Adrian's feet on a semi-regular basis, he scarcely ate anything himself.

They were in the habit of resting a bit in the rainy part of the afternoon. Tom usually found them some sort of overhang—whether cave or just an elephant-ear plant depended on their luck and locale. Today they found a place where the leaves laced together tightly enough to put a thatch hut to shame. Adrian sat cross-legged on a soft, mossy spot.

Tom dragged himself over and slumped down, facing Adrian. He scratched at his ear with his hind paw, relaxing when Adrian took over. Before long, Adrian's fingers slowed from scratching to caressing, then just rested on the big cat's furry temple, content with just the physical connection. Until his fingers began to sink into Tom's skull—not just the furry coat, the actual skull!

"Yikes!" He yanked them away, peering at Tom's temple to make sure there weren't gaping holes. There weren't. "Does it hurt?"

Tom growled low in his throat, pushing his head back into Adrian's hand. Adrian watched in horrid fascination as his fingertips not so much sank into Tom's skull, but more merged with the flesh to become one—just a smooth flow of fur to flesh from Tom to Adrian and back. Talk about making a connection!

"I guess this mind-meld stuff works now even when we're awake. You wanted to show me something last time. Something about why you aren't in the army anymore. Is that what you want me to see?"

The great head nodded, jerking Adrian's arm up and down. Adrian looked deep into the cat's dark blue eyes.

Once again, the images flee past in dizzying sequence, places, faces, meals Tom had eaten, people he'd fucked. Weapons, books, more childhood memories, but mostly army. Training, barracks living, surreptitious sex in hidden places. A hand on his shoulder, drawing him aside, for a quick encounter, for a stern warning, for a secret mission.

The images settle into a desert town, dusty, dry, and surprising chilly. Tom dressing himself in civvies—khaki noticeable by its absence. Not a holiday, but an undercover mission. Rich, spicy odors perfume the air. The anthropologist in Adrian want to explore, but he's stuck seeing only what Tom saw. Had seen.

Tom heads to a bar, nursing a few beers alone. And again the next day. And the next. Frustrated. Unable to leave with mission incomplete, unable to report in for fear of discovery. Bored and antsy. A young man approaches. A handsome young man, blond hair singular in a town of swarthy people. Idle conversation, a hand brushes a hand. A hearty goodnight with a silent agreement to meet up later.

Careful. Careful. In this country, gay means jail, death. No stranger to danger, it adds spice to their clandestine meetings. Always in Tom's rooms. Always at night. Always Lazlo on top. "I don't prefer that," he explains in stilted English. Tom doesn't mind. Human touch is precious, as is his growing affection for the blond boy.

A week. Then two. After three weeks Tom can barely stand to be apart from Lazlo. His skin itches, and he can't seem to catch his breath. Love. It must be love.

"Tomorrow we go to my place." Not a question, nor an invitation. Just a statement. Tom nods.

Two hours' drive over dusty roads, passing rusting machinery and burned-out factories along the way.

"A drink." Lazlo hands Tom a glass. A sweet tea. Finding himself thirsty in this dusty land, he drinks deeply.

"What did you..." He scarcely has time to realize the tea is drugged before he passes out.

Coming to, he finds himself naked, strapped to a metal bed frame, wire coils digging into his back. A car battery and jumper cables rest on the floor nearby.

Lazlo drifts in, regarding Tom with disinterested eyes. "You were easy." He shakes back his blond hair. "They always are."

The sound of laughter. There are several other men in the room. One makes a crude comment. Dazed, still drugged, Tom didn't even know they were there. He shakes his head to clear it. It doesn't work.

A tall woman wrapped in bright cloth enters. "Out of the way, Incubus," she orders Lazlo. She walks over to the bed, looking down at Tom, her lip curling, showing sharp, uneven teeth. She unwinds a paisley shawl from her shoulders, folding it into a square. She tosses it onto the bare coils near Tom's hips and sits. "My turn." She brings her hands together in a double fist, bowing over them as if in prayer. Slowly, she raises her head and fits one hand on his sternum, the other on his temple.

Wow. No wonder Tom has a problem with this crazy mindreading shit, Adrian thought. It's so intrusive. He wondered if he should withdraw his hand, his consciousness, but Tom had said he wanted Adrian to see this. He steeled himself and opened his mind for more.

Layer by layer, the psychic sociopath insinuates herself into Tom's confused brain, mumbling soothing phrases, telling him to relax. He struggles, trying to block her out, but it's impossible to fight off someone who's become part of you.

Images flash across his brain, fuzzy now—a memory of having his memories plundered—memories once, twice removed. She rips through his mind like a thief, tearing at things, leaving chaos in her wake. She's done this before, thwarting his efforts with ease. She's looking for something specific, stomping on memories both precious and mundane in her quest to find it.

"Ah-ha!" she shouts. Or maybe just projects her triumph into his mind. She's unearthed the information he knew she was after, the intel he's tried to hide. He runs interference, tripping her up with his scrambling thoughts, cranking up memories of rock tunes to eleven. He struggles, deliberately lacerating his back on the rusty bedsprings, throwing this mind-numbing pain at her like great white-hot missiles. This strategy slows her, but she slides under, over, and around his defenses.

Rifling through military strategies, she unearths the plan she sought, the one to take down the rebels—these rebels—at dawn. Having filched what she's come for, she flings his mind aside, leaving him bruised and aching, mentally and physically. He feels bashed and beaten.

His captors file out, leaving him tied to the bed. The next eighteen hours are a wash of misery as the coils cut into his flesh, and he further flays himself for his failure to withhold the information.

His rescue is accidental. A small group of American soldiers, retreating from their failed mission, rendezvous in the bombed out building. They find him in the cellar, quickly figuring him as the source of the rebel guerilla's information. Their "surprise" attack resulted in a large loss of life on both sides. They don't release him right away, even though they can see through the bare coils, blood dripping from his injured back onto the dirt floor.

"They tortured him," one soldier says in his defense, poking at the car battery.

"Nah, they only threatened to torture him before he cracked," said one, touching the jumper clips together. No sparks appear. "This battery's dead."

Finally untying him, his muscles scream in pain. Naked, tears of rage and frustration painting fresh tracks down his cheeks, he kneels on the filthy floor. Betrayed by love, betrayed by magic, betrayed by his own humanity, he berates himself for his weakness. He's not supposed to be the one who needs rescuing, goddamn it! He's the rescuer!

There is no trial, no investigation. Since he hadn't officially been there, how could he have officially done anything wrong? Just a fistful of paperwork offering early retirement. No cause for any undue attention. Time to go do something else with your life. A cold handshake. Dismissed.

Tears of rage and frustration tracked down Adrian's own cheeks. How could they treat Tom like this? They didn't know. They couldn't know. He tried to extract his fingers now, but a great paw, claws slightly extended, pressed down. There must be more to see.

Adrian nodded, focusing again on Tom's memories, his life.

Another hand on his shoulder—gentler this time. An offer to work. A business card reading Borderless Observers Organization. *An instinctive recoil at the thought of an organization using magic. The slow dawning of the idea that they also battled magic wrongly used—a fight Tom could get behind.*

A stately black woman. Jacqueline Batique *her card reads.*

"You will only be sent to deal with human crimes and human criminals until you are ready. The paranormal will wait."

And so he joins the shadowy organization, finding himself making friends with seers and selkies, witches and werewolves. And less corporeal colleagues he isn't sure what they are. It certainly made for a hell of an interesting company softball league.

Adrian fell back, fingers disconnecting from Tom's memory bank. He felt so many emotions: horror, anger, guilt, amazement—some his own, and some experienced vicariously through Tom. Most of all he felt love. And admiration at the resilience of this wonderful man.

CHAPTER 18

GET A WIFE!

The best laid plans of jaguars and men…

Ironically, is it was not Adrian, but Tom who had succumbed to infection, sporting a hot and swollen paw beyond Adrian's first aid training to mend. Even a few drops of the Tears of Truth brought only temporarily relief. The elixir healed the immediate infection, but with something trapped under the flesh, it only re-infected in hours. Neither Adrian nor Tom liked to use up the potion, since it was their only bargaining chip to get Chaj to change Tom back when they finally reached the Perqua village—if the young shaman even could.

They debated a while, but soon realized they needed help. Kepi and the Wallpa were the closest thing they had to friends nearby, if by friends you meant people who tried to kill you last time you were over at their place. He only hoped the Wallpa had a curative similar to the Eek.

Tom didn't bother to hide at all this time, just followed Adrian into the Wallpa village like a whipped dog. "Take me to your leader," Adrian demanded, sunlight glinting off the gold bangles and emerald earrings he now wore, the latter forced through holes unused since college.

Apparently, gold was the one thing Kepi loved even more than his chickens. "How dare you return?" was quickly replaced by, "So. How was Temple?" as soon as he saw the jewelry.

Tom and Adrian were led to the central square, fed and watered, and welcomed back as if they'd always been great pals.

The brave warriors who had previously feared and tried to kill Tom now berated Adrian for the condition he'd let the cat fall into. Tom's fine coat was matted and lackluster, his eyes cloudy and downcast.

"How could you let this happen to this noble beast?" they demanded in a variety of dialects. "We'd never let such a thing happen to our chickens!"

Adrian felt outraged, and it was all he could do to keep from bitch-slapping the closest entitled warrior.

Tom seemed to come out of his slump a bit when one of the village children escaped her mother and pounced on him like a giant stuffed toy. Soon all of the children were patting and tugging, and Tom seemed to find some peace within himself amid the riot of children.

The Wallpa *jampiri*, their medicine man, tended Tom's paw and Adrian's back, and while he didn't have Ko-hen's miracle elixir, he was able to remove a thorn that had eluded Adrian and dress Tom's paw so it might heal on its own. Amazingly, the fee for service was three gold bangles and a pair of emerald earrings, exactly the items Adrian had acquired since his last visit. Adrian kicked himself for not hiding some of his golden spoils. On the other hand, the glistening gold was probably what kept the Wallpa from killing him as soon as he arrived. Perhaps it was a fair price, after all. Perhaps they thought he had more stashed away.

Headman Kepi called for a great feast to mark the taming of the cat and the saving of the chickens. Nobody mentioned that the celebrations were a little after the fact, or that they'd driven Mis-tah Adrian and his magic cat act out of town.

So the men lounged around the fire amiably watching the children play with the man-killing, chicken-stealing creature of the jungle, while the women toiled to prepare a banquet on short notice. It was ever thus.

* * *

"Kasarakuy. Kasarakuy," Mrs. Kepi kept repeating, looking at Adrian as if he was the dumbest thing she'd ever met…right after an unusually stupid chicken.

Marriage. Marriage, Adrian translated silently. *Uh-oh. Didn't this get me into a whole shitload of trouble at the last village?* He'd had a fair amount of whatever fermented beverage they served with dinner.

(Gray, apparently, goes with both fish and fowl.) His head buzzed pleasantly in complete disharmony with his racing, panicky pulse.

Adrian shook his head fiercely, both to indicate "no" and to try and clear away the boozey cobwebs. "No. No," he said in English. *"¡No! ¡No!"* he added in Spanish. *"Ama. Ama,"* he said in Quechua. His thoughts swirled from the ceremonial liquor as he ran through every language they might know, and was just about to start on Ojibwa, which he'd learned on an anthropological dig in Northern Ontario. After the Inukshuk, who knew?

"Yeah. Yeah," Kepi said, backing up his spouse. "Need wife. Need wife now."

Adrian's language skills deserted him, and he fell back on gestures, shaking his head and palming his hands outward toward the Wallpa. Should he out himself? They'd probably just foist a husband on him instead.

He sat up straight, standing being beyond his immediate skill set, despite having sobered up somewhat since Mrs. Kepi had introduced the subject of marriage. Carefully but firmly, he said in the Quechua trade tongue, "I neither need nor want a wife." Warming to his subject, as drunks often do, he waxed, if not poetic, at least classic. Lapsing into English, he declared, "It is not actually a truth at all, universally acknowledged or otherwise, that a single man in possession of a good fortune must be in want of a wife." He burped. "'N besides, I don't got a good fortune, unless you count my—" He looked around for his stuff—lamp, machete, Tears of Truth, check. All dumped in an untidy heap near the hut the Kepi's had loaned him. "Stuff." He slumped back against his rock of choice.

Kepi and his wife sniggered together in the way of long-time couples. "Not wife for Mis-tah Adrian." They giggled hysterically at this, although the fact that they found the notion of a partner for Adrian to be so absurd was rather insulting.

"Wha—?" Adrian requested clarification.

"Peri. *Peri* need wife."

Mrs. Kepi screeched over to a nearby campfire where a number of young people were enjoying an after-dinner cocktail. A stocky young man rose and came to stand next to the seated headman, receiving a sound clout on his upper thigh by way of greeting.

He, too, giggled, and sat on the log beside Kepi.

"Peri, Son of Kepi." The headman thwacked his son across one pectoral, new gold bangles leaving red marks behind. Peri grinned in response.

"Kasarakuy. Kasarakuy," Mrs. Kepi re-introduced the topic. *"Kasarakuy. Peri, kasarakuy."* She emphasized her son's name archly. Again, Adrian felt vaguely insulted. Why wouldn't someone want to marry him? Why, in just the last village…

"Mis-tah Adrian not marry Peri." Kepi stated in English. "Mis-tah Adrian no good wife for Peri. Mis-tah Adrian not stay. Not have babies. Go with To'am."

Well, that explained why the Kepis weren't trying to marry him off to their son, and how they felt about same-sex marriage. Adrian took a look at Peri. He seemed big, cheerful, and dumb. Not unlike some of the men Adrian had dated back home. Jeeze, he really needed to break his patterns. Maybe when his decade or two of trauma therapy was over, he'd get a chance to deal with his inability to choose wisely among men. He glanced over at Tom, who was currently serving as a pillow for a group of napping toddlers. He looked away again quickly.

Peri was eyeing him speculatively. Adrian's tipsy interest in the subject was piqued, especially now that he knew he wasn't in the running to be Mrs. Kepi Junior. "You know, Peri…" he slurred in English. That the young man probably spoke even less English than his dad didn't faze Adrian a bit. "In the time-honored tradition of my father's people…" He changed seats to join the Kepi men on their log bench. "Have I got a girl for you!" He thunked Peri on the other pectoral to emphasize his point and, switching to passable Quechua, told them all about the lovely young Gaya just one village over.

The Kepis thought this was a great match and seemed particularly thrilled that she was already pregnant. A real time-saver, that. Mrs. Kepi handed Adrian another stone cup full of the highly alcoholic gray beverage. Whereas previously, it had made him gag, at this stage in the evening's festivities, it tasted great, and that was the last thing Adrian remembered about the banquet.

* * *

Adrian woke the next morning to find he'd slept *in* the firepit. A disgustingly hangover-free Mrs. Kepi nudged him awake, asking if he wanted to move or burn when she started the breakfast cookfire. The thought of breakfast sent him reeling into the nearest bushes to re-acquaint himself with everything he'd eaten in the past twelve hours.

Rowdy laughter from Kepi *père, mère* and *fils* hurt his ego and his head. Tom appeared amused as well, and that only added to the pain behind Adrian's eyes. If he'd known self-humiliation was all it took to lift Tom's spirits, he might have tried it days ago. Or not, he thought spitefully, looking around for something to take the bile taste from his mouth.

Almost as if she could read his mind, Mrs. Kepi appeared with a steaming mug of something. *"Tomay!"* she ordered. *Drink!* he mentally translated.

"Hair of the dog?" Adrian downed it, not expecting an answer. It wasn't the same as last night's liquor, except in color, but it did the trick. He felt he could eat a little, and at least the yucky taste of vomit had been replaced by a new and different yucky taste.

Instead of monkey brains, there were crispy snake strips this morning. A change, Adrian discovered, wasn't really as good as a rest. And for the record, snake strips did not taste anything like chicken.

"You know there's boat, yes?" Mrs. Kepi said, a bit of egg shining on her upper lip. "You wait here. Boat come. Take you to big village. Many white men."

"A boat?" Adrian couldn't believe it. The answer to all his prayers.

"A boat. How long? When will it get here?"

"Soon. Soon come boat."

"Yes, but how soon? How many days? How many suns?" He drew an arc in the sky east to west.

Kepi scratched his chin, consulting with Mrs. Kepi in Quechua too rapid for Adrian to follow. The chief scratched marks into the ground and glanced at the sun. "Fortnight," he answered eventually, causing Adrian to wonder again where Kepi had learned his English.

"A fortnight. That's, um, like two weeks, right? That long? Does it ever come sooner?"

The Kepis shook their heads. "No, only at this time I tell you."

Two weeks. Adrian pondered the alternatives. He could wait here for two weeks, and a boat would take him to a settlement of some sort. Someone there would have a short-wave radio or a satellite phone. *I'll be able to report the drug operation. They'll send help.*

But could it wait that long? It has already been more than two weeks since the night of his escape. How many more innocent people had been pressed into service? How many more would die? If he followed Tom, they were supposed to find Chaj and his tribe in just a few days. Then what? Should he wait, take the boat and be certain of contact with the outside world, or continue to charge through the dangerous rain forest on what might prove to be a hopeless quest? Stay or go? Which was the right answer to an impossible question?

Tom paced over and laid his huge head on Adrian's lap, gazing up at him. Adrian fed him the last of the reptilian breakfast that he'd dubbed "snake-on and eggs."

"What should I do, Tom?"

The cat nuzzled his neck, then paced toward the edge of the clearing.

"Oh, so it's up to me, is it? Thanks a lot." Could he leave Tom? Now, after all they'd been through? Knowing what he knew about him?

He stood, turning to the Kepis. "I think we'll be going. *Diospagarasunki,* again for the food and for fixing Tom's paw."

They rounded up Peri and set out for the Eek village. The Wallpa and the Eek knew each other, but the Eek were, according to Kepi, a more migrant people and had not been in this area for many seasons. There was an almost festive air about the journey, and many Wallpa young people accompanied them into the jungle, wishing to see old friends and relatives on the Eek side of the family.

The sudden, threatening appearance of the *azul*-men's helicopter ended the merriment. Both the North and South Americans evaporated into the jungle like mist. Apparently, the Wallpa had had unpleasant dealings with the drug men before.

When the danger passed, Tom and Adrian emerged from the trees. Only Peri remained. The others had, he concluded, returned to the safety of their village.

Moving stealthily through the jungle, the trio stopped for lunch at a familiar stream, the now fleshless skeleton of the massive anaconda merely another signpost on their journey. Adrian was glad it no longer smelled. Tom had a much more sensitive nose, however. They settled by a shady pool both upstream and upwind.

They kept up a good pace, and soon Adrian found he was almost enjoying the journey. He knew there were massive hurdles ahead of them—they had yet to deal with the indigo factory and find a way to change Tom back again for good—but the fact that they'd made it this far and made a few friends along the way he found heartening.

Only two weeks or so ago he'd stood in the rain wanting nothing more than a clean death. Now he had purpose, companionship, a great idea for a coffee table book, and, Dr. Ko-hen-willing, a potion that might mitigate much pain and suffering throughout the world. He almost whistled as he walked.

As they trekked, Adrian discovered Peri to be fairly conversant in the Quechua dialect the Eek spoke, so was reasonably certain all he had to do was put the strapping and none-too-bright young man near the striking and desperate young girl, and hormones would do the rest. A single, commitment-minded male and a beautiful, pregnant female. What's not to like? In light of recent events back at the temple, Adrian felt uncomfortable thinking too much about this particular scenario and moved on to other concerns.

Tom seemed to have rejoined the living, taking an interest in his surroundings again. Adrian had talked to him at length outside the village about their goals and direction, and the thought of finding Chaj and his people again had seemed to cheer Tom up. After all, they had brought back the Tears of Truth, as Chaj had requested. Perhaps the wily shaman had another trick or two up his rawhide sleeve. Getting the painful thorn out of his paw had helped lift Tom's spirits, too.

Realizing he knew Chaj only from their shared visions, Adrian found himself looking forward to meeting him in person and wondered if he'd recognize the shaman without the surreal indigo lighting. Tom had tried in various ways to spell out the name of Chaj's tribe and eventually had communicated "Perqua" as the tribal appellation. Adrian was glad he'd watched a lot of *Party Game* on TV as a child...and that the tribe's name involved only six letters. Going through the alphabet over and over by slicing the air with the side of his hand was tedious to say the least.

Peri, though, seemed to find charades between a man and a jaguar hysterical. Adrian thought about it for a while and realized that maybe it actually was pretty neat, even to people who'd been raised to believe that man-to-animal transformations were, if not daily affairs, at least within the realm of possibility.

Once he had the tribe name, Peri was able to tell him a bit about them.

"Perqua great warriors," Peri said. "Save Wallpa once, save Eek many time." He went on in Quechua, with Adrian mostly understanding there was some sort of debt owed the Perqua by both tribes. "*Yuyaychaj* great *jampiri*," Peri said, waving his hands about in a sort of hocus-pocus gesture. "Not great like Mis-tah Adrian, though." He scratched his head; something with legs fell out. "Perqua funny," he began. "They think—" Peri laughed. "They think—" he tried again, laughing so hard he bent double. The third time, he wheezed, "They think *they* the one true people."

Adrian smiled politely, not really seeing the humor.

Exasperated, Peri explained. "Everyone know *Wallpa* one true people!" When Adrian requested clarification, Peri just waved him off and began poking the fire with a sharp stick.

Peri's amusement at the way he and Tom communicated set Adrian to wondering if, should Tom's transformation be further delayed, they could get a "magic act" together. At least they could be rich and famous and together, even if they couldn't actually be *together.* He stroked his hand down one hip, and his dick twitched at the attention. They hadn't taken a trip to the spirit plane since before the temple. He'd become pretty addicted to his semi-regular trysts with his dream lover. He ran a hand over his budding erection and wondered if he could convince Peri to go hunting while he and Tom took an afternoon nap. Then he berated himself at his wantonness. *Then* he chided himself at his prudishness. Then he yawned and thought about the nap again in a less sexual light. A protruding root tripped his thoughts back into the present and he collected himself, blushing a little. It wasn't so much the sex he missed, but the chance to talk with Tom.

They pulled into the Eek village on the morning of the second day. Thanks to Peri, they traveled a more direct route this time. The villages of the Eek and Wallpa were actually fairly close together. And, Peri informed them, were not that far from the Perqua and about a half-day's journey beyond lay Tanpu. The distance from Tanpu to Temple as the 'copter flies was short and straight. Adrian and Tom's sojourn through the rain forest hadn't been.

They walked tall through the village, directly to the home of Chief Eek, Lynelle and Gaya. Passing Dr. Ko-hen's hut, Adrian waved, but the guilty-looking *jampiri* fled back inside. Perhaps office hours were starting.

The oversized black jaguar walking with them helped keep the vengeful villagers at bay.

The traveling trio lined up outside the house of Eek, scratching politely on the doorframe in the grass-hut equivalent to knocking. The woven door swept back, and the Eek family trooped out, looking a little chagrined.

"Maymantataq kanki taytay?" the old man said formally.

"I have been many places since last we met," Adrian answered in Quechua. "I have seen the Temple of Transfiguration and milked the Tears of Truth, and I have seen many wonders."

"Why are you back?"

"I have brought to you a husband for your beautiful daughter." With a little showmanship, Adrian stepped back and swept Peri forward.

"I, Peri, son of Kepi of the Wallpa, marry Gaya." Peri grinned like an idiot. They'd practiced this speech over and over on the way here. Peri had stumbled over "Kepi of the Wallpa" until Adrian had been ready to scream, and Tom had disappeared into the jungle, ostensibly to pursue dinner.

Chief Eek looked thoughtfully from Adrian to Peri and back, unfazed by the presence of the jaguar. At last he said, "Your father, Kepi, is rich man. I must have dowry of—"

"I, Gaya," the object of discussion cut in quickly, suddenly proficient in the common trade dialect, "Daughter of Chief Eek. I marry Peri."

A gracefully executed body check from Lynelle overrode Chief Eek's objections. The old woman could have taught Tom a thing or two. Or even Wayne Gretsky.

And so it was that Adrian and Tom enjoyed another feast before heading into Perqua territory to find Chaj. Adrian promised himself he wouldn't indulge in local cactus liquor this time and kept that promise right through the monkey-brain appetizer and the crustacean soup. He was quite drunk by the time banana gum paste made the rounds and once more slept in the firepit, under the watchful eye of his personal spirit animal.

Before they left the next morning, Adrian spent some time with the contrite (and greatly relieved) witch doctor, Ko-hen. Adrian's pack bulged with samples and instructions for Dr. Ko-hen's Amazing Curative and, he'd discovered, Most Excellent Hangover Remedy.

CHAPTER 19

THE ODDS MUST BE CRAZY

Adrian was now the owner of more gear than he could carry. There was the lantern he'd found in the cave, a container of oil he refilled at every village, the machete he wore at his waist, his spear/staff that had been returned to him by the Eek, and some travel food. He also carried a supply of Ko-hen's remedy, as well as the Tears of Truth. Lynelle had decanted the two portions into more dependable containers than hollow gourds, although how she had come by a large selection of Tupperware was another mystery of the jungle.

By the time his new friends added in travel food and gifts for the Perqua, Adrian's pack bulged and Tom wore a pair of saddlebags like a packhorse.

Peri had fashioned a harness for Tom that featured an ingenious release loop. In a crisis, Tom need only turn his head to the right and yank the loop with his teeth to divest himself of the load. Perhaps the son of Kepi wasn't as dumb as he looked.

Tom and Adrian said goodbye to the Eek and the happily engaged Peri, setting out again just the two of them. They traveled with greater stealth now, knowing they were entering the drug lord's territory again. The helicopter dogged them continually. Once it had managed to catch Adrian in the open, a churning waterfall masking its noisy approach. There'd been gunfire, and a stone chip had scraped his arm, but Adrian had dashed back under cover of the jungle canopy before they could do real damage.

The drug-makers seemed all the more determined to catch him now, and Adrian could only imagine the heights to which their anger had grown over time. He worried about Montoya sending foot soldiers and about local tribes who might be on Deerborne's payroll. The white men could offer an Indian many things to ensure a tribe's cooperation—money, supplies, medicine, weapons, and indigo. Or iPods. Or, probably most effective, the promise that they would not be taken to the factory of death.

When Adrian had first arrived in Colombia, he'd been warned that the area was rife with angry rebels practicing guerrilla warfare. After his time in the indigo labs, though, he figured this was Montoya's way of covering up his own illicit activities. Locals gone missing? Blame the elusive insurgents. Don't look to the innocent guys who manufacture designer drugs in the jungle using shanghaied labor.

With Tom in the lead again, they covered ground quickly. They arrived at the village of the Perqua on the evening of the third day.

A shaman waited for them on the edge of the central clearing, almost as if he'd been expecting them. His face was a crosshatch of scarification, now highlighted with whorls and streaks in purples and blues. His markings were unique among the villagers and warriors milling around in the background. The smile lines, however, ruined the severe effect, and open amusement belied his solemn words.

"Qollpa." As in their dreams, the *jampiri* used Tom's Quechua name. *"Ima mask'ay?"*

He spoke in the unfamiliar, formal dialect of the Perqua, as he had in Adrian's visions. Adrian had understood the dream-speak, but could scarcely figure out the shaman's words here in the real world. *"Qollpa"* meant salty. Adrian had never figured out the significance of the appellation, but he'd developed a few ideas, and now he'd have a chance to ask. *"Ima mask'ay"* he wasn't so sure of, but based on his growing experience with Quechua dialects, he presumed Tom was being asked, "What do you seek?"

Tom opened his mouth to answer. Adrian almost expected him to respond in human voice, but only jaguar chuffs and growls came forth.

"Qollpa. Ima mask'ay?" Chaj repeated.

Tom yowled in response. Adrian thought the cat was starting to look pissed.

The third time, Chaj asked, *"Qollpa. Ima mask'ay?"* Adrian answered for his speechless companion, striding up close and personal with the medicine man.

"He seeks to be human again, Shaman of the Perqua. To live his life as the man he was born and not be forced to live out his life as an *otorongo*. He is brave and true and has suffered much to return to your village. Must he stay like this forever?" Adrian slid his pack from his shoulder, drew out the sacred container and extended it in his left hand, making sweeping, theatrical gestures with his right. "Behold, Chaj. We bring you the Tears of Truth!"

Tom roared deafeningly, emphasizing Adrian's point.

"Great," said Chaj in the Quechua dialect. Adrian now knew enough of the common trade tongue to be nearly fluent. Chaj accepted the proffered Tupperware. "I was running low. C'mon in. Meet the rest of the tribe. You haven't had dinner yet, have you? We're having monkey brains!"

* * *

Apparently, Chaj was a very powerful, if somewhat young and informal, shaman. He was the leader of the tribe as well as its spiritual guide. Adrian knew this was unusual among aboriginal tribes. Like Adrian's own homeland, they usually prefered a separation of church and state. The Perqua, obviously, were unique in many aspects. These facts, together with Chaj's supernatural abilities, caused Adrian to be wary at first, although Chaj's warm demeanor and easy smile quickly overcame his nervousness.

There was much meeting and greeting by the Perqua. They were anxious to get to know Adrian and glad to see Tom had survived his walkabout. That he hadn't managed to turn himself back into a human didn't seem to faze the Perqua at all. Warriors clapped him on his furry back and women smiled at him. A group of children tackled him, and he played with them for a few minutes before shaking them off and returning to Adrian's side. He roared to get Adrian's attention (although he always had an eye on him), and butted him in the shoulder.

"What, big guy? What?"

Adrian sighed, ready to make with the charades again when Tom began to make an unfamiliar gurgling noise in the back of his throat. Adrian thought he might be choking, but the big cat stopped and repeated it at short intervals. Tom was trying to tell him something…something Adrian wasn't quite getting.

Tom scanned the village clearing, running toward a young boy and snatching a ball cap off his non-too-clean head with his gleaming teeth. "Hey," the kid called, then realizing who had purloined his headgear, shrugged and turned back to his game. Tom paced back over and dropped the ball cap at Adrian's feet.

Adrian brushed the dirt off the logo, Ouroboros, the snake eating its own tail,wrapped around the world on a spider web. Neat. "This yours?" Adrian asked, still not getting it.

He could tell Tom was losing patience, when the big cat suddenly plunked himself on his haunches in the dirt and held one paw up to his ear. Something was very familiar about this stance, the paw to the ear… The repetitive gurgling, it was almost like humming. A tune. Dum, de dum da. Who ya… Who ya gonna call…

The hat, the theme… A metaphorical torch came on over Adrian's head as he finally got it. "Your stuff. They've got your stuff. Here. In the village." Adrian spun toward the young shaman. "Hey, Chaj. Where's the phone?"

While it wasn't exactly *Ghostbusters* headquarters, Adrian did manage to get through to BOO on the satellite phone. Apparently the Perqua had located Tom's Jeep, smashed their way in and lugged his gear back to their village. After an aborted attempt to scratch the numbers in the dirt with a single extended claw, Tom had fallen back on the old horse trick of smacking the ground to count numbers, although his lack of patience had only slowed them down.

"One-eight-hundred. Yes, I got that part. Now was that a six or a seven? Adrian had ended up scrawling the number in the hard-packed earth by the firepit. Only then did they think to hit "redial."

A man with an upper crust British accent answered, reminding Adrian of Dr. Deerborne and making him even more nervous. The call bizarrely mirrored Adrian's 9-1-1 call all those weeks ago except instead of asking, *"Do you need police, fire, or ambulance?"* this operator asked, *"Does your emergency involve telepathy, teleportation, or transmogrification?"*

Exactly what kind of organization did Tom work for?

Luckily, Adrian could answer this one from his research. "Transmogrification, please. I'm calling on behalf of Tom Ferrell."

"In that case…" The operator transferred him to a woman with a sort of international accent.

"Hello, Mr. Thornapple. I've been expecting your call. My name is Jacqueline Batique. Is he still wearing dog tags? Please read me the identification code." She didn't ask why Tom was unable to call himself.

"Are you aware, Mr. Thornapple, if his mission to stop the manufactur of illegal drugs was successful?"

"No, ma'am. They're still making indigo, and we've got to stop them."

"I'm assembling a team now. We'll be there shortly. We're about to lose this connection. Is there anything else you need to tell me?"

The low battery warning beeped, almost as if she'd expected it to.

"You should call the Colombian authorities. Maybe the U.N."

She tut-tutted. He'd never heard anyone actually tut-tut before.

"No, Mr. Thornapple. We will not be contacting any other *authorities*. In these kinds of situations, we *are* the authorities. We'll be there in approximately seventy-two hours. Do nothing until we arrive." She paused, then added, "Please." She sounded like someone very used to being obeyed. "Please tell Agent Ferrell that he is not to—"

The phone disconnected with a squawk. Adrian placed it carefully back with Tom's belongings—belongings that were rapidly reappearing, returned by a few sheepish Indians, some items a bit the worse for wear. The pile grew, including a compass, a wicked knife, boots, and among other things, pants. Adrian packed them carefully away to take with them when they left. He had not given up hope—perhaps he never would.

Just three more days to wait. It had been so long already. Those poor people still stuck in the drug lab. He wished he knew what was happening there. He worried about Doc Soc, about Silvana, the young girl who'd worked next to him, and the others.

In just three more days, Deerborne, Montoya and their henchmen would be arrested, the prisoners released and tended, the drug manufacturing halted.

Adrian wished he could relax. He rolled his shoulders and stretched his legs. He spit on a bug bite although he had long since learned saliva didn't help the itch.

Oh, great. The bugs are biting. I guess the indigo is finally out of my system. He scratched another red bump on his elbow and looked around for Tom. The jaguar sprawled in the dirt across the town square, tail thumping lazily, stirring up a tiny dust cloud. Adrian's shoulders slumped. He'd hoped the man-as-beast thing was part of a drug-induced hallucination. *Guess not.* He sighed and looked away.

Chaj had known for days that Tom and Adrian were on their way, so unlike the Eek and the Wallpa women's short-order banquets, the women of the Perqua had received plenty of notice. They'd been working on an extensive feast for days. The menu featured endless dishes that defied identification. That evening, Adrian dined well. If it wasn't actually crawling around his plate, he accepted it, ate it, and enjoyed it.

He also chugged back the harsh Perqua liquor with the confidence of a man with a sure-fire hangover remedy in his pack. He partied with the Perqua like it was 1599.

Even Tom seemed to enjoy the celebrations, although he abstained from the alcoholic beverages. It wasn't until the next morning (after Adrian had taken a few drops of Ko-hen's elixir) that they settled down with Chaj to discuss their remaining problem—what to do about Tom.

Chaj queried Adrian at length regarding their excursion. He knew Kepi and the Wallpa well, and was pleased that the Eek were back in this part of the jungle. He said something Adrian didn't quite catch. It almost sounded not like they'd been traveling for a time, but rather that they'd been traveling *through* time. Adrian assumed he'd mistranslated, deciding that "before the coming of the white man" meant an area of the rain forest the white man hadn't yet sullied. He'd had by far enough mystical stuff thrust upon him. No way was he adding time travel to the mix.

Chaj seemed to have some cursory knowledge of Tom and Adrian's adventures, but his psychic abilities must have had some limitations, since he needed a debriefing as well. It dawned on him that the same had been true of Jacqueline Batique's abilities—she knew things that affected her, like that Adrian was going to call and that the phone was going to die, but she still needed Adrian to report their jungle adventures.

He'd read Tom's mind via physical touch. Chaj and Ms. Batique seemed to be able to predict the future, to some extent. Adrian was dying to test Chaj's talents and to figure out if they were learned, innate, or a combination. If only he'd had powers of his own. He was just a little envious. Still, now was not the time.

Under a detailed cross-examination, Adrian told Chaj about their journey to the temple, the meeting with Alexis-the-pregnant-jaguar, and their other encounters. Chaj critiqued Kepi's map, showing Adrian where he could have saved a half-day's travel by heading north rather than west around the inukshuk.

The shaman returned the map to Adrian, commending him on his handling of the situation. He was particularly pleased that Adrian had not tried any of the Tears potion himself, and that Tom had resisted the temptation to return to the pool and recommence his interrupted metamorphosis.

"You both would have ended up *uma t'ojpisqa*." Chaj crossed his eyes and sucked his cheeks inward, hooting like the monkeys who ranged the canopy. Adrian was very sure *uma t'ojpisqa* meant crazy. He was very glad he'd followed the instructions on the temple walls to the glyph.

There were many more questions in all directions, usually returning to Alexis. Yes, she'd been fine when they left. Yes, she was trapped in the pool. Yes, she looked very pregnant, far too pregnant for Tom to have been the father. No, Tom said she'd never been a human being although how he'd know that was a mystery. Maybe were-cats smelled different than regular cats. Who cared? It wasn't exactly a priority at the moment.

The shaman smiled enigmatically, the smeared remains of yesterday's face-paint making him look a little foolish. Adrian felt pressure on his thigh and looked down to see a rather heavy black-furred paw pressing down.

Changing the subject, Adrian asked, "Don't you think it's time you changed Tom back into his human form?"

"Manan uqu k'awaqa raurayta atinchu," Chaj pronounced solemnly, crossing his arms across his broad chest and nodding sagely.

Adrian parsed the Quechua, sounding it out. His head shot up and he stared at the shaman in disbelief. "'You can't burn cow dung until it's dry?' What the hell does that mean, Chaj? Can you help us or not?"

Tom growled menacingly.

Adrian raked a hunk of escaping hair back toward his ponytail. It stayed less than a second before falling forward again. He reached behind him to untie the leather thong and re-fasten the tangled mass. The activity calmed him, giving his a moment to gather his whirling thoughts.

"Fo, 'emme 'et 'is fraight…"

Adrian's Quechua was accented at the best of times, and clenching a twist of leather between his teeth didn't help his enunciation. Tom swiveled his great head around, peering at Adrian. Removing the hair tie, Adrian drew a breath to begin again, "So, let me get this straight—"

A commotion outside their meeting hut interrupted Adrian and drew their attention. Two warriors, Appo and Addo, appeared at the door, pausing respectfully.

"A boy. A boy has come," Appo said.

"A boy with black skin and metal teeth," Addo added, drawing back his lips to reveal his own sharpened teeth.

Chaj gestured for them to bring the boy in. With much soft encouragement, Addo's wife ushered in a terrified youth, dressed in modern clothes, including low-slung jeans and too-big T-shirt. He looked lost and young in the oversized outfit.

The boy took a step into the hut and froze. Adrian imagined how they must look to this newcomer. Chaj, sporting blurry blue splotches of yesterday's war paint on his face, long braids, and traditional Perqua wear (which is to say not much). Adrian himself, darkly tanned, clothing in tatters, hiking boots held together with vines, ponytail and dirt completing his jungle look.

And Tom. What the hell would the kid make of Tom?

They were about to find out, because Tom rose and closed the three paces between them, butting the frightened youth in the shoulder with his furry forehead.

"Is he..." Speaking English, the boy tried again. "Is he friendly?"

Adrian nodded.

The boy reached out a tentative hand and gently stroked the top of Tom's head. Tom let out the soft growling sound that was the jaguar equivalent to purring.

"Oh, man," the boy said, throwing his arms around the huge killer's neck. He began to cry like the small child he'd so recently been.

It dawned on Adrian at this point that this boy was not South American, but American, judging from his accent, possibly New England or somewhere along the east coast. *What was he doing in Colombia? Why was he alone in the jungle? Where was his family?* Adrian waited for the boy to regain his composure before starting in with questions.

It only took a few minutes for the newcomer to remember that big boys don't cry. He wiped tears and snot on the back of his hand, and if some got on Tom's coat, the big cat didn't seem to mind. Leaving one hand on what he apparently considered a living security blanket, the boy turned to look at the two people seated nearby.

Adrian smiled encouragingly and patted the log beside him. "I speak English. My name is Adrian. This is Yuyaychaj. Chaj for short. And the furry guy you're currently petting is Tom."

The boy just stared.

"We won't hurt you. I'm Canadian." He patted the log again. "Tom, there, is American. Do you speak Quechua?"

The boy shook his head. "That's the local language, right? Their language." He inclined his head toward the warriors who squatted near the door. "I speak some Spanish, though. Best in my class." A bit of spirit sparked in his eyes, then he seemed to fold in on himself again. Reluctantly, he removed his hand from Tom's soft pelt and walked over to sit on an empty log, facing the men rather than on the log beside Adrian.

"What are you doing here?" Adrian asked. "Where's your family?"

"My dad!" Fresh tears shone in his eyes. "My dad. They got him. They got him." He looked around wildly. "My dad!" he said again, gasping in anguish, sunlight glinting off a mouthful of braces.

"Metal teeth," Addo had said. The Perqua would probably not have seen braces before. In retrospect Adrian realized most of the Indians he'd encountered, excepting Kepi, possessed fine, white teeth, although occassionally sharpened to points. He hoped somewhere in the rain forest someone—someone not like Deerborne—was studying this dental phenomenon, too. He ran his tongue over his own teeth, lightly scored where he, too, had been saddled with "metal mouth" as a teen.

"Calm down. First, tell me your name." In Quechua, Adrian asked Addo to bring them some water, then some food. Who knew how long the boy had been wandering in the jungle?

"But my dad!" The boy was nearly hysterical. Tom moved over to his side, and the wide-eyed youth grabbed a handful of fur. "They're gonna kill him!"

Adrian translated the boy's words for the Perqua tribesmen. To the boy he said, "Take deep breaths. In and out. In and out. That's it. Now, tell us your name, please." Adrian did his best to project waves of calm in the boy's direction.

"Terrance. Terrance Warren. My dad is John Warren. We're from Washington. D.C. Not the state."

What were the chances of the terrified youth stumbling into the Perqua village just when he and Tom were here?

"There are no coincidences, Adrian," Chaj intoned.

This shocked the hell out of Adrian, because he was sure he hadn't spoken out loud. And that Chaj hadn't, either. He didn't bother to translate after that.

"We're on vacation," Terrance continued. "My dad came for a conference and then we went exploring. My dad booked us a helicopter to fly us over the rain forest." He rushed on with his description of events, stopping only to accept the clay mug of water. "Thanks, dude," he said to the fierce warrior who brought it.

"How old are you, Terrance?" Adrian asked, although it wasn't exactly germane to the discussion.

"Fourteen. Almost fifteen. Well, soon, anyway."

"You're a very brave bo—man, Terrance. Go on. What happened to your dad?"

"Our helicopter. It had engine trouble or something. We landed in the jungle. We thought we'd have to walk back." He looked like he might cry again. Tom butted his shoulder gently. Terrance laid a hand on Tom's coat and continued his story. "Then this other helicopter came along and we thought we were rescued. They had machine guns 'n' stuff, and they took us back to this, like, village. At first, they were nice to us, and the guy said they were studying plants and medicines in the jungle. That this part of the jungle had, like, no malaria or anything, and he was trying to figure out why not. He seemed nice, you know?"

Adrian nodded. "Yeah. We do know. That would be Dr. Deerborne." Under his breath, he added, "The nice research scientist who makes killer drugs and condones slave labor and torture." He looked at Tom, who nodded.

"Yeah. That's him. He promised to take us to Bogotá in a couple of days and gave us a nice room and everything. But I..."

Terrance began to tear up again. Adrian was nearly as good with kids as he was with cats—which was to say he liked them and all, but hadn't much experience with them, especially those in that delicate between time where they were as liable to respond like a child as an adult. He'd hated his own teens and hoped this young man was having a better time of it.

Luckily, Tom seemed better with kids. He nuzzled Terrance's cheek and laid his great head on the boy's shoulder, his soft black pelt merging seamlessly with the young lad's close-cropped 'fro.

Terrance buried his face in Tom's fur for a moment, before regaining enough composure to continue.

"I didn't mean anything, you know? I was just exploring. Nobody told me not to look around or anything. It just, like, happened."

"What happened, Terrance?" Adrian asked.

"I found this lab, you know. Like at first I thought they were making medicine. The rain forest stuff for malaria like the doctor said. But then I saw the people who worked there were hurt and in trouble. A man got beaten. I don't know why." Terrance drew a shuddery breath. "These people, they didn't look so good. And there were guards with guns makin' 'em work." He looked uncertainly at Adrian.

"I know, Terrance. I know. I've been there myself." Terrance looked suspicious. "As a worker. I escaped, too."

Terrance narrowed his eyes and drew back a bit. "You're the guy they're looking for, aren't you? You got away? How? I don't believe you! I think you're one of them." He looked around wildly, gaze jumping from man to man. He huddled back against Tom as if it were he and Tom against the bad guys.

Adrian gusted out a big sigh. Rising, he turned his back to the circle and hauled his T-shirt up at the back. After he heard Terrance gasp, he sat again. Hopefully, the many scars would fade in time but right now they were a quick way to win the lad's trust. He hadn't lifted his shirt high enough to show Alexis's claw marks. He didn't want to have to explain jaguar wounds to the frightened young man cuddling a jaguar.

"No, I'm just like you. The lucky one who got away. Go on, please," Adrian coaxed.

Calming down, Terrance took a huge gulp from the clay mug he'd been given. "Okay." He took a couple of deep breaths as Adrian had shown him. "After I found the lab, I went and got my dad and brought him back and showed him. But he's real big, and I guess they saw us. They sneaked up on us with guns. They locked us up, took our stuff, and made us work in the labs, too. Dad said not to breathe the indigo in 'cause it was, like, drugs they were making and not the medicine kind, you know?"

Adrian nodded.

"We worked a couple of days, doing some stuff to these plant leaves. My hands were really sore." He held up his hands, palm outward, the pink flesh of his palms cracked and blistered, oozing pus and blood where the scabs had broken open.

"Oh, God. You should have said something earlier. I have something for that. Addo, could you please bring me…" Before he could finish his sentence, Addo's wife appeared at the door bearing the battered Tupperware container filled with Ko-hen's magic elixir. Picking out the larger of the bugs that were, apparently, an important part of the mixture, Adrian spread it thinly on Terrance's palms.

"Are you hurt anywhere else?" He remembered how the men had been under orders not to rape the women. He hoped like hell Montoya's crazy sense of honor applied to young boys as well.

"No, sir. They let my dad take my beatings for me." He must have been beyond grief at this point, because he just stared at Adrian, trembling a little. Or maybe there's been a little something in the water he'd been gulping. The blue rings ringing his dark irises remained faint, his exposure fairly brief.

"How did you get out, Terrance?"

"There was this little window in the bathroom, and my dad was tall enough to reach it, and I'm, you know, small for my age." He squirmed in his seat, unable to leave his teenage angst behind him.

"I just fit, and my dad made me go. He made me. I don't even know if he's all right. You gotta help him. You gotta!"

"Did you see an Asian man there? About fifty? Speaks English?"

"Yeah. The professor. The first time they tried to whip me, my dad wasn't around. He threw himself at this really mean guy. Took the beating for me. He could barely walk the next day. He really saved me."

So Doc Soc was still alive then, thank God. And he'd sacrificed himself to save Terrance. Adrian wondered how many of the other captives he'd worked alongside were still alive. He'd hurried to the best of his ability and what the really weird circumstances would allow, but the trip to the temple and back had taken way too long. A lifetime—no, a death sentence—for a worker.

"So you climbed out the window. Then what?"

"I hid. In a pile of garbage. I can make myself real small." He hunched in on himself in demonstration. "I heard them talking. In Spanish, but I figured out most of it. They said since I'd escaped and might find help, they only had time to finish this batch of the drugs they were making… *Azul* the workers called it. Dad said it was a new drug called indigo he'd heard about on the news. Then they were going to blow up the lab and kill all the workers. Tomorrow! *Tomorrow!* My dad! My dad's in there. You've got to help him!"

"Yes, we'll help," Chaj said. "We'll go tonight." And though the boy spoke no Quechua, he seemed to understand.

Adrian sighed, noticing a few more Indians had entered the hut. He rose to address them, not worrying about the language. He just spoke from the heart, knowing they'd get it.

"I never wanted any of this. I just wanted to explore the rain forest a little. Maybe find something of anthropological interest. Then I got stuck in the drug lab, and all I wanted was to get out. Then I escaped, and all I wanted to do was report it all to the authorities.

Well, I've done that, and they're not going to arrive in time, so I'm done with going through channels. I'm done with authorities of any kind—normal or paranormal. As of tonight, *we* are the authorities. Me, Tom, and anyone else that wants to come along!" He spread his arms wide. "Tonight we're taking those fuckers down!"

Adrian fisted the air, Terrance aping the gesture. Tom roared his approval, and the warriors ululated war cries.

Outside, the women went to fetch the jungle equivalent of first aid kits. It was going to be a long night.

CHAPTER 20

PRAISE THE HORDE

Planning the raid on the indigo factory should have been near impossible, considering two languages were involved, and their chief strategist had neither language nor opposable thumbs. Still, the Perqua had been planning raids for centuries, and their warriors were hardly ceremonial. They'd invented guerrilla techniques that were successful even against enemies armed with guns and helicopters.

Once Tom got the hang of it, he managed to use a sharp claw as a stylus. If Adrian had still harbored any secret worries that Tom was just a well-trained and clever beast, the claw-rendered maps and skilful diagrams laid those to rest. Although there had been times on the trail, especially at the temple, when Tom had devolved into more cat than man, those few moments when he'd been partially transformed had re-booted his system. He demonstrated remarkable leadership skills, working closely with Chaj. The Indians had no trouble taking direction from a jaguar. Adrian wondered how often these kinds of things happened.

By the time they were done with the planning, the dirt floor of the village square resembled a football coach's playbook, pages torn out and scattered at random.

They were now the proud owners of all sorts of attack strategies and rescue plans, but everything hinged on getting someone inside the electrified compound. Since immunity to electricity hadn't manifested as anyone's secret jungle superpower, they needed the guard to open the gate.

"We'll need a decoy," Addo said.

"I'll do it!" Adrian looked around to see who'd volunteered, realizing every single person around the circle had spoken up, including himself.

"You'll be shot on sight," Chaj said. "It must be the boy. Terrence will survive."

Adrian had learned that although Chaj didn't have total clairvoyance, when he knew something, he was rarely wrong. Still, "survive" was hardly reassuring. Adrian would have preferred the young shaman to pronounce, *Terrence will emerge without a scratch and go on to have a happy life and a fulfilling career.* Was that so much to ask?

Chaj predicted instant death for any of the Indians who approached and were seen, since relations between the tribes and the *azul*-men were hostile. They would be gunned down in the dirt, just like Adrian. And it certainly couldn't be Tom. The only way they'd open the gate for the giant maneater would be to go out and skin him after he'd been shot dead, dead, dead.

So Terrance it was. There was no other way. Adrian had finally agreed only when all other options had been exhausted.

Adrian left the war council to inform Terrance of their decision.

"Allll-riight!" the boy whooped. "Thanks, man!"

"It wasn't my idea." Adrian grasped Terrance's thin shoulders and looked deep into his eyes, waiting for the young man to settle and meet his gaze. A small part of Adrian's mind noted that the blue rings were almost gone.

"You will follow orders, and not put yourself in harm's way. Tom tried to take down the drug factory before, solo. It had accomplished nothing other than giving me the chance to escape. An operation like Montoya's drug lab needs a totally coordinated attack to bring it down. Got that?"

"Yeah, I guess." Terrence went from ecstatic to sullen in one smooth move. "It's *my* dad."

"Yes, it is. And we're all pitching in to help rescue him. In the meantime," Adrian added, "you can help with the preparations. Go and help Appo and Addo with the weapons."

"Okay. Sergeant Adrian, *sir!"* Terrance saluted sharply. Apparently his sulking had a very limited shelf-life. He laughed and raced toward the weapons area. Too late, Adrian realized he'd sent Terrance to dip arrows into a bubbling vat of curare. *Please, God, don't let him get cocky with the stuff.*

As if sensing Adrian's concern, Addo shouted, "Is not poison, Adrian. Just puts enemy to sleep."

What? Were all the Perqua psychic or something? Or was his mother-henning just that easy to read even from across the village square? He sighed, forcing his shoulders to relax. He'd been tense so long he couldn't remember what safe and unworried felt like. Maybe this time tomorrow he would remember. But for now, he was just glad the curare was not poison. Better than guns, since the curare could be set to "stun."

Adrian's own role was to precede the warriors into the compound and take out the generators. No power meant no lights, no alarms, no electrified fences. Since he was the only adult available who understood modern technology, he'd have to be first in. If need be, he could always grab a gun and shoot the damn generator. Now, if only he knew enough about things electrical to recognize a generator when he saw one… Oh, and also how to shoot.

He'd been told by both Tom and Chaj that he didn't need to join the battle, that they'd muddle through without him. He wasn't a warrior, Chaj had said. He could wait behind with the old folk, the pregnant women, and the young children.

The person Adrian had been when he'd stepped off the plane in Bogotá mere weeks ago might have taken them up on it—believing in leaving things to the experts. But that Adrian had faded, little by little, first in the drug labs, then later as he and Tom had charged along the unmarked trails of the rain forest.

"You're right," he responded. "I'm not a warrior. But I'm still as much a part of this operation as anyone else here. I know I can contribute. Hey!" he shouted. "Can I get a show of hands? Anyone else here know how to take out their electrical system?"

A few people glanced his way before returning to their preparations for war. Nobody raised a hand except one silver-haired granny who wanted them to try her tree-frog casserole. It was quite tasty.

The fact that Adrian really didn't know how to take out the generator either wasn't a deterrent. He was newly toughened, smart, resourceful, and had more knowledge of modern technology than anyone else with opposable thumbs.

"Whither thou goest…" he informed Tom. The cat nodded once,

although whether he got the biblical reference and all it implied, Adrian couldn't tell.

Adrian looked up, roused from his musings and from sharpening his machete by the sounds of greeting and laughter. The Perqua gathered near the firepit, milling about like a reception line at a wedding. Adrian strode across the clearing to check on Terrance, finding Tom, too, had stationed himself at the boy's side.

"Reinforcements," Addo's wife said, walking past them with an armload of fragrant flatbread. It took Adrian a second to parse the Quechua.

"Did you know about this?" Adrian asked Tom in English, fingers running through the soft fur.

Before the cat could mime a response, a familiar voice rang out, "Hey, Adrian! To'am!" followed by the Quechua equivalent of "long time no see." Peri stepped from a small knot of Indians. A stream of warriors flowed along behind him. Adrian saw some he recognized, including Gaya's three brothers, as well as some he didn't, guessing from their clothing and markings that they hailed from tribes he hadn't encountered. Bringing up the rear was the infamous Dr. Ko-hen, laden with plants and bowls, and yet more Tupperware. Did someone hold the Colombian franchise? Adrian made a mental note to check the company's website next time he had net access.

Adrian had no time to wonder how all these warriors had known they were needed before he was engulfed in a bear hug from the happy, if a little smelly, warrior. "Thanks again for the wife and child," Peri yelled in the Quechua trade tongue, squeezing Adrian much too hard.

Adrian pushed back a little, grabbing Peri's gaze and holding it. "You do know it's not my kid, right?"

Peri laughed and pounded Adrian on the back, nearly sending him sprawling. "Nah. She told me who father is." He turned and waved at Dr. Ko-hen. The Eek *jampiri* waved back warily, as if not quite sure of the whole "no hard feelings" thing on Peri's part. "Besides," Peri continued. "You *kusisqa.* Like boys. Marry To'am."

Ignoring Adrian's sputtered response, Peri turned to solemnly shake paw with Tom, "So, To'am," Peri asked. "Where do you want us?"

While Tom reworked his strategies to deploy his new troops, Ko-hen and Chaj disappeared. Several hours and some very bad odors later, they reappeared with a carved wooden bowl full of something called *rikuchiy*

In the now-familiar mixture of languages, Adrian learned that *rikuchiy*—literally "to show"—was a traditional concoction that allowed the user to see in the dark. Adrian figured it could be magic, or maybe it worked like that stuff the eye doctor gives you to dilate your pupils. Maybe both.

To apply it, the *jampiri* used a folded palm leaf, the unmeasured liquid dripping down the frond and along the stem that rested on the corner of the eye. Adrian queued up for his, hoping there wasn't anything about his Canadian DNA that would cause the stuff to work differently on him. He figured he'd really need to see in the dark tonight.

"Jesus, fuck, that burns!" Adrian bellowed, cupping his hands over his eyes, afraid to rub them in case that caused more damage. At first, he thought he'd never see again. After a few minutes, though, his vision became less murky, then clearer than it had ever been before! He could now see the jungle's dense green walls with greater texture and dimension, picking out individual leaves and even tiny crawling insects. He decided it was worth it. Temporarily, at least. He wondered if Tom saw like this all the time while wearing the cat form.

The *rikuchiy* was another amazing find he would bring home, along with Ko-hen's curative and Kepi's map to the Temple of Transformation. The karmic wheel was turning, and the good of this expedition in the jungles of Colombia was starting to outweigh the bad, especially once they brought down the *azul*-men.

"You'll want to go there, next," Addo's wife directed Adrian, pointing to a path that led into the jungle. Adrian followed the trail, passing over some very odd tracks in the dirt. They were big and vaguely human, but with weird, enlarged outlines. They resembled the supposed Yeti tracks found in snow. A dense whitish fog cloaked the pathway, reeking of burning rubber. Adrian choked on the horrible smell, eyes watering anew.

He arrived at a smoky clearing to see a bubbling, steaming pot disconcertingly like the ones in which cartoon cannibals boiled explorers. Luckily, no pith helmets floated on the surface amid the smattering of unfortunate insects.

A man Adrian hadn't noticed before was ladling out some of the gooey liquid into inch-deep wooden moulds. After a slight cooling period, warriors dipped their feet in it, then hastily leapt into a low trough of water. When they stepped out again, a thin layer of the murky mixture adhered to soles of their feet. The latest warrior to step out of the trough flexed his toes, the new layer bending and twisting as he did, staying firmly attached. It was like having custom-made sneakers, only without the shoes!

"Caucho," the cobbler explained. "Rubber. Give me your shoes."

Adrian's hiking boots were barely holding it together. Wear and tear and rain forest rot had reduced them to mere soles and straps. A piece of rope from the Eek and some cord from the Wallpa held them on his feet. He sat on the dusty trail and peeled them off.

The rubber man took them gingerly, as if he could possibly smell the ill-used footwear over the stench of the boiling rubber. He shoved something that looked like carved wooden feet gleaming with oil into each boot and dipped the boots directly into the steaming caldron, then tossed them into the dirt to cool.

"Like new." He grinned, showing teeth filed to evil-looking points. He must be from yet another tribe, Adrian guessed, although whether the man was just an itinerant cobbler passing through or had arrived in time for the great battle, he'd never know.

Collecting his newly vulcanized boots and returning the foot molds, Adrian tied his boots together with the last of their original laces, slung them over his shoulder and headed back into the village. His bare feet had toughened up enough that walking on the worn pathway presented little hardship.

Battle preparations seemed to be winding down, so he sat on a rock and watched. He tested the sharpness of his machete one last time and went to collect his share of curare-tipped darts from Terrance and the boys.

CHAPTER 21

LOVE IS A FOUR-LEGGED WORD

The sun faded quickly, marking the close of the day and the end of the preparations for the coming battle. A hasty feast had been prepared—not a heavy meal, nor a lot of drinking. Many warriors donned body armor. Bark breastplates and some dull gray chain mail made appearances as the last of the sunlight slanted through the trees. Adrian thought the protective mesh might have belonged to the original Spanish explorers…until he got a closer look and realized it was made of those little pull-tabs from pop cans folded down and overlapping like fish scales. The usage was ingenious and he grieved again for his lost cameras, imaging a photo spread on old ways meeting new. His imaginary camera whirred as he snapped a few more mental pictures.

Some warriors painted themselves and each other; symbols of jaguars and the eye of truth made a strong appearance. Adrian himself sported streaky paw prints in the indigo ink used by the Perqua. Unlike some of the dyes, the inky blue one wore off quickly. Adrian figured wild designs on each cheek would only undermine his credibility when the Colombian authorities finally showed up. Although he no longer thought of waiting for them to start the take-down, he did envision holding onto Deerborne, Montoya, and their gang until the authorities could take them into custody. They'd want a statement. He'd probably have to return to testify.

A few of the young folk slipped away in the darkness. The Quechua equivalent of "Harder! Harder!" rang out from a nearby hut, thatch not being exactly soundproof.

The sounds of lovemaking made Adrian sigh and long for Tom. He recalled their first meeting on the plane to Bogotá weeks ago—how many now? He wasn't exactly sure. He wished he'd thought to check the little date display on Tom's satellite phone when he'd called Borderless Observers Organization. Still, as long as they were in time to rescue the workers, that was the only time that mattered.

He ambled to the edge of the clearing, finding himself a nice mostly insect-free log to sit on to watch the final preparations and celebrations from a distance—near them, but not in their midst. He still felt very much the outsider, no matter how welcoming their Indian friends had been. A damp nose in his ear was a welcome distraction and he nuzzled Tom back.

"No. I'm fine. I'm just…nervous. Unlike you and your life of danger, in my life the most horrific thing I encountered in a day is discovering my cheese had gone moldy."

Tom chuffed out a cough-laugh, batting Adrian's shoulder with a velvet paw, claws carefully sheathed.

Adrian thought of his life back in Toronto and of Violet dying in his arms, a terrible portent of all the difficulties to come. Maybe moldy cheese hadn't been his worst nightmare.

He wrapped his arms around Tom's huge neck, squeezing hard, wiping unshed tears on the soft fur. Not tears, of course, but just his eyes watering from the *rikuchiy*. The dull edge of the dog tags dug into his shoulder, pressing against old wounds, but he didn't care. He clung to the hope that Chaj could and would reverse the transformation once they'd won their battle. He'd tried to pin the shaman down, get him to commit, or at least say he'd think about it. He'd been cagey and vague, saying only that Tom must change in order to change. And that he must go forward in order to go backward. Great, more fucking rhetoric!

Goddamn shamen. Shamans. Whatever the plural was.

He silenced his inner proofreader with a swift mental kick. Ko-hen hadn't been any more forthcoming about the transfiguration, distracting Adrian with a quick lesson in elixir-making.

Adrian clung to Tom a little longer. Whether he was worrying about the coming battle or mourning his loss of innocence, he couldn't have said. Eventually, he pulled back.

"Sorry, Tom. I just…" His voice cracked, so he shut up.

Tom head-butted him in the shoulder, gently. Using one forepaw, he began to brush the dead leaves and stones away from a patch of dirt in front of Adrian. He extended a single claw, scratching at the hard-packed earth. The same razor-sharp claw that had earlier sketched complex battle plans clearly and precisely in the dirt now skidded and scuffed while trying to draw what appeared to be a basic shape.

Adrian studied the asymmetrical circle, wondering what Tom was trying to say. It was a little late to be revising their plan of attack. He peered at Tom, but suddenly the jaguar's paw became a thing a great interest, and he refused to meet Adrian's eyes.

"Oh." Adrian gasped. He'd been trying so hard to parse Tom's meaning, seeking out the designs that he'd seen carved into the walls of cave and temple, he almost failed to recognize a symbol from his own culture.

Tom looked uncertain, maybe a bit miffed at Adrian's slow reaction. He must have misinterpreted Adrian's confusion as denial. He reached out his paw to wipe away the crude drawing, but Adrian caught his foreleg before he could erase the lopsided heart.

"I love you, too, Tom. I..." Then there was nothing more to say.

CHAPTER 22

A FIGHT FOR SORE EYES

Little moonlight filtered through the canopy into the jungle, but around the fenced-off compound where the vegetation had been brutally ripped away, it cast a dim pall. A few floodlights added their bug-dappled brightness, leaving pools of light and canyons of shadow. The rain forest guerillas took up their posts, keeping well out of the lighted areas.

Adrian stared across the deforested area. When he'd first arrived in Tanpu, the factory had seemed normal to his city-bred senses, if a little out of place. Now he viewed it with an eye accustomed to the lush health of the rain forest, and it seemed like a parasitic cancer feeding off its host until it died.

The area outside the chain link fence was devoid of any greenery, as if the malevolence of the factory itself killed any living thing that got too near. The Jeep and truck tires had cut deep gashes in the red soil until the whole area looked like a blood-soaked lunar landscape.

At first, he'd thought the electrified fence was to keep out wild beasts and rebel insurgents. After his enslavement, he'd realized the fencing trapped the conscripted workers in as much as it kept the jungle denizens out.

A flicker of light drew his attention away from the factory and up toward Deerborne's mansion. The plan was that a few of the older warriors—past their prime but not yet ready for retirement—would apprehend the insane scientist. They'd hold him within his own home. The mansion would serve as an emergency medical facility for the rescued workers.

Adrian shuddered, glad he didn't have to deal with the mad Englishman himself. Montoya was straightforward—selfish and cruel—a textbook sociopath from Adrian's Psych 101 class. Deerborne, though, was complicated and unsettling. A good man who'd become twisted by honorable goals and selfish dreams, his brilliant mind warped and distorted, addled by the indigo he'd ingested at first unwittingly, then later as an addict. Deerborne must have known of the pain and anguish of his captives, yet chose to ignore the evils done by Montoya and his minions. He'd let Elvis Montoya whisper evil into his ear and come to believe that his noble cause was worth the pain, suffering, and even the death of a few Indians here, a few druggies back home. Both men profited mightily from the sale of the drugs. Both men deserved punishment fitting their crimes.

The fucking guards, too! Adrian thought, recalling Juan Carlos molesting young Silvana until she cried.

Once all Adrian had wanted was to turn these evil men over to the authorities. Now he wished for a more personal justice. If the wrong person crossed him tonight, he wasn't sure what he'd do. He barely recognized the man he'd become, but he liked and admired him. In fact, it was more that he barely recognized the man he'd been. He spat on the ground and shifted his stance.

Adrian strained to hear anything that would tell him the status of their operation, but he could barely hear the warriors that flanked him, let alone Tom's movements as the big cat circled the camp. Too bad the *jampiri* didn't have a secret potion for boosting hearing the way the *rikuchiy* enhanced sight. Or maybe they did. He would ask Chaj or Ko-hen later.

Tom suddenly appeared, giving the nodding signal that meant it was done. For a moment Adrian panicked, worried the blood dripping from Tom's jaws and paws was the cat's own. But no, Tom paced back into the shadows, awaiting their next step. There had been no tranquilizer darts for the watchmen. Tom had silently taken them out—forever.

Adrian shuddered, drawing a shaky breath. He needed to focus on the task at hand. He rubbed sweat from his forehead, his hand coming away smeared with face-paint, blue for the Perqua, black for the Eek, reddish-brown—the color of chickens—for Kepi's Wallpa. It seemed they'd each adopted him, admiring his courage and his partnership with the great *otorongo*.

A small figure detached itself from the jungle, limping toward the guardhouse. Terrance was the bravest young man Adrian had ever seen. The limp was feigned, but the tears were real.

"My dad! My dad! *¡Mi Papá!"* Terrance sobbed, remembering his lines even under these terrifying circumstances.

Montoya had recruited the most heartless bastards for his operation. Rather than coming out to help the seemingly injured boy, the guard came out to better laugh at Terrance's gimpy gait. In the end, it didn't matter why the guard opened the gate and stepped outside the compound, only that he did. A dark shadow flew into the clearing, leapt upon the guard and ripped out his throat all in a single, graceful blur, an inky smudge against the darkness, a silhouette against the floodlights. In another instant, Tom had dragged the torn and bleeding body out of sight.

Adrian dashed to Terrance's side, quickly turning the boy away from the scene.

"You were great! Flawless!" Adrian whispered. "You're dad will be so proud."

He handed Terrance off to Addo's wife, who spoke the Perqua word for "shock," wrapped the boy in a dark alpaca blanket, and led him away. So far things were going according to plan, and the next move was Adrian's.

He'd been so focused on Tom, on Terrance, and on the plan that he hadn't had time to think about his own feelings. He was loath to set foot back inside the hated compound, but he steeled himself, calling on every bit of inner strength. More slowly than he would have liked, he stepped through the gate.

Keeping to the shadows, Adrian retraced his escape route of many weeks earlier, eventually locating the humming generator. Damn. It had no apparent "off" switch or easily snipped wires, and he had nothing to cut them with if there had been. A machete might slice through a wire, but he'd probably be electrocuted in the process. He peered around, then slowly, cautiously started exploring the immediate area, watchful of any guards.

It took only minutes to locate a large supply of explosives casually piled under a tarp. Adrian recalled an overheard conversation where Montoya had spoken of using grenades to clear the jungle. Maybe these were the leftovers, or perhaps they were selling weapons to real guerrillas. At this point he spared it scarcely a thought, having found exactly what he was looking for. He mouthed a silent prayer to the gods of these jungles and pried the lid off the watertight box labeled *GRANADAS.*

Adrian wasn't sure how a grenade worked, but he'd seen enough movies to have an idea—he only hoped the movie depictions were accurate. He pulled the pin with his teeth, feeling like the hero of every war epic he'd ever seen. Quickly he tossed the deadly thing at the generator, diving behind a transport truck as he did so.

The entire world became noise, the explosion so thunderous it felt malevolent—so much for the element of surprise! Adrian wished he'd had a chance to warn Tom, whose hearing was so sensitive. The truck Adrian had put between himself and the explosion rocked dangerously in his direction, and for a terrible moment he thought he'd be squashed under tons of metal. How ironic would that be? To have come through all the trials the drug lords and the rain forest could throw at him, only to be squashed beneath a piece of technology from his own culture.

He had just moved from ironic observance to desperate prayer when gravity yanked the swaying truck back onto its four wheels with a teeth-rattling jolt. Adrian was sure it must have made a great crashing and groaning sound, but it would be a few long minutes before the ringing in his ears faded and he heard anything again.

Dirt and flaming debris rained down like the proverbial apocalypse. The night reeked of sulfur and chemicals, and the fumes coated the inside of his nose and mouth, reaching his lungs and choking him. Fire and brimstone, Adrian thought. Now he felt less like Colonel Hogan and more like an avenging angel. The lights had gone out with the explosion, but as the smoke dissipated and his tearing eyes cleared, he reconnoitered as best he could without showing himself.

He'd had no concept how much damage a single grenade would do, or maybe it had set off some kind of reaction within the generator. He was thankful he'd hidden behind the solid metal truck. Yards and yards of chain link fence had been shredded and blasted flat. A storage shed and a line of latrines burned brightly in the night. The generator and the ground that had supported it were missing altogether. Only a smoking pit remained. Adrian was glad the munitions lay a good way off, or the entire encampment would have gone boom like the mother of all fireworks displays.

The *azul*-men rushed from their barracks, running to stare at the fiery pit where their generator had been. The flaming latrines provided enough light for those without enhanced vision to stumble about in the darkness. Adrian watched from the safety of the truck cab he'd crawled into. Montoya appeared in a silk bathrobe, shouting questions and orders. He slapped at his neck. A second later he slumped to the ground, followed quickly by many of his men.

Curare "mosquitoes," Adrian thought. While real bugs were repelled by the *ayahuasca*-laden indigo, not so the Indian darts.

Exiting the questionable safety of the truck, Adrian rendezvoused with Addo and Appo, at the laboratory doors. Sparks flew as Appo chopped at the padlock with a flint axe. A few good blows and the lock shattered, man's earliest technology triumphing over modern devices.

Once they'd opened the door, a stream of terrified men and women emerged from the underground indigo labs. They'd obviously panicked at the explosion followed by the loss of light. They must have found their way by feel to the exit of their tiny, familiar world. Some of the captives were hysterical, fearing yet another torturous episode in their hellish existence. A few Perqua women who'd come along on the rescue mission assisted, reassuring their jungle brethren they were there to help.

The warriors and Tom roamed the jungle, tracking any remaining *azul*-men, knocking them out and trussing them up. Adrian looked grimly forward to a face-to-face encounter with Deerborne and Montoya.

Among those helping the weak and injured laborers escape from the underground factory was a huge black man speaking soothingly, although pointlessly, in English.

"John Warren?" Adrian called, hurrying to his side. The man towered over Adrian.

"Terry? My son—"

"Is safe. He was amazingly brave and helped save everyone here. Come with me. I'll take you to him."

Adrian started off at a trot, anxious to reach the rendezvous spot near the front of the compound.

"Hey. Wait up!" Warren called. "I can't see in the dark."

Returning to Warren, Adrian held out his hand. The two North Americans gripped each other's hands tightly for a long moment, establishing far more of a connection than the usual handshake.

"I can, John. Tonight I can see in the dark," he reassured Terrance's father. "I talk with the spirits and walk with the jaguar. I have been many places and seen many things. I'm Canadian," he added.

John just nodded. He seemed like a man without disbelief at the moment. "Thank you…?" His voice trailed off in question.

"I'm Adrian Thornapple. Terrance is this way."

"Terrance," John repeated. Adrian figured with all they'd been through, the young man would never be "Terry" again.

Settling John's hand firmly on his shoulder, Adrian set out again at a walk, despite the adrenaline coursing through his system. He picked up the pace when he discovered the ground-eating strides taken by a man the size of John Warren. Even Tom would need to trot to keep up.

They left the darkened compound and headed to Deerborne's mansion, their prearranged meeting place. It must have had its own generator, or more likely, an emergency backup, as the lights glowed dimly, illuminating the crowd of filthy, damaged workers who gathered in the massive living room.

"Dad!" The young man handed the Tupperware container he was holding to the Eek *jampiri* and flew into his father's arms.

"Terrance." The tall man buried his face in his son's hair.

Adrian brushed away a tear, his hand coming away smeared with tribal war paint. He wiped it on his torn pants; what was one more stain?

When the Warren men were ready, Adrian offered to show them where they could spend the remainder of the night.

"No way," Terrance said. "There's work to be done here." He dragged his father over to Ko-hen, and they were immediately put to use helping the wounded and the sick.

Adrian glanced around, wondering if he should offer to help, too. The sick and beaten factory workers and a few injured warriors sprawled on chairs, divans, sofas, and on silk sheets laid the floor of the grand parlor, its fancy furnishings pressed into medical service or shoved out of the way.

Three medicine men triaged and treated the wounded. That Chaj was there was no surprise, and he could already smell Ko-hen's universal curative even over the reek of unwashed bodies. He froze, though, at the sight of Dr. Basil Deerborne, looking unwashed and ill himself, joining the *jampiri* in tending the sick. Adrian watched in disbelieve that the workers were letting Deerborne touch them, letting him live.

Adrian stood, trembling, staring at the man who had run him off his property, shot Tom, and turned a blind eye to the imprisonment and torture. Deerborne's back was toward him, and as he worked, the cuts in the back of his shirt shifted to show the whip marks on his back.

Some looked infected.

A hand clasped Adrian's shoulder, and he spun to see Doc Soc, thin beyond skinny, sick and bruised looking. The professor had been stocky and fit before; now he resembled a near-empty tube of toothpaste that had been randomly squeezed. Adrian wanted to hug his friend, so glad at seeing him alive, but he was afraid to touch the wounded and frail man for fear of hurting him further. He let Doc Soc hug him instead.

Pulling back, the professor said, "He meant well, Adrian. He was trying to save millions. To Deerborne's twisted mind, what were a few Indians? He lost control. Of the operation. Of Montoya." He stared at Adrian dully. "They told him no one was being hurt. They put drugs in his food and lied to him. When he found out and threatened to report them, Montoya put him to work, too."

Adrian's eyes narrowed in disbelief. The unavoidable blue rings haloed the Asian's dark eyes. "It's true. He's been with us since you left. He managed to convince some of Montoya's overseers to go a little easier on us. The beatings stopped, mostly." A few dark lines on Doc's neck put the lie to that. "Nobody's died or been hobbled since you left."

Adrian wasn't sure why Doc was defending Deerborne, but he felt a huge sense of relief in hearing that his own escape hadn't resulted in harsher treatment for the prisoners. He backed away. Deerborne alive he could deal with. He couldn't yet forgive him. Let the authorities or the gods handle this one. He sure as hell couldn't.

He fled back to their camp, sick and shivering.

CHAPTER 23

TRIAL BY FURY

Back at the temporary encampment, Adrian found himself restless and unable to settle. He wanted to help, to contribute in some way. He had been wandering around the camp for an hour or so when Appo stepped out of the jungle and stood solemnly before him.

"Come with me, Adrian," Appo said in Quechua.

Adrian nodded and reached for his spear, leaving the sleeping camp to follow the warrior.

The sky was just starting to pink up when they arrived at a small clearing. Appo indicated to Adrian to go forward, while the warrior faded back into the jungle. Thanks to dawn's weak light filtering through the canopy and the residual properties of the *rikuchiy,* Adrian could easily make out the figure bound to a tree.

Montoya slouched against a gnarled old tree, hands tied behind him, belly overhanging his belt, in stark contrast to the malnourished workers he'd beaten and enslaved. Adrian felt a tiny surge of glee upon seeing the man bleeding in one or two places.

When Montoya saw Adrian, his eyes widened—at least, the one not swollen shut did.

"Remember me, Elvis?" Adrian asked casually. "I'm the one that got away. And that little slip-up has come back to bite you on the ass. Literally!"

Montoya whimpered as Tom appeared at Adrian's side. Adrian

stroked the soft fur, fingers tangling in the chain that held the dog tags.

Tom paced over to the bound man, sniffed his hand. He looked at Adrian as if awaiting instructions. Or approval.

Like most bullies, Montoya crumbled when the tables were turned. He begged, threatened, and offered bribes. With utter disdain Adrian horked on the ground next to the evil man's foot. *"Binchuka!"* he spat, using the Quechua word for a local poisonous bug that fed off excrement. Adrian turned to leave the clearing.

"Don't leave me with the jaguar. *Madre de Dios,* have mercy. Call him off!"

"Sorry, Elvis. It's not like I have any control over him. He's his own man." Adrian turned back for a moment. "No, this isn't right." He pulled his machete from a sheath at his belt and strode toward Montoya. The Colombian edged away, straining at his bonds.

"Now, wait a moment. I'm rich. I have powerful connections. Can't we—"

Adrian stepped to one side, slashing the ropes that bound Montoya with a single swipe of the blade. "There," he said. "Now you have the same fighting chance I did when you and three armed men chased me down in the jungle."

"You can't leave me here, I beg you." Montoya jerked his chin in the direction of the jungle cat who paced about the little clearing, tail twitching, fangs gleaming. "That thing will kill me."

Adrian re-sheathed his knife and looked at the man who had enslaved, murdered, tortured, and maimed people for fun and profit. "I certainly hope so." He turned away and started back toward Tanpu.

He was almost out of earshot when the shouts for mercy became screams of terror. Then ceased altogether.

Adrian walked back through the jungle alone.

* * *

One of the rescued laborers turned out to be a mechanic. Alejandro de Luna had signed on with Deerborne back when he had first set up in Tanpu, prior to his illegal diversification. It was from Alejandro that Adrian finally got the backstory on Deerborne and how he'd blundered down the slippery slope from legitimate research scientist to international drug lord.

Alejandro told them that when Deerborne had run through his personal trust fund, his wealthy family had cut him off. While his pursuit of an anti-malarial and other jungle cures was very noble, they weren't prepared to bankroll him nor bankrupt themselves for what they considered a foolish boondoggle. If a country had a problem disease, wise people stayed away. Malaria was practically unheard of on the French Riviera, or in Paris, London, New York, or Rome.

News of Deerborne's financial straits had spread, and one day while in Bogotá begging his bankers for yet another extension, he'd been approached by Elvis Montoya. Montoya, too, came from a wealthy family—third generation cocaine dealers. Deerborne had heard not only of Deerborne's financial predicament, but also that he'd accidentally created a powerful hallucinogen as a bi-product of his anti-malarial work.

It was a short road from Montoya's offer of no-strings-attached financial support for Deerborne's noble cause to setting up the drug lab in the far corner of the jungle compound. Montoya successfully manipulated Deerborne until they'd reached the set-up Adrian had stumbled upon.

Montoya had brought in his own henchmen, enslaving most of Deerborne's original workers, Alejandro among them. Alejandro was the only one left now of the original group.

Not long after Adrian's escape, Deerborne had confronted Montoya, demanding he close down the operation or at least treat the workers better. He threatened to go to the authorities if Montoya continued. Had he been in his right mind, he would have done so without first threatening Montoya. Montoya's solution had been easy—just lock the doctor up, too. He had the indigo formula. What else did he need Deerborne for?

Alejandro jury-rigged a power source using car batteries and managed to get a message to Bogotá via the camp's undamaged communications equipment. They notified the local authorities, as well as the American and Canadian consulates.

Not long thereafter, Colombian officials, U.S. military, even Canadian peacekeeping forces streamed into the encampment, the media close behind. The newcomers arrived in noisy helicopters and bounced down roads in armored trucks. The Red Cross sent in medical personnel, and those who needed further care—such as having misaligned bones set to rights—were airlifted back to Bogotá. The healthier Indians just melted into the jungle as soon as they'd had a good meal or two.

Montoya's right hand man, Juan Carlos, died of a snakebite while in custody. Silvana, the young girl he'd molested in the factory stood by, watching as the kindly Red Cross doctor zipped the body bag over Juan Carlos's blackened and bloated face. Adrian moved to her side to comfort her, encouraging her to turn away without touching her. He was glad he hadn't when the snakeskin choker adorning her neck writhed and hissed. Adrian nodded, moving well out of striking distance and, escorted her to the canteen for a Coke, but not before a little detour to return her passenger to his natural environment.

"Has anyone seen Basil? I mean Dr. Deerborne?" Dr. Tremblay, the Red Cross physician asked. "He said he was going to get some supplies he had stored in an out-building. That was several hours ago. You don't suppose he was accidently shipped out with the riff-raff do you?"

A thorough search of the village turned up evidence that Deerborne had shipped himself out, making a break for it into the jungle. Adrian wondered if his efforts to help the injured workers had only been an act to earn himself enough freedom to escape.

He figured Deerborne must still have a great deal of indigo in his system, just like Adrian had the night of his escape. He doubted Deerborne would have similar luck finding a protector. Adrian hated that Deerborne had even the remotest chance at freedom even though he understood how things had gone wrong for the scientist. Deerborne was a selfish and entitled man who cared little even for those whose lives he saved. Maybe he'd learn to play well with others if he, too, got changed into a beast of the jungle. Something in the slug family, maybe.

Adrian, Doc Soc, John, and Terrance received permission to leave the country provided they gave depositions now and were prepared to return to testify if needed.

Adrian obfuscated to all and sundry, tap-dancing around the journalists and the authorities—those same authorities he'd so wanted to reach, he now wanted to avoid. Any discussions of shape-shifting, visions, mind reading, or animal spirits would get him in the wrong kinds of papers, ruin his career, and land him in the loony bin, where, when he stopped to think about it all, he sometimes thought he really belonged.

A tall black woman arrived in a helicopter sporting the same logo Adrian had seen on Tom's ball cap back in the Perqua village—the world ringed by a snake biting its tail, on a spider web background. It was indeed seventy-two hours since he'd spoken to Borderless Observers Organization on the satellite phone. She introduced herself as Jacqueline Batique, Executive Director of BOO. The military people avoided her while the Red Cross people welcomed her.

She asked to speak with those who had worked for Montoya, voluntarily or otherwise. She spent time first with the overseers who had kidnapped and enslaved the workers they needed. Locked in a makeshift cell, the few remaining "bosses" awaited transport to a Colombian detention facility for processing. Hostile at first, she had only to lay a hand on a man's shoulder before he became docile and forthcoming. Adrian didn't see this firsthand, but heard the soldiers who stood guard discussing it.

Then she spoke with the workers, Doc Soc, Adrian, Alejandro, and the Warrens, as well as those Indians who were still around. She questioned each person in their native tongue, although mostly she sat quietly with them, occasionally laying her fingertips on their temples.

When it was his turn, she invited Adrian into her private tent. It seemed only a short time later that he found himself outside again. She shook his hand and smiled, thanking him for his cooperation.

"I understand you are a very good photographer."

Adrian felt a little disoriented, surprised to see night coming on so quickly. Hadn't he only been in there a few minutes? "Uh, yeah. I like to take pictures. Sure."

"I would like you to have this." The camera she held out to him was so state of the art, so expensive, so far out of his reach, he hadn't even bothered to drool over them in the photography magazines.

"I couldn't possibly accept—"

She gasped his hand and placed the camera within it, closing his fingers around the shiny chrome case. "I know you will make good use of this."

He spent the next four hours snapping photos of everything and everybody until people began to get annoyed.

He joined the Warrens for dinner. John had wanted to get Terrance as far away from Colombia as possible, but Terrance begged to stay. The trauma counselor with the Red Cross unit advised John to let him. Terrance needed closure.

"Let him stay for the good parts," the doctor said, "since he'd suffered through the bad."

In private conversation, John confessed his concerns about Terrance's mental state. It seemed the lad continually referred to someone named Tom. "Who's this Tom character, and why haven't I met him?"

Adrian assured John that Tom was an American operative who had assisted them in the planning and execution of the rescue mission, but had then returned to his assigned duties.

"Why does he keep saying this Tom was soft and cuddly?" John worried as only the father of a teenager can.

The Red Cross doctor, Dr. Tremblay, quickly came to see the value of Ko-hen's healing potion on the rescued laborers whose sores and wounds were festering and raw. Almost every one healed cleanly. After careful observation, Adrian suggested to Ko-hen that he might wish to share his formula with her. Mrs. Ko-hen, who showed up unexpectedly, took more convincing that her philandering husband should spend so much time in the company of the pretty French doctor. Eventually, though, it was decided Dr. Tremblay would accompany the Eek back to their village to learn more about Dr. Ko-hen's Amazing Elixir and Guaranteed Hangover Remedy.

* * *

Tom had killed before. Bare hands. Bare fangs. It made little difference. It was ghastly. It was regrettable. It was done.

Military trained since his late teens, Tom could compartmentalize with the best of them.

He spat in the dirt, eyeing the spittle, glad it was no longer pink with Montoya's blood. Sniffing the air, he followed the scent of water to a nearby stream, lapping until his belly bloated and threatened to overflow. Then he drank some more and heaved until his stomach was empty.

When the afternoon rains came, he put his face up to the torrent and let it sluice away dust, blood, and guilt. It helped that cats have no conscience at all.

CHAPTER 24

REGENERATION GAP

After a few days, neither Adrian nor the Warrens had much to contribute to the rescue operation. They'd dictated depositions, unloaded supplies, burned skids of indigo bricks (staying well upwind), and dug latrines. It was time for them to leave.

Each evening Adrian hiked a short way into the jungle. Each night, the jaguar appeared, and they'd sit together while Adrian talked himself out, Tom nodding at the appropriate places. Each night, Adrian went to sleep hoping to meet up with Tom on the spirit plane, but he'd slept well, with only normal dreams, waking refreshed and alone.

He couldn't leave without Tom, but he couldn't stay here in the jungle, either. Doc Soc had been medevaced out days ago, suffering from malnutrition and shock. The professor had declared he was never leaving home again and planned on writing "a boring and stuffy" book about his experiences in the rain forest. Adrian knew his friend would be back on the anthropological trail before the year was out.

Adrian needed to go home, if only to deal with his apartment, his bills, and his cat. Using his severance monies, he'd paid his rent a couple of months in advance and left some money with Wendy to cover Pixel's upkeep, but that wasn't going to last. Plus his parents were beside themselves.

He'd borrowed a satellite phone to call them and found them threatening to come get him. They'd even completed the paperwork to get their first-ever passports! Their local news station had run reports of the take-down, including footage of the big smoking mess that had once been the drug factory. To say they were frantic would be an understatement. A phone call or an email wasn't enough. They needed to see their only child.

He'd promised Tom he'd never leave him, but what future did their relationship have, man and jaguar? He'd assumed Chaj would change Tom back once the battle was over, but the young shaman had disappeared along with the rest of the Indians once the workers were tended to.

He didn't understand why the BOO people weren't as worried as he was. He addressed this with Jacqueline Batique, but she assured him Tom was fine. "I am sorry, Adrian. Only the one who changed him can change him back."

They needed to find Chaj!

Since his obligations in Tanpu were finished, he planned to set off for the Perqua camp at dawn.

That night at dinner, Ms. Batique informed them she and the rest of the BOO crew would be leaving shortly. Cold sweat dampened Adrian's waistband despite the humidity. One by one all his allies and acquaintances were leaving him. How long could he stay? How long before Tom went totally native and ran off and left him, too?

"We'll wait for you to go into the jungle one more time, Adrian." Somehow Ms. Batique made it was more like a command than an offer to accommodate his schedule.

Adrian recalled that the mixed-tribe army had set out at sunset for Tanpu and had arrived sometime after midnight, so he figured it for a half-day's walk from Tanpu to the Perqua village. Despite Terrance's insistence that seeing the Perqua village again would be highly educational, the Warren men stayed behind.

"Adrian must go alone." When Ms. Batique spoke, even Terrance stopped arguing.

Adrian headed out of the encampment at dawn, the jungle closing behind him like a curtain on civilization. He took a moment to study the breath-taking beauty of the rain forest, welcoming and familiar now, no longer terrifying and claustrophobic. He set out with hope and, before long, with his furry travel companion.

They'd walked about three hours, making them about three-quarters of the way to the Perqua village when Chaj appeared.

"Qollpa. Ima mask'ay?" Chaj asked, as he had the first time he and

Adrian had met in person.

This time Adrian answered on the first ring. "He seeks his humanity, Chaj. He's losing himself. Forgetting how to be a man. Soon there'll be nothing left of Tom Ferrell but the dog tags." He reached out and stroked Tom's great head.

"Adrian Thornapple. *Ima mask'ay?"* Chaj asked.

"What do I seek?" Adrian repeated. "I seek the real Tom Ferrell, the man I have grown to love." He circled Tom's neck with his arm, leaning into the half-embrace.

"Do you know why, Adrian Thornapple, I call him *Qollpa?"*

"It means 'salty,' right?" Adrian looked down. A large ant lugged a fallen comrade across the trail. "I assume because this far inland, salt is a precious commodity."

Chaj threw back his head and laughed, war-paint symbols crinkling into Rorschach-style blotches. "Yeah. Right. That's it exactly. And also? Because it's great in small doses, but too much is really hard to take."

Adrian clutched at Tom's fur, insulted on his friend's behalf. He sneaked a peak at Tom. The big cat shoulder's drooped, as if he was preparing to hear bad news.

"Do you know why, Adrian Thornapple, *Qollpa* took the form of his spirit-self in the first place?"

Frustrated with the cross-examination, but unwilling to do anything to offend the shaman, Adrian considered and answered, "His bullet wound was infected. You kept him alive."

"Pffftt." Chaj spat in the dirt. "My magic is stronger than that. I could have cured the fever in time, but time is not as plentiful as magic. Try again."

So not to save his life, then. Hadn't Tom told him that was why? Adrian searched his vague recollections of the dream-talks he and Tom had shared on the spirit plane. "Oh, I got it." He snapped his fingers. "You changed him to teach him a lesson. He was rigid and uncooperative and didn't play well with others. Needs own catbox."

"That is also not why he changed, although I believe he has benefited greatly from the experience."

"Because you wanted him to stick around?" Adrian was running out of possible answers. He expected a buzzer to sound any moment telling he was out of time. And out of luck.

"We have come to value Tom's skills and wisdom. We would be pleased if he would stay and spread his seed among our tribe. We have not had a changed one among us in many generations." He smiled a new kind of grin. "It would really stick it to the Eek."

If the only way to convince Chaj to change him back was to promise he'd be village stud, what could Adrian say? There'd been no promises, no commitment. Jealous and heartsick, Adrian's throat tightened. He'd promised he'd never leave Tom, but how could he stay?

"Qollpa," Chaj faced the jaguar directly. "Once you told me you did not need the Perqua. Do you still feel this way?"

Tom roared in response. Whether he meant yes or no, who could tell?

"Qollpa," Chaj said again. "I cannot change you back. It was never in my power to do so. That was why I had you travel to the Temple."

"You mean you changed him knowing you couldn't change him back?" Adrian gasped, appalled. "Why you son-of-a—"

Tom roared, making Adrian's point for him.

Chaj looked at Adrian, puzzled. "But I didn't change him. Never said I did." He spread his empty hands. "If I had, I could change him back like this." He snapped his fingers, aping Adrian's earlier gesture

"What? *What?"* Adrian grabbed onto Tom so tight he nearly ripped out a handful of hair. Tom made a mewling sound that had to be the jaguar version of "What? *What?"*

"If you didn't change him, who did?"

Chaj shrugged again. "Every magic is different. Maybe deep down, he *wants* to stay in the cat form."

Oh, great. Freud in face paint.

"He can stay with us as long as he likes," Chaj added. "You, too, Adrian."

"Tom," Adrian said gently, nails digging into his palm to help control his rage and sorrow. "You can't go home like this. As long as you're stuck in cat form, you'd be better off here. Think of the good you can do. You can help people. Be like a, I don't know, a one-man army or something."

It was all Adrian could do to put his own feelings aside. Metal bands seemed to be contracting around his chest. "Maybe, in time, you'll change back. Maybe it just has to wear off or something."

Tom roared again, his huge frame shaking under Adrian's hand. "You're right. I'll go home, but only to clear things up and see if I can find out anything on transmogrification. Those people you work with will know something." Adrian paused, plans for fixing this frothing around his brain. "You'll wait for me, won't you? Wait here?"

Tom nodded his great head, blue eyes never leaving Adrian's.

Letting go of the breath he hadn't realized he'd been holding, he lightened up his hold on Tom's ruff. Okay, they had a plan now. He could work with that. Tom would wait while Adrian did the research.

Secretly, he had a back-up plan, a desperate plan he hadn't even shared with Tom. If they couldn't turn Tom back to a man, he'd make Chaj turn him into a jaguar, too. So they could be together. He hoped it wouldn't come to that. That he wouldn't have to say goodbye to friends and family and spend his days in constant peril in the jungle. He shoved Plan B onto his mental backburner, not willing to think about it now.

Research. He was a scientist. He could do research. In the meantime, Tom could stay with the Perqua and…

"The Perqua will have another changed one soon," Chaj announced, interrupting Adrian's planning. "We no longer have need of *Qollpa.* He may go." The shaman smiled as if he was offering Adrian a gift.

"But I just said he couldn't. That he…"

That was it, the last straw. This freakin' control-freak, spirit-world-walking, magic-wielding dickhead who'd worked side-by-side with Tom to take out the drug lords, was now discarding him? Casting him away?

Adrian ground his teeth and made an indefinable sound of rage in the back of his throat—his own personal roar! He raised his fists to threaten Chaj, to implore the gods, catching the metal dog tag chain in the process. Entwined around Adrian's fingers, the chain pulled taut, snapping and sliding from the fur. The stainless steel dog tags flashed in the sunlight as they slid off the chain and to the ground.

"Listen, you bastard!" Adrian shouted in English, knowing Chaj would understand no matter what. "You can't just fuck with people's lives like this. Why you—"

"And so," Chaj interrupted, calm and smug. "You have removed the last trace of humanity from the beast you have come to love." Chaj pointed at the ground. Drawing a breath to continue his rant, Adrian glanced down at the dog tags lying in the dirt at Tom's feet.

Tom's feet? Wha— Not paws, but feet. Size elevens, from the look of them. Slowly Adrian raised his eyes, his gaze traveling up powerful legs, impressive groin, over the muscled, scarred chest to arrive at last at the beautiful face. Special Agent Thomas J. Ferrell of Borderless Observers Org., IDC: 129-45-6009, blood type 0+, stood on the jungle trail before him, naked, unshaven, scarred, and dirty, and looking better than anything Adrian had ever seen.

"H—" Tom's voice caught, rusty from disuse, or maybe from roaring. He took another run at it. "Hi, Adrian."

He raised a hand to Adrian's face, stopping just shy of touching him.

"Tom." Adrian could barely breathe.

"The power to turn back into a man was always with you, *Qollpa.* Just as you changed yourself in your moment of need."

Adrian thought he'd scream. "What the— Why the hell didn't you tell us?"

"Oh. Figured you knew." Chaj, puffed out his cheeks. "Uh, sorry?" he added with an apologetic shrug.

Chaj's blush reminded Adrian just how young he really was—probably younger than Adrian himself. Whoever had started his shaman training wasn't around now. Chaj was both shaman and leader of a tribe in danger of extinction. Adrian guessed he'd forgive the guy—eventually—for assuming the details of shape-shifting were common knowledge; after all, in his world, they were.

Adrian squinted at Chaj. The shaman was fading, just as he had in Adrian's dreams.

"What did you mean the Perqua will soon have a jaguar warrior of their own?" Tom asked.

"Even now Addo and Appo travel to the Temple of Transfiguration. I will join them there, and we will bring back the spotted jaguar Adrian named Alexis to bring strong, new blood to the Perqua," Chaj answered, body faded from the waist down now, just a ghostly torso, arms and head.

"But she's a jaguar. How can she help the tribe?" Tom asked.

There was nothing left but a talking head now. It shook itself ruefully, *tsking*. "Always arrogant, *Qollpa.* Do you think the transformation works only from man to animal?"

Tom and Adrian watched as the face evaporated, leaving just the shaman's smile. "You'll miss being able to lick your own *sogay, Qollpa.* Perhaps Adrian will do it for you."

Then there was only Chaj's warm laughter echoing in the jungle.

* * *

"Hi, Adrian," Tom said again, his eyes locking on Adrian's.

"Um. Hi." After weeks of close travel with the jaguar and dream-lovemaking on the spirit plan, Adrian felt nervous at being alone, finally, with Tom, the man, the real thing. The first time he'd seen Tom since he'd come to mean so much to Adrian. It seemed a long time since their inauspicious first time in the airplane bathroom.

Tom leaned over, running his hand over Adrian's hair, tugging on the leather thong that bound it back in a ponytail. He inhaled deeply, eyes closed. "You smell good, Adrian."

Adrian smiled, heart beating a frantic tattoo. He touched Tom's chest, running his fingers down his torso to the eggplant-colored bullet scar.

Tom shivered at the touch. He pulled Adrian to him gently, wrapping his arms around him, sighing and holding on. "Thank you. Thank you for…everything. No one's ever stuck by me like you have."

Not sure how to respond, but pretty sure *Hey, no problemo, buddy-boy* wouldn't cut it, Adrian remained silent. He returned the hug and just held on, mouth turned up in a thankful smile. If his eyes watered a bit, it must be delayed affects from the *rikuchiy*. He'd hugged Tom many times over the last few weeks. It was so good to be hugged back.

They stayed locked in their human embrace for long moments, then Adrian felt something warm and wet swipe his neck.

"Taste good, too." Tom made a sound in the back of his throat that was almost a purr.

With the next lick, Adrian shivered with pleasure. Despite his return to human form, there was still something cat-like about Tom.

When Tom nibbled at his ear, Arian prayed Tom would hang on to his feline inclinations.

Tom spent a long time licking and scenting Adrian, traveling down his body until he was kneeling before him. Tugging on his wrist, he coaxed Adrian to join him on the ground. The jungle floor looked less than appealing, and Adrian fetched the pack he'd discarded when Chaj had appeared to them.

"I was taking this blanket back to Addo's wife. She left it with Terrance the night of the raid. Since we won't be visiting the village now…" He spread the alpaca-wool blanket on a relatively clear space just out of sight of the trail. Kneeling on the blanket, he turned back to Tom. He could almost see the outline of tail lashing with impatience.

"There now. Isn't that—"

Tom attacked, pouncing on Adrian like the jaguar he'd so recently been, forcing Adrian back onto the blanket, nipping, licking, even clawing. He tore at Adrian's clothing as awkwardly as if he still had paws rather than hands.

Frustrated with buttons and zippers, he sat back and roared.

Adrian had never been more turned on in his life.

In their dreams, their mating dance had been seamless, effortless. Clothing had fallen away unnoticed, hands, mouths, and cocks everywhere at once. Suddenly, all the practical needs of sex seemed intrusive, maddening.

Adrian would have gladly let Tom rip away all his clothing, but they could hardly rejoin the rescue group naked, so he held Tom back with one hand while awkwardly unbuttoning, unbuckling, and unzipping with the other.

Once they were both naked, Tom again set about his primal mating and claiming—scenting, tasting, biting. Adrian writhed on the blanket, shocked at how erotic he found his submission. One small part of his brain acknowledged that this was their first time, or rather their first time since they'd fallen in love, and the submission was apparently important to Tom. Next time, though, Adrian was getting on top!

Remembering the she-cat's behavior, Adrian rose on hands and knees. Tom mirrored his stance. Adrian dragged his body along Tom's several times.

With a roar-purr that sounded more cat than human, Tom gently pushed Adrian onto his stomach. Seizing Adrian's hips, Tom began to bite and lick, running a quick, maddening tongue all over his lover.

Almost mindless, Adrian mumbled thanks to the jungle gods.

Far too soon, and not nearly fast enough, Tom moved up Adrian's body, positioning himself above him. He rubbed his cock along the shadowy crevice two, three times, nudging teasingly.

Then Tom pulled back, resting on his haunches, panting, straining.

"What are you waiting for?" Adrian panted, his submissiveness disappearing the instant his needs became thwarted. "Do it," he ordered. "Take it. Take it," he echoed Tom's orders from their dream sex.

"We need…" Tom gasped, his control, his humanity, obviously hanging by a thread.

"Right!" Adrian squirmed around so he could grab his pack without leaving his position. "Here." Nearly wordless with desire and need, he thrust a condom at Tom. The Red Cross nurse had given him dozens to distribute to the Indians.

"Do it!" Adrian ordered again, locating a single-use package of lubricant from the first aid supplies Dr. Tremblay had included for the

Perqua.

He heard the package tearing and smelled the incongruous scent of latex against the living odors of the jungle. He moaned in ecstasy and anticipation as Tom knelt between his legs and eased slick fingers into him. Moaning and writhing seemed to be his best course of action, so he returned to it. This time it was Adrian making the roar-purr sounds.

He rubbed and strained, hips thrusting upward, searching for more. Tom withdrew his fingers and, after flipping Adrian over onto his back, he yanked Adrian's legs up over his shoulders. "I want to see you," he growled.

Adrian strained forward, to try to rub against him, already missing the stroking fingers. He was beyond speech or thought now, and could only trust that Tom would give him what he needed.

Slowly, Tom pressed his way in. The sharp burn reminded Adrian this was real, very different from their dream sex, where there'd been only pleasure. Now he took a deep breath and tried to relax his straining muscles, glad Tom had chosen face-to-face this time, rather than mounting him from behind as a jungle beast would.

Tom pushed a little harder, and his cock slid home, where he paused, trembling with exertion, letting Adrian get used to him.

Despite the stretching burn, Adrian had never felt so good. He might have wished Tom a little less well endowed, but at least he no longer had the barbed and hairy penis of the jaguar! Not that they had ever been tempted to have inter-species sex, but he had noticed.

Adrian gave a small nod to show he was ready. Tom began with gentle, short thrusts. Always impatient, Adrian shoved back—time to get this show on the road!

Tom responded with ever-increasing rhythmic strokes, deeper, more vigorous, until he was pounding in relentless thrusts, moaning, purring, murmuring Arian's name. He reached between them, wrapping his fist tightly around Adrian's straining cock. Perfection!

A single tear painted a shiny trail down Adrian's cheek as their emotional connection equaled and surpassed their physical connection. He would never leave Tom. Never. Never. Wouldn't. Couldn't. Not now. Now. Now! Now!

He groaned aloud as he came, his orgasm pushing Tom over the edge to join him in rapture and love.

CHAPTER 25

NOT PLAYING WITH A FULL DICK

He must have slept for a while, waking to find Tom watching him. Tom smiled a nervous, boyish smile. Adrian answered with a shy smile of his own.

Snagging his pack again, Adrian produced Wallpa travel cakes (chicken-flavored) and military field rations.

"MREs, huh. Now I know I'm back." Tom grimaced, but reached for the food.

"You have to admit, though," Adrian said around a mouthful of lasagna with a five-year shelf life. "It's kind of a nice change after a steady diet of monkey brains and fried lizard. Tastes like chicken, my ass."

"You got that right. Your ass tastes much better." He patted Adrian's thigh. Adrian wished for a mirror or a lot more flexibility so he could see if actual teeth marks graced his butt cheeks.

Tom tossed an arm over Adrian's shoulder and finished his meal one-handed.

They bathed in a nearby stream, commending Chaj on his choice of location for his intervention. He'd left them with a nice place to get re-acquainted and spend the night. The scent of lavender filled the air—healthy lavender, not the rotting scent reminiscent of indigo. The riverbank was covered with *ayahuasca,* which explained why the bugs weren't eating them alive. Neither man bothered to dress at all. They held each other and talked long into the night, and when sleep finally found them, they slept in each other's arms, glad of arms and not paws anymore.

There were no dreams that night, either instructional or sensual. The men had everything they needed in a grassy clearing on an alpaca blanket.

* * *

The next morning they made love again, this time slowly, gently, some of the urgency abated. Tom was very glad he once again had thumbs. And less sharp teeth, until it came time to open another package of MREs. Then razor sharp teeth would have come in handy but Adrian had his machete, of course, so they managed.

Locating Adrian's scattered clothing took a few minutes, despite Tom's excellent tracking abilities. Most of the fastenings were intact, although a few buttons would remain forever among the rotting vegetation on the rain forest floor.

Among the items stuffed in Adrian's backpack was some of the clothing the Perqua had liberated from Tom's Jeep.

"I've been carrying it around case you came down with a sudden case of humanity." Like a jungle Mary Poppins, he produced Tom's boots, khakis and a clean T-shirt (also khaki).

"Thanks." Tom pulled on his clothes.

Adrian left the backpack containing the blanket, condoms, and a few other trinkets, on the trail. "They'll find it."

Although they were only an hour or two from the Perqua village, they chose to return to Tanpu.

"Goodbye, my friends," Adrian shouted in the direction of the village. A cloud of squawking birds fled the noise.

Tanpu was approximately three hours away. Without the baggage, they should have made good time.

Should have. Instead, the hike back took twice as long as the trip in, what with continual stopping to caress and kiss and reassure each other that their connection was real, deep, and mutual.

As they approached Tanpu, shouts and laughter, as well as the sound of generators and equipment drifted toward them.

When Tom heard the voices, he stopped, chest tightening.

"I've been living in the jungle for a while, Adrian. Honestly, I'm a little overwhelmed. It's just…all those people. The smells. All that noisy equipment."

He shrugged, not meeting Adrian's eyes.

"No problem. We can have a little more alone time." Adrian grinned. "You've been missing in action a while now. What're a few more hours?"

"You know," Adrian began, following Tom down a trail that appeared to loop around Tanpu. "I just remembered a weird conversation I had with your boss before I left this morning."

"Yeah?" Tom called back over his shoulder. He couldn't imagine a conversation with Jacqueline Batique that wasn't weird.

"I told her I was coming to find you, and we were going to take a real hard line with Chaj, but I didn't hold out a lot of hope. I said there was a good chance you'd have to stay with the Perqua." Adrian's voice shook a little. Tom walked on, Adrian following as he had for the past few weeks.

"I thought she might leap in with a plan or a cure, Tom. All she'd said was, 'Take your time. I'll see the three of you when you return.'"

Tom stopped. Adrian nearly plowed into him. "Three of us? What do you supposed she meant by—"

"Hall-ooo. Halloo, there. Help me. I require assistance!" Deerborne staggered out of the bushes, clutching at trees and vines. And his crotch.

Adrian stepped closer, but Tom held him back. Nobody in their right mind would trust this man anymore. He snatched Adrian's machete free of its sheath.

Deerborne staggered up to them, falling to his knees on the dusty trail.

At first, Tom thought it a trick of the sun. Deerborne's blue-ringed eyes floated on a background of yellow. In fact, his entire skin was yellow. And sort of gray at the same time.

"Deerborne. You look like hell." Adrian felt the man's forehead. "You're burning up. Is it malaria?"

Wouldn't that be divine justice? Tom thought. The man had spent his fortune, ruined his career, and caused who knows how much pain and suffering in order to save the world from malaria and now he was sick with it.

"No. No. I've ingested far too much *ayahuasca*." Deerborne's eyes glowed feverishly. "I was crossing a river and stopped to urinate. A small fish actually swam up my urine stream and into my penis! It happened so quickly. I believe it's take up residence there as I haven't peed at all since." He looked down at his crotch. "Help me. You must help me. Please."

Adrian hesitated. He recalled Doc Soc talking about the dick-fish—the *carnero*—when he'd first called to convince Adrian to come on the expedition. If only Adrian had stuck by his guns and said no, none of this would have happened. He'd never have met... He glanced at Tom.

Tom just shrugged. "Leave him," he said, but made no move to step away.

Adrian nodded once, grasping the kneeling man's arm. "Take his other arm, Tom."

"But he shot me. I nearly died."

"I know. Take his other arm anyway."

Tom whined like an angry kitty, but tucked the machete away and grasped Deerborne's other arm. Together they hauled the sick man to his feet and began the slow journey to Tanpu.

They'd lugged him no more than fifteen minutes when two Red Cross workers appeared on the trail, bearing a stretcher.

"Ms. Batique told us to come. I guess you guys have walkie-talkies, right."

"Sure." Tom looked away. "Special miniature ones. Implants." He touched his free hand to his temple.

"Yeah. Implants. Right," Adrian added.

The medics just shrugged and loaded Deerborne onto the stretcher. Deerborne began a litany that alternated between sincere apologies and equally sincere complaints. "Could you try to keep me steady there, boys? I'm a very ill man, you know."

CHAPTER 26

THE POSTMORTEM ALWAYS RINGS TWICE

Adrian and Tom spelled the Red Cross workers, taking turns, two at a time, bearing the stretcher. Arriving back at the camp, they left Deerborne to the Red Cross and went to report in. They found John and Terrance Warren helping out at the canteen.

"Hey, guys," Adrian called to get their attention. "I'd like you to meet—"

"Tom!" Terrance charged up to the forbidding and grimy man, grasping him around the ribcage in a bear hug. "I knew you'd be all right."

"How did you…" Adrian began, but Terrance gave him that teenager look as if he were about to ask the dumbest question ever. Adrian clamped his mouth shut. The rain forest seemed to bring out the mystical in a lot of people.

"So this is Tom," John said, extending one hand while attempting to peel his son off the newcomer with the other.

"It's nice to meet you, sir," Tom replied.

"John," the taller man corrected.

"John." Tom clasped the extended hand.

Adrian clapped both men on the back. "I don't know about you guys, but if I don't get some caffeine stat, that nice Red Cross doctor is going to have another patient on her hands." He threw the back of his hand up against his forehead, Camille-style, and mimed dying a tragic death.

Gesturing toward the battered chrome percolator, John Warren said, "I do believe I smell fresh coffee brewing. This way to the café du Tanpu."

Once seated and caffeinated, the men discussed their immediate futures.

"We're heading back tomorrow. We've briefed and de-briefed and been brief, and I think we're about briefed out. Isn't that right, son?" John patted Terrance's shoulder.

"I've been telling them all about the Perqua and their weapons and that stuff you guys put in your eyes. They took notes and everything!" Terrance's own eyes were bright, and he bounced a little as he talked. It sounded like Terrance was having a blast, despite some ongoing whining about missing all the best parties and other social events back home. Unsurprisingly, he wasn't whining about missing school.

Adrian shifted in his seat, something digging into his abdomen. Remembering the lizard that had made itself at home in his pants back when his good friends the Eek had tied him to a tree and left him to die, he leapt up and dug beneath his waistband. "I have got to get new pants," he declared, extracting a small plastic rectangle from the hidden pocket. He'd been given a pair of jeans to wear while these were being washed and mended, but he couldn't seem to give his old ones up; to do so felt as if he were abandoning an old friend. They'd been through so much together.

"Hey. It's my eight-gig memory card. I can't believe it's survived everything I've been through." He polished the hard plastic case on his T-shirt. "I think it might have a few pictures I took when I first got here. That might come in handy for the articles I want to write. There could even be some pictures I took of the compound on here that could be used in the trials."

Pursing his lips, he blew the last of the lint from the little plastic case. He snapped it open and shook the card into his palm. Thanks to the sturdy, waterproof case, the memory device looked like the day he'd bought it. He inserted it into the camera Jacqueline Batique had given him, taking special care to ensure the connectors were clean and made good contact.

The harsh field lights in the mess tent rendered the tiny display screen difficult to view. Arian futzed with the angle until he found a glare-reducing angle and began scrolling through his pictures. A few shots showed Bogotá and San Arbol, plus a few taken on the drive to Tanpu. That seemed years ago, when it had been only a little over a month in total.

He shuddered at the candid shots of Elvis Montoya. How greedy did a guy have to be to snag the few dollars Adrian had paid him for taxiing him to Tanpu when he already possessed millions? Recalling Montoya's ultimate fate, Adrian shuddered. He glanced at Tom, wondering how the ex-jaguar was coping. Tom seemed fine, listening to Terrance describe his flight from the drug factory through the jungle the night of his escape. Adrian had already heard the story several times. It became a little more miraculous with every telling. Still, the boy had found safe passage directly to the Perqua, and that was pretty much the definition of a miracle.

Adrian chuckled. He was no longer surprised by much of anything.

He flipped quickly to the next shots. Two of the drug lab back when he'd thought it a rubber-processing plant or something. Two more of the thatched cabin he'd been assigned when he first arrived and was again occupying. The last shot was of the lizard that came with the cabin. "Lee-zard," Montoya had called it. Little had he known what a truly charming host Montoya would turn out to be.

Or was that the last picture? He pressed the advance button. Then again, and again.

The small screen showed detailed shots of the interior of the lab. How could they possibly be on this memory card? Here was one of Montoya and his heavily armed men standing in the rain, having trapped him between a rock and a raging river.

He remembered putting the memory card in his pocket as an extra the night he was captured. It wouldn't have been in the camera Montoya stole, but stowed in Adrian's pocket the entire time. What else was on here? His finger trembled. It took three tries to hit the advance button.

The cave where he'd awoken after his escape. The view out over the rain forest from the cave's front door. The pictographs, photographed from all sorts of angles, so clear he could read them—a man turns himself into a jaguar in order to save his lover. God, if only he'd known that back then!

He suddenly needed to breathe again because at some point he'd stopped.

"Oh, my, God! They're here! They're all here!"

"What are?" Tom laid his hand on Adrian's arm. "You don't look so good. Are you okay?"

"The pictures! All the pictures I framed in my head along the way.

Look! Here's the view from the cave where I first woke up. Some great shots of the pictographs, although how that was taken in the dim lighting is beyond me. Here's a shot back at the mountain from the trail when we first set out. I'll bet the Perqua could help us find it again. What a treasure that cave art would be to the world." He flipped through the shots so fast it was like his life flashing before his eyes—or at least the last few weeks.

"Look. Here's the Eek, the Wallpa, and the Perqua. There's a great shot of Kepi and his chickens. Here's Gaya and Peri all happy together. Here's the inukshuk. And a great one of the decomposing snake. Look how huge it is!"

The pictures went on and on—the landmarks and milestones of their trek through the rain forest, the ruined temple and the spotted jaguar, the smelly hermit and the wonders they'd seen along the way.

The tiny digital readout said the card was completely full. There were dozens of pictures. Adrian reached the final picture. Tom, in all his furry glory, sitting lazily on a rock, dog tags glinting in the sun, Adrian sprawled next to him, a big, open grin on his tanned and grimy face.

He turned the camera for Tom to see.

"Well, this one's certainly suitable for framing." Tom laughed, handing the camera first to the Warren men. Tom had explained his transformation to John Warren to reassure him that Terrance wasn't crazy. Somehow he felt his explanation might not have had the intended outcome.

"But if I'm *in* the picture, who the hell took it?" Adrian asked.

"Uh, timer?" Tom scratched his shoulder "My boss is going to confiscate the memory card, you know."

"Yeah, I figure." Adrian sighed. "Maybe they'll let me keep this one picture."

"Why not just upload it all to my laptop?" Terrance looked from one adult to the other, his amazement at their brainlessness written clearly on his young features. "What? One of the warriors found it among Montoya's things. And I know that guy from the Colombian newspaper has connector cables."

Before the Warrens left next day, Adrian had turned the memory card over to Tom's boss. He patted the borrowed flash drive in his pocket and hugged Terrance until he squirmed away. "You're a genius."

"And a very brave one." Tom added.

"I hope you can use a brave genius in your outfit, Captain Ferrell," John said, shaking Tom's hand. "Because Terrance announced last night he'll be joining BOO..." He rolled his eyes. "As soon as he's finished college."

Tom looked delighted. "Is that so? Well, you'd better get back and finish high school first, young man. But when it's time, we'll come looking for you. We can use someone who keeps his head in a crisis and believes the unbelievable." He shook the teenager's hand. "Stay in school and stay in touch."

"No problemo. Ms. Batique gave me her personal email address. She says I'm gonna go far."

* * *

Adrian borrowed a satellite phone from BOO again, this time to check in with Wendy. When he'd spoken to his parents, they'd promised to call her and let her know he was okay. He needed to touch base with his friend, though, and experience a bit of vicarious normalcy, even if just by long distance.

"Yeah, Pixel's fine. I'm fine, too, by the way."

He could hear the big gray cat yowling in the background once Wendy had informed the cat who was on the phone. It felt odd to be called "Daddy."

"I know this isn't the moment..." Wendy's voice crackled over the wires. "But can I keep him? I mean you never wanted a cat anyway, right. You had that incident with the kiddie pool and the curling iron and the Siamese."

"Persian," he corrected. He thought for a moment. He hated to deny her anything; she'd always been such a good friend. He took a deep breath. "No. I'm sorry, but Pixel is my cat. We've bonded. I can't just go around making pledges of lifelong...whatever, relationships, and then dumping them on the first pretty lap that comes along." He felt bad, but if there was anything he'd learned out of his entire rain forest experience, it was to stand up for what he believed in. "But I'll tell you what. I'm on my way home now. I've gotta start looking for another job, but maybe this Saturday we can go to the Humane Society and rescue a kitty."

"Oh, maybe a black one." He could hear purring in the background.

"Sure. I know black's your favorite color. All your furniture and most of your clothes are black."

"Right. So Pixel's light gray fur shows up on, like, everything. I'll see you in a few days. I've missed you so much!"

"Me, too. And I have so much to tell you."

"Did you meet anyone?"

"Did I? Yeah, I did. But you know those foreign flings. We're heading home to different countries, hell, different hemispheres. I—" Adrian's breath caught in a near-sob. "Gotta go," he choked and hit the disconnect button, returning the phone.

* * *

After much hugging and promising to keep in touch, the Warrens left, hitching a ride on an Air Force chopper. Terrence grinned and waved until they were completely out of sight.

A few hours later, the BOO helicopter touched down in the muddy area serving as Tanpu's municipal parking. The pilot, Joe Schwartz, announced he'd be flying Ms. Batique, Tom and Adrian directly to Bogotá, skipping San Arbol. Adrian wasn't sure how come he'd taken a flight from Bogotá to San Arbol and a drive to Tanpu on the way out if it was only a few hours flying time, but he'd given up worrying. Maybe Joe was the best damn pilot in the world, or maybe he knew some secret wormhole over the Amazon basin. Adrian was beyond wonder and beyond caring now.

Ms. Batique had arranged a replacement passport and airline ticket back to Toronto. He accepted it, unable to meet her gaze. They'd split up at Atlanta, Ms. Batique and Tom heading back to their island base and exotic lives. And Adrian? He'd go home. Alone.

The BOO flight back to Bogotá was another experience, entirely. On the drive out, the industrialization had seemed normal, a positive step, even. How could it not? His only frame of reference had been coming from an industrialized nation himself. Long before he was born, his country had blasted its way through rocks, sliced through forests, choked and polluted some of the finest fresh waterways in the world, not to mention devastating the animal and native populations. Forests had given way to farmland. He'd often heard Canadians lording their natural-resource-based economy over the American military-industrial complex, but were they really so much better?

Now on his return trip, having come out of a nearly unspoiled section of the rain forest, his perspective had shifted. Where before he'd seen progress, he now saw devastation. As they flew over the rubber-harvesting areas, Adrian gasped. The great gashes in the trees felt sinister, as if money-grubbing vampires bled away the very souls of the forest. The farmland looked so flat and barren compared to the jungle that had stood on the same ground only a few years before. He could almost see the ghosts of the trees and vines. The unruly waterways that had wound their way through the rain forest were now straight cement lines, speckled with rusting soda cans and other offal of the industrialized world.

The city itself, as they approached, seemed devoid of life, despite the continuous flow of traffic. It had seemed so charming when he'd first arrived—a quaint third-world town. Now it looked like any other city in the world, full of crime and hunger, cement and asphalt. The few trees that lined the pot-holed streets seemed twisted and maimed. Tears trickled down his cheeks as they landed at the airport. Tom looked stricken as well, saying nothing, grasping Adrian's hand tightly the whole way.

CHAPTER 27

WHEN PUSH COMES TO LOVE

Adrian's brave front threatened to collapse during their stopover at the Atlanta airport. Suddenly his Air Canada ticket and boarding pass to Toronto absorbed all his attention. *Just a few more hours, and I'll be home.*

He couldn't stop himself from glancing over to where Tom and Jacqueline Batique chatted softly. They'd found a relatively quiet spot to have "a word." He knew BOO's headquarters were located on the tiny island nation of Azunya. He'd googled Azunya on a borrowed computer, finding it described as a tax-free paradise just off the Caymans. The Azunya Tourist Board website played tinkly Caribbean music and encouraged visitors. A flashing banner warned that it was *carnero* season, so swimmers and boaters should be careful of this deadly fish that swarmed the surrounding waters. It seemed this fish would enter the body via the penis…

Adrian thought that was weird because he'd researched the *carnero* back in Toronto when Doc Soc had first mentioned it and it had said that it only lived in fresh waters found in the Amazon basin. The website didn't mention when *carnero* season ended, either. It was almost as if they wanted to deter tourist from coming.

"Hey, buddy." Tom sat on the leatherette bench. The metal armrest between them seemed like a heavy-handed metaphor for their upcoming separation. "The boss-lady wants a word. I'll watch your stuff."

Adrian tried to get a read off Tom's expression, but the man's face was less revealing than the jaguar's had been. *She probably just wants to say it's been swell.* He ambled over, hating long goodbyes.

She gesturing to the spot recently vacated by Tom. "Have a seat, won't you?" A tired-looking mother of three toddlers, one screaming, two arguing, arrived, about to take up residence on the bench across from them. Jacqueline caught the woman's eye.

The woman froze, intoning in a robotic voice, "We're going to go sit somewhere else." The children followed their mother's gaze. Upon making eye contact with Jacqueline, they stopped their crying and yelling and moved into an orderly line, filing across the departure area after their mother.

Adrian looked back at Jacqueline, who met his gaze primly.

"These are not the seats they're looking for," she paraphrased.

Adrian burst out laughing. Viewing her as a Jedi knight made her a lot less scary.

"I'll be brief, Adrian. Depending on the outcome of this conversation, I'll either have worlds of time to speak with you further, or I'll never see you again."

She seemed to be waiting for a response even though it wasn't a question.

"Uh, okay," he finally said.

"I have reports of your behavior since coming to South America. Indeed I have reports of your entire life."

Adrian squirmed in his seat like a school kid. "Well, um…" he said, then clamped his mouth closed so sharply his teeth clinked together. If she was going to criticize him, he wasn't handing her any additional ammunition.

Silence stretched between them. Overhead, the speakers churned out scratchy announcements about flights arriving, flights leaving. When it mentioned "Toronto," Adrian tuned in. *"Attention Air Canada passengers on flight 8622 to Toronto. There has been a change in departure information. Please proceed to Concourse D, Gate D37. Your flight departs in 15 minutes."*

"I guess I better be going. It's been swell." He figured someone should say it. He stood and held out his hand, wiped it on his jeans and held it out again. She took it, but rather than shake it, she clasped it and stood, rising to her full height, bringing them eye level. Or maybe she was a wee bit taller. He glanced down, absently noting she wore flats.

"Adrian. I need you to make a decision. I want you to work for me. Work with Borderless Observers Organization."

"I, uh." He was doing real well today conversationally. He noticed she hadn't played the *work with Tom* card.

"No. I want you to decide on your own. Where you want to be. Who you want to be. We do good work all over the world, but we do it in relative secrecy. There will be no accolades, no fame." She released his hand. He was still looking at her shoes, although seeing nothing. Using her manicured index finger, she raised his chin to meet her eyes. It dawned on him he hadn't spoken that last aloud, yet she'd addressed it. No fair.

"You'll have to get used to it. Hone your own skills."

"I have no skills. Your people are seers and shape-shifters and—" He glanced around, eyes darting from person to person around the lounge area. "I have nothing to offer."

"Let me see. To start with, you are a trained anthropologist. You have extensive experience handling personnel matters from your employment in human resources. You are brave, loyal, compassionate, ethical and honorable."

"But—"

One look and he clapped his mouth shut again. "You have a facility for languages, both oral and written. You accurately read the pictographs in the cave and the carvings in the Temple. You became fluent in both Quechua and Spanish in a matter of weeks."

"Come to think of it," Adrian toyed with his ponytail. "I did, didn't I?"

"Yes, you did. I should add humble to the list although I prefer my operatives to be a little more self-aware." Her smile removed some of the bite from her words. "You have some telepathic potential, as evidenced by your dream-walks and your ability to access memories."

"But you already have seers and telepaths on your staff. Better ones than me." He felt like he was back in his old job of HR Manager, trying to talk some executive out of empire-building at the company's expense.

"What is most interesting to me, though, is an ability I have never encountered before."

Again, she left him standing in silence. The overhead speaker announced his flight again—he had less than ten minutes to get to the other end of the airport.

He considered. What could he do that others couldn't? Did he even know the extent of the talents employed at BOO?

What can I... what do I... He snapped his fingers. “I can take pictures with my brain!”

She nodded, tiny smile playing around the corners of her lips. “I believe with training, we can couple your psychic abilities with your visual recording talent and you can learn to project those pictures over great distances. We would find that useful. At present, we can view people’s memories, but we do not have a method of recording them. Translating thoughts to static media would be most useful.”

“Email!” Adrian cried, unconcerned when nearby airport patrons glanced his way. “I bet I could learn to email you what I see. Like all I have to do is carry around a Blackberry.”

Jacqueline’s smile widened. “Now you are proving yourself a valuable asset. However…”

“What? Er, do go on, please.” He shifted nervously from boot to boot.

“Five minutes until AC flight 8622 departs for Toronto.”

He was going to miss his flight. He really didn’t have the money to waste on Air Canada’s ridiculously pricey change fees.

“I have spoken with Professor Kawasaki, and he told me you sometimes have trouble making decisions. I can’t have that. I need to know you can make a quick decision, even one that affects your entire fut—”

“Yes,” he interrupted. “Yes. I will join BOO. But right now I need to go back to Canada, deal with my apartment, my family, my best friend, and my cat.” He waved his airline ticket back and forth. “I gotta go. I need to say goodbye to Tom and get my luggage.” He looked back to where he’d been sitting. The bench was empty. “Where is—”

“You had best hurry, do you not think?”

“But Tom. My stuff. I—”

“Go. We will be in touch.” She surprised the hell out of him by leaning over and kissing him on the cheek. “Thank you for taking such good care of Thomas. *Au revoir.”*

Still stunned from the unexpected kiss, not to mention the life-changing job offer, Adrian charged down the corridor toward his flight, knapsack bouncing against his back. The healing scratches itched like crazy.

He located concourse D, only to realize Gate 37 was the last possible gate. *Well, I’m in pretty good shape these days, I’ll just run.*

He arrived at Gate 37, gasping, holding up ticket and passport. The usually cranky Air Canada staff smiled and welcomed him. "Right this way, Mr. Thornapple. We've been holding the flight for you." He leaned against the counter, panting while they processed his ticket.

"Who is this guy?" one of the flight attendants whispered. Adrian could hear him though.

"I dunno," replied her coworker, making tick marks on a clipboard, "but the call came from on high. He's really cute. So was that other guy they had us watching for." To Adrian he said, "You've been upgraded to first class. Enjoy your flight."

Of all the amazing things Adrian had experienced in the last month-and-a-half, this was perhaps the most miraculous of all. "Thank you. Thank you!" Adrian retrieved his documents and practically skipped down the embarkation corridor.

The other passengers had already taken their seats. Adrian located his row near the front of the plane. A handsome man with military bearing occupied the window seat.

"Pardon me, is this seat taken?" Adrian asked.

"I've been saving it for you." Tom patted the seat, moving the crossed belts out of the way. Adrian popped his backpack into the overhead compartment and dropped into the seat.

"So…" Adrian grinned at his seatmate. "Going to Toronto for business or pleasure?"

"Pleasure," Tom answered, grinning. "And then we can get on with business."

"And what business would that be?"

"Why the saving-the-world business, of course." He leaned over and kissed Adrian. "We're gonna make a great team! And besides, we can't spend all our time having sex in the bathroom."

* * *

The flight home was predictably dull, with the exception of the sex in the bathroom. This time Tom bottomed, insisting turnabout's fair play.

Adrian enjoyed the shrimp cocktail.

There was, as expected, a hassle over luggage. Customs wanted to check every bag arriving from Colombia, but Tom waved some sort of magic badge, and they walked away unsearched.

"You'll get one, too."

"BOO sounds better all the time, what with first class travel and expedited service."

"Yeah. That *is* great. The danger, injury and possible death…not so much." He tugged Adrian's ponytail to show he was kidding. Mostly.

They rolled out of the passengers-only area, past the check-in counters, and toward the taxi stand, tired and anxious to get home.

Unexpectedly, Adrian halted, snatching at Tom's sleeve, yanking him to a stop.

"That guy," he whispered, pointing at a scruffy-looking man heading toward the Air Canada check-in. The guy stopped at one of the self-service kiosks, looking confusedly from his passport to the electronic instructions.

"What about him?" Tom asked, turning to one side and glancing at the man sideways.

"It's the guy. Skip. The boyfriend. The indigo dealer." Adrian's breath came raggedly, and his heart leapt around his chest. "His girlfriend, Violet. She died."

"Right." Tom nodded. "He'll recognize you, so I'll go stall him. You get Security."

"So *now* you want to go to the authorities." Adrian couldn't help the little dig. He bypassed a long line of customers, all of whom raised their eyes from their Blackberries to glare at him.

"Sir. You'll need to go to the back of the—"

"Call Security now," he whispered.

"Sir, if you'll just step over—"

"Just do it!" He slapped his hand down on the counter. "Now!" The Canadian in him got the better of him, though. "Please."

She picked up the phone and dialed. One of her colleagues glanced over. "Daisy. Take over my customers, please." Then into the phone. "Security to the Air Canada check-in counter, please. Yes, immediately." She stared into his eyes, and it dawned on him she was calling Security *on him.* Well, he could work with that.

"I'll be over there where that scruffy-looking man in the Leafs ball cap *who is wanted for murder* is talking to my boyfriend." Adrian sauntered away. She'd tell Security what he'd said, and they'd probably nab both him and Skip. And Tom. Didn't matter, as long as they got Skip.

It didn't go down quite like that. Security arrived and asked Adrian to accompany them, ignoring his protests that they should grab Skip, instead.

Skip must have figured the helpful guy showing him how to use the kiosk to produce his boarding pass was actually stalling him. He made a move to leave. Tom tackled him. Security finally caught a clue and ended up taking all three men into custody. It took several phone calls, another flash of Tom's badge, and a visit from the RCMP to straighten it out.

"Thank you kindly," the Mountie commended Adrian and Tom. "This man is wanted for questioning in regard to a recent drug overdose."

"I know." Adrian hung his head, rubbing his sore wrists where they'd been cuffed. "I know." His wallet was one of several things that had mysteriously turned up after the rescue mission. He pulled it out now. From among the ephemera of modern life he retrieved a business card—*Officer Robyn Warner, Toronto P.D.* "She'll fill you in."

They left their contact information with Constable Kowalski, and finally, finally, exited Pearson International. Tired, hungry, and anxious to be home, Adrian guided Tom to the taxi line-up, reminding him he was supposed to lead sometimes.

"Limo, Mr. Thornapple?" a man said, smiling broadly, white teeth gleaming.

"Yes, but..." He glanced at Tom, then back at the driver. "Mo" his brass name badge read. "It's already paid for, right, Mo?"

"Yes, sir. Please to be coming this way."

"Well, Tom. Welcome to Canada. Let's get my cat and go home. Oh, and wait till you meet the parents. You can be the one to break it to them that their son is going to go live with you in another hemisphere and work for a shadowy organization where I'll be risking life and limb on a semi-regular basis."

Tom climbed in after Adrian, sitting far closer to him than was necessary in the spacious limousine. "Maybe we should work up to meeting the parents. I might not be as brave as you think. Let's start by getting your cat. I'm good with cats."

"So am I, Tom. So am I."

STORM GRANT

Storm Grant is a writer of short and long tales, her work spanning both genres and genders. Storm's stories offer titillation and merriment, and in a few cases, horror. In the last few years, she's published with several publishers, and now Amber Quill.

Storm is a board member of the Toronto chapter of the RWA, a general member of the FF&P chapter, and a founding member of the Rainbow Romance Writers chapter. Her business degree has seen much use over the three decades she's spent working in marketing and administration. She lives in Toronto, Canada, with her husband and a miscellany of rescued pets and a rather messy house.

Follow Storm's life and writing career at her blog, storm-grant.livejournal.com, or email her at storm.grant@gmail.com. Oh, and Twitter, of course: twitter.com/StormGrant.